THE
FINAL
DAYS
OF
MAGIC

THE
FINAL
DAYS
OF
MAGIC

**A WITCHES OF
NEW ORLEANS
NOVEL**

J. D. HORN

Text copyright © 2019 by Jack Douglas Horn
All rights reserved.

Published by 47North, Seattle

www.apub.com

Amazon, the Amazon logo, and 47North are trademarks of Amazon.com, Inc., or its affiliates.

ISBN-13: 9781542040143 (hardcover)
ISBN-10: 1542040140 (hardcover)
ISBN-13: 9781542040136 (paperback)
ISBN-10: 1542040132 (paperback)

Cover design by Rex Bonomelli

Printed in the United States of America
First edition

To the witches, both real and imaginary.
I hope I've done you proud.

CHARACTER LIST

THE MARIN FAMILY

Celestin Marin—Patriarch of the Marin family and deposed head of the Chanticleer Coven, once New Orleans's most powerful and influential coven. Celestin, intent on commanding the power promised in *The Book of the Unwinding*—a legendary grimoire that reveals the secrets of how to survive and prosper in the final days of magic—murdered his own son and grandson and slaughtered many of the region's witches at the ball intended to memorialize him. In revenge, his body was cut up, and the pieces passed out as magical relics.

Laure Marin—Celestin's deceased wife. Obsessed with another woman's husband, Laure encouraged her rival to work a risky spell outside the auspices of the coven, claiming it would protect their children by suspending the dangerous *The Book of the Unwinding* between realities. The spell led to Laure's commitment to a psychiatric facility for witches and her rival's death. Laure died in the institution nearly twenty years ago. Laure was the mother of Nicholas, Vincent, and Fleur.

Nicholas Marin—Celestin and Laure's elder son. Nicholas challenged Celestin to become the head of the Chanticleer Coven but has now lost the coven and the one woman with whom he may have found love. Nicholas is the father of two sons: Luc and Hugo.

Astrid Andersen Marin—Nicholas's missing wife. Though Astrid was once regarded as a fragile, artistic witch who used her magic to escape the Marin family intrigues, her surviving children have come to understand she, too, attempted to gain control of *The Book of the Unwinding*. Instead, the grimoire now has her under its control.

Luc Marin—Astrid and Nicholas's eldest child, and failed challenger to his father's position as head of the Chanticleers. Celestin murdered Luc as part of his plan to access the magic held in *The Book of the Unwinding*.

Hugo Marin—Astrid and Nicholas's younger son. Hugo has long relied on drink and drugs to mask his own sensitive nature.

Alice Marin—Raised to believe herself to be Astrid and Nicholas's daughter, Alice has learned that she's the product of an affair between Astrid and Celestin. Alice has made her way back from the Dreaming Road but may have brought some of its darkness back with her.

Vincent Marin—Celestin and Laure's middle child. Murdered by Celestin, who then assumed his identity. Vincent was blessed with a lack of magic that for a while allowed him to lead an independent life of his own choosing. Unmarried and childless, he long tried to act as a father figure for Nicholas's neglected children.

Fleur Marin Endicott—Celestin and Laure's youngest child. Celestin forced her into a marriage of convenience with a Washington up-and-comer, Warren Endicott. As that marriage comes to its dissolution, Fleur is determined to become her own woman. But after the slaughter of witches, she finds herself facing much greater challenges than building a new life.

Lucy Endicott—Like a millennial Mephistopheles, Fleur's outwardly superficial and undeniably spoiled teenage daughter feigns indifference, but always finds ways to improve the lives of those around her.

THE SIMEON—PERRAULT FAMILY

Soulange Simeon—The spell that led to Laure Marin's commitment also caused the death of this once great Voodoo practitioner. Bad blood has run between the families ever since Soulange was found dead and Laure wandering mad out on New Orleans's haunted Grunch Road. With her daughter Lisette's help, Soulange's spirit derailed Celestin's scheme at the slaughter of witches. Soulange was the original proprietor of the famous French Quarter Voodoo supply store, Vèvè.

Alcide Simeon—Soulange's husband, musician. Blames the Marin family for his wife's death.

Lisette Simeon Perrault—Soulange and Alcide's daughter, Lisette has run Vèvè since her mother's death. Though struggling to recover from a stroke triggered by dark magic, Lisette has uncovered a connection between the twilight of magic and the founding of New Orleans.

Isadore Perrault—Lisette's husband and owner of one of New Orleans's premier landscaping companies. Although Isadore takes pride in having a true partnership with Lisette, he defers to her in matters of religion.

Manon Perrault—Lisette and Isadore's elder child, Manon is a no-nonsense self-starter who has recently completed her undergraduate degree in business. She is preparing to marry her partner, Michael, and is expecting their first child.

Remy Perrault—Lisette and Isadore's teenage son. A visual artist, Remy has recently begun to attend college.

THE WITCHES OF NEW ORLEANS

Evangeline Caissy—Stereotypes would imply that the solitary witch, a red-headed Cajun, is more temper than heart, but her past has taught her both patience and compassion. A former exotic dancer, Evangeline now runs her own Bourbon Street club, Bonnes Nouvelles. She finds herself at the center of machinations put in play centuries before her birth.

Mathilde, Margot, Marceline, and Mireille—The sister witches. Having arrived on the banks of the Mississippi before New Orleans became an American city, the four sister witches are New Orleans's first and oldest sorceresses. They are heartless, ruthless, and capable of changing form to meet their needs. Mireille, the youngest of the sister witches and Evangeline's mother, died after falling for a storefront church preacher and turning against magic. The surviving three acted as Celestin's accomplices at the slaughter of witches.

Frank Demagnan—The slight, though preternaturally strong, funeral director whose family had met the mortuary needs of the witches of New Orleans for as long as there had been witches in the Crescent City until the day he found himself victim of another's dark magic.

The Chanticleer Coven—Once dozens strong, at the time of the slaughter of witches, the moribund coven had dwindled to the Marin family and eight degraded witches: second in command, covetous **Gabriel Prosper** and his sister **Julia**, the vain and punctilious **Monsieur Jacques**, the steadfast and sturdy sergeant-at-arms **Jeanette**, the elderly and addled **Rose Gramont**, Rose's much younger self-appointed caretaker **Guillaume (Guy) Brunet**, and a brother and sister duo known as "**les Jumeaux**" or "**the Twins**," who strive to function as a single, indivisible entity. Only the Twins survived the slaughter unchanged. Rose Gramont found herself rejuvenated, both in body and in magic, from the charged blood of the murdered witches, and she has joined forces with her former friend, Astrid.

Nathalie Boudreau—Part-time chauffeur, full-time psychic, Nathalie has a sixth sense that lands her in situations her good sense would tell her to avoid. Assisting Soulange and Lisette in their battle against Celestin has awoken Nathalie's own dormant magic, even as Alice Marin has reawakened her heart.

Lincoln Boudreau—Nathalie's cousin. Charming and flirtatious, Lincoln is a street musician who has Evangeline Caissy in his sights. He also has a secret.

Washington (Wiley) Boudreau—Lincoln's younger brother and fellow performer. Hardheaded and passionate, Wiley shares his brother's secret.

Michael Parrish—Manon Perrault's fiancé, Michael has been conspiring with Astrid against the Perrault family.

and

Babau Jean—Also known as "John the Bogey," Babau Jean is New Orleans's own born and bred bogeyman. Go on. Turn out the lights. Face the mirror. Call his name three times. He'll see you.

DECEMBER 19

ONE

Lisette Perrault remembered a time when she wasn't filled with rage. Golden in hindsight, grotesque in light of what was to follow, those final days of contentment were now fixed in her memory, preserved, though extinct, like an ancient bug trapped in amber.

Since the stroke, Lisette's left arm hung limp at her side. She used her right hand to raise the arm and position it, forearm up, on the cold metal surface of an industrial workbench. A half-empty fifth of rum sat beside it.

The old man watched, nodding and grinning around the bit of his unlit corncob pipe, as Lisette took the single-edged razor blade between her thumb and forefinger and rested one sharp point against her skin. Overhead, a failing fluorescent light blinked on and off, its buzzing an incessant lamentation to protest its own mortality. Her heart beating out of her chest, she paused and glanced around the shop floor of the former factory that now housed her husband Isadore's landscaping company. This was the last place her daughter's fiancé, Michael Parrish, would think to look for her. Hell, until she heard herself giving the taxi driver the address, she hadn't expected to find herself here either.

Now, she realized the old factory was probably the last place on earth she felt at all safe.

Her mother's shop—*her* shop—had been desecrated, and no number of new fixtures or fresh coats of paint could keep her mind's eye from seeing the racial slurs and symbols of hatred sprayed on its walls.

Her once beloved home offered no sanctuary. The enemy now lived there, beneath her roof, acting as her caregiver. Feigning devotion, while preventing her recovery.

She drew a breath, then cut the first slit—long enough and deep enough to leave a scar. To leave a scar was the point. This wound and the six to follow, each in honor of Erzulie Dantor, would form a *gad*, part invocation, part petition for protection. A curse had been placed on Lisette, and tonight she was appealing to Erzulie Dantor to rid her and her family of the man who'd laid it.

The stroke hadn't only affected her arm. It had also gifted her with a tremor, a halting step, and slurred speech. Perhaps Dantor, whose tongue had been cut out by those she'd trusted, would feel a stronger affinity for her because of it. Besides, Dantor was a mother, too—a mother who protected her children with the same fierceness Lisette felt burning in her own breast.

It had taken a visit from Papa Legba himself to awaken Lisette to the truth about Michael. Lisette wouldn't have accepted the revelation from any other source, even her own best instincts, as Michael's power allowed him to make a person see him in whatever light he wanted. He'd deceived her for years, and she hadn't had a single inkling.

Lisette should have acted sooner, but he'd kept her just weak enough to make sure she was housebound. And neither her husband, Isadore, nor her son, Remy, would listen to any word spoken against Michael; they had both fallen under his thrall. Only Lisette's father seemed immune to Michael's influence, and Michael did his best to keep her and her dad separated. Lisette knew the only reason she'd managed to slip away tonight was because Michael would've never suspected she'd leave Manon's side at such a time.

The pain and the sight of her own blood oozing up from the wound fed her anger.

The bastard will pay, and Erzulie Dantor will be the one to collect what is due.

Lisette wasn't sure if the thought belonged to her or to the old man. He regarded her with glistening dark eyes, his look telling her it didn't matter. He was with her, and she with him. For now, there was no separation. He reached up and pushed back the straw fedora he wore. Only then did she notice the black-and-red band encircling its crown.

Blood ran in a solid trickle down her forearm. A red pool began to form on the workbench's surface, her lifeblood's coppery scent now competing with the pungent, almost peppery smell of gasoline and sharp green perfume of cut grass that, regardless of season, permeated the building. Above them all floated the crisp chemical pine of a hanging car freshener one of Isadore's workers had hung on the tinsel Christmas tree Isadore insisted on setting out every year. It stood this year, as every year, beside the entrance of the staff breakroom, about five yards from her current workbench. The tacky antique held no lights, just twenty or so sparse green branches adorned with the perennial dollar-store silk ball ornaments—red, green, and a champagne color that might have once been gold. The angel on top regarded the scene enacted before her in frozen horror.

Lisette damned the angel for judging. She made the second gash.

The old man chewed on his pipe and squinted, as if he were considering a puzzling question. He drew the pipe from his mouth, used his free hand to grasp the mug that contained the other half of the rum, and lifted it to his lips for a quick, though appreciative, sip. As the old man returned the mug to the table, Lisette considered the words printed on its side.

Hell, yeah. She hated Mondays, too. And of late, every other damned day of the week.

From the moment Lisette had spotted her father, Alcide Simeon, teetering along drunk down Chartres Street, determined to play Celestin Marin's soul into hell with the unfamiliar silver trumpet in his hand, her world had grown more tumultuous with each passing day, the unthinkable manifesting itself with a disconcerting, disheartening regularity. Each week brought a new earthquake to shake and fracture her once firm foundation. Her bedrock had crumbled into shifting sand.

And now her baby girl was dying.

Severe preeclampsia. At this very moment, Lisette's girl was in the emergency room at Touro. The good doctors there were doing their damnedest to save both Manon and her unborn child. *Michael's unborn child.* CT scans, and ultrasounds, and cardio-somethings-or-other. Fancy tests could diagnose Manon's condition, but no medical intervention could strike at the root cause: the baby's father.

It was up to Lisette to do that. She made the third and fourth cuts in quick succession, a feeling like an icy finger tracing down her spine even as her arm caught fire.

Leaving Manon, slipping away from Isadore and Remy, had pretty near ripped her heart out, but until she could protect herself, she could do nothing for her daughter. Still, the sight of Isadore hunched over in the waiting room, his fists clenched, his skin ashen, would haunt her the rest of her life. She couldn't even let herself consider what her baby girl must be going through.

Ends and means, Devil and deep blue. She'd sort through rights and wrongs once she got the job done. Lisette drew the sharp edge along her forearm once more.

The old man rocked back on his stool, nodding in approval at the growing tally. She'd cut her arm clean off if that's what it took to keep Manon in this world. She would not let her daughter die.

Lisette had died, briefly.

Michael was the one who'd killed her.

A bead of sweat formed on her forehead as the second thought trampled over the first.

There had been no pearly gates opening wide, no bright light reaching out to embrace her. Instead she'd found herself in a strange world where fire burned cold and dark. Now, whenever she closed her eyes, she saw the exquisite, fearsome face of the fair witch who'd hovered above her, leading a versicle and response recantation of the spell for which Lisette's mother had given her life—a spell to hold *The Book of the Unwinding* locked between realities.

The witches had returned Lisette to life as a means to counter her mother's magic, rendering her mother's self-sacrifice meaningless. To them, Lisette was a pawn. A key to turn in a lock. Their counterspell required only that they resuscitate her. They'd shown indifference to, or perhaps had even taken delight in, sending her back damaged.

The rising dark tide of greed and violence, lawlessness and disdain for common decency reported in the daily paper and on the evening news bore witness to the fact that the wicked had been successful in their efforts to return the foul book to this world. Where it all would end, she couldn't hazard a guess, but tonight was about shoring up the levees that protected her and her own.

Another slash. She fumbled with the razor, the blade slick with her own blood. She registered a metallic glint as it dropped to the floor. The old man pulled a fresh blade from behind the band on his hat, then leaned forward to offer it to her. Lisette reached out to accept the new razor, a sensation like static electricity shooting through her as their fingers brushed. In that instant, any semblance of his being a man fell away. She caught a glimpse behind the facade, and she understood Papa as the entity he was. She sensed the evil, the crawling chaos he alone held back.

Annihilation.

The word flickered in her mind, then the curtain fell and once again before her sat an old man. He lay his pipe on the table, its corncob bowl resting in a finger of her blood. He doffed his hat and laughed, seeming pleased by her flash of insight.

He nodded at the blade poised in her fingers, and Lisette fixed her eyes on his, taking strength from the surety she sensed there. She pressed the point of the blade into her skin, the deepest cut of all, and tugged it through her flesh with a savagery fed by her own rage. She lay the blade down beside her wounded arm, then dipped her forefinger into the pool of blood. She traced a heart pierced by a dagger, a simplified rendition of Erzulie Dantor's vèvè, then grasped the rum bottle and emptied its remaining contents over her wounds to feed the gad. She gasped, wincing at the fresh fire. The clear rum washed across the workbench's top, diluting her spilled blood as it dripped from the table to the floor, transforming the trickle into a stream.

Lisette reached over to the stool she'd stationed beside her, catching hold of one of the clean microfiber towels she'd retrieved from Isadore's stash in the cleaning supply closet. That went on top of her forearm—the first step in a makeshift bandage. She layered three more towels over it, then snatched up the roll of silver duct tape from which she'd already unrolled a six-inch lead. She attached the tip of the tape to the exposed skin of her wrist, unwinding the spool as she wrapped the tape around the towels.

"What have you done to yourself?" Michael asked, appearing, it seemed, from nowhere. He crossed to her and took hold of her left hand. "My God." She had to give the devil his due. He sounded sincere. Like he really gave a damn. Lisette glanced around his shoulder at the old man. Papa held a finger to his lips. Only then did she realize Michael was unaware of the old man's presence.

"You followed me," Lisette said, watching Michael's eyes dart around the gore.

"No," he said, focusing first on her face, then on her taped arm. His complexion went gray; he was in true shock. "Yes," he said, his forehead wrinkling, lips parting. "But only after we realized you'd gone missing." His features smoothed as he regained his equilibrium. "Isadore sent me to find you, since certain staff at the hospital don't quite consider 'fiancé' to be family." Lisette suspected the boy was lying on both counts, but it didn't matter. She was happy to have him away from Manon.

Michael took the spool of tape from her and began wrapping it around her arm, tighter and tighter. Finally, he bent over and bit into the tape, breaking the strand. "Tourniquet," he said, rushing around the shop floor till he found a mower belt. He retrieved the blade she'd dropped from the floor and cut through the loop, then slipped the belt high around her arm, tugging the ends tight and tying it. He repeated the movement twice, leaving the remaining belt to dangle.

The old man rose from his perch and circled around the table to stand at the unaware Michael's side. He nodded, a signal the time had come to speak. "What type of spell did you use?" she said. She spoke the words slowly and in a loud voice, the way her speech therapist had taught her. Still, the words slurred into one another.

Michael's head jerked back, and he examined her with a counterfeit concern. "Spell?" Butter wouldn't melt in this bastard's mouth. Lisette could see an aura like heat rising off blacktop develop around him. Michael was trying to nudge her perception of him away from suspicion and toward gratitude.

Gratitude. Lisette nearly snorted. "What type of spell did you use to find me?" He stood before her dumbfounded. This surprise, she intuited, was real. He took a step back, the better to study her. Or maybe to strike.

"My eyes are open," she said. "I see you as you are, witch. And your attacks on my family end right here." Her words might not have been clear, but by God, she knew he understood her intent.

Michael froze for a moment, then howled with laughter. "Well, get a load of you, Mother Perrault." An inquisitive look rose to his face. "It's okay for me to call you 'mother,' right? I mean, your daughter and I would already be married if she didn't keep putting me off because you're in such poor shape."

Lisette suddenly realized the delay of the nuptials had nothing to do with her health. Deep down, Manon sensed something was off. A tiny part of her daughter was fighting back against this witch's mind control. Lisette felt sure of it. Manon might've gotten free of him if he'd been less determined, but Michael had kept the crosshairs of his power fixed on her.

Tiny wrinkles formed at the corners of Michael's eyes as his face lit up with glee. "Of course, we both know you're never going to recover. Not completely. But you aren't going to die . . . again. At least not until I'm tired of playing with you."

Michael fell silent, then began cracking up again. His amusement infuriated her. "I'm sorry," he said, though there was no regret in his voice, "but 'spell'?" He paused, looking at her as if she were a total fool. "You stupid bitch. I used my phone to locate yours. I turned on your share-location setting when I helped you set it up." The aura that had formed around him had grown denser, darker, raw. "Isn't technology great?"

Lisette recognized this strange fire enveloping him. It was the same cold energy that had lit the twilight realm where the witches had caught her soul and sent it back to her hobbled body. Lisette felt her resolve crumble, fear gripping her heart.

"Now, I tell you what," he said, speaking in a sugary, patient tone like he was addressing a child. "The two of us are going to put this unpleasantness behind us." He held out his hand. "Come on. Take it." He shook his hand at her. "Come on," he repeated, this time with greater firmness. "I don't know how you saw through my magic, but I can make you forget. Put us back on a good footing."

"Never." Lisette shook her head. "Never."

The old man circled around her, but she ignored the movement, not wanting to alert Michael to his presence.

"Come on. We don't want to miss the show now, do we?"

Her tongue felt as if it were carved of wood. She shook her head again. This time not in protest, but to signal a lack of comprehension. He smirked at her. The arrogant son of a bitch actually smirked. "The big miscarriage. It's all been leading to this. Gonna be heartrending."

"But," Lisette said in utter amazement, "it's your child."

He shrugged. "That little clot has served its purpose. If it were up to me, I would've flushed it down the pipes weeks ago, but I had to wait for the go-ahead from the higher-ups." He smirked. "Or lower-downs. It's all a matter of perspective." He reached out to her once more. "Last chance. Take my hand, and I'll let Manon survive this horrible, horrible ordeal. Try my patience further, and I'll put an end to her, too. I don't want to, but you're making me." He looked at her with mock sympathy. "After all, it would be a terrible waste of a fine piece of ass."

He lunged forward and caught hold of her injured arm with both hands, squeezing until the pain drove her to her knees. "There, Mother." He nodded down at her. "It's gonna be all right now." The black fire surrounding him concentrated on his arms, then crept down, coalescing around his hands.

Lisette had never—in this world—felt such cold. Agonizing. Sharpening, rather than calming, the searing of her cuts.

She sensed the old man coming closer. In her peripheral vision, she saw him place his hands on either side of her head, close but not touching. The cold darkness that had begun to creep up her arm stopped its ascent. Michael regarded her with confusion, then startled, jerking his head up.

His expression turned to rage as he released her.

Gunfire.

One instant Lisette was gazing up at the fury twisting Michael's face. The next he was falling back, the splattered remains of the right side of his head trimming the tinsel Christmas tree. Lisette followed the angel's eyes and looked back over her shoulder. The old man was gone, replaced by another.

Her father's silver hair lit up like a halo beneath the dying fluorescent bulb's final flash.

TWO

Nathalie Boudreau hated the sound of jingle bells. She gripped the wheel of her SUV tighter and smiled, casting a quick glance back at the pair of middle-aged women she'd picked up outside the light show in City Park.

The women had taken to the "don we now" bit with gusto. They wore sparkly snowflake sweaters—one in blue, one in white—and matching red-and-green felt elf hats ornamented with jingle bells around the bands. As a finishing touch, each hat was tipped with another, larger bell in place of a tassel or pom-pom. They were visitors from Little Rock, one divorced, one widowed. First time for both in New Orleans, or "N'awlins" as they insisted the city was known to the natives. They were having such fun saying it to each other, Nathalie didn't have the heart to set them straight. They were nice enough ladies, really, good people, both of them. Nathalie could tell. And she sure bore them no ill will.

All the same, she really hated the sound of jingle bells.

Still, the bells weren't the whole of it. She hated the holidays, everything about them. In fact, she hated the whole dang month of

December. But Nathalie would also hate to bring these nice women down, so she ignored the arrhythmic tinkling and sang along with her passengers to the carol playing on the radio.

Nathalie felt a hand on her upper arm and glanced up into her rearview mirror. One elf was focused on her phone's screen, but the other was leaning forward, craning her head around the side of Nathalie's headrest.

"Doesn't this music just put you in the holiday spirit?"

Spirits. Nathalie repressed a shudder. Spirits were the very reason she hated the holidays. Every year Nathalie pasted a jolly smile on her face and responded in kind whenever someone wished her a merry Christmas or happy holidays, but the twinkling lights and tinkling bells seemed to summon the most unsavory of ghosts.

She'd grown up witnessing apparitions, but she'd learned right quick most people didn't see everyone she did, and those who didn't did not like to be alerted to what they were missing. She could still feel the sharp sting of her mama's slap almost thirty years on.

"Why, how could it not?" Nathalie responded, doing her best to match the woman's sugarplum enthusiasm. Not quite a lie, but still a good distance from the truth. Her ride-along elf, pleased by the dissimulation, gave her arm a gentle squeeze, then leaned back.

Over the years, Nathalie had gotten used to seeing spirits, the fresher ones often stumbling around disoriented, sometimes hostile due to their confusion. She could spot one as easily on Independence Day as on the Feast of the Immaculate Conception, but the ghosts of December, they were something different. The spirits she spotted in December were the ugly ones—menacing, raging, desperate—and the closer it got to the winter solstice, the more violent they became. Maybe it was the sharpened emotions, heightened expectations, and inevitable disappointments of the season that fed their anger in much the same way as the holidays affected many of the living. These were the spirits who held on to this world, the ones who sensed they were better off here than with whatever might be waiting for them on the other side. From the warped thoughts and fractured, furious energy Nathalie picked up from them, she thought the ghosts of December might be right.

It struck her that she hadn't spotted a single demented specter this season. Maybe she hadn't noticed them because she was in a better frame of mind. She was happier this winter than she'd ever been. She had Alice now, or at least had the chance of having Alice, and starting New Year's Eve, she'd be working for Evangeline Caissy at her club. Not just working the door like she'd been doing on and off since Thanksgiving, but as the club's assistant manager. Both gifts had come unexpectedly on the last day of November, starting with Alice's apologetic, almost embarrassed request for help transporting a table and chairs from a consignment store in the Faubourg Lafayette to her new apartment in the Quarter.

If Nathalie wasn't too busy. If she didn't mind.

Nathalie would've moved a mountain for Alice. Nathalie's assistance had earned her a mushroom po'boy at the diner on Dauphine, from which Nathalie had claimed as a souvenir a coaster in the shape of a defiant boy with akimbo arms, his hands pushed deep into the pockets of his suitcoat. Perhaps it had granted her luck, because she'd had a cup of coffee with Alice at the same place two days later, and nearly every day after that, too.

Ms. Caissy had rung her up the same night. Another happy chat had come of that, this time over vodka and tonic, the vodka for Ms. Caissy and the tonic for Nathalie—she was driving, after all.

Things were good, or at least they were getting good. Only she had a relentless gnawing cold in her gut warning her the spirits' absence had nothing to do with her. This year the spirits were lying low, or maybe even moving on, to avoid something way scarier than them.

Nathalie turned off Canal Street and made two quick rights to arrive at the hotel's entrance. "Here you are," she said, with no small sense of relief to be ridding herself of the jinglejangling.

"You should pop in for a moment," Elf One said, "and have a look at how they decorated the lobby. They did a marvelous job."

"It's true. It is enchanting," her friend said, drawling out the last word for emphasis.

Even though Nathalie had lived pretty near her entire life a stone's throw in one direction or another from this hotel, she'd never actually visited its annual holiday display. "Yeah, I know," she said, letting her bright tone imply she had. "They're famous for that."

A gentleman in a black top hat approached the SUV and opened its rear door. The women piled out in a tinkling chorus of thank-yous—a handful aimed at Nathalie, the rest at the hotel's doorman—and happy holidays, intended, Nathalie felt sure, for her benefit. She waited, watching the women until they'd passed through the hotel's polished brass doors, a sudden odd concern for their safety rising in her like sap.

The sound of gunfire made her jolt, and she slipped down low in her seat, scanning her surroundings for its source. No one else reacted. The doorman stood before the hotel, grinning and greeting passersby, then rushed to open the door for a guest carrying a multitude of shopping bags. A growing sense of dread bubbled up in her.

She took a few deep breaths to slow her heartbeat, ready to call it a night and head home despite the one silver lining in the dark cloud of December: the bounty of fares. She reached over to sign out of the driving app even as her phone began to ring. A local number. She didn't recognize it. She didn't need to. She sensed who was on the other end.

Her finger hovered over the red button, inviting her to decline the call, but Nathalie resisted the impulse and tapped the green button instead. "Mrs. Perrault?"

There was a moment of silence, then Lisette Perrault's panicked voice exploded through the speaker. "I'm sorry," she said, almost shouting. There was a pause, and just as Nathalie was about to respond, Lisette continued. "I'm sorry. I know I shouldn't involve you. I do. But I don't know who else to call."

"I'm sorry, ma'am. Involve me in what? Are you okay?"

"No," came the sharp, angry response. "I am not okay."

Nathalie could hear Lisette's labored breathing. "Where are you?" Nathalie asked, certain she'd regret getting caught up in whatever was going on, but even more sure she'd never forgive herself if she didn't try to help. "Are you at your shop?" Nathalie sure hoped not. Ever since she was young, she'd done her best to avoid Vèvè. The faces that peered out of its paned windows onto Chartres Street still sent chills down her spine.

"No. We're at my husband's business," Lisette said without elucidating on the cryptic "we." "Over in Elmwood." Her tone, though softening, still rang with agitation.

"I can find it," Nathalie said. "Is someone hurt? Do you want me to call an ambulance?"

The distant rumble of Lisette's dark laughter startled her. "No, *ma chère*, it is way too late for that."

Too late. A vision flashed through her mind. An enigmatic older man in a straw fedora. Lisette's father, the Quarter's famous trumpet player. She recognized him from the memorial for Alice's uncle Vincent, which she'd attended before she even met Alice. She saw the steely glint of hatred in his eyes, the pistol in his hand.

Nathalie startled at the peal of gunshot even though she now recognized it as an echo of an earlier and distant event.

"Can I trust you?" Lisette's words broke through Nathalie's muddled vision. She repeated herself when Nathalie failed to respond, fear and fury twining together in her voice.

"I'll come," Nathalie said. "I'll see what I can do." She was getting a bit too good at answering direct questions with near truths. "I'll be there as soon as I can."

Another silence, and the call ended.

Nathalie didn't need to pull up the address of Perrault Landscaping, not now that she'd picked up on Lisette's anguish. A direct channel, as unyielding and as dangerous as a train track's electrified conductor rail, would deliver her right to Lisette's side. Nathalie signaled and checked for oncoming cars before pulling out into traffic, then let the dark gravity of Lisette's emotions take over as navigator.

Nathalie pulled into the parking lot of one of the smaller industrial buildings on Sams Avenue, her headlights revealing a tan box dominated on one side by a tall gray roller door illuminated by a security light, and on the other by a forest-green canopy sheltering the main entrance. Two green-and-white heavy-duty pickups had been stationed within view of the blinking red light of a security camera. Another camera pointed down at the main door.

Whatever Lisette had gotten herself into here tonight, there could be evidence of it on those cameras if the footage wasn't deleted. And maybe even if it was—an inquiring mind might notice the gap carved into the recording. Nathalie killed her engine and dug beneath her seat, fishing out an old baseball cap she kept on hand for when it rained. She put the cap on and pulled the bill down to shield her face from the camera. She slipped out of the vehicle and eased the door almost closed, then leaned against it so the latch caught with a quiet click. Only then did it strike her that she was trying to sneak into a place to which she'd been summoned.

She pulled the cap's bill a bit farther down to cover more of her face, then noticed a third security camera pointing straight at her vehicle, privileged with a full-frontal view of her license plate.

"Well, double damn," she muttered under her breath, and glared directly at the camera. A shower of white sparks rained down in unison from each of the three devices. "So, we're gonna start up with that again," she said, angry at herself, at Lisette Perrault, and at her own once dormant, now capricious power, jarred loose by her first encounter with Lisette and her mother—yet another spirit.

She slipped under the green canopy and tugged on the door handle. The door rattled but remained closed. She noticed a button to the side of the door and pushed it. A moment later she heard a quick buzz followed by a click.

A disheartening sense of déjà vu told her she might not ought to open the door, but she was here, and she was needed. She grasped the handle again and, overestimating the strength it would take to open the door, swung it wide.

Nathalie had seen things before, real bad things, especially in the last five months or so. The tableau that greeted her, she decided in a flash, landed squarely at number two, right after watching the reanimated corpse of her former boss crabwalk across the floor on limbs first severed and then reattached the wrong way, left to right and forward to back.

No, Nathalie told herself, trying to siphon a grain of optimism from the situation, compared to that, the sight of Lisette Perrault on her knees, covered in blood spatter and struggling with one arm to drag a corpse onto an uncooperative blue plastic tarp was a cakewalk.

Lisette broke off from her efforts and looked up at Nathalie with an ashen face and haunted eyes. "He wasn't a good man," she said, the pronouncement ringing with the finality of a full explanation, then renewed her labors.

Hell, maybe it was explanation enough.

"No, ma'am," Nathalie said, choking back the bile rising in her throat. "I'm guessing he wasn't or we wouldn't be here." Nathalie drew closer to the body, too close. She could see a good portion of the man's head had been blown off, and the stench of murder gripped her stomach and gave it a good shake. Nathalie's attention glided up from the floor to a blood-coated workbench, then to a fake Christmas tree topped by an angel whose face had been painted with an eternally alarmed expression that probably mirrored her own.

"Help me," Lisette said, a desperate keening in her voice as she fought to gain traction in an oval of congealing blood.

Nathalie noticed Lisette's left arm, wrapped in silver duct tape and tied off with a length of rubber. Blood was seeping out of each end of the metallic bandage and in a spiral along its winding seam. Nathalie rushed forward, her new sneaker pressing a flawless imprint of its tread into the gore, triggering memories of every single police procedural she'd ever read or watched.

"You're hurt," she said, taking a step back. Only then did she realize she'd managed to leave a textbook-perfect blood transfer print on what had, a second before, been a patch of clean floor. Hell, if she was implicated, the quality of the evidence she was creating against herself would probably be perfect enough to convince any sane juror she'd been framed. She shook the thought off and focused on the only person in the room who seemed more terrified than she was.

Nathalie approached Lisette the way she would a frightened child. "He hurt you," she said. She squatted beside her and slipped an arm around her waist, then rose and stepped back, bringing Lisette with her. The body slipped to the floor. "This was self-defense," she said, easing Lisette onto a stool beside the bloodied workbench.

The sound of a leather sole slapping the concrete spun Nathalie around.

"Yes, young lady," came a man's weary voice from a patch of shadow at the far end of the floor. "It was. Everything you say is true, although not in the way you think."

The voice belonged to Lisette's father. Alcide Simeon—his name came to her. Mr. Simeon stepped forward into the light, though to Nathalie it seemed a finger of the shadow followed him like gum stuck to the heel of his shoe. He still held the pistol that Nathalie assumed had done the damage.

Nathalie offered one opportunity to ambush her per customer. If Mr. Simeon was here, like in her vision, then the elderly man in the fedora was more than likely lurking somewhere, too. She glanced around the space, scanning for the missing man. "Where's your friend?" she addressed Mr. Simeon. "Is he still here?"

The silver-haired man's head tilted back, a line creasing his forehead as he, too, began to survey the push and riding lawn mowers stowed along the room's perimeter. "Friend? What friend?"

"The old guy. No offense," she added with the same breath. "In the hat."

A look passed between father and daughter.

"Only been two men here tonight. Him"—he nodded down at the body—"and me."

The way he'd lingered on the word "men" told her she wasn't the only one good at deflecting direct questions. Nathalie was, she reckoned, witnessing karma in action.

"We owe her more than equivocation." Lisette addressed the words to her father, then turned her face to Nathalie. "What you perceived as a man," she said, "is anything but. I won't skimp on clarification once we've dealt with this situation, but now I've got more pressing issues."

"You talk some sense to my girl. She's thinking she can clean all this," he said, brandishing the pistol in a wide sweep encompassing half the room, "up. Make it like nothing happened. But sooner or later, and it's gonna be sooner, truth'll out."

"You should probably put that down, sir," Nathalie said with a nod toward the gun.

He looked down at it with surprise, as if he'd forgotten he held it in his grip. He bent down with some effort, bracing himself by placing his free hand on his left knee, and laid the gun on a clean stretch of the concrete floor. Hand on knee, he pushed himself up. "If it isn't the police who come for me"—he planted his gaze on Nathalie—"it's gonna be one of you." He studied her face and then shook his head. "Don't be coy with me, young lady. You know what I mean."

"Well, no, sir, I—"

"Witches." He shouted the word at her, then his lips curled up like he'd tasted something bitter. "One of you witches."

"Oh, okay," she said, rattled less by the unexpected novelty of being called a witch than by the sense of rightness with which the label struck her. "You have nothing to worry about from me," she said, trying to reassure herself as much as to convince Mr. Simeon. "Mrs. Perrault trusted me enough to call me . . ." Her words trailed off as the single part of her mind that wasn't reeling picked that precise moment to raise a pertinent question. She turned her focus to Lisette. "Why did you call me?"

Lisette regarded her with a cautious look. "Because you saw much worse than this the night you helped my mama and me. You've kept quiet about that. I'm hoping you'll do the same now."

Her memories from the night Nathalie had agreed to serve as Mrs. Simeon's *chwal* remained a bit dim, at least those made while Mrs. Simeon had controlled Nathalie's body. Still, enough of what she had witnessed the night of the witches' ball burst into her consciousness to kick even the sight of Frank's tortured corpse to second place on her list of horrors. The scene before her now ranked a distant third.

"I did this." Mr. Simeon's voice pulled Nathalie back. "I will take responsibility for it. I need you," he began, crossing the room till he stood beside his daughter, "to see to my girl."

Nathalie caught sight of a swirling movement on the far side of the shop floor. She craned her neck and focused on the area. The finger of shadow that had attached to Mr. Simeon resolved itself as an arm. Like one bubble breaking free of another, an outline of a man pulled itself up and out of the surrounding darkness, falling forward onto its hands and feet. The smell of sulfur rose up all around them.

This, Nathalie realized, was the bigger and badder thing her regular spirits were avoiding. A demon. And it didn't count as her first. Her mind flashed to the night of the conjuring at Grunch Road, when she'd narrowly succeeded in preventing a shadow demon from dragging Alice down into the crumbling earth.

She stumbled backward, pointing at the entity, first mouthing and then yelling "there, there," once her wind caught up with her panic.

A second entity broke free from the shadow, this one screeching and squealing as a third demon forced its way around it. They lumbered forward, their humanoid shapes fading into an amorphous mist that joined together as one and crept across the floor, covering the body.

Lisette jumped up, knocking over the stool she'd been sitting on. Mr. Simeon caught hold of his daughter. "You're doing this," he called to Nathalie, as he dragged Lisette back. His accusation held more hope than rancor.

Better the devil you know . . . Nathalie thought as the unified shadow creature grew, lengthening, spuming till it swallowed not only the body, but also the gore-covered workbench. "We should go," she said, already in retreat toward the entrance. She glanced back at the front entrance to see another dark mist roiling there behind them.

Nathalie spun toward the rear door, which, for the moment, stood clear. "Move," she yelled as she bounded over to Lisette and her father, bowling into them and pushing them in the direction of the exit even as she reached out to right them. She sent a burst of energy ahead, a solid punch that blew the rear exit door off its hinges, leaving their path wide open. "Now *that*," she spoke directly into Mr. Simeon's ear, "I did do." She steered them toward the opening.

A force reached out and slammed them to the floor, knocking the wind out of her. She felt a hand grab her ankle, its grip a burning cold like dry ice. She pushed up onto her hands and knees and tried to pull away, but the hand yanked her back, pulling her a good twenty feet from the door.

She looked up to discover the creeping shadow had swallowed the workbench and was working its way up the artificial tree. As she watched, helpless, it climbed to the highest bough and cascaded over the plastic angel. It then slid down the other side of the tree and along the floor until it rested within an arm's length of Lisette and her dad. Then Nathalie saw the elderly man from her vision circle the two, tracing a barrier around them with his cane. He turned to the shadow, holding his cane high, and advanced on it.

The shadow pulled back in a sudden great wave, taking with it all it had touched. The blood-spattered tree and its unfortunate angel, the gory workbench, the body, the blood that had pooled around it. These things diffused and became part of the mist that continued to recede until it had begun to pass through the building's solid walls. Nathalie felt the grip around her ankle loosen, and she jumped up and bolted forward. Her uneven stride caused her to glance down as she ran, only to realize her shoe, the one she'd trailed through the blood, was missing.

In the moment before the shadow completely disappeared through the wall, something shot out from within it and fell with a hollow sound to the floor. The object bounced up and came down again about a yard from Nathalie's unshod foot.

The plastic angel gazed up at her in wonder.

THREE

Alice Marin stood on the fourth-floor balcony, looking down at the view. From one angle, a view of St. Louis Cathedral's steeples—rising above the neighboring building's duo HVAC units—and from the other, the twin spans of the Crescent City Connection cantilever bridge straddling the Mississippi. She grasped the window's casing and closed her eyes, leaning forward and breathing in the river's muddy scent on the breeze, trying to convince herself she was finally home. She opened her eyes and turned away from the window. One plain truth could not be ignored: if she were home, she wouldn't have agreed to pay an astronomically high rent so she could lease a partially furnished apartment on a month-to-month basis.

She needed to keep her options open, a sense of possibility alive, even if that meant having one foot out the door. She couldn't bear to be confined again—not in an asylum, not on the Dreaming Road, not even in her once-upon-a-time hometown.

The apartment was dark except for the French Quarter's ambient, all-night glow, and a short strand of battery-powered lights that coiled in a sloppy spiral around a miniature rosemary Christmas tree—a sweet gift from the ever-prudent Nathalie. Nathalie, tense and voluble, had been tentative about offering her the gift, shifting it from hand to hand. Before Alice could even speak, she'd provided her with a hundred excuses not to accept it, even grumbling that she hated the holidays herself, so she didn't know what had possessed her to buy it. Still, Nathalie had glowed with pleasure when Alice took the plant from her, then leaned in and kissed her.

After their meal that afternoon, Nathalie walked her home from their cafe. Yes, in spite of herself, Alice had begun to think of the coffee shop on the edge of the Marigny as theirs. When they reached Alice's door, Nathalie fished a pack of miniature lights out of her pocket. "Maybe these are stupid," she said, pressing the lights into Alice's free hand. "I couldn't decide." She hesitated, then dared another quick peck on Alice's lips before startling at the sound of the cathedral's bells and darting away, calling back over her shoulder that she was late to a meeting with her boss, with Evangeline. Nathalie had left Alice— plant and possibly stupid lights in hand—on her doorstep, laughing. Alice realized that since she'd returned from the Dreaming Road, she'd only laughed, at least with sincerity, twice. Both times were because of Nathalie.

She approached the plant and gently rubbed a few of its leaves between her thumb and forefinger. She lifted her hand to her nose to savor the fragrance.

Rosemary.

Alice suspected Nathalie had perceived its magical properties as a ward against evil spirits and nightmares, just as Nathalie had intuited how to draw closer to her without making her feel cornered. Alice would set the pace, if there was a pace to be set. This was Nathalie's real gift to her.

◆ ◆ ◆

The lights on the plant flickered, and the air grew heavier, denser, the sensation erasing the smile she'd felt lingering on her lips. Though she had not seen him since before her years-long imprisonment on the Dreaming Road, Alice needed no visual confirmation of his presence. She sensed him staring up at her window, the intensity of his gaze enough to affect her apartment's ambiance.

Rosemary, effective against evil spirits and nightmares, but not against a callous, prideful ass like Nicholas Marin.

Alice crossed the room and snatched up a key ring with a hand trembling not from fear, but from fury. She leaned out the window and flung the keys, aiming for Nicholas's face, her smug target lit by the glow of a lamppost lantern. Her aim was true, but he stepped back, leaving them to land at his feet.

Offering him the keys, even as a missile, was nothing more than a symbolic gesture. If he wanted to enter, he needed neither her permission nor her keys. Nicholas was renowned for coaxing locks open. He bent down and picked them up, then looked back up at her, shaking his head. The ever-patient father disappointed by a little girl's tantrum.

Only he wasn't her father. He was her half brother. Still, that knowledge couldn't undo the years of history between them. Regardless of their true relationship, a part of her would always see him as the father who'd abandoned her. And Nicholas, she understood, would always use the ambiguity of their relationship to keep her off-kilter.

Alice flipped on a lamp, and Daniel's crooked, self-conscious smile greeted her. No photos of Daniel existed; servitor spirits couldn't be photographed. His image was always blurred, as if the camera's shutter couldn't blink fast enough. She'd been working on this painting of him for weeks, determined to catch his essence before his image slipped from her memory.

Alice was wearing the shorty pajamas that Lucy, her self-appointed personal shopper, had purchased on her behalf. She tugged the oversize gray sweatshirt that her cousin Lucy had advised her to burn over the pajamas. Alice told herself she donned the sweatshirt because she felt a chill, but there was no denying the extra layer, a polyester-cotton blend breastplate, made her feel less vulnerable.

She stood there, facing the door, waiting for the sound of the key in the lock. Then, feeling foolish, she advanced and swung the door open at the same moment Nicholas reached it.

They stood there, silent, glaring at each other, waiting . . . but for what? For the other to blink first? Everything she wanted to say to him, every word she had rehearsed in anticipation of this moment failed her. Alice felt her anger begin to turn to tears. That she would not allow to happen. She spun on her heel and strode back into her apartment. *Her* apartment. She drew a feeble courage from the knowledge she was the mistress of this shabby, threadbare domain.

She heard the clack of the closing door, followed by the sound of footsteps that signaled he was drawing near. Alice turned back to find his eyes weren't focused on her but darting around her quarters.

"You didn't have to do this," he said, disdain obvious in his glance, if not his tone. "Move into . . . ," he gestured with a rolling wave of his hand around them, "into private quarters. My house will always be yours."

"Your house was never mine," Alice said, pleased that even though her mind was raging, her voice remained cool. There would be no tears. Not now. And certainly not for him to witness.

Nicholas didn't respond beyond a steely glint in his eyes. He turned his attention to the rosemary tree. "Cute," he said with an intonation that could either show sincerity or cloak sarcasm. "She gave it to you?"

"Yes," Alice said, sharpening her tone as she spoke, "*she* did." It seemed purposeless to ask him how he'd learned of Nathalie. Perhaps he'd had the decency to alert his *other* sister of his homecoming before inflicting himself on Alice. Perhaps someone else had told him. There was no shortage of loose tongues, not with so many failing witches seeking to ingratiate themselves with those who still had power. Perhaps he'd been spying on her since her return to the common world. It didn't matter. Not really. All that mattered was that she move him off the topic of Nathalie before he sullied her name by speaking it.

Her curtness chafed him. "*She,*" he parroted her, "isn't right for you."

Alice barked out an indignant laugh. "Now you want to play father?"

"To start with," he said, brushing off her derision, "you're twenty-two. She's thirty-three. The age difference is . . . inappropriate. Distasteful." He gave each syllable of the word its full measure.

"You're old enough to be Evangeline Caissy's father," she said, noticing he winced at her name. "That didn't stop you from seeing her."

"No," he said, his usual ramrod-straight posture curving into a question mark. "But it did, in the end, factor into the failure of the relationship." He paused, his softening gaze suggesting he was reliving the romance's denouement. "Although the final nail in the coffin was her implying I'd murdered my own son." He shook his head. "There is no coming back from that." A lopsided grin joined his narrowing eyes to show he'd regained the arrogance of which regret, or perhaps simple wounded pride, had, for an instant, deprived him.

Alice rushed to speak before he could return to his unwelcome offering of counsel. "I lived seven years on the Dreaming Road in the time since you took off on your pilgrimage. In my mind I feel much closer to her age—"

"Regardless, your birth certificate still says you're twenty-two."

"My birth certificate still says you're my father." This blow landed. He fell silent, scanning her face as if she were a puzzle to solve.

He crossed to the round, possibly vintage, chrome and red Formica dining table straddling the bare floorboards of the kitchen area and the dingy beige of the worn shag rug that demarcated the living area. He pulled out one of the plastic stacking chairs—also red, but not vintage, just cheap—and sat. "You know nothing about her. About her family. There are matters surrounding the Boudreau family to which you should be made privy—"

"Wait." Alice held up a hand to stop him. Now she got it. "This isn't about Nathalie. It's about Lincoln. Lincoln and Evangeline. You're hoping to manipulate me into trying to drive them apart. And if doing so hurts my relationship with Nathalie, well, you'd consider me justifiable collateral damage. Again." Nicholas kicked out his legs and huffed as if from exasperation. "Admit it. It's killing you to see her with someone else. With someone who makes her happy."

Nicholas flushed red and opened his mouth to speak, but then appeared to think better of it. His shoulders slumped as his expression shifted from irritation to sadness. "This isn't about Evangeline. But you're right that it's about Lincoln. And his brother"—he paused, waving his hand, pretending to search for the name—"Washington."

"Wiley," Alice said. "He goes by Wiley. And he's a good guy. He's good for Hugo."

"He's unworthy of Hugo . . ." Nicholas let his words trail off, letting what was left unsaid be heard loud and clear. He waited for her reaction, but Alice refused to take the bait. "They're killers," he said in a low, matter-of-fact voice that left no room to think he might be joking. "Executioners, to be precise."

"Executioners?"

He shrugged. "Magic is about to flatline, but the Boudreaus have always been good soldiers. To the last man." He paused, then fixed her with his gaze. "To the last witch."

"I don't know what you're trying to convince me of, but—"

"There are laws. Laws of conduct among witches. Many byzantine, most overlooked and by and large unenforced, but there remain a handful that are considered immutable."

"Such as?"

"Such as 'Thou shalt not assist thy not-altogether-dead grandfather in the slaughter of witches at his own memorial ball.'" He rapped his knuckles on the table and grimaced. "I do apologize. I should have said 'father,' not 'grandfather'—I understand you relished passing on that sordid tidbit to the masses." He raised his hand to his heart, an involuntary gesture she felt sure.

For a moment she wondered if this act could be more than a prideful man's reaction to public humiliation, if it betrayed an ambivalence on his part as well. Perhaps he regretted his lies. His desertion. That he couldn't find it in his heart to love her.

"Everyone knows Celestin took me to the Dreaming Road by force. That I didn't play a role in the massacre."

"Oh, do they?" he said, feigning innocence. "Even after what you got up to at Précieux Sang, ripping the gates off their hinges? You were foolish to indulge in such theatrics before magic-starved witches."

"It wasn't theatrics. I wanted to send the message that I wouldn't let myself be *anyone's* victim, ever . . ." She fell silent, acknowledging to herself that the message hadn't been for the benefit of the toothless witches who'd gathered in the cemetery, hoping to walk away with a magical relic, ready to snatch up fingers, ears, or even a pinkie toe. The message was for Celestin, a farewell to ring through every cell of his consciousness-haunted corpse as the witches carved it up and parceled it out.

"And quite the message you sent, too," Nicholas said, his words trampling over her thoughts. "You're strong. You're powerful. More powerful than most of the witches in the Gulf region combined." He paused, a glint in his black eyes. "You're hard." This he said with a timbre that hinted at pride. Then he smirked and mimed hacking off his left hand and tossing it into the crowd, a parody of her dismembering his . . . their father's body. "You could be, no, you are dangerous."

She looked back on the day and for an instant saw herself as another might. She must have been, as Fleur had later told her, horrifying. *Glorious.* She'd only been brought back from the perfect hell Celestin had built for her on the Dreaming Road hours before. Daniel had given his life to save her, and if it weren't for Nathalie, they would have lost Hugo, too—a fact she ought to share with the man who stood before her criticizing the woman who'd saved his child, now his only child. Alice had been traumatized, maybe even a bit out of her mind. Would she act in the same manner today if given the chance to reconsider? Once again she felt the heft of the athame in her hand. In her imagination, she could see the gleam of the dying sun on its fine blade. Her hand moved, a nearly involuntary action, and again she felt the blade slice in a single swift stroke through withering flesh and brittle bone.

Nicholas studied her face, then nodded as if in agreement with himself.

"You've got a lot of your mother in you. You do," he said, emphasizing the last two words as if he anticipated an objection.

Ambivalence prevented her from doing so. She felt butterflies in her stomach and placed a hand over the fluttering spot. She hoped she did share her mother's strength but feared the seeds of Astrid Andersen Marin's darkness might be germinating within her. Maybe it was only her time in the hospital on Sinclair, the years when her magic had been tamped down and kept in check, that had kept those seeds from reaching maturity and bearing fruit.

Now it felt as if nothing could constrain her.

"There are laws," he said, wagging an accusatory finger at her, as if he were certain she'd broken more than a few. "And there are those who enforce them." He cocked an eyebrow. "Strange, isn't it? There are only"—he paused, making a show of counting his fingers—"five witches of any true ability left in New Orleans, and three of them are sharing their beds with a Boudreau?"

The butterflies in her stomach caught fire. Alice wasn't, not yet. Maybe not ever. But her love life was none of his business.

"I must admit," he said with exaggerated nodding, "I am beginning to feel a bit left out. I wouldn't mind having a go at the younger Boudreau boy myself." A sly smile rose to his face as he savored her surprise. "Not all of us are as narrow in our tastes as you and our hapless Hugo seem to be."

Her blushing discomfort sated his desire to shock her. "I'm sorry," he said, though his tone was anything but apologetic. "I'd assumed anyone who's spent seven years on the Dreaming Road would have a more cosmopolitan perspective on matters of the flesh." He'd succeeded in driving home his point about her immaturity and the common-world age difference between Nathalie and herself. He leaned toward her. "Or are you, the worldly-wise habitué of the Dreaming Road, uncomfortable discussing sexuality with me because an infinitesimal part of you still sees me as your father . . . despite your very public disavowal?"

He covered his face with his hands, giving her the impression that he had revealed more than he would like about his own hurt. When he lowered his hands, his face had lost all vitality. He looked older. He looked tired. "I didn't come to fight with you. The fact is I didn't even come to comment on your life choices. I only came because I wanted to warn you that your actions may have unintended consequences. You've brought a lot of attention on yourself. And with a serial killer for a patriarch, we Marins were already under intense scrutiny."

A vague-enough admonition. Alice reasoned the true goal of this encounter was to frighten her so that she would seek shelter under the canopy of Nicholas's protection. His visit was a last-ditch effort to regain control over her. The thought should have rekindled the flame of her anger, but it didn't. Maybe because she no longer felt afraid.

Alice realized she, too, had lost her will to battle. Rather than vengeance, she wanted answers. She might never have such a ripe opportunity to get them.

"I met her, you know," Alice said. "I met Astrid. On the Dreaming Road."

His eyes widened ever so slightly. A sign, Alice took it, of true surprise.

"And how is my dear, devoted wife?" His tone was biting, but Alice could sense the news had thrown him. Alice couldn't tell whether he truly still cared about Astrid or if he was simply buying time to regain his footing.

"She's gone now," Alice said, searching his expression for the answer to that question. She saw only amused incredulity. His disbelief felt like a challenge. "The world Astrid inhabited was collapsing around us as we spoke. She had no way out—"

"Oh, she had a way out. Astrid always has a scapegoat for the Devil and a life raft for the deep blue sea. I suspect she'll still be carrying on long after the human race has died out, and radioactive cockroaches rule the world."

"She confessed everything to me."

"You may rest assured anything she said to you was either a lie or a misdirection." He paused, seeming to reconsider. "Maybe you aren't so much like her after all. You enjoy a capacity for truth Astrid was born without."

"Says the man who pretended to be my father." The only thing Astrid had ever given Alice, perhaps the only thing she ever had to give Alice, was her story. Alice was unwilling to let Nicholas strip away the value of Astrid's bequeathal by shedding doubt on it.

"Says the man who tried his best to be a father to you."

Alice startled, stunned by the assertion. "You must be joking."

"No need to provoke or dissimulate. I see you are seeking an answer to the big why—Sinclair Isle, and its psychiatric care for those deranged with magic, as well as those deranged by magic. Why did I abandon a perfectly sane little girl there? The answer is simple, whether you choose to accept it or not." He leaned back in the chair and crossed his arms over his chest. "I put you there to keep you safe. Safe from Celestin, certainly, but most of all from Astrid. I knew she'd find her way back. Eventually. Once she got her claws into *The Book of the Unwinding*."

He sighed and forced his body into a less defensive pose, uncrossing his arms and folding his hands on the table. "I'm not certain for what purpose, but Celestin and Astrid made you to serve as a tool. Of one thing you may rest assured, your mother had a use for you. Otherwise, you would never have been born. Separating you from them, from your magic by means of the hospital's safeguards, seemed to be the best way to ensure your safety, and"—he shrugged—"the well-being of the rest of us. Don't forget, the heir to magic can't have children. If Astrid still had her sights set on capturing the last breath of magic, she would have mowed both you and Hugo down without a second thought. And if Celestin believed he might be the lucky witch, he would've done the same—to all of us."

"They had a falling out," Alice said. "Celestin trapped her on the Dreaming Road, just like he—"

"I," Nicholas said, holding up his hands to stop her. "*I* trapped Astrid on the Dreaming Road. Luc's tenth birthday. You—you were a newborn. I came upon her reading to the three of you from *The Lesser Key of Darkness*, letting Luc turn the pages as if it were a children's picture book." A slight shake of the head signaled that he still couldn't comprehend Astrid's actions. "'A present,' she called it. I snatched the book away and tried to burn it in the fireplace. Luc tried to dodge around me and rescue his gift. Hugo did as Hugo does—he escaped the room. You lay in the bassinet wailing. I had a full blaze in the fireplace, but *The Key* wouldn't burn. The flames danced around it, but they wouldn't touch it.

"Astrid bounded around the room, screaming as if I'd set her alight rather than that damnable grimoire. She didn't stop shrieking until she managed to recover the book. That's when I realized the degree to which Astrid was connected to *The Key*. I began laying the trap. It took a few months, but I succeeded. She fought like the hellcat she was . . . is, but I succeeded. I forced her psyche from the common world onto the Dreaming Road—or at least the hinterlands. Had I known Babau Jean

35

had turned it into his own private whorehouse, I might have pushed even harder, but I only recently learned that tidbit about the Storyville construct from your loquacious cousin."

Ah, Lucy had been his source of information. Alice felt certain there had been no ill intent on Lucy's part, only her customary lack of discretion.

Nicholas fell silent, his eyes landing on the easel standing in the corner. "It's a shame about Daniel," he said, his voice hushed in a moment of quiet candor.

Alice tried to blink back a tear, but the thought of her former nanny and oldest friend giving himself up to save her tore her apart every time it bubbled up in her mind.

To her surprise, she witnessed a tear trace a path down Nicholas's cheek. "He was one of a kind, our Daniel," he said, wiping away the offending tear and rising. "I'm sorry for disturbing you so late. This reunion might have gone better in the light of day."

"I doubt it," Alice said without rancor, her response bringing a laugh from Nicholas.

"No, I'm sure you're right." He turned toward the door.

"You think they might be coming after me?" she called after him. He looked over his shoulder at her. "The Boudreau brothers?"

He shook his head as he made his way to the door. "Not after you, my dear. You could handle them. I fear they're 'coming after' Fleur."

"Fleur? Why would they want to harm her?"

"You know why," he said, stopping to look back as he grasped the knob. "The spell she worked. For Lucy. To bring one person back to life, she would've had to sacrifice another." He opened the door, turning away. "Our sweet Fleur," he said as he stepped over the threshold, "is a murderess."

FOUR

Blood. Sex. Dreaming.
Intoxication. Adoration.
Deprivation.
Madness.

Astrid Andersen Marin rested one pale hand on the moonlit, silver trunk of a bald cypress, reaching out with the other to touch the words flickering before her, their fire cold and blacker than the midnight-blue night air in which they hovered.

They evanesced at her touch, others coalescing to take their place.

These are the gates to magic,
of which Madness is the greatest,
for Madness is the utter surrender to Magic.

The words dissipated as a young man, a teenager, crabwalked toward her at a furious clip, his broad shoulders straining the fabric of his royal blue-and-white letterman's jacket. A *shing* resounded as Babau

Jean's razor-blade smile showed itself on her lips. The boy cried out at the sight of her and pushed back in the opposite direction, trying to launch himself toward safety, but instead landed flat on his back before her feet. Astrid gazed down at him, a beautiful boy with a square jaw and thick, curling locks that gleamed golden even in the cooling light of the moon. His body was strong, athletic, pleasing in proportion—a true Adonis. He might have escaped Grunch Road had he not twisted his ankle on a treacherous tree root.

There is neither a left-hand nor a right-hand path.
Threefold, singular, serpentine, the way of Truth.

The young woman who'd come with him to Grunch Road had shown herself to be more fleet of foot than her lover. Astrid smiled, pleased the female offering would provide Rose with a much-needed challenge. Rose dearly loved to exercise her newly limber body, but she'd been let go from Bonnes Nouvelles for getting into a fistfight with another one of the dancers. Astrid hoped tonight's outing would bring an end to her tiresome pouting.

The boy screamed as a shrieking Rose gained on him, then she swung the sharp blade of her ax low, silencing him. Rose snatched the head up by its curls and sniffed the wind. "Here, girly, girly," Rose called out. "Your boyfriend has a kiss for you." She laughed, a cackle really. Dark magic—and the Book had revealed to Astrid that all magic is, at its root, dark—could steal the warmth from a witch's laughter, leaving it nothing but a screech to send shivers down a lesser being's spine.

Listening through Babau Jean's sensitive ears, Astrid heard the laughter have this exact effect on the young woman, who had, like a fool, hidden rather than attempt to circle back to the car. The terrified girl failed to suppress a sound that fell somewhere between a gasp and moan. Rose bounded forward, making a beeline toward the source of the noise, rising a foot off the ground as she did.

Another scream. Another silence.

Murder was the first act of magic.
Murder will be the last.
Every time.

Every time. Two most revelatory words. This had all happened before—the fall of the King of Bones and Ashes, the rise of the Queen of Heaven. The agonized union of opposites. A dissonance that conveyed magic, a stream of pure potential, into the common world.

The inconsolable maiden who weeps at the gate
for her missing bridegroom
Is the whore who coupled with the groom for silver,
And the huntress who ensnared and devoured him, who rent
him from limb to limb.
Kiss her bloody lips, surrender to her noxious seduction,
for She is Holy.
She is Magic.

Once Astrid had dreamed of becoming the Queen, but the Book would not have her. It offered her instead the role of mater dolorosa. In the end—and this was the end—she'd proved nothing more than a blind midwife.

Evangeline Caissy, the swamp witch, would be Queen. Preposterous, but Astrid sensed Evangeline had been born, perhaps even bred, to play the role. Evangeline's mother, Mireille, had carried the spark of *The Book of the Unwinding* inside her to these shores, much as she had later carried Evangeline in her womb. The Book had been present at Evangeline's conception, perhaps had even had a hand in molding her. Certainly, an affinity existed between the Book and the Caissy girl, well, really woman now.

Myrrha finds in the night what Psyche loses in the light.
The goring beast, the glory of the King of Bones and Ashes.
He who steals his father's fire,
to light the heavens and set the world ablaze.

Rose trudged backward, dragging the girl's remains along with her, and dropped the body alongside that of the boy. She scanned their surroundings until she spotted a tree stump, upon which she then sat. Resting the ax's blade between her knees and its handle between her chin and shoulder, she began pushing an implement she'd called a "bastard file" along the bit of the blade. The instrument made a whisking sound like Babau Jean's teeth as it sharpened the edge.

Astrid knew this wasn't an act of maintenance. It was foreplay.

Eventually, the scraping stopped, and the witch stood and cast a glance at Astrid before meandering off in the direction of the thin, crooked finger of lagoon that bisected the dirt lane known as Grunch Road. Sacrifice was, after all, thirsty work.

Psyche's dim torch lights Infinity in fear,
Her blade poised to carve the boundless into chaos.
Chaos is Potentiality fleeing Reason.

When Astrid first read *The Book of the Unwinding*, its message had been inked by the mist of Eli Landry's blood. Astrid recognized what she was now witnessing was an illusion, an afterimage, of the text she'd been blessed to receive. For all the lies told and conjectures made over the centuries about the Book, she'd found one to be true: the Book could only be read once.

Yes, she'd sacrificed everything for a book that could be read once.

That single reading merited each and every forfeit.

Madness is never blinded by reality.

Astrid repeated the thought aloud, the word "never" a tickle on the tongue.

The utterance acted like a charm, revealing a man who stood silent, observing, on the clearing's periphery. The light of the waxing moon seemed to melt around him rather than illuminate his features, but Astrid didn't need to see his face to recognize him. She knew Him. For whom He pretended to be. For what He was—and for what hid behind that. He had placed her foot on the first step of her descent. It seemed only fitting He should witness the end of her journey.

The darkest heart rejoices at its own bereavement.
The darkest heart, unflinching, sees Truth.

As a restorer of magical texts, Astrid had encountered hundreds of grimoires, preserved dozens, and returned many one-of-a-kind works to functionality, if not their original condition. Even now, she carried in her mind a catalog of all extant, lost, and legendary grimoires.

She had once included *The Book of the Unwinding* in this last category.

Astrid was on the cusp of finishing her apprenticeship at the Atelier Magnusson when a down-at-the-heels old man swept into the workshop with the presumptuousness of royalty in exile. He wore a threadbare brown wool jacket with cream pinstripes, its elbows shiny from long and—as evinced by the musk it exuded—constant wear, and too-large pants of maroon polyester. In his mottled hand, he clutched a battered, leather-bound, and, Astrid could spot from ten paces, counterfeit copy of *The Lesser Key.* The poor fool, she surmised, had squandered the last of his resources on the shoddy forgery.

Astrid had encountered *The Lesser Key* twice before, once protected by wards and unbreakable glass during her studies, and again while taking inventory of her deceased aunt's collection. Astrid had acquired her love for books, of both the arcane and common variety, from her aunt.

The Lesser Key exuded an undeniable magnetism, one strong enough to capture the imagination of the credulous, and to bend the will of the weak. Potent enough even to ensnare many otherwise astute witches. Sensing *The Lesser Key*'s allure, Astrid had dared to take hold of her aunt's copy and witness firsthand the tiny cilia-like shadows reaching out to test and seduce those it might. But she had not been seduced by the book's prickling overture. If anything, its predatory approach and trickster energy had repulsed her. She'd included her aunt's edition of the work among the texts to be turned over to the occult library in Blåkulla.

After experiencing *The Lesser Key* herself, she conjectured the tract had been created as a kind of insidious hoax. Its purpose was most likely to collect magic from beguiled witches, or perhaps, crueler even, it had been created for no other reason than to ensnare the dupable.

Desolate and deceived, the witches who'd fallen prey to *The Lesser Key* held on to the delusion that the time and effort put into obtaining and studying this thin volume must be worth something. Like many other fanatics disappointed by a doomsday prophet, these witches maintained hope by assuring themselves the great revelation for which they'd been striving lay just around the bend. If the payout couldn't be found in the pages of *The Lesser Key*, those pages must point to a greater mystery. The tract's very title hinted a greater key existed. This attempt to keep hope alive, she'd once believed, was the origin of the legend of *The Book of the Unwinding*.

A mercurial fairy tale, she had long believed *The Book of the Unwinding* to be, as slippery and ever-changing as the myth of the golden city of El Dorado, and as gratifying as the stories of the land of milk and honey, Cockaigne. Astrid had laughed at the witches who scoured every historical source: diaries and court records, correspondences—both personal letters and Church encyclicals—even bills of lading and ship manifests. Regarded warily those who'd unearthed graves, some ancient, many fresh. Scorned those who'd attempted true sortilege, offering up their very essence as reward to any entity powerful enough to act as guide. She'd held all those who tried to pick up on the Book's trail in contempt—albeit a quiet contempt, as many of the Atelier's most eminent clients fell into one or more of these camps.

All revelation is betrayal.
Apostasy. Abandon. Abnegation. Annihilation.
The four pillars of Revelation.

And so she believed the tatty old man who'd come to her with the imposter tucked beneath his arm was one of the legion who'd been ensnared by a cheap bit of flash. He ignored her male colleague, who'd approached him with a guarded offer of assistance—an offer that cloaked his intention to maneuver the threadbare visitor back toward the exit for ease of ejection—and addressed Astrid. "I'd like to know your opinion of this. It seems to be very old, and perhaps of some value, cultural if not pecuniary," he said in perfect, though oddly accented, Swedish.

Many witches remained capable of magic-enabled polyglottery, and others of projecting meaning so their native words would be understood by their interlocutor, even though the commonality of these gifts was fading along with the magic that made them possible. The visitor was using neither of these powers. Astrid decided he had learned her language through study and practice. A witch who did things the hard way all along would, no doubt, fare better than most in the final days of magic.

Enlightenment is the absolute betrayal,
for which the serpent's head is crushed.

43

He held the book out, offering it to her. When she didn't move to accept it, he said, "I'm sure you'll find it of interest. It isn't the *hoax* you believe it to be."

She caught her breath, divining the elderly witch had not just picked up on her current snap judgment as to his book's authenticity, but rather her broader suspicions about *The Lesser Key*.

"Perhaps our young friend would like to take a break." He turned to her colleague. "It's a fine day. Quite warm," the old man said, using, no doubt, the tone the serpent had used when seducing Eve. Astrid cast an eye out the window, expecting to see the same drizzle that had been falling all morning long, and was surprised to see a patch of blue sky. "The kind of day"—the visitor's voice brought her attention back to him—"that causes one's sap to rise, no?" He patted her coworker on the back, the gentle force proving to be the final push her colleague needed.

They waited in an unplanned conspiratorial silence until they were alone, the old man beaming at her, and she doing her best to keep her expression impassive. He introduced himself, an odd name that might have been either his given or family. It slipped through her memory almost the moment she heard it.

He proffered the book once more, urging her on with an impatient nod. She held back, uncertain. Surely, she had better things to do during her final days at the atelier than disabusing an old fool of his fantasies. She attempted to stare him down, hoping he'd take the clue and excuse himself, but he didn't flinch.

She decided to make quick work of the task—perform a perfunctory examination, pronounce it a fake, and offer the old man a 200-krona note, enough to purchase his dinner, perhaps even breakfast, too, if he dined frugally. With a quick sigh, she accepted the book from him.

The moment she touched its leather cover—the moment it touched her—she knew there was something different about this book.

It had a pulse.

The idea that this was the actual work and every other edition of *The Lesser Key* known to the world was a forgery flooded through her. The old man regarded her with a knowing smile and a devilish twinkle in his eye, but he remained as silent and as still as stone. The book reclaimed her attention.

Astrid drew a breath and opened it, discovering inside vellum pages, cut in a manner that told her this work had begun as a scroll; it was a codex rather than a traditional book. The pages were hand-scripted in what she first took to be carmine ink, then recognized as blood. She looked up with surprise. One heard of such things in folklore, but in reality, even in her line of work, such a thing was rare. Rarer still, the blood was not stagnant. Rather, it coursed through the written words. This circulation gave the book its pulse.

The Lesser Key's pages fanned apart without a touch, the book falling open to its center, its beating heart. Images of Inanna and Damuzi danced around each other, their circling movement creating a downward spiral, leading her—or rather inviting her—down into an abyss. The old man snatched the book from her grasp and closed it.

She gaped at him in wonder and envy, advancing on him, ready to murder him on the spot to take ownership of it. He placed it—pleased, it seemed—into her clutching hands. "It looks like *The Key* has found the one it sought," he said, giving what seemed to her a mocking bow before fading into nothingness.

His odd exit should have given her pause, but she felt only relief. It was hers. She wrapped her arms around the gift and held it to her heart. The rhythm of its pulse fell in sync with her own, or perhaps her heartbeat had taken on the cadence of the book.

She never saw the old man again. Until now, though she recognized He had always been near. In the common world. On the Dreaming Road. With invisible, boundless strings, He had led her, His puppet, here to this very clearing, to this very moment.

The proud river is enslaved, shackled,
silenced by the silt it has swallowed.
The savage is tamed, and the earth crumbles
beneath its masters.

Magic wasn't dying. Magic wasn't fading. Reality floated in the sea of infinite possibility, closed off for the most part. This undiluted, malleable potential trickling into the common world had become known as "magic." A person capable of sensing this flow and molding it to their own purposes, a "witch." Only the means of conveyance, the rent in the fabric of reality that allowed seepage of undiluted potentiality from beyond, was closing, healing, forcing the flow of magic into an ever-constricting channel. And witches were to blame, at least those witches not willing to make sacrifices to keep the gash wide.

The time for sacrifice had come once again.

Astrid heard a rustling and looked up to find the old man gone, having once again disappeared as he had the day he'd given her the Key. *Of course, Evangeline.* The realization came to Astrid as her mind turned from thoughts of her son, the King of Bones and Ashes, to Evangeline Caissy, the bayou Queen of Heaven. In a flash, the old man's choice became clear.

The old man and Evangeline.

Only now did she recognize a family resemblance.

DECEMBER 20

FIVE

Evangeline Caissy awoke with the sun on her face, a resolute beam finding the sole angle that allowed it to reach over the rooftop of the neighboring building and down through her private garden to pierce a pane of her bedroom's French doors. The warmth, the golden glow, should have been pleasant, but like at the Newgrange burial mound on winter solstice morning, it tickled the back of the grave and called forth an uneasy awareness.

In the night, as Lincoln lay beside her, Evangeline had dreamed of her dead lover.

She couldn't remember how it had begun. It felt almost as if Luc had insinuated himself into the progression of a mundane dream. With a flash of his blue-black eyes, he drew closer, and closer yet, and then became the night sky, lit only by a sprinkling of stars. Through the omniscience of dream, she knew there were seven stars, even though the dream defied the waking logic required for counting. One by one they fell, leaving behind a void that was not empty, but rather a realm of eternal potential. Nothing had yet been created, and all was possible.

Transcendent. That was the word.

In the dream, Evangeline had accepted Luc for what he'd become. Perhaps even loved him for it. As the details returned to her, her pulse rose, and a cold finger traced down her spine. She spun over to find her cat once again staring at her from Lincoln's empty pillow.

Sugar regarded her with contemptuous, knowing, peridot-green eyes.

Man you will keep.

Sugar had taken to Lincoln with the same degree of ferocity with which she had rejected Nicholas. "Man you will keep" was how Sugar's name for Lincoln presented itself in Evangeline's mind, though the phrase could either be a prediction based on the cat's longtime, intimate knowledge of Evangeline's psyche or, more likely, given Sugar's affection for Lincoln combined with her imperious nature, a simple command. *Man you will keep.*

Evangeline reached over to run her hand down the cat's back. Sugar accepted the show of affection with an air of noblesse oblige, then, with a cool meow, rose and slunk away. Evangeline hadn't yet earned a pardon for temporarily turning the cat over to Hugo and Daniel's care.

Daniel. Poor fellow. Odd fellow. Not really a fellow at all.

Daniel had started out as nothing more than conjured energy, a servitor spirit created to act as nanny to the Marin children. He'd raised Luc. And Hugo. He would've raised Alice, too, if she hadn't been taken from him. Several weeks had now passed since he'd given himself to free Alice from the Dreaming Road.

Evangeline rose and dressed, tugging on some jeans and Lincoln's gray hoodie. His scent, trapped in the fabric, comforted her, pushing away the dream and the feelings of guilt attached to it. A pair of shoes and she was out the door, making her way to Bourbon Street, following behind a street washer that left the fragrance of dish soap–scented urine in its wake.

She noticed something amiss the moment she set foot on the bawdy end of Bourbon Street. Bonnes Nouvelles was still blocks away, but the club was close enough for her to spot Lincoln outside, grasping the handle of a bucket with his left hand and scrubbing the windows with a brush.

A pair of women came up behind him and paused. One shrugged and shook her head, causing the elf hat she wore to jingle. They carried on toward Evangeline. The taller of the two nodded a tinkling greeting at the same moment her friend spoke a word that stopped Evangeline in her tracks. "Babylon."

"I'm sorry?" she said.

"No, sweetie, you're good," the taller woman said, misinterpreting Evangeline's question for an apology and stepping down off the curb to make way for Evangeline. "You please excuse us two hicks."

"Merry Christmas," her friend called back to Evangeline.

"Merry Christmas." Evangeline gave the rote response without even considering the meaning of the phrase. She walked through her own words, growing angrier with each pounding step until she arrived at Bonnes Nouvelles.

Lincoln had managed to scrape most of the tag off the window glass, but the muntin strips holding the individual panes in place still bore the scarlet paint. Enough of the scrawl remained for Evangeline to see the women she'd passed had guessed correctly. Someone had sprayed the word "Babylon" across the front of the club.

There was no question in her mind as to who'd done it. For five years Reverend Bill had made a habit of camping out in front of Bonnes Nouvelles, preaching against her and predicting her imminent downfall, though of late, Evangeline found herself missing his contemptuous harangues. A couple of months earlier, the good reverend had lost what little alcohol-drenched mind he'd had left. Oh, sure, he still called her "the Great Whore," but the term had changed somehow from an affront to a veneration.

"I'm sorry, *coeur*," Lincoln said, lowering his scrub brush and offering her a wan smile. "I'd hoped to get this taken care of before you woke up. But it looks like it's going to take some paint. Maybe some primer first, too." He dropped the brush into the bucket, then set the bucket down on the sidewalk. "On the bright side, it seems I still have a bit of magic left in me. I had a premonition something was wrong around here. I didn't see the details like I used to, but—"

"You would have told me?" Evangeline said, her anger at the vandal shifting onto the closest target. "You weren't just going to fix things for the little woman?"

"No," he said with an uneasy laugh. He approached her and placed his hands on her shoulders. "I wouldn't have kept you in the dark, though I'd hoped to clean it up before you had to see it. That's what people who love each other do, you know. They take care of each other."

Her face flushed hot, and she felt her pulse in her neck. There she stood, staring up into the face of the only man who'd ever loved her enough to put her first, and still she wanted to strike out. Her dream of Luc crept back into her thoughts, bringing six suitcases of guilt along with it.

She was angry. There was no two ways about it. She was angry with the sanctimonious son of a bitch who'd defaced her club, and she was angry with herself for what felt like an emotional infidelity. But she wasn't angry with Lincoln. "No," she said, "I'm the one who's sorry."

She leaned into his chest, and he tightened his arms around her. "I know," he whispered into her ear, "you can take care of yourself. God knows you always have. All I'm asking is for you to let me in. To let me help." He kissed her temple before relaxing his embrace. "Okay?" he said, first nodding his own head, then, with a sly smile, catching her chin between his thumb and index finger and nodding her head as well.

She reached up and took his hand in hers. It felt rough and strong and sticky from the soapy water he'd been using to remove the paint. It was real. Not the phantom limb of some ghost her subconscious had manufactured and trotted out to punish her for being happy. And she was, she realized, happy, for the first time in her whole dang life.

She kissed his hand, and he laughed when she made a face, tasting the cleaner.

"That's how romance works in the real world. Here, share some of that with me," he said and tugged her in for a kiss on the lips.

She let herself relax into him, felt his heart beat an inch or two above her own. "Don't worry about fixing this. I'll call the owner. It's about time they paid for a little maintenance on this place."

She felt Lincoln stiffen. "I don't think that's necessary. It'll get done quicker if I take care of it."

She took a step back and studied first his cautious expression and then his darkening aura. "You're keeping something from me."

He took a deep breath and shrugged. "Why, yes. Yes, I am, but right now you have a more pressing problem." He nodded toward the window. "I got your friend the parson locked up in the storage cage, and you need to decide what we're going to do with him."

Evangeline felt her ire rise once more. She shook her head at Lincoln, but bit her tongue as she pushed past him.

The storeroom was dark. One of the two overhead lamps, the one directly over the cage, had burned out, and the other was dimming as if the light was being drained from it.

She smelled the old man before she picked out his crumpled form from the shadows. He was lying on the floor on his back, his arms stretched out to his sides, his legs crossed so one foot rested on the other. Reverend Bill noticed her arrival within seconds and rolled over, pushing up onto his knees.

"'And upon her forehead,'" he called out, his voice ringing through the storeroom, "'was a name written, Mystery, Babylon the Great, The Mother of Harlots and Abominations of the Earth.'"

Evangeline recognized his words. They came from the book of Revelation, the source of many of her father's favorite sermons and her earliest night terrors. Reverend Bill's fevered mind had upgraded her from a common Jezebel to the mistress of the Armageddon, the woman who rode the scarlet seven-headed beast.

"'They will bring her to ruin and leave her naked,'" he said, his eyes widening as his mouth pulled up into a tight, toothy smile. "'. . . they will eat her flesh . . .'" He licked his lips, running his tongue a full circle. "'. . . and burn her with fire.'"

Lincoln, who'd followed her in, slammed the cage. "My fist is gonna write a few things on your forehead if you don't shut the hell up."

The old man ignored Lincoln and gazed up at Evangeline with a ferocity of adoration that could only come with madness. "'The inconsolable maiden,'" he began, his voice softening to a near whisper, "'who weeps at the gate for her missing bridegroom, is the whore who coupled with the groom for silver, and the huntress who ensnared and devoured him, who rent him from limb to limb.'" This did not come from Revelation. Evangeline knew the words didn't come from the Bible at all. She couldn't pinpoint their source; still, they were strangely familiar to her, more resonant to her than John the Revelator's eschatology. "'Kiss her bloody lips, surrender to her noxious seduction, for She is Holy. She is Magic.'"

Reverend Bill raised his eyes, and Evangeline recognized the strange fire burning in them. It was the same light that used to play in her father's eyes when drink combined with religious fervor.

"This *couillon* is not your father," Lincoln said. The idea that he might have picked up on her thoughts from her expression, from knowing her, scared her more than the notion that he might have read her thoughts.

"Open the cage," she said.

"We can't just turn him loose."

"We can't keep him locked up in here either."

Lincoln pulled the key out from the pocket of his jeans. He stood there for a moment, not moving, gazing down at it.

"Lincoln."

Evangeline held her hand out for the key, but he didn't offer it to her. In fact, he gripped it even tighter. She fixed him with her gaze. Lincoln's jaw worked side to side like he was chewing his pride into small enough bites to swallow. It took another several seconds of silent challenge, but finally he reached out and dropped the key into her still-upturned palm.

She turned to the door and opened the lock. "Get up, Bill." She swung the door open, but the old man didn't budge. "I said get up." The old man pushed up to his feet.

"We could call the police," Lincoln said. "Turn him over to them."

She ignored Lincoln's plea and positioned herself before the door. She began to pull Lincoln's borrowed shirt up over her head.

"What the hell are you doing?" Lincoln said, though she felt sure he had already guessed.

She kicked off her sneakers and, balancing first on one leg, then on the other, tugged off her pants. Her thin cotton panties were the only thing protecting the man from the thing he hated most. She pulled them down, then kicked them to the side.

She stood naked before the old man.

The old hypocrite regarded her with a savage yet fearful expression, at once disgusted and lustful. A woman was to remain covered or be undressed by force. A small, indignant cry escaped him.

"Is this what you're so afraid of, Bill? Is a woman's body, is my body, so repulsive, so tempting? Can I cause all of mankind to fall into sin?" She lunged forward, and Reverend Bill scampered back into the cage until his back bumped into the shelves of alcohol. "Am I a whore because I'm not ashamed? Because let me tell you, Bill, if this body frightens you, then let's see how you like this."

Her head snapped back, and her arms bent behind her, her fingers twisting, reshaping themselves. Thick black feathers began to push out through her skin.

"Two bottles, Bill," she said as her human form began to fall away. "Any two you want. Even the good stuff." Her field of vision widened, and she wasn't so sure her last words had come out in human language. She flapped her wings and rose up into the air.

The old man turned back and, with no deliberation, snatched the closest bottles. But he didn't flee as Evangeline had expected him to. Instead, he stepped from the cage and bowed his head. "My Queen," he said.

Behind the madness, through the debauched reverence, Evangeline recognized the spark of triumph.

SIX

The hidden passage running between Celestin's former study and the delicate, oval ladies' card room had become Fleur Marin's personal chamber of horrors. It served as a safe place to store anything she didn't want her daughter, Lucy, to see. An open secret, the passage held no intrigue for Lucy, who'd grown up aware of its presence. She'd inspected it at her leisure, found it boring, and that was that.

Still, Fleur took the precaution of setting a simple ward in place to turn Lucy's attention away. Not so much a manipulation of her daughter as an offering of something shiny to catch her attention whenever she hesitated near the passage's entrance.

Fleur had decided to take up dress design once more, an aspiration discouraged decades ago by her own mother. She leaned several bolts of fabric, the props for her "second act," as she'd begun to speak of it, against the wall to create a secondary barrier should her ward fail.

Lucy rarely went out any more. She spent a lot of time online, poring over her D.C. friends' social media. She spent a lot of time standing mere feet from this room, complaining to Fleur about everything she was missing at "home."

Fleur had at first labored under the foolish fantasy Lucy would want to enroll at Fleur's own alma mater here in New Orleans. Maybe the problem was that the school was girls only. Or perhaps Lucy's resistance was for sartorial reasons, be it the plaid uniform students had to wear, or the tradition of wearing pink dresses to graduation—Fleur suspected it had been a fatal mistake to share the photo of herself done up in full delicate Southern belle fashion. But mostly, Fleur realized, Lucy simply hadn't wanted to be the new girl, certainly not in her final year. In the end, she'd given in to her daughter's insistence on a private tutor.

Lucy's world seemed to be growing smaller each day, but, at least for now, that might be for the best.

Fleur had long ago placed a spell on her daughter, one that would keep anyone with psychic abilities from picking up on the truth. But she'd been scraping the bottom of the barrel for months when it came to power. Even with the bump she'd gained from holding her father's head as a relic, Fleur had been forced to direct most of her dwindling magic to the act of keeping her daughter's heart beating, and less and less to maintaining the mask.

Alice's friend, Nathalie, had zeroed in on Lucy's condition the night they'd come together to bring Alice back from the Dreaming Road. Later, Fleur had questioned—no, interrogated—the woman about what she'd seen, what had given them away. "It started out as a feeling," Nathalie confessed, "but when I took the time to look, really look, I could see her energy didn't square up right. It was too loose, too messy. Kind of like those fitted sheets. You know, they come folded just so, but once you take them out of the packaging, you can spend all day trying, but you ain't never gonna get them back to the way they started."

Alice, too, had intuited a disconnect, though her description was more succinct. "It feels," Alice had told her, "like Lucy is haunting her body rather than living in it."

Perhaps it was, in part, because she was currently sharing the small space with her nephew Hugo, but the narrow hall felt close, stifling, a claustrophobic hell of Fleur's own making. She looked at the pedestal table that held her father's severed head. The dazzling beam of the portable LED lamp Hugo had strung from the ceiling cast the head's silhouette, larger than life, larger than death, on the wall behind it. Fleur had a moment of déjà vu, flashing back to an elementary school art project in which she'd traced the outline of her father's profile on white construction paper, then cut it out and pasted it on a black sheet of paper.

Fleur had justified claiming Celestin's head by thinking of him as a monster, but remembering him in a tender moment made her feel less like a monster's daughter and more like a monster in her own right.

She turned away, moving her focus back to the source of the light. The lamp dangled halfway between floor and ceiling, its cord curled around a strong hook that had, no doubt, held lanterns before the house was hooked up to the electrical grid. Once Hugo finished his project, he would take down the lamp, leaving the passage, and Celestin, once again in darkness.

"I need to know you're sure about this," she said, turning her gaze back to Hugo, working shirtless, his torso glistening in the bright white light. "There'll be no turning back, not once you pass your magic on to me."

Hugo lowered the brush he was using on the plaster wall and twisted to face her. "Right now, I'm only sure of two things, and one of them is I want to do anything I can to help you protect that overindulged imp you call a daughter. As an old friend was fond of saying, 'A good nemesis is hard to come by.'"

Fleur teared up at Hugo's generosity, even as she smiled at his allusion to Daniel. Or, who knew? Maybe it was the other way around.

"Besides, I'm not giving you all of it. I'm keeping one last trick up my sleeve for an old friend I owe a good turn." A bead of sweat trickled down Hugo's forehead, and he wiped it away with the back of the hand that held the brush. He bent and dipped the brush into the quart of red paint at his feet, then rose and made three quick slashes across the intricate symbol he'd composed by painting one letter over another. "There, that should do it." He stepped back from his design to study it, then reached for the lamp. He snatched the light down from the hook and held it closer to the shimmering symbol. "Not magic, just the paint," he said, moving the light in and out to highlight the sparkle. "Scarlet glitter." He turned the beam on Celestin's profile. "He yelled at me once because I let a friend paint my nails with red glitter polish. Yelled at my friend, too."

Fleur shook her head. "He yelled at you because he perceived it as a slight to his own precious masculinity. It would've never occurred to him to let children be children. Was your little girlfriend terribly upset?"

"Who said I was a child? Who said it was a girl?" Hugo winked at her.

Fleur laughed in spite of herself. "I should've guessed as much. On both counts." She approached him and claimed the lamp. "What exactly have you created here?"

"It's a contract," Hugo said, "between you and me."

"This . . ." Fleur searched for a neutral term for "monstrosity." Points and curls sticking out in all directions, the symbol struck her as a graceless, ugly thing, despite its shimmer.

"Sigil. It's a sigil, *chère Tatie*. Written in the 'alphabet of desire'—not as sexy as it sounds. It's chaos magic, which is not as end-of-the-worldy as it sounds. At least not yet. Something I picked up while visiting Alice in the nuthouse on the Island of Misfit Toys. There are sigils all over Sinclair."

Of course, Fleur knew of Austin Osman Spare and the method of magic he'd engineered. She was also aware of its use in the shrinking system of witch-only hospitals and sanitariums such as the recently abandoned one on Sinclair Isle. She'd intended to ask for specifics on what he'd built into the symbol, but all men, even the more enlightened ones like Hugo, shared the deep-seated need to explain; doing so gave them the sense of imposing order on chaos. As the wife of a politician, Fleur had long ago become inured to humoring this frailty. Besides, she had another reason to play dumb. She kept her expression and her tone neutral. "Okay, the sigil is finished, then?"

Hugo nodded. "All that's left is the forgetting."

"I'm sorry—"

"A conscious focus will keep it from working. It's a watched-kettle kind of thing. After the sigil passes into our subconscious minds, into our dreams, the effects of our contract will then manifest in the common world. Except for the one thimble's worth of power I'm holding back, you'll own the dregs of my magic, and you're welcome to them. If it does any good for you and the blonde devilkin you hatched, then that'll be the only happiness it ever brought me." He began examining the flecks of red paint on his hand.

"May I ask what you intend to use it for? Your 'thimble's worth'?"

"A farewell gift. For an old friend." He looked up, smiling. "A friend who'd slap me if she heard me call her 'old.'"

Fleur glanced back at Celestin's head, looking like a marble bust, the white light accentuating the pallor of the skin. "Am I evil? A ghoul?"

"Maybe," Hugo said, the intonation of the word flat and humorless. Although her nephew made a habit of teasing her, hell, of teasing everyone, he had not spoken in jest. The Marin family had long been known to behave in a monstrous fashion. She sensed Hugo would be disappointed, though not surprised, to hear her confess to any crime. "For what?" he asked.

For the briefest moment, she considered speaking the truth, owning up to the heinous act only a monster or a desperate mother could have committed. Discretion had always proved her truest friend, so she swallowed her confession. Instead, she said, "For only caring that the relic's power is fading much faster than I'd hoped." She looked back to Hugo, who answered her with a shrug.

"For being capable of regarding my father's head as a relic." Her heart felt cool, her conscience clear. "For claiming anyone's head as a relic."

"Well, if that makes you a fiend, then you come by your wickedness naturally."

This time Fleur *was* at a loss. "How so?"

"You mean Celestin never showed you the family history book? Musty. Crumbling. Looks old enough to be bound in dinosaur?" He pointed toward the opening to Celestin's study. "Probably still in there."

"No." Fleur cast a resentful glance at the relic. "For Celestin, knowledge was the purview of the males in the family. We 'girls' were meant to be pretty, not smart, and certainly not educated. He was fond of telling me '*La tête vide s'échappe des rides.*'"

"You know I never really caught on to the French thing, right?"

"It means something along the lines of 'An empty head eludes wrinkles.'"

"Charming. I have some sparkle paint left over if you'd like to give the old man a coat or two of it."

"As tempting as the idea may be, perhaps you could skip the makeover and provide me with the salient points of our family history."

"Salient? I'm starting to think I never really caught on to the English thing either . . ."

"Give me the highlights."

"Oh, well, there's a lot of history, so a lot of highlights, but I was thinking of the first bit."

"The first bit . . . ," Fleur prompted him.

"Yes. The origin of the illustrious, bloodthirsty Marin clan." He bent over and rested the paintbrush sideways across the quart can. "You know the story of John the Baptist, right? I mean you must. And the woman who danced to get him beheaded." He looked over at Celestin. "No offense to present company."

"Salome, yes . . ."

"Well, our sweet Salome was a mere pawn. She was just doing what Mommy told her to. It was her mother who wanted John's head as a paperweight. You remember Mommy Dearest's name?"

Fleur didn't really feel like racking her brain to pull up the trivia, but with all Hugo was doing for her, she felt she owed him the enjoyment of sharing his story as he saw fit. She pulled up the name Herod first. He was the king in the tale. His wife had a similar name. "Herodias," she said, feeling a surprising rush from this minor victory.

Hugo repeated the name, stretching it out. "Herodias. Make you think of anything? Anything witchy, that is?"

Fleur ran the name through her mind a few times. "No," she said. "It doesn't ring any bells . . . or books or candles, for that matter."

Hugo smiled, pleased, it seemed, she was getting into the spirit of the tale. "Well," he said, his tone reminiscent of someone sharing a juicy bit of gossip, "when things went south for Herodias's new man, Antipas, Caligula exiled the pair, the world's most famous relic stashed in Mrs. Antipas's overnight bag, to southern France—to the heart of what would become Cathar country."

"The Cathar Heresy," Fleur said. "They considered John the Baptist to be the true messiah."

"Yes, or perhaps an emissary of the Devil. Sometimes both at the same time. Confusing and contradictory . . ."

"As religions tend to be." An idea struck. "The Cathars. Theodosius. The monk who wrote *The Book of the Unwinding*. He was a Cathar, no?"

"Sort of, but no. You're off a few centuries, even though you're spot on when it comes to what Theodosius believed. He's often referred to as a 'Cathar apologist,' but I'd say he was closer to being a neo-Cathar."

"Are you saying the mad monk was our ancestor?"

"Colder. Colder."

"Okay, smarty-pants, how do the Cathars fit into our family history? We were Cathars way back in the when?" she said, appropriating Lucy's term for anything that had happened before 2005.

Hugo made a buzzing noise. "Oh, so wrong, but thanks for playing."

"Listen, it's hot. I didn't sleep last night . . ."

"All right, all right," Hugo said with mock pique. "Herodias. Her name evolved over time to one I'm sure you'll recognize—Aradia. You know, from *The Gospel of the Witches.*"

Of course Fleur knew of Aradia. The first witch, Aradia was thought by some to be the goddess Diana's daughter. Others considered her an aspect of the goddess herself. *The Gospel of the Witches*, a tract attributed to a coven of witches from Tuscany, was a dumbed-down contemporary rehashing of centuries-old lore.

"That's how it fits into the Marin family history. Aradia, at least according to family legend, was our founding matriarch. The witches' goddess, the Baptist's head, and Theodosius and his Cathars. Would've made for a great family crest." He snatched up his T-shirt from the floor and pulled it on. "Shall we?"

Fleur nodded her assent, her mind occupied with the questions prompted by Hugo's story. She watched as he popped the lid back on the paint and put it and the brush back into the paper sack in which he'd brought them.

He winked and unplugged the lamp. The world around them went black, but in moments Fleur grew accustomed to the darkness. Hugo moved past her and opened the door to the study. The soft, gray light that filtered into the passage fell short of reaching Celestin.

Hugo, holding the door for her, turned back. "An interesting coincidence, isn't it? Evangeline's name. It means 'good news,' like the name of her club. But it also means 'gospel.'"

The Gospel of the Witches. And there Fleur found it, the epiphany she had been waiting for. She'd only just begun to spin the thought around in her mind when the sunlight filtering in through the open windows—windows she had left shuttered—blinded her.

"Hello, *ma chère*," Nicholas said. "Is it too early for a brandy?"

SEVEN

Lisette Perrault had no memory of it happening, but the Boudreau girl must have taken her into the employee shower to wash off the gore. Even though Lisette might never feel clean again, the waste of Michael—his dried blood, the flecks of gray matter, and the tiny fragments of bone that had landed on her—was gone. The clothes she'd worn the night before had been replaced by one of the spare uniforms Isadore kept on hand in his office.

She'd retained only a quick flash of the ride home: Nathalie turning the radio to one of the news stations, then snapping it off at the tinkling of jingle bells.

Before leaving, Nathalie brewed Lisette a cup of hot tea, which she spilled out and replaced with whisky the second the girl was out the door. She sipped the whisky as she waited for the sun to rise. Her father must have gone off on his own, because she'd been alone with Nathalie in the car.

When she jumped at a shadow—her *own* shadow—she pushed the rest of the whisky away.

◆ ◆ ◆

Lisette dressed in slacks, blouse, and a cardigan. She studied herself in the mirror, trying first with her fingers, then with a wide-toothed comb to work through the tangles the harried shampooing had left behind. She gave up and wrapped a royal blue scarf over her hair, tying the cloth into a tignon turban. Lisette thought of the day her mother had taught her how to tie the tignon, how she'd explained that this form of headdress, intended as a mark of shame, had become a symbol of pride. She wished her mother were with her now, then realized there was only one place where she might still feel Soulange Simeon's presence.

She found her cane, propped up against the kitchen table, and took to the street, locking the door behind her.

She might not be—might never be—as she was before Michael triggered the stroke, but some justice had been done; his death had already accelerated her recovery. She could've managed without her cane, but she gripped its handle and made a great show of leaning on it as she made her way down Chartres Street to her shop. Vèvè. Those same people who'd been turning away as she struggled—some to hide their discomfort, others to hide their satisfaction at seeing the great mambo humiliated—would stare agog if they were to witness a too-quick improvement.

A chilling sense of déjà vu came over her as she flipped on the lights and stepped into the store. Shards of broken glass glinted on the floor, and the scent of spray paint filled the air. The main altar had been moved from near Vèvè's entrance to the far wall. The familiar venerations of the loa were missing, replaced by now-extinguished pink and white candles and a single image.

This was not the work of some racist vandal, though. Lisette recognized in a flash Remy's style in the filigree heart common to all the loa who shared the name Erzulie. The vèvè painted above the altar, with its three eight-pointed asterisms that resembled snowflakes more than stars, two banner-bearing staves, and opposing trefoils—one pointing up to the heavens, the other pointing to the earth—belonged to Erzulie Mapiangue, not to Erzulie Dantor, whose help Lisette had sought. Beneath it, Remy had painted the words "*Notre Dame du Perpétuel Secours.*" Our Lady of Perpetual Help. Mapiangue was the loa who eased the pain of labor and protected birthing mothers and newborns.

The altar was covered in red velveteen fabric bearing, at its center, the image of the Black Madonna, Our Lady of Czestochowa, a syncretism between Voodoo and Catholicism.

Lisette noticed a plastic sheath of red roses, the kind grocery stores sold, resting on top of a shelf at her side. The glass at her feet lay in a drying puddle of amber liquid, the remnants of the sacrifice of a dark spiced rum the underage Remy must have charmed some shopkeeper into allowing him to purchase.

Remy had done well, keeping the offering separate from the symbols of veneration. Most loa accepted the offerings on the altar, but Mapiangue required that the objects used to venerate her be kept apart from the offerings made to her.

"I should've burned this place to the ground." Her father's voice came from behind the counter. Lisette should have realized this was where he'd end up—the place where he felt closest to her mother. After all, that's why she'd come here, too. "Years ago." He stared at the vèvès in the window, his face hardening with hate. He'd aged at least a decade since last night. His eyes were tired, rimmed with red. "I should've known if they'd take her from me, they'd try to take you, too. Oh, I'm not talking about the Marins this time. I'm talking about these spirits of yours." He pointed at the panes with a shaking finger. "They've got some kind of game going on. One that began before there were people like you and your mama to serve them. Hell, long before there were people, period." He began clenching and loosening his fist, as if his hand craved something solid to strike out against.

"I don't regret killing the boy." He circled around the counter, then leaned back against it. "I only regret not killing him sooner. Maybe if I'd realized . . . if I'd acted . . ." He reached up and wiped away an errant tear with his sleeve. "I thought I could put an end to this. Protect you and Manon. She still talking about giving up the baby?"

"She is," Lisette responded.

Lisette had received the news secondhand from her husband. "If the little one makes it." Her heart throbbed as she said these words. Until now, she hadn't acknowledged, even to herself, that her granddaughter—thirteen weeks premature, two pounds and twelve ounces—might never leave neonatal intensive care.

Manon wouldn't see Lisette. Manon wouldn't visit the baby either. Michael's death had broken his hold over Manon, the snapping of the magical cords that had bound and controlled her alerting her to his demise and allowing her to know him for the monster he had been. With Michael no longer around, she had settled for blaming Lisette—and her own newborn daughter—for his sins.

"For the best, if it doesn't live," Alcide said. "Child's only half us. It's half them, too."

Lisette felt a rush of heat claw up her spine. In that moment, she hated her father. "The hell you say." She averted her gaze and poked at the broken glass with the toe of her shoe. She would phone Remy. Have him come and help her invoke yet another Erzulie, Erzulie Mansur— Erzulie the Blessed—and petition her to kindle a mother's love in Manon's heart.

"May not matter one way or the other soon," Alcide said, drawing her attention back to him.

"And what is that supposed to mean?"

"She told me things," her father said. "Your *maman* showed me things about this city, back when I still cared to listen. Things she thought you weren't yet ready to understand. Things I hoped you would never have to learn." He focused on her arm. "But you're in too deep now, and the only way out is through . . ." His words trailed off as he scanned the glass-strewn floor. He turned back to the counter, gazing down at a brightly colored map laid out on the surface. "Come here, girl. I got something I need to show you."

"Right now you have nothing I care to see."

"You think, *ma fille*"—he looked up and nodded to the vèvè on the wall—"Remy acted completely on his own? You think I learned nothing from decades with your mother? I was willing to try anything. To do anything. I brought Remy here. He followed *my* instructions."

She hesitated, angry, and realized she was looking to take her anger out on him much as Manon was taking hers out on her. Still, knowing what she was doing and being able to stop herself from doing it were two different lands divided by a wide gulf. She crossed to his side but avoided making eye contact. She focused instead on the map. It was similar to the one Papa Legba had used to demonstrate the connection between the environs of Jackson Square and his personal vèvè. This one, too, was glossy and covered with cartoon-style art. Still, it was one of the better tourist maps that went beyond the Vieux Carré to include the whole city. She gazed down at the symbol he'd added to the map with the thick black line of a permanent marker. Her father had drawn a different vèvè—Baron Samedi's—superimposing the vertical bar of its cross over Canal Street.

"The Gates of Guinee," she said. Anyone with more than a passing interest in the occult had heard the story that the gates to the spirit world could be found by aligning the center of Samedi's vèvè with Canal Street. The vèvè's seven stars were said to mark the locations of the gates.

Lisette had always considered the story nothing more than non-sense for tourists, but Papa Legba had shown her how his own vèvè aligned with the area around Jackson Square. She realized she'd be both stubborn and foolish not to hear her father out. "I always believed they were only a metaphor for the seven days after death."

"That they might be, but your *maman* always swore to me they're real, too, and spread out over the city, with the first gate in New Orleans's first cemetery."

She traced her finger over the map, pausing at each of the seven stars. She was willing to consider the possibility there was at least some truth to the story. Still, her common sense raised an objection. "But Daddy," she said, surprised to find herself leaning into his shoulder for comfort, "if the gates were real—and that easy to find—they would have been located centuries ago."

He slid the marked-up map aside to reveal a fresh one beneath it. He traced his finger up St. Peter Street. "The city used to end at a moat a bit beyond what is now Dauphine Street. On the other side of the water, that's where they put the original cemetery, in the area between what is now Burgundy and Rampart." He began to trace out the shape of Samedi's cross. "It isn't Canal Street the gates center on—it's Orleans."

Lisette watched as he finished his quick sketch, the seven stars falling at points around Orleans Street. "The Gates of Guinee," she said, feeling a sensation that lay between a vibration and a shiver pass through her. She sensed deep in her marrow her father was right.

"That's right," he said, "though your *maman* always said 'gates' wasn't the right word. She always called them 'the seven wounds.'" He looked down at her arm. "Show it to me," he said, "the gad."

Lisette hesitated, but then removed her cardigan and rolled up the sleeve of her blouse. She peeled away the bandages Nathalie had plastered over the wounds and was surprised to see the seven gashes of the gad were already scabbing over—the accelerated healing possibly due to the girl's unexpected magic. Her father looked down at it, the pain in his eyes as intense as the pain in her mutilated flesh.

"Wounds. Gates. Either or both, the witches, like your friend Fleur Marin, want to open them wide." He reached out and gingerly traced a finger along the deepest of the wounds. His tone was sharp, but his touch was gentle. He pulled the sleeve down over the cuts. "I'm afraid, *ma fille*, that gad might make you the key."

"No, Daddy. This gad was meant to protect us. You interrupted before Dantor could intervene with Michael. Papa Legba was opening the way for her."

"I never saw Legba," he said, his voice low. "Not once in all my years with your *maman*. And I didn't see your Legba last night either."

A single word caught her attention. "*My* Legba?"

"I never saw Legba," he repeated himself as if she hadn't spoken. "But I felt him. That thing there with you last night, *chou*, was not Papa Legba."

He tapped each of the stars with the tip of his marker. "This is where the gates were."

"Were?" Lisette said, her head whirling. The night of the massacre at the ball for Celestin Marin, Legba had been present. Her mother had seemed certain of it. But Lisette had only witnessed his totem, a wiry-haired little mutt that looked very much like the dog that had accompanied *her* Legba . . . very much like. Not the same. Not upon reflection. Her Legba's dog looked much better fed. "What happened to them, Daddy? What happened to the gates?"

He grasped her left hand but didn't speak. He didn't need to. She felt the seven cuts she'd carved into her own flesh each take on a separate pulse.

EIGHT

Their café was on the edge of the Marigny, but still well within earshot of the bells of St. Louis Cathedral. Alice grasped the handle of the eatery's door just as the bells began to peal nine.

Most mornings Nathalie beat Alice there, and Alice would arrive to find her nursing a mug of steaming black coffee and entertaining herself by building pyramids out of sugar packets. Nathalie would always look up, beaming at her the second she came through the door. They sat at the same table every time.

Nathalie was late today, or at least later than usual.

Of course, they'd fallen into this easy pattern without ever deliberately pinning down specifics of time, or even place, so technically neither of them could be late.

The waitress—her name tag read "Sue," though Alice sensed it wasn't her real name, that there was a past from which she was hiding—nodded her greeting and reached for a mug. She was anticipating the decaffeinated green tea Alice drank every morning, a justification, or perhaps a preemptive act of penance, for the chocolate chip pancakes that had become her regular order.

Nathalie always grimaced at her tea.

Nathalie never felt the need to justify anything she enjoyed; Nathalie simply enjoyed.

Alice took a seat at the table—their table—and began pulling the weeds of suspicion Nicholas had sowed in her mind. Alice grabbed the largest by its roots first. She couldn't bring herself to conceive of the Boudreau brothers, Lincoln and Wiley, as executioners, but then again—the part of her that always insisted on playing devil's advocate challenged—she couldn't bring herself to think of Fleur as a necromancer even though this she knew to be true.

Alice had come to trust Nathalie implicitly, in part due to their shared experience as outsiders. While she liked the Boudreau brothers, she knew she could never completely trust anyone who'd grown up feeling as if they belonged. If there were even an inkling of truth to what Nicholas had said about Lincoln and Wiley, and Nathalie caught a whiff of it, she would come directly to her. Of that much Alice was certain. But could it be possible that Lincoln and Wiley were using their cousin as an unwitting accomplice in slipping the noose around Fleur's neck? It was all too ridiculous, and Alice felt a flash of anger at herself for letting Nicholas get to her.

Alice heard the door open and she looked up, disappointed when an old man stumbled in, the reek of stale sweat and fresh whisky crossing the threshold with him. His patchy hair made Alice think of a monk's tonsure, with a shiny bald patch on top and an unkempt, finger-in-the-light-socket white fringe wrapping around his temples. He wore a soiled brown jacket with tan stripes that looked like cold leftovers from a moth's buffet.

The man pushed deeper into the café and took a seat one table over from Alice, putting himself between her and the door. He jabbed his hand into his jacket pocket and pulled out a fistful of coins. He let them rain—silver, nickel, and copper, some too large or too small to be American currency—onto the tabletop, then reached into the other pocket and extracted a few wadded-up bills.

Alice had never seen the man here before, but "Sue" seemed to be familiar with him. She dropped off Alice's mug of green tea, then crossed to his table and fingered through the coins, pulling some closer, pushing others back to her patron. She picked up the crumpled paper and unfolded the three bills, smoothing each of them out by running it back and forth over the edge of the table, then scooped up the acceptable currency and left the table, returning only a few moments later with a plate of eggs, bacon, and hash browns. "Back in a second with your biscuit, Bill," she said. "You want coffee?" This Bill fellow responded with a shake of his head.

It was rude to stare at the unfortunate man, so Alice focused instead on the door, keeping an eye out for Nathalie's arrival. Then she realized she was staring past the presumed vagrant if not at him, which might seem the same from his perspective. She lowered her eyes and grasped her mug between both hands, sliding it closer to her. She studied her image mirrored in the liquid until she saw through herself, then stopped seeing herself altogether. For one brief, disconcerting moment she had the sensation of fading away.

She jolted and looked back up to find the old man watching her, smiling. He nodded as if in agreement, though she had no idea with what.

It dawned on her that he seemed to recognize her even though his features were unfamiliar to her. She sensed no magic from him, but perhaps he'd once been a witch. He appeared to be around Celestin's age and may have been a former associate, or possibly an enemy. Of course, the answer could be simpler. She may have passed by the man as he sat on a corner asking for handouts. She always made a point to drop something into an upturned palm, though she reckoned now this constituted less an act of true charity than an attempt to salve her conscience. If she really cared, she'd remember if she'd placed coin or bill in this man's outstretched hand. She made a resolution to pay more attention going forward.

The door opened again, and her eyes darted to it. But it wasn't Nathalie, only a thick, bearded guy in a tank top. Alice had to hand it to the guy. Even in late December, he seemed committed to showing off the tattoos that ran from his shoulders down to his wrists. Seemingly oblivious to her gaze, he turned to make his way toward the padded bench that ran the length of the far wall.

Alice's phone vibrated, sliding a bit on the smooth tabletop as it did. She reached out to grasp it, her shoulders relaxing as she read Nathalie's name on the screen. She realized she was smiling. "I'm about to start without you," Alice said with mock impatience.

"Oh, gosh. I am so sorry," Nathalie said, sounding as if she had taken Alice's tone seriously. "I was hoping I could catch you before you left your place. I'm not gonna be able to make it today," she said, sounding more excited than sorry. "Something just happened. Something amazing, really. I'm on my way up to Natchitoches."

As Nathalie spoke, Alice's eyes drifted back to the old man. He sat there in silence, knife in one hand, fork in the other, his face turned slightly down as he focused on the plate before him. Still, Alice could see his lips moving, as if in a tardy and silent blessing, and for the briefest of moments Alice had the impression that they moved in sync with Nathalie's words, almost as if he were speaking the words himself.

"Oh," Alice said, shaking off the illusion and reaching deep into herself to try to match Nathalie's enthusiasm, or at least hide her own disappointment. "What is it? What happened?"

"The Boudreaus contacted me."

Alice had a sinking feeling in her stomach.

"My family," Nathalie continued, her pleasure at saying the words palpable.

Alice understood Nathalie's hunger for a sense of connection to them, but the timing . . .

"They asked me up for a visit. Just a short one," Nathalie said, sounding defensive, or like she was grappling with her own disappointment that the Boudreaus had set a definite limit on her welcome. "I'll be back tomorrow."

"A holiday gathering?" Alice said, doing her best to keep her voice light.

"Nah," Nathalie said, then added, "well, maybe. I don't know. There might be a bit of that, too." She sounded less than pleased at the prospect. "But they got some kind of big meeting going on tonight, and they want me . . ." It touched Alice's heart to hear Nathalie's voice break. "They want me to come up and join them. They called me up, out of the blue. I wasn't supposed to tell anyone about it, but I knew you'd wonder where I'd disappeared to. At least I hoped you would." Alice was teetering between inquiring into the Boudreaus' wish to keep the meeting clandestine and reassuring Nathalie that she would feel lost without her, when Nathalie spoke again, her tone going flat. "Listen," she said, "I know it's stupid of me to get my hopes up. They've never given a damn about me before, but—"

"I'm sure," Alice cut her off, deciding not to risk Nathalie's fragile joy by giving voice to Nicholas's suspicions—at least for the present, "Lincoln and Wiley have let them know what a wonderful person you are. That they've been missing out."

"I don't know about that . . . ," Nathalie responded, sounding happy and a little embarrassed at the same time. Alice could almost hear her blushing.

"I'm quite sure of it," Alice said.

"Sorry," Nathalie said. "Didn't catch that. I'll call you back in a bit. I think I'm heading into a dead—"

The sound of a chair scraping on the floor drowned out Nathalie's words. The old man pushed up from his table and, stumbling a bit, turned toward the door.

"Hurry back," Alice said, then realized Nathalie was gone.

NINE

Fleur could barely breathe. For five years, Nicholas had helped maintain the spell that kept Lucy alive by skimming a bit of power from the Chanticleer Coven's every working. He always spoke of their "little arrangement" with an air of magnanimity, but he spoke of it often. Mostly offhand comments which were laden with a clear import: what he so generously gave, he could snap away at will.

But this summer everything had changed. Nicholas had lost control of the moribund coven the same day their father slaughtered most of its remaining members. Of course, Nicholas hadn't known of the massacre when he'd gone on his off-the-grid walkabout. He had fallen to the one-two punch of his dethronement and being dumped by Evangeline Caissy. The region's surviving witches thought Nicholas had taken off to lick his wounds, or to hide his shame, perhaps even to the Dreaming Road.

Of course, Nicholas had played the role of the great martyr, using Lucy's need as a cover for his flight and Fleur as the sole witness to his altruism. Fleur was happy to play along. She didn't give a damn, as long as Lucy might benefit from his absence.

Did Nicholas's return signify success or surrender?

"Good to see you, son," Nicholas said, his gaze fixing not on her, but on Hugo.

Fleur held back, hoping absence might have made Hugo's heart grow fonder toward her brother—despite everything, Nicholas was his father—but Hugo only shrugged. "Then you'll love how I look from the leaving side," he said, studiously avoiding his gaze. Without another word, he passed by his father and exited the room. Fleur heard Hugo make a gruff, unintelligible comment in response to Lucy's muffled voice. The front door slammed.

Nicholas regarded her with a veneer of amusement, one eyebrow raised as he shook his head and chuckled, but his mirth was only for show. She knew her brother, probably better than anyone else left on this earth. He'd been hoping, if not for a rapprochement with his son, at least for a cessation of hostilities. Perhaps there was a certain level of paternal affection involved, though Fleur suspected it came in second to Nicholas's need to be admired. Revered.

Nicholas seemed to realize she was peeking behind his casual facade; he turned away and crossed to the eighteenth-century *table à quadrille brisé* on which their female ancestors once played now nearly forgotten card games such as brusquembille and aluette, the cards of the latter capable of doubling as a tarot deck. Fleur had taken the table over as a design space. She'd covered its surface with sketches and cloth swatches and paint chips for the renovation she intended to make on the manse.

He knew the jitters were about to cause her to climb out of her own skin, but still he gazed at her as unblinking and unmoved as the Sphinx. He was toying with her, making her wait like a dog with a treat balanced on its muzzle. She could almost hear him commanding, "Wait for it."

She couldn't stand it another moment. He'd won this staring match. "Have you . . . ?" Fleur was on the verge of asking him if he'd found the magical solution for which he'd been searching, but he held up a cautioning hand.

"Wow," Lucy said, sweeping into the room. "What crawled up Hugo's . . ." She stopped as she noticed Nicholas. "Oh." For a moment Fleur's voluble daughter was struck dumb. But only for a moment. "This close to Christmas, I was hoping for a visit from the jolly Saint Nick, but I guess we'll have to make do with you. Greetings, Uncle." She cupped a hand to the side of her face, shielding her mouth from Nicholas. "He is," she began in a stage whisper, "still my uncle, right? Not my stepbrother twice removed or anything?"

Nicholas shot Fleur a pained smile. "Yes, Lutine," he said, using his favorite nickname for Lucy, "I am still your uncle."

Fleur was both pleased and somewhat surprised to sense Nicholas felt an honest affection for his niece. With Lucy's father a thousand miles away on the map and a million miles away in terms of an emotional connection, Lucy could benefit from a solid relationship with her uncle. Fleur felt a tinge of sadness as she realized how much better Vincent had been suited to playing an avuncular role in Lucy's life.

"Thinking of redoing the old pile?" Nicholas began examining the sketches, lifting them one by one and holding them up to the natural light that filtered through the window.

"More than thinking. Please don't interfere. *Tu m'écoutes, Nicho?*" She punctuated her plea with a long-abandoned childhood nickname, an appeal to any small spark of affection that might still glow in his heart.

He answered with a nod and returned the sketches to the table. "You'll need to deal with the foundation before tackling"—he waved his hand over the designs—"the cosmetics. There are some substantial cracks." Nicholas wanted to believe he was so very different from their father, but Fleur could see he still regarded her, as Celestin had, as *la belle bécasse*, pretty but empty-headed.

"The contractor will be starting after the New Year," Fleur said. "The gentleman who took over Vincent's business," she added to lay the blame where it belonged—squarely at Nicholas's feet. Due to an inheritance scheme set up almost two centuries earlier, ownership of the house fell to the eldest son in each generation. Vincent would have shored the foundation up long ago if Nicholas had let him, but their elder brother had never made a secret of his loathing for the family's historical home. Nicholas had even castigated a stunned Vincent for making necessary repairs after Katrina. After that, he'd refused to allow any upkeep on the structure. Left unloved for more than a decade, it counted as a wonder that the house had fared as well as it did in the New Orleans climate.

"I leave it in your capable hands, then," he said, though his emphasis on the word "capable" telegraphed that he considered her anything but. He was leaving the restoration to her partially because he thought she'd find herself in over her head. "But you must realize, you're only buying time. It's more than the foundation of the house crumbling; it's the land beneath it."

"Um," Lucy began. Fleur could tell from her daughter's wrinkled brow that she was spooked. "Is it safe to stay here, or are we going all House of Usher?"

"We are," Fleur said, with a challenging side-glance at her brother, "as safe here as anywhere else in southern Louisiana. The Mississippi River is alluvial. The sediment it carries would, if nature were allowed her way, build shifting banks and determine the path of the river's flow. When they fixed the river's course, the engineers created a situation where the water table beneath New Orleans started falling, taking the land lower with it. Unintended consequences are sometimes poetic." She allowed herself one small warning jab at her brother: "The very thing that makes it possible to prevent the land from flooding is causing the land to crumble beneath us."

"You are *so* not making me feel better . . ."

"And on the other end," Nicholas added, "the Atchafalaya is silting up. The next big flood may change the river's course anyway and wipe out a couple of towns along the way as it does."

Fleur could see a spark rise to Lucy's eyes. "Kind of like what Alice has been saying about magic."

"You've been speaking to Alice . . . about magic?" Fleur had been encouraging Lucy to spend time with her cousin, but she'd assumed Lucy would encourage Alice to develop a healthy respect for consumerism, not that Alice would enlighten Lucy about the occult, perhaps more than was safe. Her daughter had an uncanny ability to pick up on subtle clues, at least when she wasn't practicing a willing obliviousness.

"Is that so unexpected? She knows things. And it isn't like we have oodles of other interests in common."

"It's good you are, it's only . . . Well, never mind. What did Alice tell you?"

"That magic is meant to be wild and untamed. That it's something you can tap into, but never control. At least not forever. Maybe magic isn't dying. Maybe its course is silting up."

Nicholas regarded his niece with surprise, as if he'd encountered a donkey quoting Shakespeare.

"What?" Lucy said, picking up on his incredulity.

"Nothing," he said, coming alert, a spark of pride rising to his eyes. "Nothing at all. It's only I'm happy to see you taking an interest . . . at long last." Behind her daughter's back, Fleur arched her eyebrows at him and gave a quick shake of her head. As Lucy turned toward her, she managed to cover the expression by brushing back her bangs.

"Perhaps I would have a long time ago if I were really a part of the family," Lucy began. "Well, you know what I mean. If I were like the rest of you."

"You are a part of this family," Nicholas said, "though at times it seems you're the only one who wants to be." His lips curled up into something that resembled a conciliatory smile. "Listen," he said, shifting his focus back to Fleur. "I wanted to stop by and let you know in person that I'm back. We have a lot to talk about, but at the moment

I'm a bit pressed. You see, I have an event I'd like your help with, and the clock is ticking."

This was not a request; it was a command.

"What kind of event?" Fleur could feel herself beginning the smooth shift into the guise of politician's wife. She'd been groomed, if not born, to stand at the side of a powerful man doing his best to win over other powerful men.

"I'm hoping you'll join me—well, actually I'm hoping all of the region's remaining witches will join me—in reviving a lapsed tradition." His face brightened as he reached into his coat pocket and retrieved what appeared to be a bit of glossy card stock. He gave it a quick glance, then held it out to her. She took it, expecting an invitation, but instead she found herself holding an old Polaroid photograph from the late seventies of the three Marin children—Nicholas, Vincent, and herself—in costume.

"Oh, Nicholas," Fleur said, her own delight surprising her. "The Longest Night?" She stared down at the picture, trying to make a connection between the girl dressed as a tiny Morgan le Fay and herself. With Nicholas, it came with greater ease. He was older than she, and in the photo had already begun to display many of the traits he was to carry into adulthood. Young Nicholas's costume consisted of a red bodysuit with a pointed tail, a headband with horns, and a black trident. His hand rested on her shoulder. Vincent stood beside them, though at more of a distance, as if he, like Lucy, felt he wasn't really a part of the magic. He was dressed in a black suit and held a leatherbound journal in one hand and an oversize quill in the other. Fleur didn't remember seeing him in the costume, but she recognized it as the Dark Man with his book of damned souls.

Lucy crept up beside her and took Fleur's hand. "Cute," she said, taking the photograph from her. "Halloween?"

"Not Halloween," Fleur said, "but close. It's witches' Halloween. The real one, the winter solstice. It's the longest night of the year, hence 'the Longest Night.'" She looked up at Nicholas and added, "Tomorrow night."

"Non-witches used to bar their shutters from dusk till dawn," he said. "Of course, the night became watered down over the ages until it lost its significance."

"Like Halloween," Lucy said. "The other real one."

"We used to call it 'la Defilé des Maléfiques,'" Nicholas continued, ignoring Lucy's quip, "because it's the night where we embrace the image of evil projected onto us."

"My, how terribly liberating."

"No." Fleur fought against her daughter's propensity to make snap, final judgments. "I know it may sound silly, but it truly is a marvelous sight. *Une procession aux flambeaux*—a torchlit procession."

"Once we used actual torches," Nicholas added, at the worst possible moment if he wanted to convince Lucy the event could have any cool factor, "though as far back as I can remember it's been a few candles mixed in with flashlights. Safer for everyone, considering the shaky grips and unsteady walks of some of our fellows."

"The Longest Night," Fleur offered, "always used to bring the covens together."

"That is precisely my goal." His look seemed to telegraph a thought to Fleur. Her heart leaped as she realized this somehow fit into a plan to help Lucy. A devil's grin flashed on his lips in the moment before his face smoothed into the mask of a beatific angel. "I hope to bring those of us left together. Build a new coven out of the ashes."

Fleur doubted her brother would get much further than she had, but for all Nicholas's faults, he was an excellent leader. If anyone could find a way to resurrect a sense of commonality in the fractured community, it was her brother. Even so, his efforts seemed to be too little, too late. The witching community had been teetering along the line between moribund and extinct even before the slaughter. Most of the witches left had been too old or antisocial to attend Celestin's memorial ball.

"Our elders will appreciate the nostalgia of the event," Nicholas said, as if he could glean her thoughts at will. "Especially the burning of a wicker man. And our friends who prefer a solitary path will, I hope, enjoy the anonymity of the event, as well as their ability to slip away once they've had their fill of human interaction."

"You certainly have my support," Fleur said. A look of amusement rose to his eyes. He found it funny she spoke as if she had a choice.

"Then perhaps you and Eli will do the honor of lighting the effigy."

Fleur felt her mouth go dry. "Eli has been out of reach for a while now. At least for me."

"Oh, I'm sorry. He'd mooned over you for so long, I'd assumed that given a second chance—"

"Listen, Mom . . ." Lucy jumped in, Fleur felt sure, to rescue her, then paused as if to regroup. "Don't get me wrong. Love the idea of parental-condoned mischief. Love"—she lingered on the word—"it. But about this Longest Night thing . . ." Lucy's words drifted off, and she cast a coy glance at the floor. The combination signaled her lack of interest in the affair.

"Yes, what about it?"

"The Marins, we're not exactly well-loved since your dad kind of, well, massacred a lot of people. And by 'a lot,' I mean 'a lot.'"

"No, *ma lutine*, we are not."

"Maybe we should pass on this parade or whatever it is . . ."

"It is a procession," Fleur corrected Lucy, "not a parade."

"And the oh so significant difference would be?"

"A parade," Nicholas began, "is for the spectators' entertainment. A procession is for the edification of its participants."

"Okay, sure." Lucy gave Nicholas her signature eye roll. "I am always up for edification, but maybe there's a way more fun and far less opportunity-for-revenge option to pull the old gang back together?"

"You don't have to worry about your safety." Nicholas cast a glance toward the hidden passageway. "Celestin has paid the price. The others' acceptance of his body for use as relics has paid for our pardon."

"Ugh. I don't want to think about it. Bits and pieces of Celestin—"

"Changing hands like currency. And currency is what his body has become."

"But he can't feel anything, right?" She focused on Fleur. "You like exorcised his head, right, so he's . . . well, whatever, so he isn't . . ."

"Yes, Lucy. We've discussed this." Fleur fixed Nicholas with a perhaps too-innocent gaze.

"I still don't know how Alice—"

"Don't judge her, dear." Fleur hoped to put Lucy off the subject. Parental judgment usually drove her to change topics or to storm off. Right now, Fleur would settle for either.

"I'm not judging her. Not really. Not much. I mean, part of me is in awe of her, and part of me is terrified. But all the same. I know this Longest Night fun run is like a holiday tradition—"

"Oh, it's more than a tradition," Nicholas said. "It's a sacred duty."

"A sacred duty we've never participated in."

"A sacred duty you've never participated in. I've walked the path many times."

"I'm guessing like maybe twice since 1982, though, right?"

"We haven't celebrated Longest Night since . . ." Fleur tried to pinpoint a year. "Well, I can't really remember. Since we were children." She looked to Nicholas for confirmation.

Lucy folded her arms across her chest and glared at Fleur. "I rest my case."

"So, I've lapsed," Fleur said, returning her daughter's deadpan expression. "I'm home now, and ready to return to the fold. After all, the Chanticleer Coven used to lead the procession, and we Marins—"

"Yeah, yeah. We led the Chanticleers. Okay, but burning a wicker man? It's like some kind of lame outsider art."

"It's a leftover practice from the old days," Fleur said. "Lore has it when magic was stronger and reality more pliable, witches would turn themselves into will-o'-the-wisps on the Longest Night. We'd lead a wayfarer astray and burn him as a sacrifice to take the place of the fallen sun god in the underworld."

"Charming."

"A Longest Night celebration is more than a bit of local color, you know," Nicholas explained. "It was once worldwide. Witches everywhere would venture out, doing their part to return the light to the earth."

"Checking in to make sure we're clear on a point—you both understand this is all metaphor, right? The world is going to wobble back up whether or not a bunch of senile old sorcerers teeter along the river carrying an open flame."

Nicholas raised an eyebrow. "Are you so sure of that?" he said. "Many once considered witches' duty, their only duty, to be the bringers of light. Your grandmother Laure's side of the family had the tradition of naming the firstborn boy and girl of each generation a variant of Luc or Lucille because of it."

"Oh, I thought there was some dusty old ancestor lingering on the edge of soon-to-be-forgotten history."

"Well, legend has it there once was." Nicholas's mischievous grin resurrected itself. "He, too, was a rebel. Like you."

Lucy rolled her eyes. "Yeah, more like Luc."

Nicholas rocked back, genuinely stricken.

Her face froze. "I'm sorry. I so did not mean to go there. My mouth was in motion, and my brain couldn't shut it down in time."

It took Nicholas a beat to recover. "It's all right. Luc was our . . . Phaëthon," he said, opting to substitute Apollo's ill-fated son for his better-known and far more Catholic counterpart. "Come on. Frankly, this may be the last year the procession ever takes place. Anywhere."

"You'll enjoy it," Fleur coaxed her daughter. "It will speak to your taste for the dramatic. The site of the bonfire at the end is even called 'the End of the World.' I'd like to share the tradition with you. Please? For me?"

"Ugh," Lucy said with mock exasperation, "save the maternal guilt. I'll go."

Nicholas applauded, then folded his hands and bowed to them. He drew near and kissed Fleur's cheek. "Wear your flats, ladies," he said as he exited the room. "We'll be walking a distance and crossing over train tracks."

"Hmmm," Lucy said, turning to Fleur. "Tell you what. I'm in a generous mood, so I'll let you off with new Louboutin sneakers."

She shrugged. "Deal."

A young man appeared in the doorway. "Excuse me, ladies. The gentleman told me I could come through." In the crook of his left arm he carried an enormous and extravagant bouquet of probably three dozen roses. In his right hand was a small, square cardboard box.

"Someone must be feeling guilty," he said, meaning it as a joke.

"See," Lucy said, advancing on the poor man as if she were a tiger stalking prey, "I told you Eli would come crawling back." She snatched the card from the large bouquet and tugged the message from its envelope. "Oh," she said, her face falling. "They're from Dad." A sharper shade of disappointment slid across her face. "They're for me." She let the card drop to the floor and left the room.

"Oh, geez," the delivery man said, "I'm sorry. I didn't really think—"

"It's fine. Don't worry. You couldn't have known." Fleur circled around to her worktable, then dug beneath some samples for her wallet. She found a twenty and crossed to the delivery man. He was still struggling under the weight of the large bouquet. "Oh, I apologize," she said, still trying to look pleased by the delivery. "Please, put those down anywhere you can find a space."

The man's face telegraphed relief, and he set the larger part of the burden down on a side table. "I think," he said, proffering the box he still held, "this one is for you."

Fleur accepted the box, handing over the tip in exchange. "Thank you for bringing these. I'm sure the holiday season is very busy for you."

"It's my job," he said with a shrug.

Fleur nodded. "Do let me show you out."

"That's okay, ma'am. I can find my way." He went to the door, then turned back. "You have a nice Christmas, okay?" he said.

"You, too," Fleur responded, surprised to find a sincere smile rising to her lips. She waited, listening intently for the sound of the door closing behind him. Only then did she dare read the message accompanying the box. It read, "A bit of magic of my own, for the rarest of flowers. W." She opened the lid of the box. Inside lay a single camellia flower, a Middlemist's Red, exceptionally rare in any season, in December a near impossibility. An outwardly loving gesture which, in fact, underscored that Warren was now wealthy and influential enough to no longer need the Marins.

This was the bastard's way of announcing the divorce was final. The doorbell rang again. This delivery would be the settlement papers. At least Fleur wouldn't have to tip.

TEN

Evangeline turned her face away as Lincoln leaned in to kiss her goodbye.

The Boudreaus had summoned him and Wiley up to Natchitoches to attend an impromptu family meeting, or—given the secrecy that seemed to overhang it—cabal.

Evangeline focused on Sugar, curled up and sleeping on Lincoln's sweatshirt, which Evangeline had shed like a skin and dropped onto the sofa. When she'd pulled the shirt on that morning, its gray fleece and Lincoln's scent had comforted her. Walking home, she'd felt suffocated, and she had begun tugging it over her head even as she crossed the threshold. She'd gone into the bedroom to dig out the ancient white T-shirt she liked to wear when nothing else seemed to fit, then returned to find Lincoln staring down at his phone. The summons had come by text, which didn't mesh well with the rustic image Evangeline's imagination had conjured of the Boudreau clan.

Lincoln's lips brushed her cheek. "If I had a choice," he said softly in her ear, "I wouldn't go."

He had a choice. There was always a choice. But she didn't challenge him. She'd lost any right to challenge him. The confrontation with Reverend Bill should have wiped away all thought of Luc Marin, but instead something about the look in the old man's eyes had sharpened the edges of her dream. The sense of Luc insinuated itself a bit deeper into Evangeline's awareness with each passing hour, sticking there, sharp and irritating like burr grass on a tube sock.

"You're mad at me."

She tried to convince herself it was true. He and Wiley were leaving her short at the club, after all, and Lincoln claimed he "couldn't" tell her what the family meeting was about. But she hadn't turned away in anger; she'd turned her face because of the irrational fear that—even though she'd only dreamed it—Lincoln might taste Luc Marin's kiss lingering on her lips.

Another pang of guilt. Now, *that* made her angry.

She shouldn't feel guilty for thinking of Luc, for dreaming of him, for wishing his life hadn't been cut short. Luc had been her first love. Still, Evangeline didn't dare look at Lincoln straight on, afraid he'd realize she was looking through him and at the memory of a man dead going on a decade.

"I'm not angry," she said, but she pulled back when he tried to kiss her again. He reached out and caught her chin between his thumb and forefinger, turning her face to him.

Irritation rippled across his features, then melted away into hurt. He nodded and sighed. "I'll be back by dinnertime tomorrow," he said, releasing her.

When she didn't respond, he started to turn away. "Wait," she said, and reached up to run her fingers through his thick mass of blond cowlicks. She came so close to a confession, but the words got caught in her throat. If she told him he was competing with a dead boyfriend, she doubted he'd take it well. Men were men. His pride would build a wall between them.

She needed to sort her emotions out on her own before involving him in them.

"Drive careful," she said, and lay her other hand on his chest, a sign of affection and a barrier between them.

Evangeline fastened the shutters and locked her Creole cottage's twin front doors. She pushed the living room furniture against the walls and rolled up the area rug, then lit a single white jar candle, her breath still coming heavy from the exertion.

She scooped up a protesting Sugar and deposited her in the bedroom, closing the door. The cat hissed, hurling a barrage of expletive images that challenged Evangeline's intelligence, sanity, and scruples equally and at the same time. Sugar couldn't possibly comprehend what Evangeline was doing. Evangeline herself didn't understand; she was acting on instinct.

She stopped as she passed through her kitchen and dug in the junk drawer until she turned up a piece of chalk abandoned by the young daughter of one of her former dancers. The girl had spent an afternoon with Evangeline once while her mother sorted out some legal or medical difficulty. Evangeline couldn't remember which. Astonishing as it seemed, the little girl she remembered was probably in high school now.

Evangeline returned to the living room and knelt in the center of the floor, sketching out, as best she could manage freehand, an old-school pentagram. Only then did she allow herself to acknowledge what she was doing.

She pushed back from the pentagram and sat with her back against the wall, resting.

Sugar launched a fresh volley of recriminations from behind the closed bedroom door. Evangeline blocked out the barbed images framed as dire warnings and pulled her knees into her chest, wrapping her arms around them. She closed her eyes and endeavored to reconstruct a memory she'd long tried to erase—her last conversation—all right, quarrel—with Luc.

It had taken place in the small upper-floor apartment on Barracks Street she and Luc had shared after Katrina. He had become obsessed with wresting control of the Chanticleer Coven from Nicholas, and Celestin had encouraged his rebellion at every step. Evangeline could have easily defeated any flesh-and-blood challenge to her relationship with Luc, but she didn't stand a chance against the mania his grandfather was fanning into flame.

It was absurd. A ridiculous and wasteful gesture. Even then it had been clear that the once powerful band of witches had fallen into a decline for which there was no hope of reversal. But for Luc, controlling the coven had never been about power. It had been about proving something to Nicholas. About punishing him for driving his mother, Astrid, away.

That day, the day of their last fight, she told Luc that if he went through with the insanity and issued a challenge to Nicholas—a challenge meant to leave one of them victor and the other dead—he shouldn't come back. At the time, she'd had no doubt he would be the victor. She'd believed in Luc that much. He was so sure of himself, so full of fire. She'd worried he wouldn't be able to cope with the guilt of killing his father.

Luc had laughed at her ultimatum, confident he could depose his father as the head of the Chanticleers, then win Evangeline back. He'd believed in himself that much, too.

Nicholas had surprised them both—twice. He'd bested Luc, then offered his hand to him in forgiveness. In a different world, father and son might have one day made their peace, but Celestin had forestalled that happier conclusion by murdering Luc in cold blood. Only Alice had seen him do it. Alice, who'd been the first to carve up his corpse at Précieux Sang. Though she wished she could have spared Luc's sister that pain, Evangeline couldn't be happier they'd butchered that bastard's corpse, and that he'd been aware of every cut.

"I'm sorry," Luc's voice reached her, not triggered by memory but coming to her from the center of the pentagram. These were the words she'd wanted to hear most, so it came as no surprise that they should be his first.

The Luc in her living room would say what she desired to hear, tell her what she believed to be true. The Luc in her living room wasn't really Luc.

She had to fully own that, in her heart, before she let herself look at him.

It was an open secret among witches that most of what went under the cover of necromancy, although it did rely on actual magic, was nonetheless still a fraud.

Witches didn't raise the dead.

No, Evangeline corrected herself, witches didn't raise the dead *often*.

But that hadn't stopped witches throughout the ages from pretending that they did, either for profit or out of sympathy. A witch could take a mourner's memories and shape them into a simulacrum, a seemingly intelligent, interactive, sometimes even tangible double of the deceased, but the "returned" was really nothing more than a puppet molded from ectoplasm. Such chicanery was even viewed as benevolent, for it gave the mourner closure—a chance to say the things that in life had gone unsaid, to ask the questions that had gone unasked.

This conjuring was known as an Endor spell, named after the biblical story about King Saul's attempt to contact the spirit of the prophet

Samuel. According to the canon, the witch panicked when she recognized King Saul, but the true source of her dread was that Samuel's actual spirit materialized. It would've been like fishing in a slow creek with a cane pole and landing a whale.

"You haven't changed."

This made her laugh. The thought that her own vanity should float so near the surface. She'd been twenty-three when Luc died, and she'd been dragged along a decade's worth of rough road since.

"Why did you call me here if you won't talk to me?" It was his voice, all right, the perfect timbre, the perfect rhythm, and a hint of amused arrogance. "You've certainly waited long enough to reach out." The patronizing irritation in his tone sounded so much like the real Luc that her eyes snapped open.

"Ah, there's my girl," he said.

The Luc before her was the twenty-one-year-old she remembered, only he glowed with his own interior light, brighter and steadier than the candle's flame.

"I'm not a girl," she said.

"I can see that," he said. "But are you still mine?"

Evangeline hugged her knees tighter in the heavy silence that followed.

"I see then. That's what this visit is meant to determine." He ran a finger down his forearm, seemingly surprised by its solidity. He tried to step outside the pentagram, but the tip of his toe stubbed the air like he'd kicked a solid wall. He flashed her a sly, challenging smile that stirred something deep within her, something she'd forgotten or at least buried deeply in her mind. For a moment she was tempted to cross the boundary and go to him, but then she remembered the man she saw before her only existed in the form of imagination people speak of as "memory." Luc was no longer real, but Lincoln was.

"I've met a man," she said, her mouth going dry. "A good man . . . who's good to me. And good *for* me, too."

"Then he must not be a Marin," he said, pausing to let the knife he'd just plunged into her heart turn. "Yes, I know about you and Nicholas."

Of course he would. This Luc could see deeper into her psyche than she could herself, because that's where he came from. "Do you love him, this new beau of yours?" "Beau." He might have said "lover," or perhaps the ill-fitting word "friend," but he'd chosen "beau," a word that both acknowledged and mocked her relationship to Lincoln.

"New." She chose to focus on that word instead. "It's all new. Too new, maybe. But I think I do. Love him."

"Like you thought you loved me."

She bristled. "I did love you. But you're gone."

"Dead, sweetie. Not gone. No need to parse words."

Of course, that was exactly what she had been doing. The first bitterness that came with an Endor spell was it left you to argue with a candid, all-knowing mirror. She ignored the quip. "You've been gone a long time now. And I wasted a lot of that time."

"You wasted time mourning me?"

"I didn't mean that. I meant I wasted it with Nicholas."

"Same thing, really. We both know what that was about. Punishment."

Evangeline felt that knife twist again, pushing in deeper. "It started that way. I wanted to punish you."

"Punish me?" He shook his head and snorted. "That slow train wreck of a tryst you shared with Nicholas was never about punishing me. It was about punishing yourself. And Nicholas, too. Holding him close so that neither of you could ever forget that you'd failed me."

That was a bit more truth than she could handle in this moment. She threw up her hands, ready to send the wraith back into her subconscious, but then he spoke. "What is it you need from me?"

She lowered her hands, but she could no longer look at him. "I need you to remind me why I loved you, so I can let you go."

"Come on," he said, barking out a laugh of disbelief. "That's an easy one. I represented everything you felt you weren't. Wealth, privilege, a sense of entitlement. I was the lord of a feast where you always felt like a beggar. I was your Prince Charming, come to raise you up. Being my girl meant you got to stand in the glow of all that. I deemed you worthy to stand by my side, so you were just as good as anyone else."

"Was it . . . was I really as mercenary as that?"

He shook his head. "Of course not, at least not quite. But you needed me to peel away those layers before you could see beneath them. You loved me because you knew I saw that special spark in you. The strength, the smarts, the power everyone else overlooked. And I think I loved you because you reminded me of my mother. Or at least my idealized version of her." His inky black eyes glowed a bit more brightly. "What a time the two of you might have had. God knows that's really why Celestin and Nicholas wanted me to have nothing to do with you. That's why they tried to demean you by calling you a 'swamp witch.'"

Evangeline wasn't sure how to feel about her deeper psyche comparing herself to Astrid Andersen Marin, but that was baggage she'd have to unpack another day.

"The spark you say you loved. He sees it, too. And he loves that I'm powerful not because of what I can do for him, but because of what I can do for myself and others."

"But?"

"But I've begun sabotaging myself . . . my relationship with . . ."

"You can say his name. I know I just spoke of myself as Prince Charming, but this isn't an old fairy tale. I won't use his name to lure him to his doom."

"I know I can say his name, it's only when I try to open my heart up to him . . . completely . . . you're still in the way."

"Then either there's something you miss about me, or something you distrust about him."

The final bitterness of an Endor spell was that once the key truth was spoken, the spell itself was broken, and the mourner was left alone with fresh feelings of loss. "Though I'd like to think," the conjured specter said as he faded away before her, "it might be a bit of both."

ELEVEN

"Papa-san has returned." Hugo stood in Alice's doorway, holding a blue duffel bag over his shoulder. With a tilt of his head, he asked to enter, and Alice stepped aside to let him pass.

"I know," she said, as he dropped the bag onto her dining table. "I tried to call you twice last night, and again this morning, but you didn't answer your phone."

He looked back at her. "I have a phone?"

"That explains why your voice mailbox wasn't set up. I tried texting, too, but—"

"Daniel." He cut her off with a shrug. "Any number you have would be for the phone I gave him. He fielded all my calls." Hugo smiled. "And occasionally handled the . . . um . . . overflow for me."

"Okay, that was more information than I would have liked."

"I do apologize for offending your delicate sensibilities," he said, placing a hand over his heart, "but get over it. Daniel had many facets, and like it or not, one of them was a randy buck. Now, jumping back to the present, your father-brother"—his brow furrowed as if he were debating a point within himself—"brother-father? Do we start with the long-accepted relationship or the actual gnarled branch on the family tree?"

"How about we stick to Nicholas?"

"Sure thing, sister-aunt. Nicholas is moving back in, so I need to be moving out." He looked around the apartment. "Okay if I hang out here for a day . . . or twenty?"

"You're always welcome." Alice's apartment was fine for one. It would be tight for two. She knew he'd be more comfortable with Fleur in the grand Garden District house, but she also knew his request had nothing to do with needing shelter. Her brother, she realized, needed her.

"You say that now," he said, already unzipping his bag, "but in three days when you're picking up my dirty socks and watching me drink the last of the milk straight from the carton—"

"How about we don't let it get to that?"

"Hey," he said, "I can try, but some things are out of my control." He hefted the bag up and dumped its contents onto the table. Glass vials, bottles of pills, plastic bags of powders, and what Alice guessed were dried psilocybin mushrooms and psychedelic herbs. He gave her a mischievous grin. "Brought the whole pharmacy. By the way, I'll need to borrow some socks for you to tidy up." He winked. "Kidding. My suitcase is in the lobby. Wanted to make sure I was welcome before I lugged it up. By the way, you know they make buildings with elevators now, right?"

"What's all this for?" Alice said, not surprised that Hugo had a large stash of drugs, but disappointed he'd been inconsiderate enough to bring them into her new space. She had grown up in a psychiatric hospital where medications were forced on you, where clearness of thought was a privilege only granted to the docile. The thought of narcotics for recreational use struck her as inconceivable.

"I dunno. What is any of it for?" He reached into the pile, sifting through it until he came upon a small brown glass vial filled with a liquid. He unscrewed the cap, releasing a scent not unlike one of the cleaning fluids used by Sinclair's janitorial staff. He lifted the bottle to his nose, sniffing its contents with each nostril. He shook his head and shuddered, but a wide grin spread across his face. "I started using them to reach altered states to enhance my spells. You get it, right? Launching my rocket where there's less gravity to drag it back down." His glee was short-lived. His expression turned somber as he recapped the bottle and set it on the table. "Then I started using them to reach altered states, period. Thought all of this might be of some use to you, since you and Evangeline appear to be in the running for last witch standing."

He was right. Alice had always been able to sense the strength of other witches. A remnant of bright sparks still hovered in the ether, the most brilliant Alice herself and Evangeline, but every day a few more lights blinked out. The snuffed lights did not, as far as she could tell, signify deaths or witches taking to the Dreaming Road. The witches remained alive and present, but their powers had failed them. She turned her focus on the shimmer she knew to represent Hugo, surprised to catch an image of a star swallowing a star. His magic, she realized, was being appropriated by another. By Fleur.

"Hugo—"

He seemed to read the revelation in her eyes and held up a hand to stop her. "It's okay," he said. "It was my idea. A donation given freely and for a good cause."

"A good cause?"

"Lucy. She's dead. Or she should be. But I suspect you already knew that. It's why you granted Fleur the prime cut of Celestin. The thing is," he said, spinning a chair around, then dropping onto its seat, "Fleur told me. I can't help but wonder how you found out."

Alice hesitated, unsure she should discuss Lucy with him before first talking with Fleur. "I don't know," she finally said. "I sensed it. When I focused on her, I could see this weird corona around her, like she didn't quite fit in her skin."

She pulled out the chair opposite him and sat down at the table. "How does it feel to be losing your magic?"

"Well, Doctor," he said, feigning a German accent for some reason, "I feel just fracking fine." He leaned in. "Really," he said with his normal inflection, "I say good riddance." Alice sensed he meant it. "I mean, magic never brought me anything but grief anyway." He draped his arms over the back of the chair, the same way Nicholas had done the night before. Hugo was of course much younger, and his coloring was fair, but otherwise the son was a perfect twin to his father. So many tiny behaviors, learned or innate, betrayed one's parentage. "Besides," he continued, "I haven't been able to count on it since . . . well, you know . . . out on Grunch Road. Shorting out on me without warning. If what little I have left can keep the brat around a while longer, Fleur is welcome to it."

"Nicholas said Fleur had to kill to bring Lucy back."

"Well, I don't know the details, but resurrection spells . . . they always require a trade. I figured she must have taken someone out."

"And this thought doesn't bother you?"

"Even desperate, she would have been discerning. I'm sure it was no one nice, and knowing our—excuse me—my *tatie*, probably no one attractive either."

"Lucy should have been born a witch. That means Fleur would have had to sacrifice another witch. She could be burned for—"

"Yeah, yeah, how terribly *Malleus Maleficarum*. But who's gonna find out? And how? And even if they did, there aren't enough witches left with big-enough balls," he held up his hands, "or—not to be sexist—ovaries to even try to go after her. Her magic may be on the wane, but her money isn't."

Alice bit her lip. She wanted to believe there was no need to worry, but Nicholas's accusations continued to haunt her.

"Listen," Hugo said with a sigh, "witches always used to talk a good game, condemning blood magic, but that was all bull. The real reason necromancy was forbidden is because its holy grail is to capture the essence of a great magician—the ultimate relic—and trap it in an alabaster urn or a precious stone like a firefly in a Mason jar. No one wants to be *that* magician." Alice's mind flashed on the famed diamond of the now extinct Silverbell Coven. Of course, that was why the stone had been coveted. "But times have changed. Nobody is going to care if Fleur recycled the spark of a witch no one has missed in going on two decades to resurrect her child. A lot of witches have been doing a hell of a lot worse for a paltry amount of power. Besides, even if somebody might care, nobody but us knows."

And there it was. "Nicholas says the Boudreau family knows. He says that's why Lincoln and Wiley came to New Orleans."

Hugo's eyes went wide as his jaw dropped. He tilted his head and looked at her with the confused irritation of a dog hearing a high-pitched noise. "Oh," he said and nodded. He leaned back as his confusion gave way to anger, his widened eyes narrowing to slits. "This is about Evangeline." He wagged his finger at her, another gesture he'd picked up from his father. "This is classic Nicholas. If he can infect you with distrust for Lincoln, the virus might start to spread." He shook his head and puffed out air. "Nicholas doesn't want Evangeline for himself. He doesn't love her. He just doesn't want her to be loved."

"There's something else," she said. "I told you Astrid claimed Celestin trapped her on the Dreaming Road."

"As punishment for not being willing to sacrifice you." The price required of the heir to *The Book of Unwinding*.

Alice fell silent. She'd clung to this one shred of evidence that Astrid hadn't been a complete monster. She bit her lip. "Nicholas says otherwise. He says he put her there to protect us—you, me, and Luc. He says he caught Astrid reading to us from *The Lesser Key of Darkness*. Nicholas threw the book in the fire, but it wouldn't burn."

Hugo's gaze went distant and a line formed between his brows. He shook his head and focused on Alice. "Sounds like quite the dramatic confrontation, but I don't remember anything like it ever happening."

"Then he's lying?"

"Oh, I didn't say that. It's quite possible it did. It's only I don't remember much from that period. Don't care to, really."

"Then it seems we'll never know what happened."

Hugo pushed a path through his mound of illicit pharmaceuticals to find Alice's hand. "Listen. You're wondering which of them is lying, Astrid or Nicholas. Chances are it's both of them, through shading and omission if not through outright duplicity. You're the artist here. Finding truth in this family is like showing the outline of an object by using the negative space around it. You may never see the truth itself, but you might be able to guess at its shape based on the lies surrounding it."

"What do you believe?"

"I believe," he said, releasing her hand, "some of the far-fetched campfire tales about the final days of magic might not be complete fantasies. I believe it may actually come down to a final witch who will catch magic's dying breath and either bring magic back to the world or preside over its—or rather our—extinction. I believe, my dear sister-aunt, that you might end up being that witch, and I believe Nicholas—having arrived at that same conclusion—will say and do anything to slither back from your bad side. Oh, and I believe I'm over calling you 'sister-aunt.'" He shrugged. "It's been fun, but now it's done."

"Well, there's one bit of good news."

"I realize now I lied to you about something," he said, strumming his fingers on the tabletop. "We had crap for parents." He leaned forward and clasped his hands together, staring down at them. "Not surprising, since it seems they had crap for parents, too. Astrid was gone. Whether Celestin took her, or Nicholas trapped her, or she merrily deserted us all on her own, she was gone. And Nicholas, it felt like he was never there either. I mean, after Astrid left, I was afraid my hand would pass right through him if I tried to touch him." His gaze rose and landed on the portrait she'd done of Daniel. "But I lied about magic never bringing me happiness. It did once."

"Daniel," she said, realizing he had been their only true parent, acting as both mother and father to them.

"I miss him, and it hurts like a mother—" he stopped himself. A sad smile rose to his lips.

They both knew Daniel had not approved of profanity. "Simple, ugly words for simple, ugly minds," he'd say before marching the offender to a thesaurus to make them find a more precise, less vulgar word. As a little girl, Alice had added the word "infernal" to her vocabulary as the Daniel-approved substitute for "damned." That she'd heard Nicholas saying "damned" had proved a far less incontrovertible defense than she'd expected it would.

"It hurts . . . a lot. He was more than a conjure. I keep hoping he'll pop back up, nattering on about how I can't even put away the laundry he's washed and folded for me. Before, when he was gone, I could still sense him, flitting around the periphery. I even caught sight of him every so often. But this time there's nothing." He rocked back and forth a bit, his regard hardening as his mouth pulled into a tight pucker. "I think I need to say goodbye to him."

Alice reached around the mound of narcotics and placed her hand over his. "We should hold a memorial for him."

A spark returned to Hugo's eyes. "No," he said, "not a memorial. A wake."

TWELVE

Nathalie heard an insect-like whirring, punctuated by a metallic rattling that seemed to be synchronized to an almost imperceptible fluctuation in the brightness of the faint light beyond her closed eyelids. The air around her felt stifling and dank at the same time. Swampy. At regular intervals, a weak breeze slithered over her skin.

Nathalie stitched the various impressions together into a reasonable explanation. There was a fan, oscillating, causing aluminum blinds to tap against a window frame.

A flash of her SUV cruising along 10. Heading east, out to Grunch Road.

Why had she been headed there?

Alice. Something about Alice.

She remembered finding Mrs. Perrault looking like a writhing Pietà, struggling to drag a corpse onto a plastic tarp. A creeping black mist that devoured everything, the corpse, the tarp, the blood, and—Nathalie remembered as she wiggled the toes on her bare right foot—her shoe.

Then it hit her. The creeping black mist. The demon that had tried to drag Alice into the pit. They had felt the same. Nathalie was heading out to Grunch Road to look for evidence before worrying Alice. But she hadn't made it there.

Hitting an invisible barrier at fifty miles an hour and flipping ass over latchkey. The windshield shattering into a million tiny prisms.

Nathalie felt for the earth around her, still halfway expecting asphalt, but she was lying on an uncovered mattress, low enough her hand draped over its side and touched a wooden floor. Her skin felt damp and sticky, clammy, like waking after a fever has broken.

Her SUV skidding along on its roof, spinning three-sixties as it did so.

She felt weighed down, pinned in place not so much by gravity as by a heavy scent, at once earthy and spicy, musty but laced with incongruous sweet notes of honey and citrus.

She opened her eyes.

Dull gray light. Dusk? White ceiling.

Mold growing overhead formed an image, like one of those inkblot things, a Rorschach. To Nathalie's confused mind, desperate to impose meaning on her disorientation, the shape the mold formed was at once the all-seeing eye, the eye of Horus, and the ichthus pendant she'd received as a confirmation gift.

Thinking she might die. Wondering if she might already be dead. Praying she wouldn't end up a ghost of December.

Nathalie tried to rise, but nausea washed over her and knocked her back. Hard. The room didn't so much spin as rock. She became consciously aware of an eyeball-busting headache.

Darkness. Waking with a gasp, the breath too painful to push back out as a scream.

She pushed back against the pain, trying to reconstruct the sequence of events that would explain where she was and how she'd gotten here.

Hanging upside down, restrained by her safety belt.

Beyond that, Nathalie had floated in darkness, not the safe sea of the womb, but a cold, airless nothing. Despite the surfeit of light, she'd witnessed silver, glitter-like flecks falling all around her, giving her the sensation of being trapped in an ink-filled snow globe.

She'd reached out—not with her hand, but with her mind—and caught hold of one of the glints. Nathalie had found herself looking in at a teary teenage boy looking out. The glint was both a mirror and a window. In that singular moment, Nathalie could feel the energy of the boy's raw, red-faced self-loathing flowing through the mirror into her, burning and bitter, yet as fortifying as her morning coffee.

Nathalie had startled as terrifying memories from her childhood surged in. Babau Jean scratching—*clawing*—at the wrong side of her bedroom mirror.

The glass had cracked and splintered in her grasp, sending a shock through her. That shock was what had first made her aware of this place.

She heard a shuffling—leather-soled shoes on creaking, rotting wood. The scent of honeyed citrus and, it dawned on her, bay leaves, grew stronger. A shadow fell over her. It put her in mind of another shadow, so Nathalie tried to rise again, this time with more grit, but she only succeeded in forcing herself up on her elbows and pushing back an inch or two. The room reeled around her, and she collapsed back onto the thin, musky mattress. She tried to speak. She tried to scream, but nothing came out beyond panicked, meeping gasps.

"*Mais, ma fillette,*" a patronizing voice said, stretching the final syllables into a slow, husky glissando, "*t'souviens-toi pas de ton tonton Emil?*"

A man with a deeply tanned, deeply lined face bent over her. His hair was a thick, steel gray mass of untamed cowlicks, his eyes as blue and bright and unnerving as police car lights in a rearview mirror. He looked far too happy, his expression exaggerated like the face you'd make when playing peekaboo with a baby.

This man on his knees, peering in at her, grinning.

She saw the glint of a ruby ring as a pale hand reached over her. Felt his palm over her forehead. Cool. Calming. Still, Nathalie's mind protested she wasn't a little girl, not by anyone's standards, and although there was something familiar about his face, she'd never heard of an Uncle Emil on either side of her family.

She got another whiff of his cloying aftershave. The perfume was strong, kind of like he'd bathed in it, but it failed to mask his close-up scent of sour sweat and menace. Her eyes traveled from his strong, calloused hand up his thick forearm to a rounded, solid bicep. He wore a tight, graying T-shirt. His hair might be gray, and his face weathered, but the rippling beneath that shirt showed his muscles were still wound as tight as rubber bands inside a golf ball.

"I'm very sorry, sir. I'm sure it's my fault," Nathalie said, slipping into the politeness she reserved for passengers who made her uncomfortable enough to begin calculating the minimum force it would require to fight them off, should the need arrive. "But I don't know you."

He shook his head as his mouth pulled into a sad, or perhaps disapproving, pucker. "'Course you don't, *sha*. But it ain't your fault. That's your bitch mother's doing. Took you away from your family. Took you and your papa, both. Never got around to sending either of you back, neither." He seemed to study the space around her, scanning it from left to right like he was reading a text printed in the air. "Shame she didn't hang herself years before she finally got around to it."

Nathalie couldn't find words. Yes. Her mother had hanged herself. In Corpus Christi. After Katrina. In Nathalie's mother's sister's attic— her mother's sister, not her aunt. Nathalie had sensed the passing but might never have known the details if a note from the sister hadn't arrived two years later, after having followed her to Natchitoches, back to New Orleans, and through three different apartment moves around the city. The thin, worn envelope had carried a dozen forwarding stamps on its face. Inside was a news clipping and a yellow sticky note with the words "This is on you" printed in red felt-tip.

"You weren't right. Never were." Her mother's flat, sour-breathed lamentation sounded anew from this man's mouth. "I knew it from the second they put you in my arms."

Somehow, this man had zeroed in on the single most painful memory Nathalie held of her mother. This was the day her mama had sent Nathalie to live on the streets. Nathalie had been fourteen.

She found herself reliving the moment in a visceral way that went beyond mere memory. Her mama had met her on the front steps of their house that day. She could still see the faded floral cotton shift dress her mama had worn beneath a threadbare maroon cardigan—despite the steam rising up after the rain from the late July sidewalk. "I should've grabbed you up by the ankles when I could still swing you and bashed your brains against a wall."

The memory cut off, but Nathalie felt her own lips moving, silently mouthing the words that remained burned into her. "If I'd known what you'd grow into, I would've. It would have been a kindness."

Her mother hadn't been talking about magic.

Emil laughed. "Your *maman* had the ideal neck for hanging. Scrawny, pale, too long. Bet it snapped"—he said, snapping the fingers of his free hand as he spoke the word—"like a twig."

"Stop it," Nathalie said, her shocked rage pushing her upright, doing what fear and willpower could not. Nathalie held her hand out toward him; sizzling red sparks danced along her fingertips.

"*Regarde,*" he said with a derisive snort, "*la chatonne sait sortir ses griffes.*" He focused on her hand, and it began to tremble. "You aren't like your spindly little *maman*, though, you got a sturdy Boudreau neck, and a sensible Boudreau head riding on it. That's why you aren't going to try any more of your nonsense on *Tonton* Emil again, you hear?" Her hand spasmed into a painful cramp. "I asked you if you heard me."

She felt like her fingers were being crushed and pulled apart at the same time. The agony came over her so fast and strong, it took Nathalie a moment to realize that Emil was causing it, that he was punishing her. "Yes. Yes."

"Yes what, *sha*?"

"I heard you," she gasped out and the pain fell away.

He sat on his haunches and gazed into her eyes. "Ah, *fillette*, you couldn't know no better," he said, his tone a parody of tenderness, conciliatory to the point of saccharine. "I should have sought you out sooner, but before . . ." He shrugged. "Well, it's only that you bloomed so late I figured you might be too much your *maman*, and not enough Boudreau. At least the part of Boudreau that matters."

She closed her eyes and drew in one deep breath after another, letting them out slowly, doing her best to calm her pulse, to calm her mind, to regain control of her faculties. But then a realization hit her. "You crashed my car." Her eyes popped open, and she was too danged mad to care about the way her whole head felt like it might pop open, too. "You could've killed me."

"*Mais non, sha. Jamais.* Just needed to get your attention." His voice was calm, but Nathalie could hear the patience draining from it as he spoke, like he was answering the umpteenth question from an overly curious child. "Now you sit still for a moment." Before she could pull back, his hands shot out and grasped the sides of her head. At first, she felt only panic, but then the thundering in her head gave way, and her vision righted itself. The head-to-toe soreness she felt eased away and was replaced by a sense of vitality. Nathalie hadn't felt this good since she was a teenager.

"There you are." He pulled his hands away and beamed down at her. "Your *tonton* added a few years back to make up for . . . the in-con-ven-i-en-ce," he said, lingering on the word, morphing each and every vowel he could into its nasal French cousin, even managing to add two extra syllables.

"What do you mean?"

"I mean you wakin' up tomorrow younger than you did today . . . provided, that is, you wake up at all." He held up a cautioning hand. "Not a threat. At least not from me. Just telling you something that, deep down, you already know."

Without even trying, Nathalie could pick up precise details about the near future of any random stranger, but it was rare for her to get an insight into what was coming her own way.

This time Nathalie thought maybe this guy was right.

She could feel a premonition brewing; she had ever since she'd dropped Mrs. Perrault off at her house late last night. Her mind applauded itself as it put this missing piece of the puzzle back into place, then stopped as it dawned on her she had no idea how long she'd been out. Might have been last night, might have been last year.

It was this sense of an approaching crisis, a big one involving Alice, that had sent her out to Grunch Road.

"Those demons you came across with the Voodoo woman," he began, then wagged a finger in her face. "No use trying to lie to me. I've always been able to see through you," he said, "and *through you*, too." He held up his hand and turned it so she could see the gleam of the ruby he wore on his ring finger. "I can see through anyone's . . . well, most anyone's eyes, thanks to this." He drew closer and held his hand out so she could examine it. "*C'est un joli truc, non?*"

No. The stone wasn't the least bit pretty. It took an act of will for Nathalie to look at it at all. "It's like some kind of enchanted ruby?" She'd said "enchanted," although she was thinking "cursed."

"Can't really say it's enchanted. Hell, it ain't even a ruby. It's the eyeball of one of those shadow demons. Not easy to come by. You gotta catch the thing as it's slipping from le Chemin . . . or as you city folk say, the Dreaming Road, into this world."

"You killed one of them?" Nathalie added this variable to her calculation of the man's strength.

"'Course not. No need. I cut out the eye and let it loose. When its buddies saw the damned thing had been wounded, they took care of the killing for me." He lifted the ring to his lips and kissed the stone. "Nasty little *couillons*, but then they've been refined to be."

"Refined?"

"'Course, *sha*. Your Dreaming Road, that's what it does. Story goes when a witch takes to the Road, it's the magic that gets burned away." He pursed his lips in disapproval and shook his head. "Ain't the magic. It's the humanity that gets smelted away. The impurities of conscience and compassion"—he clapped his hands together, then held them out to her, empty palms up—"poof. Gone. Road leaves nothing behind except the magic and an empty, angry, controllable"—he paused on this word—"spirit. Ten of those, and you can take on an army. A hundred, you could take down the world."

"But I thought the witches who went there could never return."

"Oh, *sha*. They don't. Not really. What does slip back in ain't the same as what went out."

"Alice came back," Nathalie thought aloud, regretting having spoken Alice's name the second the words were out.

Emil cocked an eyebrow. "Did she really now?"

Nathalie cautioned her fool mouth to keep shut, but she felt compelled to explain about Alice, to defend her. To wipe the sneer off his face. "We rescued her. Her family and I."

Emil remained silent, though his eyes began glistening with humor.

"We brought her back from the Dreaming Road."

"No one's ever been pulled back from the Dreaming Road, unless the Road wanted them to be pulled."

"That's not true. We used 'the gravity of rightful destiny.'" Nathalie could nearly hear Daniel's voice as she spoke the words. "My destiny, our destiny, Alice and mine."

He smirked at her. "Now, who put such nonsense in your head?"

"Daniel . . ." She hesitated, wondering how best to explain who Daniel was, what he was. "Our friend Daniel." It felt weird calling Daniel a friend. In the short time Nathalie had known the guy, she'd felt unnerved by him. But he'd given himself to rescue Alice, and that was enough for her. They might not have been friends while Daniel was still alive, but, Nathalie made up her mind right there on the fly, they were friends now.

"Your friend Daniel?" Emil said, shaking his head, his eyes narrowing in contempt. "You mean the servitor spirit, the one created by your Alice's *maman?*"

This Emil wasn't trying to get information from her. He was trying to give her the impression he was far more in the know than she herself was.

"You didn't pull Alice Marin back. The Road spat her out of its own accord. She's one of them, your *petite amie.*"

"What do you mean 'one of them?'"

"One of those shadows. She's the worst of the bunch. They're an army, and your Alice is their general. That Daniel spook. Your girl's friends and family. They done played you for a fool."

"That isn't true. You're making this up."

"Ain't making nothing up. Not me." His aftershave started to remind her less of cologne and more of the mortuary soap Frank Demagnan had used to prepare bodies. "Seeing clearly, that's all. You know you right 'bout one thing. That gravity of rightful destiny has pulled you and Alice Marin together, but your destiny ain't to love that thing. Your destiny is to kill it."

"I would never hurt her."

He leaned forward and guffawed, nearly bending all the way over as he did so. He allowed himself a good long laugh, glancing up at her a few times as he did. Finally, his mirth faded, replaced by something else. Sadness? Sympathy?

•

"I know what you're going through, girl. It kind of does feel like love, don't it? The pull between the hunter and the prey. But it's gonna be her or you. She's the one who ain't gonna leave you with a choice."

"You're wrong," Nathalie said, stopping short of saying what she was really thinking. This guy was beyond *dingue*. He was a dangerous crazy, the kind of crazy that does not like being called crazy.

"You'd never get what you think you want from that girl. Not even if she had it in her to give it to you." He shook his head. "No, *ma fillette*. You don't want to love that thing. You want to end her. You ain't never gonna feel complete until her blood is on your hands. That's how it works with some of us, *chérie*, folk like you and me. The only one we can love is the one we're born to kill."

Nathalie jumped up, determined to fight her way out if she had to, but he stepped aside. She pointed herself toward the door, but he reached out and grabbed her by the wrist.

"You don't want to believe me, I understand that. But I know what I'm talking about. This"—he held the ring up before her once again— "came from my wife."

Nathalie felt her stomach churning. She shook off his grip and advanced on the door. She was mad enough, frightened enough, to rip it clean off its hinges if she had to, but the door wasn't locked. It flung open so hard, the knob punched the interior wall.

The last rays of the day's low winter sun shone through the opening, and Nathalie gave a quick but heartfelt thanks for the breeze that accompanied them.

Nathalie was about to cross the threshold when she stopped cold, unable to believe what she was seeing. In front of her were about a dozen men who, at first flush, looked enough alike to be brothers, or certainly at least cousins—*her* cousins. She scanned their faces, looking for Lincoln or Wiley, but neither was to be found.

The men wandered around the overgrown patch of grass before her. They each wore a type of camouflage pattern, some the familiar hunting one designed to blend in with leaves and bark, others with dull, brick-like markings that looked like they'd work better in urban environments. Each man carried a semiautomatic rifle strapped across his chest.

Emil drew up behind her. As the men took note of his presence, they jerked to attention and saluted him.

"*Bienvenue, ma fillette*," he said, "to the new world order."

THIRTEEN

Evangeline lined up a row of lowball glasses along the bar, beneath Daniel's benevolent gaze and crooked, self-conscious smile, rendered so perfectly in the portrait Alice had painted of him. It was an appropriate tribute given that another portrait, one Astrid had painted, had helped bring him to life. And it was that "life" those who loved Daniel would be gathering here at Bonnes Nouvelles to celebrate.

She felt the weight of a stare and, by instinct, sought out its source. Her eyes fell once again on the portrait. It sat flanked by a pair of white votive candles in clear glass holders left over from the day Evangeline had first met Lincoln, here at this very bar, when the sparks between them had been enough to kill the power on the entire block.

Was she afraid of losing control as she had in that moment?

The conjured Luc's parting words haunted her. It was true— Evangeline was holding back, refusing to trust Lincoln completely. But did she fear the man who could cause her to lose control, or did she fear what she might become if she lowered her guard too far?

She opened a bottle of Irish whiskey and, by sound alone, poured two fingers into the closest glass. Daniel hadn't been Irish, of course, but he'd spent most of his existence believing he was a ghost from the Emerald Isle, thanks to the backstory Nicholas and Astrid had given him, and what he'd believed to be true about himself had continued to color him long after he'd learned it was a lie. Maybe that's what Evangeline found most human about him.

She set the bottle on the bar and lifted the glass, saluting Daniel, then widening the gesture to include Bonnes Nouvelles as well. She sipped the whiskey, grimacing at the taste. Honey, vanilla, and orange, with a soupçon of cat piss.

Vodka. Unflavored and ice-cold. That was her poison.

The door swept open with magnificent force. Evangeline looked over to find the Vieux Carré's own Miss LaLaurie Mansheon, a six-foot-four wall of solid muscle draped in a teal chiffon halter-style gown, hurrying toward her in six-and-a-half-inch stiletto-heel platform pumps that conspired to raise the drag queen's stature to nearly the seven-foot mark. LaLaurie drew near and, beaming down at Evangeline, lifted a heavily bejeweled hand and brushed back a wayward tress of her long lace-front wig that had been styled in easy beach waves and dyed a shade not so different from Evangeline's own natural auburn. "I hope you appreciate the homage."

Evangeline laughed and raised her glass again, this time to LaLaurie. "Indeed, I do."

"I know y'all are shutting down early tonight for your"—she waved a hand in the direction of Daniel's portrait—"private event, but I wanted to pop in and tell you goodbye in person."

"Goodbye?"

"Yeah, there's a sea of ignorant and ugly out there, and it feels like high tide is rolling in. Gonna get out of here for a while. Go out and visit my family in Oakland."

"I thought your people were from Mississippi. I didn't know you had relatives in California."

"I didn't say 'relatives.' I said 'family.' You know there's a difference, girl."

"Indeed, I do," Evangeline repeated herself and grasped the whiskey bottle. "Care to join me?"

"Oh, good Lord, girl. No. I have one more set to perform and a six a.m. flight I gotta be on." She nodded at Daniel's portrait. "I'm sorry for your loss."

"I'm sorry we're losing you."

"Aren't you sweet. You may not be losing me. Least not for forever." LaLaurie cast a quick glance around the club.

Evangeline assumed she was looking for Hugo. "He's in the storeroom with Alice trying to unearth our old karaoke machine."

"Hmmm . . . ?"

"Hugo."

"Oh, that one." LaLaurie waved her hand in the air, the overhead light setting fire to the stones in each of her five rings. "He's all wrapped up in that new 'friend' of his. All tough and manly, just like the straight boys who'd like to kill them both. Guys like Hugo could never . . . well. He ain't even gonna notice this old girl is gone."

"That isn't true. At least the part about missing you."

LaLaurie flashed her a wide smile. "Yeah, I guess you're right. But no. I'm not looking for the Marin . . . boy. I'm taking the old place in. It's only now I'm leaving, I'm starting to feel nostalgic. You know I first started coming here back when they still called the place 'The Black Cat.'" A bejeweled nail pointed to the stage. "Back when you yourself, Miss Evangeline, was up there working that pole like a fireman sliding down to a four-alarm fire. You sure were something back then," she said, then seemed to recognize it as a left-handed compliment. "Not that you aren't now," she added.

"Strange, I don't remember you—"

"And you're wondering how you could have missed all this." LaLaurie struck a dramatic pose and made a sweeping gesture that took her in from the top of her wig to the soles of her stilettos. She chuckled. "Nah, you didn't miss anything. I used to come here in boy drag, to look after my sister—my real sister, not the blood one. Maybe you remember her? Tiny little thing." LaLaurie raised her hand to the level of Evangeline's shoulders. "Bright green eyes and long black hair with a streak of red in it. Called herself Regine. She could pass, so she used to dance here a bit. I kept watch in case any of the boys got a little too free with their hands and ran across, well, you know, her boys."

Evangeline did in fact recall the dancer, clearly enough to feel surprise Regine had passed beneath the radar of not just her ordinary five senses, but her extrasensory perception, too. "Yes, I do remember Regine," she said. "I haven't thought of her in forever, though. How is she?"

"Damned if I know. She drifted away during Katrina. Probably ended up married to some farmer and teaching Sunday school in Bazine, Kansas. She got out the week before. Me, I was fool enough to have faith in . . . well, you know."

Evangeline, uncertain what the queen was getting at, shook her head. "The government."

LaLaurie barked out a laugh. "Yeah. Butter wouldn't melt in your mouth, would it?" She leaned in. "I mean people like Hugo, and you. And probably that fellow in the picture there, too. I know what you are. I know what you all are."

Hugo entered, a dusty cardboard box in his arms and Alice at his side.

"Well, well, well," he said, nearly bowling Alice over as he pawned the box off on her. "I was wondering if you were going to haul that sagging camel toe tuck of yours in to say goodbye before you took off."

"You knew I was leaving?" A spark of hope betrayed the queen by slipping out from behind her feigned nonchalance. Evangeline's heart nearly broke for LaLaurie. Hugo loved her, all right, as best he could and with his entire guarded heart. But the love Hugo had for her was not the kind LaLaurie had always dreamed it would grow into.

"Posters with your pancaked puss over the words 'Farewell Tour' are pasted all over the friggin' Quarter. By the way, two dive bars do not a tour make."

"You could have come to one of them. It would've saved me having to hike all over the blessed city in these shoes." LaLaurie gave Evangeline a sidelong glance that acknowledged she'd busted herself. Yes, LaLaurie would have walked a hundred miles in those shoes to hear Hugo say he'd miss her. Evangeline looked down, acting like she hadn't picked up on the slip.

"When have I ever made your life easier?" Hugo asked.

"There was that one time on August sixth, two thousand and never."

Hugo drew near the queen. "Best day of my life."

LaLaurie blinked her beaded eyelashes with pleasure as Hugo reached into his pocket and fished out a wadded-up dollar from his pocket. "They got a lottery out there in California, don't they?"

"You know they do."

"You take this," Hugo said, flattening the dollar and offering it to LaLaurie. Evangeline saw a spark move from the tip of Hugo's finger and stretch out to envelope the bill. "You play it on the big lottery. Not some damned scratch-off. And don't you use it for anything else. You promise. The day you get there."

"About time you got around to giving me a tip." LaLaurie glanced at the bill before slipping it into her padded bra. She pursed her lips. "Costs two dollars to play, but I guess I'll have to make up the difference on my lonesome."

"I reckon you will. But one of the two will be that one. Promise me."

"All right. I promise." She shrugged her steely shoulders. "Big draw. No scratch. Too stingy to dig a bit deeper in that pocket of his." This last bit she muttered. "The day"—her voice rose as she patted her wig—"the very second I get there." She grabbed Hugo's wrist, focusing on his watch. "Is that the time? I got to get back for my next set."

It was clear LaLaurie had only wanted to touch Hugo. She released him, slowly, with great tenderness, and strode to the door like she was working a catwalk. Evangeline picked up on a stray thought. LaLaurie had rehearsed this moment in her mind. Dozens, maybe hundreds of times. LaLaurie reached the door and grasped the handle, then looked back over her shoulder with a graceful twist of her neck.

"Bye, Norman," Hugo said, stretching the name out.

LaLaurie's eyes flashed, but her lips curled up into a tight smile. "You are such a malevolent little bastard. But I still love you."

She turned back and pushed the door open.

"Love you more," Hugo mumbled under his breath.

"I heard that," she said, then stepped aside, holding the door open for Fleur, whose arms were laden with a bouquet half her size.

Fleur ducked beneath LaLaurie's arm. "Thank you."

"Mmmhmmm," LaLaurie's voice trailed off, and the door closed.

"Hugo?" Fleur said. "Could you . . . ?" Hugo rushed forward and relieved her of the load, setting the vase on the end of the bar.

"Your friend," Alice said, joining her brother, balancing the box she'd been holding on a barstool. "She'll never spend that dollar. She'll hold on to it forever."

Hugo tapped a glass. "Barkeep?" He watched as Evangeline poured a shot for him. "She will . . . someday. She'll drop it on the lottery. When she's ready to move on for real. By letting go, she shall receive." He grabbed the glass and drank it down.

"Not everyone is as cavalier as you, dear nephew," Fleur said. She looked diminished. Her aura seemed to consume the light around her, giving Evangeline the impression she had been outlined in black ink. Without even trying, Evangeline picked up on her feelings—concern, fear, wounded pride.

Fleur's eyes met hers. "My divorce was finalized today. Warren's wedding is Christmas Day."

"Where's the brat?" Hugo said.

"That's why I'm running late . . . and Lucy didn't come. We're having a bit of a disagreement. Warren sent flowers to each of us today. Hers included an invitation, a surprisingly sincere-sounding one, to participate in the nuptials."

"She wants to go to Warren's wedding?" Hugo said, incredulous.

"She wants to go home. Even if it means living with her father and his child bride."

"The father she wanted to put a blood curse on not six months ago," Alice said with the unintentional bluntness of someone to whom being able to speak her mind was still a novelty.

"We've worked through all that. She and Warren have been video chatting over the last several weeks. At my urging." Fleur rushed out the next words, and Evangeline didn't need to use her power to discern she was trying to fend off Hugo's expression of . . . what? Surprise? Sympathy? Contempt? "She and Warren need each other. I'm not going to let anyone's pride—hers, his, or mine—put a wall between them. I only wish it were possible for Lucy to attend the wedding."

"But why—" Evangeline began, regretting the intercession the very second her lips began to move. This situation was in no way her business or her concern.

"You're a class act, *Tatie*," Hugo said, rescuing Fleur and Evangeline both. He planted a quick kiss on Fleur's temple.

Fleur's eyes filled with gratitude, but the warm glow was short-lived. She brushed her bangs back, and it was gone. "And still my daughter isn't speaking to me." Fleur turned her gaze toward her. "Bar's open?"

Evangeline poured her a whiskey and slid it over. Fleur lifted the glass to her lips and sipped. Her shoulders relaxed. She focused on the painting on the bar. "It's hard to think of Daniel as dead," Fleur said, casting a quick glance around to determine who was in earshot. "I'd only just begun to think of him as alive."

"But he was alive," Hugo said. "A man, not a disposable servitor spirit. He may have started out that way, but he developed a rich interior life." A smile quivered on his lips. "He was even capable of duplicity." He knocked back his whiskey and grimaced. "Nicholas and Astrid didn't give him any of that, you know. And he didn't get it from that damnable book Astrid used to create him either."

"No," Alice said, focusing on the painting she'd done of Daniel, "somehow Daniel had a spark of his own."

"You really captured his essence." Fleur moved side to side as she considered the portrait. "You have a real talent, our Alice. It takes great skill to make it seem as if the subject's eyes are following you."

Hadn't Evangeline thought the same? But this painting went far beyond that. Daniel's eyes did more than follow you. They looked through you.

Fleur glanced around the club. "Is it only the four of us? I'd assumed Nathalie and the Brothers Boudreau would be joining us."

Evangeline expected Hugo to jump in with an answer, but instead he fell silent. A shadow crossed over his face, and he reached for the whiskey bottle.

Fleur gave her a cautious, confused look. Evangeline shrugged.

Another moment of awkward silence, and Evangeline decided to answer. "Lincoln and Wiley have been called up to Natchitoches."

"'Called up' is an odd phrasing. You make it sound like the draft."

"It seems it's more of a formal end-of-year meeting than a Christmas visit. Lincoln described it as a compulsory family cabal with jambalaya and *bouille*."

"And Nathalie?"

"She, too," Alice said, "was invited. Or drafted, though she was happy to volunteer. It's been good for her, connecting with Wiley and Lincoln. It's built a bridge between Nathalie and the rest of the Boudreaus."

"But Nathalie is such a lovely woman," Fleur said. "Why would a bridge even be necessary?"

Alice fell silent, and Evangeline sensed she was debating whether it was appropriate to be discussing Nathalie in her absence.

Hugo had no such qualms. "Nathalie's mother," he said, "was an outsider, an unpopular one. The Boudreaus haven't exactly shunned Nathalie over the years, but they've never reached out to her either. Not even when she went up to Natchitoches after Katrina."

"Nathalie has been on her own since she was fourteen," Alice said, as much a simple statement of fact as a condemnation of the larger Boudreau family.

Evangeline sensed another level of meaning, too. Alice was speaking from the center of her own pain, having been deserted by her family . . . and by Evangeline, too.

"Beautiful," Evangeline said, tracing a finger along the petals of a flower that resembled a rose except for its coloring, which fell somewhere between blue and deep violet. It wasn't a lie. The bouquet was lovely, but she'd only spoken of it to fill the silence, and because she sensed Fleur could use another shot of validation.

"Blue Rose lisianthus." Fleur tapped a wine-colored nail against a similar bloom. "I know he was fond of them. The bright blue ones are bachelor's buttons," she said, first gazing sadly at Daniel's portrait, then smirking, "in honor of his status as a confirmed bachelor."

"And the green ones?" Evangeline asked, to continue Fleur's distraction.

Fleur turned to her with what seemed a genuine smile. "Bells of Ireland. Of course, he wasn't really Irish. If anything he was a caricature of the Irish, but the idea of a connection to faraway Éire was, I understand, once very important to him." She took another sip of her whiskey, then reached out to examine the bottle. "It appears great minds do think alike."

Hugo grunted, then craned his neck as he looked out the window to the street.

A drab young woman had arrived at the door. She tugged it open and stepped into the bar. She wore no makeup. The glow of the club's predominantly blue-tinted LED lights rendered her complexion a snowy pale. Her brown hair was pulled back in a tight bun. A second woman around the same age followed her into the bar. They wore identical white, long-sleeved, bow-at-the-neck blouses, paired with calf-length skirts. The second woman waited by the door, holding it open, perhaps to facilitate a hasty escape.

Evangeline found the pair somehow familiar, but she couldn't place them. She was about to tell them the club was closed for a private function when Hugo spoke up.

"Sorry, ladies," he said, eying them up and down. "Dancer auditions are on the third Thursday of the month."

"Hugo—" She began to chastise him but fell dumb at the sight of Nicholas in the doorway.

"They're with me." Nicholas walked, full swagger, up to the bar. He acted as if they should applaud the restoration of the rightful monarch.

"You're not welcome here," Hugo said, puffing up and positioning himself like a territorial cock protecting his hens. "And neither are your beige brides of Dracula."

Nicholas responded by reaching out and drawing his son into a tight embrace. He nuzzled Hugo's hair, though his gaze remained fixed on Evangeline. Nicholas wanted her to experience his regret, his guilt. To understand how desperately he'd missed his son. How deeply he'd missed her.

Nicholas released Hugo, and Hugo staggered back. The show of paternal affection had landed with more force than any punch could have. Nicholas slipped an arm around Fleur's shoulder, giving her a gentle squeeze, then focused on Daniel's portrait. "Odd you could love the creation and still hold the creator in such contempt. I know you believe I treated him callously, perhaps even resent me for his end, but I gave him life. I gave him purpose. And for how the rest of it turned out, what can I say? There's no denying I have an inflated ego, but I never wanted to play God."

Nicholas looked at Evangeline with the same self-assuredness that had always at once repulsed and attracted her.

"Oh, come now. I don't expect a hero's welcome, but we've all made mistakes. You two"—he pointed back and forth at Hugo and her— "deemed me capable of murdering my own son and conspired against me." He released Fleur and looked down at her. "And you allowed pieces of our father's body to be passed out like party favors while I was off searching for a way to . . ." He hesitated as Fleur's expression turned to stone. "To find a solution," he continued, "to our predicament. All in all, I think you should laud me for my magnanimity, or at least pour me a drink."

Evangeline was happy for the suggestion. It gave her something to do. She grabbed the bottle by the neck and eyeballed a half jigger of whiskey. She slid the glass toward him, cringing when his fingers traced over hers. She snapped her hand back and turned to his companions. "Drink?"

"No, no," Nicholas answered for them. "It's requisite they maintain a sober mind for the sake of—"

"It's you," Alice blurted out, tilting her head as she examined the young women. "You were at Précieux Sang, at Celestin's trial."

In a flash, Evangeline, too, recognized the women. They were the Goth girls Alice had warned away before taking the knife to Celestin's corpse. But their black coats, thick eyeliner, and lavender hair were gone, replaced by this garb that made them look like missionaries.

Nicholas's eyes caught hers, a mischievous glint in them. *Missionaries.* He'd planted the image in her mind. He'd never possessed such an ability before. Nicholas flashed her a tight, knowing smile and opened his mind up to her like a movie screen. With a single thought, he laid it all bare before her.

Yes, these women were missionaries, all right, of a faith Nicholas himself was founding. He had found a way to recharge his failing batteries. Vampirism through adoration, similar to the way performers feed off the energy of the audience—only intentionally, and without any thought of giving anything back. These women were his acolytes, and if Nicholas had made his triumphant return, Evangeline was sure they were only two from among a legion.

Blood. Sex. Dreaming.
Intoxication. Adoration. Deprivation. Madness.
These are the gates to magic.

The words came to her in a separate stream. Had Nicholas projected them, or had they surfaced from somewhere in her own mind? Before Evangeline could delve deeper to discover their source, Nicholas raised his glass in salute. "To Daniel."

There was a moment of uncertainty, then Fleur seconded him. "To Daniel. It takes a special person to learn he doesn't exist, then go on with his life anyway."

Hugo seemed to float up through a cloud of confused resentment, but he, too, raised his glass. "To the only father I ever knew. And mother, too, for that matter."

"Well," Nicholas said, "there is that." He returned his tumbler to the bar. "I'll leave you to your further reminiscences, but first I must admit I had an ulterior motive for crashing your celebration of our dear Daniel."

"Anyone surprised here?" Hugo turned from Evangeline to Alice to his aunt. He focused on Nicholas's acolytes. "Watchtower Twins? No?"

Nicholas ignored Hugo's sarcasm. "I'm hoping you'll join me, well, actually, I'm hoping all of the region's remaining witches will join together in reviving a lapsed tradition. The Longest Night."

Hugo snorted. "I think you're forgetting dear old *grand-père* Celestin slaughtered half the witches between Galveston and Biloxi. Unlikely the survivors are going to show up for a sequel."

"Celestin's atrocities are the very reason I think rekindling this tradition is important. Of course, Celestin didn't act alone." He turned his focus to Evangeline. "Your aunts colluded with him. A joyful Longest Night celebration would give us all an opportunity to repair our image, and, more importantly, help our community heal."

"You have my support," Fleur said, then turned to her nephew and niece. "Oh, come on. It's exactly what we need. All of us. It's like a roving masked ball meets Burning Man. Not only are intoxicants and devilry condoned, they're encouraged. You'll love it. Especially you, Hugo."

It struck Evangeline that Fleur was working too hard to sell this idea. Nicholas, she surmised, had already gotten Fleur's buy-in, and no doubt his sister had proposed Daniel's wake as the perfect place for him to buttonhole them. All of them together, all of them emotionally vulnerable. Taking advantage of their vulnerability didn't feel like something Fleur would involve herself in naturally. Evangeline studied the two as they stood near each other, watching the ebb and flow of energy between them. Evangeline could see it written in their auras. Nicholas was holding something over his sister's head.

"I won't beg," Nicholas said, "but do know you're welcome. More than welcome. Your support would mean the world to me, as it would give me hope perhaps not all is lost between us. That my relationships with each of you might still be salvageable."

"That," Alice began, "is a lot of weight to place on a single evening—"

"Relax, Nicholas," Hugo said, cutting his sister off. "Fleur had me at Molly and mischief." He shrugged. "How bad could it be anyway?" he said, looking everywhere except at his father. "Oh, yeah. That's right. It could be hell on earth. Literally." He caught hold of Alice's hand and tugged her toward the door. Alice cast a surprised glance back at them as her brother conducted her out the door and onto the street.

Nicholas turned to Evangeline, a silent question hanging between them.

"Lincoln and I will both be there. You can count on *us*."

FOURTEEN

It was 12:15 a.m. A paper cup half-full of cold coffee sat beside the vending-machine pimento-cheese sandwich Remy had brought Lisette before heading out at the end of visiting hours. The unopened plastic wedge that held the sandwich pointed like a planchette toward the silent, glowing flat-screen television built into the dark, wood-veneer cabinet to her left. To her right, a man lay stretched out on the short leg of the gray, padded, L-shaped banquette. He snored softly.

Mama? A single-word text from Manon popped up on her phone.

Lisette typed her response. *Yes, baby. Mama's here.* And then she waited for what seemed a thousand years.

I need you. Can you come? Then *I know it's late.*

Mama is just downstairs, Lisette responded, then worried that might sound presumptuous. *I knew you didn't want to see me, but I was hoping.* She'd already scrambled to her feet as she typed the first response, but now she paused, frightened she might have put Manon off. Another eternity passed.

Her answer finally came. *I love you. I'm sorry.* It had been worth the wait.

Lisette ran toward the elevator bank, not worrying whether she looked like a mad woman, not worrying about displaying her remarkable recovery in the very hospital where she'd been treated after her stroke. She darted into an elevator car before its doors had fully opened. She caught sight of her blurred reflection as the doors closed. She'd developed a new nervous tic overnight, tugging down the sleeve of her sweater to make sure the gad remained hidden. She gave into the urge once more, knowing it would help her regain her composure before the doors opened on the maternity ward. The staff wouldn't look too well on a grandmother who was foaming at the mouth.

Isadore was waiting for her when she stepped out. He looked worse than exhausted—unshaven, rumpled, still wearing the same shirt and jeans he'd had on when Michael had summoned them to the hospital. He motioned with a thumb over his shoulder. "She's that way," he said, his voice hushed in deference to both the setting and the hour. "Three doors down on the left."

"You talked her into seeing me?" Lisette said, doing her best not to let her anxiety punch up the volume of her voice.

Isadore rubbed his hand down his face, then gave her a wan smile. "No. I know better than to try talking either of you into anything. She came around on her own." He stepped around her and pressed the call button for the elevator.

"Aren't you coming with me?" Her voice had started out low but rose till her last word pealed like a bell.

The attendant at the nurses' station lifted his finger to his lips. Lisette mouthed the word "sorry."

"No," Isadore whispered. "It's past visiting hours. Only one of us can stay with her, and she wants her mama." He leaned in and planted a kiss on her forehead. "Don't be scared," he said. "The storm is over."

"How can you be so sure?"

"I've got decades of experience predicting the weather," he said as the elevator doors opened. He stepped into the car, then turned back.

As the doors began to close on him, he leaned forward. "After all, like mother, like daughter."

Any other day, she might have bristled at his parting quip. Tonight, the familiarity of his good-natured ribbing comforted her. Lisette was, she realized, afraid. Afraid she might make a misstep, that she might say or do something that would set her fragile daughter off and alienate her once again. She turned, bracing herself for whatever was to come.

She made her way down the hall, the soles of the new sneakers she'd bought to replace her blood-soaked pair squeaking with each step. In the lobby, where it didn't matter one whit, they'd lived up to their name. Here, they seemed determined to compete with Gabriel's trumpet.

Lisette approached the opening of the third door and peered in. The subdued nighttime lighting revealed Manon wasn't in bed as Lisette would've expected at this hour. Instead, she sat in the guest chair, waiting for her. Manon wore a robe, a new one Lisette had never seen, pastel pink with oversize white and yellow daisies, and matching padded slippers. Lisette couldn't imagine anything less like her daughter. Maybe Isadore had sent Remy out to do the shopping, or maybe one of Manon's school friends had dropped off the ensemble. From her own stint at this same hospital, Lisette knew anything was better than the ass-flaps-in-the-wind gowns they gave you to wear.

Lisette stepped over the threshold and waited, studying her daughter for any sign she wasn't happy to see her. Manon's gaze, at first distant, sharpened as it registered her presence. "I am so scared, Mama," she said, holding out a hand that Lisette rushed over to grasp. "How am I going to do it?" Manon's shoulders hunched forward, and her chin dropped nearer her chest. She seemed to be crumbling in on herself. "How am I going to love this baby? What if I can't?"

Lisette squeezed her daughter's hand, then lifted it to her lips. Manon's eyes drifted up to hers, full of the same expectant look she used to get as Lisette patched her up from some childhood accident. She wanted her mother to promise her everything would be all right, maybe even expected it. But this wasn't a scraped knee. Sweet nothings would get them nowhere.

Maybe Lisette's father was right. Maybe the child would be better off with a different family, a normal family that knew nothing of magic. She felt her heart tighten in her chest at the thought. She didn't believe it. Not really. Despite everything, Lisette felt the baby girl would be better off with them. Despite everything, she didn't think it would take an intervention from Erzulie Mansur to open Manon's heart.

"How," Lisette began, reaching out, stroking Manon's hair, "do you feel when you look at her?"

Manon pulled back. "I haven't seen her. It's wrong of me, I know. I needed . . . I need you to go with me."

Lisette nodded. "That's why I'm here. To help you do whatever it is you need to do. Regardless of what that is."

Manon's focus softened, but a crease formed between her brows. "What if she doesn't live?"

"Of course she's going to live." Lisette spoke as if that were the most nonsensical thing her daughter had ever said, then forced a smile. She wanted to tell Manon that her being near the child, loving her, would probably play as big a role in her survival as anything the doctors could do. She knew better than to say it, though. If the child lived, that would be one thing. If the child died, she would have saddled Manon with a lifetime of questioning, a lifetime of guilt.

"When can we go?" she asked.

Manon stared at her blankly. "Go?"

"To see the baby."

"Oh." Manon gave a small nod. "The nurse, she said anytime. They got her in a private room in the NICU. They do that here," Manon said, then choked, "for the most fragile ones."

The nurse, a young woman wearing blue hospital scrubs, met them as they approached the baby's room. Lisette imagined she saw a look of relief in the woman's black eyes. "She's been waiting to see you," the nurse said. Then, seeming to read something in Manon's expression, she moved into business mode. "I'll need you both to wash your hands." She handed Lisette two plastic bags, each containing a sky-blue disposable gown, made, it seemed, from the same material as the bags in which they were packaged. "And put these on over your clothes."

The woman paused as she went to a sink stationed in the hall outside the row of private nurseries and turned on the water. Lisette at first assumed it was for them, but then the nurse soaped up her own hands and put them under the stream. "You're feeling healthy, right?" This question was aimed at Lisette.

Truth be told, Lisette felt like she'd ridden an express train halfway to dead, but she knew the nurse needed to be sure the baby wouldn't be exposed to infection. "Tired," Lisette allowed herself a partial confession, "but no, I've been well." *Other than the stroke that nearly killed me and the self-surgery I've done on my arm.*

The nurse's face flashed a doubtful expression, her mouth pulling into a pinched, tight line as her gaze zeroed in on Lisette. For a moment, Lisette wondered if the woman had picked up on the thoughts she hadn't expressed, at least not aloud. "You're sure? It's crucial—"

"I am. I'm sure. I'm sorry, it's only I've been . . ." Lisette paused and wrapped her arm around Manon's shoulders, "we've been going through hell."

The nurse nodded, her features smoothing, losing any air of suspicion. "I understand," she said, but the words sounded perfunctory, as if she didn't understand at all.

139

"She's so small," Manon said, seemingly surprised. "So small," she repeated herself, this second time with fear building in her voice.

"She's a fighter," the nurse said, speaking with a sterner tone than Lisette would have liked. "That's what she is." The woman reached a hand into each of the incubator's hand ports. "She needs to know she's got someone to fight for."

No one could fault the nurse on her professionalism. She was working hard, though maybe not hard enough, to conceal her contempt for the mother who wouldn't be present for her daughter, for the grandmother who hadn't been present for hers. Lisette wanted to speak up, to try to explain their situation in a way that wouldn't prompt the nurse to make a call to child protective services.

The caretaker looked back over her shoulder at them. "Place your hand like this. One on each side. And talk to her." She zeroed in on Manon. "She knows your voice. Keep calm. Keep positive. Tell her how glad you are she's in the world. Tell her how much you love her."

Manon's face crumbled and fat tears traced down her cheeks. "I am," she said, seeming to realize the truth of her words as she spoke them. "I do. I do love her."

The nurse's flinty eyes warmed, and a genuine smile twitched on her lips. "Come here and tell her that."

Lisette gave Manon a quick squeeze, then escorted her to the baby's incubator. The nurse nodded to Lisette, as if to signal she had it from here. Perhaps it was selfish, but Lisette felt relieved the nurse's newfound warmth seemed to extend to her, too. It was as if the woman was willing to cut them some slack now that she'd determined them capable of human feeling. She led Manon, guiding her hands through the ports. "There you are. Rest them by her sides."

Manon beamed down at the tiny, fragile creature.

"Look. She knows you. See how she relaxed at your touch?"

Lisette hadn't noticed any change in the child's comportment, but she had nothing against a pious lie or two, especially in a situation such as this one. The nurse met her eyes, and in that instant Lisette tried to telegraph a world of gratitude. A soft blink reminiscent of a satisfied cat seemed to serve as the nurse's acknowledgment. The woman placed a hand between Manon's shoulder blades. "I'll be right outside if you need me."

"Thank you," Lisette said, this time aloud.

Manon stirred as if from a dream. She mumbled, "Yes, thank you," her focus never straying from the baby. Lisette and Manon stood there without speaking for a few golden minutes, taking in the miracle in the plastic box.

With relief came exhaustion. The room was spacious, with a recliner for the parents to use once the baby was far enough along to be held, and a padded bench that ran along a good portion of the far wall. Lisette took a seat on the bench and waited.

Lisette didn't want to speak, for fear she'd fracture the spell the child was weaving on the mother. Finally, Manon broke the silence.

"I was thinking I might name her Joy," she said, "after Grandma Perrault."

"I think that would make your father very happy."

The thought made Lisette happy, too. Joy Perrault had been a good woman; Lisette couldn't have hoped for a better mother-in-law. She cursed the breast cancer that had taken Joy from them.

Isadore's mother had always been a bit on the quiet side. She'd grown up in the North, the Chicago area, with her widowed mother, Lucille, and another woman Lisette now realized had been Lucille's partner. Joy's older brother had been a naval officer stationed at Great Lakes. It was he who'd introduced Joy to Isadore's father.

Joy did have a couple of odd quirks—she was terrified by the scent of carnations and refused to set foot in the state of Mississippi, even though her people, the Burkes, were originally from a place there named Kilroy, no, Conroy, a dot on the map that had ceased to exist altogether after an explosion destroyed the paper mill that had been its main employer. Joy claimed her mother had forbidden her even to visit Mississippi. Said her mama had made that one stipulation before giving Joy her blessing to marry Isadore's father and move back below the Mason-Dixon Line.

Long before Lisette had ever considered Isadore in a romantic light, their families had known each other. Joy always treated Lisette's mother, Soulange, with a respectful, cautious deference despite her uneasiness about Soulange's Voodoo. Though she'd never once set foot in Vèvè, she hadn't been above coming to Soulange for counsel on everyday matters or sitting next to her at Saturday mass.

"Oh," Lisette said as she realized the subtext encoded in the choice of name. Her mother-in-law's skill for being a part of the family, but not a part of Soulange's religion, had influenced the choice.

Manon licked her lips. "I want a different kind of life for her, Mama. Not that I don't love and respect both you and Grandma Soulange. It's only . . . with her father being—"

"I get it, my girl. No need to explain." Lisette stood and drew near the incubator. She gazed down at the tiny life in the plastic box. "I want you both to distance yourself from witches and their magic. You can't do that if you follow in my footsteps." She traced a finger along the top of the incubator, pretending to herself she was touching the baby's cheek. "I've come to realize as long as a person is in service to the loa, witches are going to be circling like buzzards trying to pick at their power. These witches—they killed your grandmother. And they damned near killed the three of us, too."

"What about Vèvè? I know," she dared, as Lisette pondered her reply, "you were hoping I'd carry on the tradition."

Lisette shook her head, thinking on what she'd found when she entered the store that morning. "No, *ma chère*, I don't think the loa want you anyway. I think the mantle is falling to your brother." She sensed this to be true, and she also felt certain it was what Manon hoped to hear. Still, Lisette couldn't help but wonder if Manon might be the one who regretted this conversation one day. If, after years of hiding the truth of who she was behind the less-than-glamorous realities of business management, there wouldn't come a time when Manon might crave a bit of magic. "It's his choice to pick it up or walk away. All I can do is make sure he makes that choice with his eyes wide open."

Manon smiled at Joy, for she was Joy now. Not just "the baby," and certainly never again "it." Manon looked up at Lisette. "Would you like to . . . ," she said, taking her hands away from her little love. "I know it isn't the same as getting to hold her . . ."

"I was," Lisette said, her heart flooding with love for both of her girls, "afraid you were never going to ask."

FIFTEEN

Hugo claimed they had been invited to drop by, but Alice doubted the invitation extended to this late hour. The shutters of the house—a Gothic Revival double shotgun cottage—had been pulled closed, and the trio of lantern-like porch lights overhead was dark. She could see Hugo wouldn't be put off even by such obvious signs. He wanted to rake Nicholas over the coals, and to do so properly he needed a larger audience.

Alice stepped off the sidewalk into the street. Still booming a few blocks down, the street was subdued, if not entirely quiet, here on its more residential end. At least it was until Hugo began rapping on the house's twin front doors, moving back and forth between them as he called out to the residents.

If anything, this small gray house, crowned by a triangular central dormer that called to mind a traditional witch's hat, seemed too on-the-nose to belong to les Jumeaux, or "the Twins," as they were called when the former felt too stilted. Of the once powerful Chanticleer Coven, only the Twins and the Marins remained. With no one left to cling to the pretension of maintaining French as the coven's official language, the Twins would be unlikely to hear the French version of address moving forward.

After so many years of thinking of the Twins as a single unit, Alice had been almost surprised to learn they had given names as individuals. The sister went by "Art," short for Artemis, and her minutes-younger brother by "Polly," an adaptation of Apollo. Apollo and Artemis, sun and moon. Even if the Twins' parents had lacked the coldblooded ambition shared by Alice's parents, they must have had some pretension to greatness.

Thanks to the ever-cocky Hugo and the commotion he was causing on their darkened porch, curtains were shifting sideways and shades were being raised, only they were in the neighboring houses. As far as the Twins' house went, there was no sign of life.

"We should go," she called to Hugo. "They're probably asleep."

"Asleep?" Hugo said, looking back over his shoulder at her. "They're witches."

"Witches sleep," Alice said, hearing the call of her own bed from only a few blocks away.

"Not the cool ones," he replied and continued with his assault on the house.

I'll huff, and I'll puff, and I'll blow your house down.

The words crept into Alice's consciousness, causing her to smile, though the smile faded as soon as she realized the voice in which she'd heard them spoken was Daniel's. The phrase came attached to a transient memory of crawling onto his lap and holding the book as he read aloud to her, but what began as memory grew feeble and was forced to rely on imagination for details. She couldn't say where actual history ended and wishful thinking began. She did remember, and this part was certain—Daniel had been very good at doing the wolf's voice.

She was about to make a case for calling it a night when the porch lights flashed on, and, like a cuckoo clock striking the hour, both doors swung open at once.

One twin stood in each doorway, dressed, not exactly to Alice's surprise, in matching short candy-apple-red silk peignoirs and white floral overlay boots, a crystal at the center of each white leather daisy. Atop their heads sat identical brunette beehive wigs, ratted high enough to house multiple colonies.

They posed, turning slightly, one left, the other right, and raised the absinthe glasses in their right hands so the light spilling out through the open doors filtered through the cloudy, chlorophyll-green spirit.

"Oh, for God's sake, guys," Hugo said. "Too much pageantry, not enough alcohol."

A curt, though still synchronized, spin on their heels, and the Twins turned back into their house, leaving the doors open behind them.

"Left or right?" Hugo said with a nod to each door.

"Does it matter?"

"Everything matters when it comes to magic. You of all people should know that." He waited for her to choose, but when she hesitated, he tacked on an explanation. "It's a little test they do, the first time someone comes to their house."

"All right, then," she said, nodding toward her choice, "left."

Hugo paused, eyebrows raising in surprise. "Really? Are you sure?"

"Why shouldn't I be?"

He shrugged. "Not judging. Wait, that's a lie. I really am, but not entirely in a bad way."

"What is this a test of?"

"Oh, c'mon. Really?" he said. When she didn't reply, he laughed. "It's pretty heavy-handed, and I'd assumed obvious. The left door, the left-handed path." He paused, seeming to wait for a reaction. "It's like a litmus test for someone's propensity to darkness, a kind of 'are you a good witch or bad witch?' appraising tool."

Alice didn't mean to cheat him out of his moment, but she'd jumped a step ahead. Looking from one door to the other, she asked,

"If the Twins are testing you as you enter their house, wouldn't the left and right be from the interior perspective?"

"Oh," Hugo said, his mouth holding the shape of the sound long enough to show Alice she'd managed to present him with an aspect of the situation he'd never considered before. He pulled an exaggerated, comic frown. "I went in the other. Well, what the hell. Doesn't matter now." He beckoned her with a wiggle of his finger, then said in a high, childlike voice, "'Why, I'm not a witch at all.'" His pitch dropped to its regular register. "Least I won't be for much longer."

Alice joined him on the porch as the overhead lights began to flash.

"All right, all right," Hugo growled, "keep your tit clamps on." He looked back at Alice. "No, seriously, I could make out the chains beneath their robes."

Alice shook her head at him in mock disgust. Unaffected, he turned and bounded, perhaps by habit, through the right door. Alice paused to consider the choice once more, then followed in Hugo's footsteps.

"If this door is good enough for you," she called to her brother as she crossed the threshold, "it'll work for me, too."

The Twins turned to stare at her with dual blank, befuddled expressions, as Hugo threw his head back and roared out a laugh. "I was only pulling your leg," he said, reaching up to wipe a tear from his eye.

Alice blushed and clenched her fists. "You are an . . . ass. You're an ass, that's what you are."

He drew closer and tapped the tip of her nose. "I'm your big brother, and I have years . . ." He paused. "Years," he repeated himself, stretching the word out into a ghostly moan, "of teasing to make up for."

"Oh," Alice said. "Lucky me."

Art arched one brow and gave a small, slow shake of her head, a muted expression, Alice decided, of sympathy. An almost imperceptible smile curled up on Polly's lips. It was a rare break in their mirroring of each other.

Alice glanced around, taking in the room.

Although most of the house appeared to maintain a true double shotgun layout, the Twins, or someone before them, had knocked through the wall in the front room, creating a large shared space with chocolate-brown walls and dark hardwood floors. The room seemed to center on a grouping of furniture. A low, three-legged, teardrop-shaped orange coffee table stood before a minimalist teal love seat and was flanked on one side by a pair of fuchsia velvet chairs—these a bit too cleverly designed in the shape of fleurs-de-lis.

The far wall was devoted to a collection of ornate masks, most, Alice guessed, of Venetian origin. Hugo pointed himself toward this display. "Father," he said, summoning Polly with a single shake of his curly blond head. "Longest Night. Masks." It seemed a kind of shorthand existed between Hugo and the Twins. Or maybe her brother had simply grown accustomed to getting his way with them without a belabored explanation. Hugo concluded with a somewhat sardonic "please," so maybe it was a little of both. All the same, it wasn't lost on her that Hugo had spoken of Nicholas as "Father." It was too late for her and Nicholas, but maybe it wasn't for Nicholas and his only surviving child. Alice only wished she didn't expect Nicholas to crush Hugo beneath his heel.

Polly waved her forward toward the wall, an evident invitation to select whichever mask she'd like to borrow. Only one option stood out to Alice—a simple, squarish half mask in bone white that called to mind the face of Babau Jean. Where she would have once found terror, she now felt an odd pang of longing.

"Would you care for some absinthe?" Art said.

Alice startled at the sound of her voice.

"Or perhaps something less decadent?" she added in response, Alice guessed, to her shocked expression.

"No," Alice said, blushing once again. "It's only I'd assumed you weren't capable of speech."

"Really, Alice, what an absurd assumption on your part. After all, we are members of the Chanticleer Coven. You even heard us sing as part of the spell working at Celestin's charade of a funeral."

"I'm sorry. I'd assumed that was part of the magic—"

"As a child," Polly jumped in, "I had a slight lisp. Our father suffered a great sense of shame because of it, seeing my lisp as evidence of this . . ." He gestured from his beehive to his boots.

"This flawlessness?" Hugo finished the thought.

Polly's face lit up with pleasure at the compliment. "You can be so sweet," he said, then added in a lower tone, "when you care to be."

Hugo shrugged. "It comes at a cost." He pointed across the room to a green glass bottle sitting on a drop leaf table pushed up against, and painted the same cocoa shade as, the wall.

Polly spun and turned his focus on her. "Really, *ma douce*, I can feel you limbering up to perform the mental acrobatics, and frankly, your efforts are exhausting me. He, she, him, her. I'm not trapped in the binary. On any given day, at any given hour, I myself might switch back and forth a dozen times. It matters far more to you than it does to me, so go with whatever you find the least taxing."

"I . . . ," Alice began, embarrassed, realizing that in the back of her mind she had begun to search for a polite way to ask.

"Father used magic"—he . . . *yes he, she decided* . . . had already moved on—"to try to fix me." Polly lifted his chin as if in defiance. "When that failed, he took to mocking me without mercy. He badgered me to the point I also developed a significant stutter. After that, I stopped speaking altogether."

His look of defiance fading, he smiled, almost apologetically, and reached up to pat the wig. "Mother engaged a speech therapist, and after a few years of work, the cat returned my tongue to me. But by then, Art and I had perfected our silent communication. We found we could carry on full conversations with only a single shared mental image. So much faster and more precise."

"I'm sorry," Alice said, filled with genuine regret for having res-urrected painful memories, but also desperate for a graceful way to extricate herself from the awkwardness of the moment. "I had no idea."

"*T'inquiète pas, chérie,*" Art said as she poured the green spirit into one of the half dozen ringed glasses arrayed around the bottle and bal-anced a flat straining spoon on its rim. "Father was a thoroughly detest-able man, but justice was served in the end." She laid a sugar cube on the spoon and reached for a carafe just large enough to hold a half cup of liquid. "We cut out his tongue." She began dripping water over the sugar. "It seemed to be the fitting thing to do—after all, we were only children at the time." She glanced up with a bright smile. "He choked to death on his own blood." She gave a slight nod toward Alice. "Right there on the floor where you're standing."

Alice took a quick step back, and her gaze fell to the floor as, in unison, Art and Polly began to titter, and Hugo let loose with a full snort. The three carried on, falling about laughing, for a solid minute. To Alice, caught on the butt end of the joke, that minute seemed to stretch out into a dozen of them.

"I do apologize," Art said, regaining composure, though nothing in her tone or her mirthful expression provided any evidence she felt regret. "It's only I found your precious gullibility too tempting." She removed the spoon from the glass and laid it on a coaster positioned between the bottle and a small silver bowl that from Alice's vantage point appeared to bear a different pattern than the spoon. Hugo walked over and reached for the glass, but Art snatched it back. "You, you rep-robate, can wait. This is for the delightful Alice."

Alice felt anything but delightful. She hesitated.

"Oh, *chérie*, don't pout. Think of our innocuous jest as your initia-tion ritual." She crossed to Alice. "Felicitations, you passed. Now"—she proffered the glass—"drink up. You barely made it in under the wire."

"Under the wire?" Alice said, lifting the glass to consider the now cloudy spirit.

"Before the end of the world. My sister is certain the world, or at least our world, is spinning down like a top," Polly said and saluted her with his own glass. "That is why tonight, the last night before the final day, we drink absinthe." He cocked his head. "*Chin chin.*"

Polly lifted the absinthe to his lips.

Alice followed suit, taking a cautious sip. The spirit was at first spicy and dry, with the flavor of anise growing in prominence as the absinthe crossed her palate. The dissolved sugar battled with, but couldn't overcome, a salty, vegetal bitterness.

"Wormwood," Art said, answering a question Alice hadn't yet formed. She'd returned to the table to mix Hugo's drink. When he took it from her, Art turned back and fixed Alice with a mischievous look. "'And the third angel sounded . . .'"

Hugo lifted his hand to his mouth, miming holding a horn. "Dootdootelydooo."

Art smirked without taking her gaze off Alice. She continued, "'and there fell a great star from heaven, burning as it were a lamp, and it fell upon the third part of the rivers, and upon the fountains of waters.'" She paused for dramatic effect. "'And the name of the star is called Wormwood: and the third part of the waters became wormwood; and many men died of the waters, because they were made bitter.'"

"Absinthe," Hugo said, stepping forward and assuming the deep, assertive voice of a commercial announcer, "the official drink of the Apocalypse."

Alice regarded Art and Hugo, calculating how the pair might be planning to turn these remarks into yet another practical joke on her. She studied the liquid in her glass. "But," Alice began, then paused to take another sip before finishing. "That isn't really *our* apocalypse, is it?"

"No?" Art said, finishing her drink, returning to the stealthy table positioned near the wall. She swirled a bit of water in the glass, preparing it, Alice surmised, for another round, then emptied the water from her glass into the silver bowl. "It feels rather personal to me." She smiled, though this time her smile didn't reach her black eyes.

"I don't understand."

"Wormwood," Hugo said, holding up his drink to the light. "It's also known as artemisia. Although artemisia took its name from Artemis the goddess, not our lovely"—he lingered on the word—"hostess." Hugo grinned. "Our Artemis isn't quite that old."

"Touché," Art responded with a throaty laugh. She appeared genuinely amused rather than resentful of Hugo's quip. She sighed, then reached up to tug off her wig, revealing a nylon cap. "Pardon, *frérot*," she addressed her brother. She dropped the wig on the table. He shrugged and removed his as well, then disappeared into another room for a minute and returned without the wig. Alice sensed she had indeed passed some kind of rite of initiation with the Twins for them to reveal themselves in any state short of perfection.

Or maybe they really did believe the world was ending, and no longer cared.

"*Alors, mes enfants*," Polly called out with an operatic trill, "you've come to choose a mask that will disguise your true identity, or perhaps"—he paused and leered at them—"one to reveal it."

"Well," Hugo said with an exaggerated sigh, "I was thinking either Bart Simpson or Vladimir Putin, but it looks like those options are out of stock."

"Perhaps a Zanni, then?" Polly suggested. "He's alternately a clever trickster or a fool."

Hugo crossed to the wall, posing with his fist under his chin as he considered his options. He reached out and touched one of the masks, a golden monstrosity with an impossibly elongated nose. "This one. I'll take the gold plague-doctor mask."

"Oh, but that isn't a Medico della Peste," Polly corrected him. "That is the Zanni. Traditionally, the longer the nose, the greater the fool. As you can see, this particular example has been blessed with a prodigious rhinal endowment."

"Don't you remember?" Art said, clasping her left hand over her right upper arm. The stance made her look like she was appraising a work of art. Polly responded with a slight rise of his eyebrows. On anyone else's face, Alice would have assumed the look a simple signal of bemusement, but given the connection between brother and sister, they could be carrying on a full conversation. Perhaps Polly didn't remember, or maybe he did, and he was warning his sister off. "Nicholas," Art continued, "wore the Zanni mask to the last Defilé des Maléfiques."

"I'm sorry," she said, addressing Hugo. "Please don't let that influence your choice. I shouldn't have said anything, only I'm always surprised to find bits of my own mother still lurking in myself." She paused as if to weigh her words. "We work so hard to exorcise our parents, to imagine ourselves as above both nature and nurture, self-generated," she said, her gaze turning tender, as if she felt sympathy for Hugo, "but still in the little things, in the areas where we're unguarded, blood will tell."

A chill ran down Alice's spine at the thought.

SIXTEEN

A look of caution passed between the Twins. "We were aware Nicholas had returned," Art said. "He paid us a visit earlier today."

"Yes," Polly said. "Far too early, in fact. But he always did keep such beastly hours." He spoke as if returning to an oft-discussed subject, but Alice had no knowledge of how Nicholas spent his days.

Art nodded. "True. It was from Nicholas I first learned there was a seven in the a.m. as well as the civilized hour."

"He was on fire," Polly began, then rushed to add, "figuratively, not literally. Out to proselytize his last-minute plan to resurrect the Longest Night." Polly reached up and ran a finger beneath his beige wig cap, scratching absentmindedly. "Of course, we all know Nicholas never leaves anything till last minute."

"Unless," Hugo said, "he doesn't want you to have long enough to think about what he's setting you up for."

"For what it's worth, he professes to be racked with regret over the ways he's failed you. He wants to make amends to you," she said, her gaze broadening to include Alice, "to you both."

"An ambitious undertaking," Alice said, a self-conscious smile twitching on her lips. "He could begin by letting us set him on fire—literally."

"Indeed," Art replied, her eyes opening a bit wider, her lips pursing into an amused pucker. She looked upon Alice with what appeared to be a new appreciation, as if she'd only just begun seeing her as anything other than a piece of Hugo's luggage. "I'd wondered what you'd done with her, Hugo. With that marvelous creature who peeled back the gates of Précieux Sang. I'd begun to think this one was a changeling. Welcome to the party, *ma chère*. This time I mean it."

Polly batted his eyelashes. "Still, Nicholas's soliloquy pulled on the heartstrings. Really, it was wonderful theater. Shame he only offered a matinee performance."

"I'm sure." Hugo's head tilted a little forward and to the side, one brow rising higher. "It fits Father's scheme . . . whatever he's up to now . . . for you to believe him."

"Here's something you can believe," Art addressed Hugo. "Every king needs an heir. You do matter to him, if only as an extension of himself."

"That much I can give you." Hugo took a drink and grimaced. "But he's not much of a king. At least not anymore."

"Ah, but that brings us back to the Longest Night," Art said. "Your father has an agenda for wanting to revive it. One that goes beyond nostalgia or healing rifts."

"Nicholas has a motive for everything he does," Alice replied, "and it's never altruism. Nor is it regret."

"But what's he looking to get out of resurrecting this moldy bit of nostalgia?" Hugo mused.

"No need to speculate, *mes chers*," Polly said. "He elaborated on his grand plan this morning." Another quick glance passed between the Twins. "He's found a solution, he believes, for our current troubles, one that's more sustainable than black-market body parts."

"In all fairness," Art said, the words spoken in a mock-conciliatory tone, "he was far humbler than that. He spoke of it as 'stopgap.'" She paused, her focus drifting back to the Zanni mask. "To give the devil his due"—this time she sounded sincere—"his plan seems feasible. In fact, I'd say it stands a very good chance of working, provided one doesn't concern oneself too much with the ethics of the thing."

"What brand of snake oil is the *petit papa Nicholas* selling?" Hugo asked.

"When it comes to magic," Art said, "the power grid is failing. He's proposing to move the witches of New Orleans—those of us left—off the grid and onto an alternative source."

"It's a plan," Polly added, "he purports to have stumbled upon after his disappearance, but if the scheme is as far along as it seems to be, it has taken some time to put in place."

"Do tell," Hugo pressed. "How does Father plan on leading us into the promised land?"

Art turned and crossed to the drinks table. "Much," she said, spilling another round of absinthe into her glass, "as the good Doctor Dupas learned to draw power from his drugged clients, Nicholas intends to feed on the energy of those who come together to adore him."

"Adore him?" Hugo said with a snort.

Art looked to her brother to provide the explanation, then busied herself with dissolving sugar into her drink.

"In short," Polly said, "Nicholas is becoming a cult leader. It's easier than you might think. The hard part is channeling the power. Not many witches are capable of acting as a transformer. That's why Dr. Dupas created our old friend Babau Jean . . . and lost control of him within months. A servitor spirit with that much power flowing through it will not remain a servitor for long."

"Nicholas is eschewing any intermediary. He, himself, will be the focus." Art took a sip of her drink, closing her eyes and smiling. "All power will flow through him." She opened her eyes but kept her focus on the glass in her hand. "As your grandfather sought to drain us, your father has plans to recharge us. Tomorrow . . . although at this hour, it's really tonight . . . he plans to use la Defilé to give us a taste of what he, if we accept him as our king, can offer."

"Maybe we should skip this roving costume party," Hugo said, holding his empty glass up to Art.

"Darling boy," she said, "one per customer. You want another, make it yourself."

"Miss la Defilé? Not on your life," Polly said, pulling several sheets of off-white packing paper from a box, then slipping the Zanni mask off the hooks that held it. "Truth is I've missed the Longest Night. Despite Nicholas's machinations and our own Cassandra's"—he cast an evil, narrowed-eye look at his sister—"predictions of certain and inescapable doom, I'm actually looking forward to it. Even if the world doesn't stop spinning, this could very well be the last Longest Night celebration." He wrapped up the mask, then tucked it into a shopping bag that featured the image of a grinning bodybuilder hiding his privates behind a Santa cap.

Hugo lumbered to the side table, his hand hesitating over the bottle of absinthe for a moment before dropping back to his side. He seemed, at last, to have begun feeling the effects of the alcohol he'd been putting away since before Daniel's wake. His eyes met Alice's, and he gave a slight shrug. "I had no idea, Polly, you were so sentimental."

"I feel," Polly said, pausing as his face began to crumple, "everything . . . deeply." He looked up with vulnerable, mournful eyes. "So very deeply." His tremolo turned to a growl, and his face to cool stone. "Though never quite as deeply as I'd like." He made a wide gesture toward the array of remaining masks. "And you?" he said, addressing Alice.

She scanned the wall, then chose, almost as a joke, the most ridiculous of them all, a cat's face with a feathered headdress. "The cat, please."

Apollo froze and shared what seemed to be a meaningful glance with his sister.

Alice had believed there were no limitations, but the duo seemed to fall into a silent debate. "It's okay," she said, thinking she must have by accident chosen one they were unhappy to lend, whether its value was of a sentimental or monetary nature. "I can wear another," she said, then added quickly to circumvent making another mistake, "Perhaps you could choose for me?"

"No, no, *petite* Alice," Polly said. "This is the mask you chose, and it is the one you must wear." He removed it from the wall slowly and regarded it with what looked to Alice like reverence.

"It's only . . . ," Art said, drawing closer. "It's only *The Gospel of the Witches* tells us the goddess Artemis once disguised herself as a cat to seduce her brother, the shining one."

Alice found herself uncertain how to respond to this unexpected bit of salaciousness.

"Not to worry," Polly said, wrapping the mask with more care than he had the Zanni. "My virtue has always remained safe with my own Artemis." He placed the mask in the bag.

His sister dismissed his interjection about their given names with an impatient wave of her hand. "Your own family's lore posits you are descendants of the result of this coupling."

"Aradia," Hugo said, nodding. His face wore an expression that somehow managed to be at once smug and disdainful.

"Of course, it's only a myth, but the stories those who came before us told do attempt to describe forces that defy a more direct explanation." Art held out her hand. "The fallen god"—starting with her thumb, she began to tick off each of her points with one of her digits—"the Queen of Heaven, your choice of disguise, your fa—brother Nicholas's attempt to resurrect the Longest Night, burning a wicker man at the bend in the river we affectionately refer to as 'the End of the World.' Mock me as Cassandra if you must—after all, no one listened to her either—but I'm more convinced than ever we're headed toward *our personal* Armageddon."

"Okay," Alice said, "but I think you're making connections where they really don't exist. Besides, I don't remember any myth involving Apollo's demise, so I don't think you can consider him a fallen god."

"Oh, *ma chère*." Her lips pulled into an embarrassed smile. "Perhaps not in the guise of Apollo, but certainly you've heard of Lucifer." She lifted her drink to her lips and made a study of Alice's features. Alice fought to maintain a passive expression.

"Perhaps," Art continued, "it is more than a myth. Perhaps *blood is telling*." She crossed the room and sat in one of the fuchsia chairs like she had ascended to a throne. "I always felt your familial strife had an air of history"—she lingered on the word—"repeating itself, as if the seed of rebellion was planted in your DNA."

Polly rested his arm on the back of his sister's chair, then produced, seemingly from nowhere, a vaporizer. He gave a slight cough, to gain Hugo's attention, and when Hugo looked his way, he put the inhaler to his lips and wiggled his fastidiously shaped eyebrows.

"Thanks, man," Hugo said. "I'm good."

"Suit yourself." Polly slipped out of the room, headed, Alice suspected, to one of the small hidden courtyards not uncommon in the Quarter.

Art gestured to the sofa, the invitation a sure sign Alice's night was far from over. "Nicholas and Celestin." She adjusted her robe so it better covered her thigh. "Luc and Nicholas, the upstart son challenging the harsh, distant father. Who knows how many generations back this particular drama has played itself out?"

Hugo dropped to the sofa, seeming pleased to dig into what Alice considered an old and best-forgotten wound. But then again, he hadn't been there to witness Luc's murder. Alice considered joining Apollo and his vaporizer.

"So, our great-great-grandpappy," Hugo said, glancing up at Alice with shining, gleeful eyes, "was literally the Devil himself." He patted the seat beside him. "That would explain a lot." Alice would have preferred to excuse herself and head home, but she found herself a victim of her own curiosity. She sat beside her brother.

"I will do you the favor of assuming you're being deliberately obtuse." Art looked from Hugo to Alice. "Do feel free to kick off your shoes and pull your feet up, *chérie*. Make yourself at home." Then back to Hugo. "I'm not talking about the Devil. I'm talking about Lucifer— the bringer of light, the initiator to hidden wisdom."

"Three blocks from here . . ." Alice let her words trail off, not having intended to speak aloud. The absinthe must have lowered her inhibitions. Realizing all eyes were fixed on her, she committed to her statement. "Three blocks from here is a building full of clerics who will be happy to remind you this 'initiation' caused the fall of man."

Hugo smiled at Alice, then turned to Artemis, raising his eyebrows and cocking his head as if daring her to accept a challenge.

"Oh," she said, relishing, it seemed, the chance to do so. "But that's their version of the story. In mine, Lucifer is a Prometheus figure, punished for illuminating that which the gods wished to keep hidden. He's the demiurge, the force that converts energy into matter. The one that spins potentiality into reality. Or at least creates the illusion of an objective reality."

Artemis delivered her discourse as if she thought Alice—whom she seemed to consider a neophyte—would find her thesis provocative, but the woman's story wasn't original. Alice knew the twin had inherited it thirdhand, the Cathars having adopted it from the Gnostics, who, in turn, had adapted it from the ancient Greek philosophers.

Alice was considering revealing the true provenance of Artemis's heresy when the sound of Daniel's voice derailed her thoughts.

No one likes a know-it-all, Alice my love.

It felt like more than an encroaching memory this time. She could almost feel Daniel's presence, but that might be expected after attending his wake, especially considering her heretofore limited experience with alcohol.

Artemis interpreted Alice's agitation as a reaction to her own words, and, encouraged by the effect she thought she was having on Alice, her voice grew more animated. "The sages used to speak of the music of the spheres, a great harmony they thought filled the universe. But that great harmony is nothing more than a fairy tale." She shifted in her chair, leaning toward Alice. "This world wasn't built upon harmony. It was created through dissonance. The reality we know couldn't exist without it."

She seemed to realize she was growing heated as she spoke. She leaned back, assuming a regal pose and an enigmatic smile that could challenge the Mona Lisa's. "That is 'the fall' of which your clerics speak. The shift from a plane of perfect and infinite potential to an imperfect and finite reality. Your priests dream of the day when this world dissolves into light, but all they're really craving is the resolution of the true original sin, the state of dissonance that allows us to exist."

Perhaps this questioning of what was and wasn't real was the reason Daniel felt so close tonight. Shreds of Art's ramblings seemed to hold a sheen of truth, but Alice suspected this was another area where truth could only be glimpsed as it flitted by on the periphery, and even then only by focusing on the negative space surrounding it.

Alice had spent most of her life questioning what was real and what was true, first in the hospital on Sinclair, and then, to an even greater degree, on the Dreaming Road. Maybe it was the late night, maybe it was the effects of the absinthe, but Alice felt a shadow lingering on the edge of her psyche. The image of a ropy black snake slithering across a snowy field flashed into her mind.

Polly returned, the scent of a peppery floral perfume attempting to override the smell of skunk rubbed in thyme that preceded him into the room.

Hugo looked up at the returning twin, sniffed, then wrinkled his nose. "Fifteen-hundred-dollars-an-ounce Caron Poivre to cover up the stink of your, wait, let me guess"—he paused and sniffed again—"thirty-five-dollars-a-pound Kush?"

Polly looked down his nose at Hugo, then waved his hand in front of himself, causing his scent to waft toward them. He turned his attention to his sister. "Have you finished with your sermon, *ma chère frangine*? Yes? Good," he said without giving her even a beat to respond. "She takes such pleasure in her blasphemy." He paused and smiled beatifically down on them. "I do hope you won't find me an inhospitable host, but dawn isn't far off and I should put these old bones to bed."

"Oh," Alice said, half-embarrassed for overstaying their welcome, but entirely happy to have been dismissed. "We're so sorry to have kept you up."

"I'm not," Hugo said, running his hand down his face, but then he stood and stretched.

"Don't forget your masks, children," Art said, pulling her legs up sideways into the chair.

Polly crossed to Alice and offered her his hand. "Lovely to see you again, Alice. It really is."

Rather than take his hand, Alice startled and rubbed her eyes. She was experiencing a hallucination, imagining the black snake from her vision had coiled around Polly's hand, pulsing and breaking into segments. "Oh, dear," Polly continued, causing Alice to look up from his hand. He was regarding her with mild concern, likely for good reason. His skin appeared to have grown translucent, and she could see the inky snake slithering just beneath it, slipping down from his head and coming out of his mouth. She had the odd impression it wasn't really Polly speaking, but the serpent revealing itself through him.

"Perhaps you should get her home," Art said. Alice glanced over to witness a serpent wriggling beneath her skin, too, down her cheek.

"I'm fine," Alice said, rising to her feet. "I'm fine," she repeated, trying to reassure herself more than the others. Her eyes fell to her own hand, only to see the snake writhing there like short, dark veins. It darted deeper, disappearing within her flesh. Her knees buckled, but she felt Hugo's arm reach out and wrap around her.

"C'mon, lightweight," Hugo said. "Let's get you to bed."

Alice nodded and, with her eyes closed, leaned against her brother's shoulder.

SEVENTEEN

It was going on three a.m., but Evangeline felt no hurry to get back to an empty—or mostly empty, if you counted Sugar—bed. *Mostly empty,* she decided. There was no way not to count a cat who delivered menacing ultimatums one moment, then called you "Mama" the next. A cat who would stretch herself across the comforter and gaze at Evangeline as unblinking, and—Evangeline occasionally suspected—all-seeing as the eternal Sphinx.

But it wasn't a too-quiet house that had kept her at Bonnes Nouvelles, her only companion the painting of Daniel she'd move to the storage room for safekeeping until Alice came back to claim it. Evangeline had stayed here tonight because she was waiting for something, though she hadn't known what until she caught sight of the girl standing across Bourbon Street, awash in the cold white of a waiting taxi's headlights, her abject gaze fixed on Evangeline, waiting and willing herself to be seen.

Lincoln had taken to calling the slight street kid "ghost girl" after Evangeline had made a number of attempts to point her out to him, only for the girl to fall back behind a wall or lose herself in a crowd before he could spot her.

Of course, she'd chosen to show herself again while Lincoln was away in Natchitoches.

Evangeline had first noticed her a couple of weeks ago. Spindly and pale, the waif wore dirty, garish, oversize sweats she'd either found on the street or stolen from a souvenir shop. She looked to be ten, maybe twelve; Evangeline found it difficult to guess her age from her size, malnourished as she appeared to be. Her straight blonde hair hung in dirty tangles. Dark purplish-brown circles cradled her eyes.

But for the color of her hair, the girl was a goddamned mirror.

A mirror that could bend time, reflecting not the woman Evangeline Caissy had grown into, but the feral adolescent she had once been.

From that first sighting, Evangeline had wanted—felt compelled even—to do something for the girl. There was no doubt her desire sprang from concern for the child's well-being, but she couldn't pretend her motivation was undiluted altruism. A good dose of yearning to set old wrongs right hitchhiked along with her philanthropy. Evangeline had gone through a lot growing up, and she'd done things she wasn't proud of in order to survive. A gnawing in her gut seemed to promise her that if she could help a child—this child in particular—she'd be cleaning the slate.

The ragamuffin had taken to slinking up and down Bourbon Street, relying on the kindness of some of its daily-changing strangers and the carelessness of others. She'd first caught Evangeline's attention as she was weaving her way, unaccompanied, through a throng of day drinkers, each toting a plastic neon-green grenade. It had taken Evangeline less than an instant to divine the girl was surveying the crowd, searching out the softest mark. No sooner had that thought registered than the child bumped into a rotund man whose overburdened Celtic cross T-shirt stuck out like a shelf over his camouflage hunting pants. On impact, he reached up with his free hand to grasp the bill of his red baseball cap, pushing past the girl as she lifted his wallet from his back pocket without ever rousing his drink-dimmed suspicion.

Evangeline had never, even for a heartbeat, considered alerting the guy to his loss. Honor among thieves, perhaps, or maybe the sympathy of someone who'd once walked in an orphan's shoes. Indeed, her first thought had been to hope the mark's bar-crawling itinerary had included a recent stop at an ATM, so the puny pickpocket's take would be worth the risk.

Even as the clown had stumbled on unaware, the girl stopped cold and turned, as if by instinct, to face the only witness to her offense. Their eyes locked, and the girl's sense of despondency punched through with such intensity that, even if Evangeline hadn't been reaching out with her empathic powers to read the girl, it would have taken her breath away. Open as Evangeline had allowed herself to be, the sensation struck her like the sudden, shrill feedback from a microphone, leaving her rattled and dizzy. Before she could recover, the girl turned away and darted down Bourbon. Evangeline lost sight of her as she flitted up St. Peter toward Congo Square, but the look in the girl's eyes—the ferocious innocence of a wounded animal—had haunted her for days.

Evangeline knew that look. She knew what it felt like to go to bed hungry for stretches of days at a time.

By the third day, you can't stop shivering. Even on the hottest night, wrapped up in a heavy, itchy gray wool army blanket that has been knocking around in this world longer than you have. How the old man who runs the convenience store by the factory catches you stealing a candy bar, then takes one look at you and hands you a loaf of bread and a gallon of milk to go with it.

How you intuit all charity is short-lived, so you learn to become a more adept thief.

Tonight, the girl had stood waiting, watching, her imploring gaze fixed on Evangeline. But before Evangeline could go to her, something caught the girl's attention from the direction of Toulouse Street. She glanced over, then turned away, her eyes grazing Evangeline once more as she began walking, a brisk but not panicked pace, in the opposite direction toward Conti.

Evangeline bolted after her without a second thought. She'd crossed over Conti before realizing she'd left Bonnes Nouvelles empty and wide open. She called after the girl to wait, but the waif took off running, increasing the distance between them each second. The girl was young and fleet, and, unlike Evangeline, she hadn't been doing shots all night. She was slipping away, already a block ahead. To Evangeline's surprise, she stopped for a moment, glancing back over her shoulder as if to ensure she was still being followed.

A clamoring rose up from the street ahead as a mixed group of drunks, male and female, in identical Santa Claus costumes, stumbled from a karaoke bar onto the street. They shouted and hurled raucous merry Christmases at all those they encountered, then started howling out a rough-voiced rendition of "Silent Night"—a cacophony that sounded more like a battle cry than a carol.

One rough Santa snatched at the girl as she tried to run past the inebriated rabble, catching her by the hand and screaming, "What do you want Santa to bring you?" The child responded with a hard kick to his groin. As he dropped to his knees before her, she tugged her hand from his grip and slapped his face. Having served up the fight, the girl now opted for flight. She sped down Bourbon at a pace Evangeline could never hope to match to the accompaniment of the man's obscenities and his gang's laughter.

Evangeline dodged across the street to avoid getting caught up in the tangle of red suits, but her effort came too late. The girl was gone. Evangeline opened herself up, sending her energy out like radar, waiting for it to bounce back.

A sense of loss, tinged with rage, punched her in the chest. Evangeline turned and began running up Bienville, away from the river. And then it happened. The transformation was nearly complete before she'd even registered it had begun. Her clothing dissipated like vapor and her field of vision widened as sprinting gave way to flight.

No compelling force or lunar phase controlled Evangeline's transformations now. There was no pain. No disembodied voice to taunt her and tempt her with promises of sweet release. No hellish fermata retarding the process until it seemed time itself stood still.

Now she could change form in a blink, but the gift came at a cost. In that blink Evangeline touched darkness, and the darkness touched her.

"Each change, *ma chère*, will make you less of what you were and more of what you will be," her mother's sister witch, the ancient Margot, had said. Margot's words had seemed not so much a warning as a blunt statement of what the crone had considered to be an inescapable truth.

Margot was gone now, as was the even more ancient, addled Mathilde. The same power that had been forcing Evangeline's tortured transformations had turned the pair to dust.

Evangeline had watched as the third sister witch, Marceline, destroyed herself. Rather than suffer the yoke that had once controlled Evangeline's mother—a necklace forged to separate a witch from her power—Marceline had offered herself as a sacrifice to the Dark Man, the all-consuming shadow that, while not the source of magic, served as the conduit through which all magic flowed, in the hope of being restored. Only after Marceline's destruction did Evangeline learn this sorceress, who'd orphaned her by snatching her father into a starless night sky and dropping him so his head burst like a hot watermelon, had been her mother's sister by blood. Her aunt.

Blood. Bad blood. Spilled blood. Anyone else might have celebrated the murderous witches' annihilation, but their deaths, especially

Marceline's, had severed the last tie Evangeline had to her mother, taking away any chance to learn who her mother had been before she'd signed her name in the Dark Man's book.

Soaring above the Vieux Carré's rooftops, Evangeline could see all—the late-night revelers bathed in a neon glow, the whirling blues and reds of police-car lights, the street corners ruled alternately by spirited musicians and insolent panhandlers, the street lamps glinting off the pocket-change tributes passersby offered both.

And, of course, her quarry. The aerial vantage had helped her spot the child in moments. The girl had passed out of the Quarter on Rampart. She paused at Canal Street, then darted against the light across six lanes of traffic and the median that separated them, creating a symphony of blaring horns and screeching brakes on both sides of the common ground. She continued until she reached Gravier, where she turned right, away from the river. Suddenly, as if she'd been winded, her pace slowed to a walk.

Arriving at the common ground separating the directions of Loyola Avenue, the child looked up and raised her hand in greeting.

The child knew her even in this form.

Evangeline swooped lower in a wide circle, catching sight of a movement in her peripheral vision as she did, a creeping shadow that took the shape of a man even as she focused on it, as if her attention had given it form. It lurched forward in a jerky bear walk along the edge of Duncan Plaza, pausing and lifting its head in a manner that reminded Evangeline of a predator sniffing the wind to catch the scent of its prey. Its neck elongated, stretching to a length far greater than any actual human being's could. Its head snaked forward and fixed on the girl, who appeared unaware of the entity's presence as she passed it. If anything, the child remained fixated on Evangeline, spinning around once and gazing up, moving along once she was sure Evangeline still followed overhead.

The staggering shadow's movements gained fluidity even as it began a violent chattering. It slipped onto the street, shielding itself needlessly behind a parked car—the girl continued, not hearing, not seeing. With a shriek, it bounded onto the roof of the car and began to turn in place, its head flailing back and forth. Evangeline realized the shadow was sounding a warning. No, it was calling others to the hunt. It pounced from the car roof to the asphalt, its landing silent.

Evangeline intuited the child's lack of fear prevented the shadow from claiming her. If the girl perceived what stalked her, she would flee, and seal her fate in doing so. Nothing was more tempting to a predator than the sight of its prey bolting in panic.

The girl approached the long-deserted Charity Hospital and slipped behind the plastic traffic barricade as two more shadows, one coming from each direction of LaSalle Street, crept up to join their brother. Another quick glance up from the child as she grasped the top of the chain-link fence and tensed, preparing to pull herself up and over it.

Evangeline also tensed, readying to swoop down between the creatures and the unsuspecting child. But rather than charge the girl, the three shadows drew toward one another, sparring, she sensed, for dominance, till two bowed their heads. A gust of wind rose up around them, carrying with it a scent as acrid as sulfur but as sweet as myrrh, as they joined together into a single black mass.

She flashed back to the day of Celestin Marin's trial. An involuntary cry, a husky corvid caw, pealed from her as she recognized this shadowy being as the demon she'd sensed lurking around the tombs of Précieux Sang Cemetery. She'd been fool enough to leave herself open, and it had reached in and rattled her bones, turning the breath in her lungs to ice. In a flash, she'd recognized it as one of the hungry shadows Fleur told her Daniel reported encountering on the Dreaming Road. This shadow had the same energy to it as the dark entity Evangeline herself had sensed lurking in Précieux Sang.

The girl froze and looked up at her.

The demon's head twisted a full rotation as its neck stretched up toward the sky. Evangeline dove down to take a defensive position between child and demon, flapping her wings and cawing with all the fury her terror could stoke.

The demon hesitated and let loose a bloodcurdling howl that seemed to combine confusion and rage with submission. It retreated, splitting into its original three components as it did.

Evangeline heard the chain-link fence behind her rattle and turned back. Her left eye saw the child had slipped over the perimeter fence and beneath a lower section of an inner fence that stretched between two of the former medical center's wings. Evangeline looked back to find the demons, too, had vanished, leaving her alone in the night.

She flapped her wings, preparing to fly over the fence and seek out the terrified child. Once over, she'd change back into her true form.

As she passed over the inner stretch of fencing, however, she caught sight of a glint of metal at the foot of the fence. On the ground where the child had slipped through the fence lay a necklace, an unclasped chain whose links Evangeline would recognize from any distance, a hideous medallion she could spot in any light.

It was the chain her own mother had forged. The chain Marceline had carried with her into the Dark Man's heart.

The girl was a mirror.

The girl was Marceline.

EIGHTEEN

WHERE THE UNUSUAL OCCURS & MIRACLES HAPPEN

Evangeline read the lettering on the wall of old Charity Hospital by the glow of a *fifolet*, a will-o'-the-wisp ball of light she'd conjured to illuminate the abandoned building's pitch-dark interior. She was sure Charity could deliver on the promised unusual, but doubted it had any miracles left to offer.

She held her mother's chain in her balled fist. Its weight seemed to grow with each passing moment. She opened her hand and gazed down at the necklace. It appeared to be nothing out of the ordinary—a medallion and a collection of links fashioned from a metal some might call silver and others pewter. Both sides would be wrong. The metal from which her mother had created the necklace didn't belong in this world.

A ceiling tile that had held on since Katrina chose the very moment she looked away to tumble down and bounce off the arm of a hideous blue faux-leather chair. A scurrying sound overhead revealed the cause of the drop.

She shuddered and willed the light to move along, a trick Luc had taught her. She floated along behind it, her feet a good foot and a half above the detritus-strewn floor. This trick she'd taught herself.

The walls of the corridor were lined with tiles, the light of her globe gleaming on their glossy surface. A few yards ahead she spotted a very human silhouette. The torso of a CPR dummy stood sentry.

It was risky to open herself up to the energies lurking in such a place, but the medical center's three towers and their connector covered a million square feet, and even though the demons had retreated, she wasn't so sure they wouldn't circle back and maybe bring reinforcements with them. She could spend hours bobbing up and down around the hospital's collection of forgotten horrors, or she could send out the tiniest ping to see what would bounce back to her.

She didn't want to risk getting swatted down like a wasp, so out of caution she sought a clear spot in the hall and lowered herself until her feet touched the floor. She dismissed her guiding light, then braced a hand against the wall's cool tile. But she was still unprepared for the force that responded to the burst of energy she sent out.

She'd feared being overwhelmed by any spirits that might still haunt these halls, but it wasn't the energy of lost souls that rebounded on her—it was the essence of the hospital itself. The building's memories had given it life, and its heart had been broken when the city deserted it. It mourned. It suffered. The grief was too intense, too palpable not to address. *I'm sorry.* Evangeline spoke the words in her mind, then found herself unable to hide the thought the hospital would no doubt someday, possibly soon, be cleared away. "I'm sorry." She repeated the words aloud.

Evangeline heard a whirring sound, and at the end of the hall, elevator doors sprung open. A light blinked on inside the car. She felt the building itself impress images onto her mind's eye. A room with peeling aqua walls. Large, irregular white patches showed through the spots where the paint had fallen away. The effect could have been monstrous, but it put Evangeline in mind of clouds in a summer sky. On one side, the room held a twin bed, a regular one, not the adjustable electric ones usually found in patient rooms. On the other side stood a wooden desk. Positioned between them was a small, round table holding one of the room's two mismatched, utterly non-infirmary-style lamps. The current had been cut to the entire floor, so neither lamp could be the source of dim, bluish light that fell short of filling the space. Despite the room's wretched state, it appeared to be clean, like someone had tried to make the space livable.

The elevator sounded a bing, expressing its willingness to carry Evangeline to the floor the room was on. Out of respect for its feelings, she decided to walk to the elevator rather than float to it, regardless of the possible tetanus risk. As she took the first step, a force that felt like a marriage of wind and static electricity blew up around her and began sweeping the debris that had collected in the hall to either side.

As she prepared to step into the elevator car, she paused and ran her hand down the wall—a soothing caress, she hoped. "You were a good friend to this city. You deserve better." She stepped into the elevator and its doors closed behind her. The car lifted up, its cables grinding like gnashing teeth, till it reached one of the upper floors. The doors opened onto darkness.

As she exited the elevator, its light flashed off, and a soft moan spilled out behind her. She felt the energy of the hospital fall back, and it struck her that the ailing hospital had expended more effort than it could afford to help her. "Thank you," she said, willing the spirit of the place a bit of healing magic to repay the favor.

She snapped her fingers to reignite the *fifolet*. Its glow illuminated a placard reading "Staff Dorm Rooms." She stared down the length of the corridor. Some rooms remained closed off, but many of the doorways gaped open before her, the rooms they opened onto silent, dark, long since abandoned.

Only one doorway was different. Through it shone a pale glow so faint Evangeline could hardly discern it. She sent her own light forward, following behind until she found herself standing at the incongruous opening. Inside the dilapidated dorm room, sitting at the desk in the glow of a camping lantern, was the child Marceline. She looked up at Evangeline, the bluish electric light accenting her large gray eyes and the dark circles beneath them.

"*Un fifolet*," Marceline said, nostalgia underlining each syllable. "We used to send out *fifolets*, Margot and I, to lure lost travelers farther into the wilds. We'd follow, watching from above, wagering on whether they would survive the journey." Her sentimental tone left no doubt these were happy memories. "I always let Margot be the one to predict their demise, even though I knew she'd win our little game seventy percent of the time. But then again, for me it was never about winning."

"Yeah." Evangeline willed the illumination to fade. "Good times." She focused on the small face before her, a shade whiter in the lantern's bluish light.

Marceline's eyes ran her up and down. "You are aware you can conjure the clothes you were wearing back?"

Evangeline blushed, not so much from modesty as from being treated as the amateur—at least compared to her aunt—she was.

"Just"—Marceline swept her hands before her—"and click your heels three times." Before Evangeline could act, Marceline's tiny face broke into a smile. "I'm only joking about the clicking, but . . ." She again made the motion with her hand.

Evangeline mimicked the gesture, and indeed, it worked. She was once again fully clothed, shirt to shoes.

"Is this some kind of glamour?" Evangeline said, her head spinning as it tried to wrap itself around the idea the little girl before her could possibly be her mother's sister, the centuries-old witch Marceline.

The girl's mouth tightened into a thin frown, and a look of caution crept into her eyes. She shook her head. "No, child." The words sounded comical coming from the waif's lips. "It is no glamour. No simple enchantment. No parlor trick."

"Prove it." Evangeline thrust the necklace at her. To her surprise, Marceline accepted it with a shrug, then slipped it around her neck and fixed its clasp. It rested on her small chest only for a moment before the links of the chain separated themselves from one another and fell with almost inaudible clinks to the floor. "It's lost its power," Evangeline said, even as she watched the links snake back together.

Marceline leaned over and caught hold of the mended chain. "*Non, ma chère,*" she said, holding the necklace out to Evangeline. "I've lost mine."

Evangeline couldn't bring herself to touch the necklace. "How can it be—"

"You were there." She laid the chain on the desk, then turned on her chair. "You witnessed the act yourself." Her legs weren't long enough for her feet to reach the floor. "I commended myself to His will, and He freed me from this damnable charm your Marin boy hung around my neck. But it pleased Him to bring me back as such." She gestured, running her hand from head to knee. "As I was on the day my sisters and I ventured into the deep, black pines to seek Him out."

"But you couldn't have been more than—"

"Ten. I was ten years old when I chose to barter my soul to the Devil, the same age as Margot. Mireille, your mother, was eight. We three considered Mathilde our leader. She was of marrying age. Almost thirteen."

"I had no idea."

"What, did you believe we were always as you'd known us to be?"

"I never really considered—"

"We were powerless, starving," Marceline cut her off, "when we met Him, though we were hardly unique in those aspects. It was winter in the year of someone else's Lord, sixteen-hundred and ninety-three. Bad weather, poor harvests, war, fear, and greed. The perfect recipe for famine—la Grande Famine. We were all four orphans, or as good as. We slipped into the forest, determined to find magic or die there from exposure. We left the village on le Jour des Saints Innocents, the Massacre of Innocents. Not a calculated move, but notable for the maudlin poetry of coincidence, no?

"We discovered we were far from the first to seek Him out. We encountered a dozen corpses, maybe more. Some strangers, some faces we'd known all our lives. Some on their knees, hands frozen together in supplication. Some half-eaten. By wolves, Mathilde told us, knowing her story was far less frightening than the reality. But I divined the truth. My stomach rumbled. Meat is meat.

"I think we amused Him, we four. The plain and once pious Mathilde, the always foolhardy and on occasion foolish Margot. Your beautiful, timid mother, Mireille, and I, the exacting little ball crusher who believed herself capable of negotiating the deal. Margot, she would have sold her soul for the guarantee of one hot meal a day. Mathilde couldn't see past the horned mask the faith she'd abandoned forced on Him. I led Him away from the others after receiving their agreement to abide by the bargain I struck. I saw the face behind the lie, and the force hiding again behind that. I sensed the depth of His power to mold reality and demanded that He make us queens rather than handmaidens. If only He had been the Devil. We might have found ourselves in the eighth circle with Erichtho, fourth pit from the left," she added with an unexpected wink, "but the depths of hell would still have provided both a level of certainty and a firm foundation. With the Dark Man there is nothing but legerdemain and shifting sand.

"I thought I'd worked through every intricacy of the negotiation. Indenture or damnation, for the other two and myself it didn't matter. But I haggled long and hard for Mireille and won her the opportunity to slip free of His bond before death. Of course, He found a way to turn that. He always finds a way to twist your dream into a curse. He left Mireille burdened by the conscience whose call we others stopped hearing—or at least attending to—over time. Much less time than you might suspect. Her burdensome conscience was what drove her to marry the preacher, hypocrite that he was, and to the creation of that damnable necklace."

"She tried to change. She wanted to."

"Yes, the poor fool tried to free herself." Marceline lay her hand beside the chain. "Through bondage. But she never stood a chance." She lifted the necklace, offering it once again to Evangeline. "*Tiens.*" She reached out and grasped Evangeline's hand, dropping the simple chain into her open palm. "Look at it. See it. Not as an instrument of torture. Not as a hated object. Not as an object at all, but as the energy of which it's composed, and the vibration of that energy."

Evangeline could feel the chain and medallion begin to pulsate, in time, she realized, with her own pulse. Its links seemed to quiver, then they emitted a blinding flash and morphed into a new necklace, a cascade of teardrop emeralds and round diamonds caught in shimmering gold. Evangeline held the jewels up, barely able to believe her eyes. She knew this necklace. She recognized it from the night of the massacre. Julia Prosper had worn these very emeralds to her own murder. Evangeline tossed the necklace to the desk, where it shimmered and returned to the simple chain that had once burned into her own flesh. "But I had this chain"—she pointed at where it lay—"with me, in my bag, when Julia entered the hall wearing the emeralds."

"They may have appeared to be separate, but they are and always have been one. They are two expressions of the same energy."

"I don't understand."

"Nor did I. Not until I passed through His heart. Before that moment, I saw myself as cursed." She shook her head, the young face taking on a weariness far beyond its apparent years. "Mireille's chain was created to separate a witch from her magic. Inanna's necklace of diamonds and emeralds—seven of each, to be precise—was manifested to allow a witch who comprehends the seven mysteries to focus her own power and claim that of others, to ascend until she touches the heavens. But the homely chain that deprives and the exquisite necklace that gives are one and the same. There is no separation. There are no dichotomies. There is only polarization."

"The seven mysteries?"

"Yes. The seven mysteries. Every culture addresses them after a fashion. The Buddhist's seven factors of enlightenment offer a release from the illusion of selfhood. The seven principles of Hermes Trismegistus promise to dissolve the illusion of a material world. The seven wounds of the cross teach Christ's followers they can redeem themselves through the surrender of self. The seven seals of John the Revelator have been interpreted a thousand ways, but all point to the end of reality as we know it. Inanna passed through seven gates of the underworld, and at each gate, the goddess surrendered another belonging, another symbol of self, to arrive at wisdom—the absolute reality of nonexistence. Not death, *tu vois*, but a descent into chaos, and at the same time a flight into the realm of infinite possibility. Like a magnet's poles—opposite but one.

"Theodosius, our famous mad monk who gave us *The Book of the Unwinding*, began as a manuscript finder for Pope Nicholas V, seeking out those texts his Holiness wouldn't want to publicly acknowledge. Theodosius had been charged with traveling to France to discover and collect any remaining tomes that had belonged to the Avignon papacy." Marceline leaned in as if to whisper a secret. "By the way," she said, "there were seven of them, you know, the popes of Avignon." She touched the side of her nose and nodded.

Evangeline remembered that a power struggle between one of the long-ago popes and a king of France had led to a brief period when the seat of power of the Catholic Church shifted from Rome to French city of Avignon, but the details of the conflict were lost to her.

"The diligent young cleric Theodosius," Marceline continued without missing a beat, as if she expected Evangeline to carry an encyclopedic knowledge of the intricate relationship between Church and State in the late Middle Ages, "was carrying out his faithful completion of this mission when the old Cathar Heresy planted new seeds in his fevered, fertile mind. He stumbled upon the mysteries through the Cathar interpretation of the story of Salome and her dance of the seven veils, a tale I would expect to resonate with you, given your chosen line of business."

Of course Evangeline knew the story. Her father had denounced the millennia-dead woman with the same fervor with which he came after the female contemporaries he judged to be harlots.

"Forget that man." Even bereft of her magic, Marceline seemed to have discerned her thoughts. "It's certain you have more Longeac in you than Caissy. Yes," she said, her chin raised in pride, "you are one of the Longeac women." She clenched her hand and touched it to her heart, an unstudied gesture that betrayed more emotion than Marceline had likely intended. "From Mende," she said, lowering her hand, recovering, "in the Lozère region. Before they named it the Lozère. The two-faced pulpiter knew that, I'm sure, but I'm not surprised he kept those facts from you." Her youthful features hardened as her cheeks flushed red. A furious loathing for Evangeline's father played in her eyes.

"Salome," Evangeline said to bring Marceline back before her rage ignited Evangeline's own, "performed a kind of striptease for the king. To capture the head of John the Baptist."

"Yes," Marceline said. A look like gratitude's poor relation crossed her face, then faded away in the next instant. "Salome danced, enticing her king, liberating herself from each of her seven veils—symbols, of course, of what stands between the seeker and her enlightenment. The Cathars, though, they went a bit further in their interpretation of the text. To them, John the Baptist had come as an emissary of the Devil, to act as foil to the Christian Messiah—the Antichrist if you will. But that wasn't the Cathars' true heresy. Their tenets posited the two personages, Christ and the Antichrist, were not individual beings, but polarizations of a single, inseparable energy."

"The necklace." Evangeline found herself drawing closer to the desk, her finger tracing the surface on which the chain lay. "Why fourteen stones?"

"The diamonds are the seven stars of le Grand Chariot, better known in this land under the prosaic name 'Big Dipper.' The seven emeralds of Inanna's necklace combine to form the emerald tablet of Hermes Trismegistus's *Kybalion*. The fourteen stones together express the Principle of Correspondence—'as above, so below.'"

The *Kybalion*, Hermes Trismegistus—names to conjure with, literally. Some considered the *Kybalion* to be the arch grimoire, the greatest modern treatise on magic, and most held Hermes Trismegistus, "Hermes the Thrice Great," to be an incarnation of the entity known in ancient Greece as Hermes, ancient Rome as Mercury, and ancient Egypt as the great god Thoth—the god of writing and father of all sciences, the architect of physical reality. Hermes Trismegistus was said to have recorded the secret of spinning the energy of the eternal chaos into matter, the supreme act of magic, on what Evangeline had always thought to be a fabled emerald tablet. But if there was even a glimmer of truth in what her aunt was telling her, the tablet was real, and connected to Evangeline.

"Is my mother's connection to the necklace the reason why I'm different?"

"I perceive you as being 'different' in many ways; I'm unsure any of them coincide with the uniqueness to which you're referring." A genuine smile. A warm smile. Evangeline sensed neither guile nor sarcasm. "Perhaps if you could pose a more succinct question."

"Magic is dying," Evangeline began.

"Magic is fading," Marceline joined her in a singsong.

"The others. Most of them have no magic of their own. They're clinging to depleted relics. But I . . ."

"You are sizzling with magic, like *une cierge magique*." She pursed her lips as she searched for the English term. "A sparkler. Yes. You are shooting sparks. Bright. Blinding."

Lincoln had advised her not to let her gains become common knowledge. She agreed that for now discretion was wise, but soon it seemed she might not have to worry. Only Alice came anywhere near her in power—Alice herself had made a point of showing her hand with the fireworks she'd displayed at Précieux Sang—and a great chasm was growing between them and the rest. Even though Nicholas's grand scheme had emboldened him, he was looking for a new battery while Evangeline could sense lightning bolts of power playing beneath her skin. Ironic the "swamp witch" might end up the last witch standing.

"What can I say, *ma chère fille*? Magic has always played favorites." Marceline studied her face. "As I descended through the heart of madness, I learned the most salient facts in regard to magic's demise." She hesitated, as if waiting for Evangeline's permission to share. Evangeline nodded. "There is something I need to show you, but it will require the eyes of another for you to see it. You must arrange a meeting with the Marin girl. Alice."

The sister witches had conspired with Celestin. Celestin, who had locked Alice away on the Dreaming Road. "I'm not sure Alice will be willing—"

"Make her be willing. Luc needs you. He needs both of you."

NINETEEN

A text from Nicholas: *I know you and Hugo are still out. I've sent the Rolls to bring you to the house.* Headlights flashed at them as she read the line. Hugo, in the middle of commenting on a leftover bill announcing LaLaurie Mansheon's farewell "tour," shielded his eyes with his hand. Alice tapped his shoulder and handed him her phone. The fresh air of the wee hours had somewhat revived her, but Rolls or no Rolls, only one destination held any interest for her—bed.

He read the message and grimaced. "Do you see now why I don't carry one of these things?" He dropped the phone back into her hand and started walking toward the car. "Well, come on then."

"Wait, you're going?"

Hugo turned to face her, walking backward toward the black sedan. "No," he said, waving her forward, "we are." Alice hesitated, but Hugo bounded ahead. A man, dressed in charcoal-gray slacks and a white button-down, popped out from behind the wheel and opened the rear door.

"'Sup?" Hugo nodded at the driver and climbed in. He stuck his head out and focused on Alice. "Come on. 'The Leader' awaits."

The car slowed to a stop before Nicholas's well-lit house, situated within view of the finger of water known as Bayou St. John. The house had sat mostly silent in the weeks following the loss of Daniel, but now seemed to be bustling with activity, even though the time was going on three a.m. As Alice leaned around Hugo to survey the situation they were walking into, the driver shifted the car into park, though he left the engine running. The man got out of the car and moments later, Alice's door swung open.

"Miss?" he said.

Alice turned first to Hugo to find him staring at the house, his silent stillness signaling his enthusiasm had flagged. "We don't have to do this," Alice said, laying her hand on his forearm. He turned to her, a counterfeit version of his earlier enthusiasm kindled on his face.

"Nah, this is going to be great," he said, opening his own door. "Just effing great."

Alice sighed and exited the vehicle. "Thank you," she said to the driver, who waited for her, standing at near attention.

"My honor, miss," he said. Alice picked up on a strange sincerity, a zeal even, in his tone. For him, she had a strong sense, these words weren't a mere pleasantry.

Alice paused and took note of the driver's appearance. He was clean-shaven, and his hair was short, neat, perfectly parted—a prudent match for his nondescript manner of dress. His eyes held an ardor that made Alice uncomfortable. The pieces slid together in her mind. Like the young women at Daniel's wake, this man was one of her father's newfound adherents.

Hugo slammed the Rolls's door, causing her to jump. She found herself instinctively backing away from the smiling, outwardly unremarkable zealot. Hugo had already made it halfway down the walk by the time he realized she wasn't following. He turned back and held out his hand toward her.

"Come on, Gretel," Hugo said. "Let's go grab some gingerbread."

◆ ◆ ◆

The door opened as they approached, one of the former Goth girls waiting in the entrance. "Welcome," she said, and as she stepped back to allow them entry, "through us, he shall do great things."

Hugo froze, his eyes locking with Alice's. One eyebrow rose as his lips pursed.

"Through us," the other young woman said, coming down the hall toward them, "he shall do great things." She stopped before them, her face beaming. "He's asked me to bring you to him."

"You're escorting me to my own father . . . in my own house?" Hugo said.

"I hope you'll forgive my presumptuousness, but Father requested it."

"Father?" Alice said, thrown off.

"I believe she means pater noster." He shook his head. "Wait. Make that pater me-ster."

It was the former Goth girls' turn to cast a cautious glance at each other.

"You are fortunate to have him as your biological father," the first said. "As we are blessed to have him as our spiritual father."

Hugo turned to Alice, his eyes wide in disbelief. He snorted out a laugh. It took all of Alice's willpower not to join him in laughter. The two women grew visibly perturbed—the first's shoulders slumped, her eyes dropping to the floor; the second's face flushed, her jaw tightening. This one, Alice decided, had more of her true self, or at least her former true self, left in her.

"Hugo," Alice said, tugging his sleeve. "I'm tired. Let's see what Nicholas wants and leave."

He looked down at her. "Sure," he said without conviction. He shifted his attention back to Nicholas's acolytes. "Listen, I feel we should apprise you that having Old Nick as any kind of father isn't going to be everything you've cracked it up to be." He glanced at Alice. "Am I right?"

Alice wondered if her performance at Précieux Sang, when she'd terrorized the pair, believing she was doing them a favor, had backfired and driven them deeper into the web Nicholas was spinning. "You should listen to him," Alice said softly to the women. "Whatever Nicholas has promised you, when he's through with you, he will be *through with you*, and you will leave empty-handed."

"And that's if you're lucky," Hugo added.

"He's waiting for you," the second girl said, undeterred. Her look of confidence seemed to say she had met a foretold challenge and passed the test. She turned and moved to lead them down the hall.

"It's okay," Hugo said, pushing past her. "I think we know the way." He looked back at Alice. "Make sure you drop breadcrumbs just in case."

The two women moved quickly, trying to advance around Hugo, but Alice held up a hand, both warning them and willing them to stop. The two froze in their tracks, their eyes flashing on her in unison. They gazed at her with a reverential wonder.

She turned away from them and continued in the direction of Nicholas's study, arriving at the moment Hugo flung open its door.

He advanced into the room already speaking. "Don't get me wrong, 'Father,'" he punched the word out to underscore the irony, "this is by far the best community-theater production of *Sweet Charity* ever, but why in the seven hells are you dragging us into it?"

Alice stopped in the doorway and watched Hugo spin around one of the chairs that sat before Nicholas's desk and drop into it, splaying his arms over the top of its backrest.

Nicholas looked past Hugo to her. "Come in, please, and close the door behind you, if you will," he said with a deference he customarily reserved for an influential stranger, someone he didn't know, but who had something he wanted. It struck Alice this was an apt description of her relationship with him. Alice closed the door softly behind her, then crossed to the empty chair and sat down. She smiled at Nicholas and waited. Alice was comfortable with silence, having spent much of her life alone.

Hugo, on the other hand . . .

"Why did you bring us here?" he asked.

Nicholas folded his hands, resting them on his desk. "I'm sure the Twins have provided you with a cursory explanation of my recent undertaking."

"You mean your cult?" Hugo said.

"'Cult' is such a charged word," Nicholas responded, a sly smirk rising to his lips. "I prefer 'society.'"

"What have you done to them?" Alice said, keeping her voice low and calm.

"Done?" he said, giving a shrug. "To whom?"

"I believe she's referring to your two vampire brides."

"They've been changed." Alice held a hand up to silence Hugo. "Don't pretend you had nothing to do with their transformation."

"On the contrary," Nicholas said, his lips pulling down, a sign of mild umbrage. "I had everything to do with it. They were lost souls on a downward spiral. I have given them purpose."

"You have given them *your* purpose," Hugo said.

"I have given them faith in something greater than themselves, a sense of wonder, a sense of security."

Alice held her tongue, giving him a chance to feel the full weight of her distaste. His mask of confidence slowly began to crack. The sharp gleam in his eyes faded. The corner of his mouth twitched. He looked down, focusing on his hands. "I took two broken girls, two broken girls who had no future before them"—his eyes rose to meet hers—"and I broke them down further, so I could begin to rebuild them." The look of self-satisfied superiority returned. "And they love me for it. Adore me. They trust me . . . completely, and they have opened themselves up to me . . . absolutely."

"And you're feeding from them," Alice said. "You're engaged in psychic vampirism." Nicholas was becoming his father, and he couldn't even see it.

A sudden revelation ripped the scales from her eyes. He *did* see it. Cults weren't built in a day. Nicholas must have put this plan of his into play long before he'd disappeared from New Orleans on the day of the massacre at Celestin's memorial ball—a slaughter he himself had narrowly missed due to the disloyalty of his coven. A slaughter for which he could in no way be held responsible. Oh, yes, he'd been both spared and acquitted, almost as if he'd anticipated the bloodshed and shielded himself from the outcome rather than attempted to prevent it. The thought sickened her.

"I'm taking the potentiality of their life force, potential that would have otherwise been wasted, and I am spinning magic from it." He paused and leaned forward. "They're not the only ones." He laughed, almost as if he couldn't believe what he was relating. "Around the country, I have hundreds of others. And with your help—"

"Ah, here it comes," Hugo said, scowling as he draped himself against his chair's backrest.

Alice held her gaze on Nicholas, who looked back and forth between the two of them, his patient, though put-upon expression seeming to ask if they'd satisfied their sanctimonious need to express contempt.

"I am sheltering the homeless, bolstering the weak, giving meaning to those most in need—"

"Wow," Hugo said, "a visit from Saint Nicholas, and it isn't even Christmas Eve."

Nicholas held up his hands in surrender, closing his eyes and shaking his head. He drew and released a deep breath, then opened his eyes. "You both need to grow up," he said, any attempt to ingratiate himself to them tossed to the wind. "Power is a pyramid. You were both born on the apex—"

"I thought I felt something sharp poking me in the ass," Hugo sniped.

"That pyramid is crumbling," Nicholas said, ignoring his son. "I'm building a new one."

"Over which you'll be the all-seeing eye," Alice said.

"It is," he said, "my pyramid, after all. I don't feel the need to justify myself. I'm not looking for your approval. Or even your gratitude. I'm giving you the chance—"

"You're just like Celestin," Alice said, not an accusation but a cold, simple acknowledgment of fact.

"Celestin stole," Nicholas said, fast and sharp. It seemed he had enough of a conscience left to be riled by the truth—though not enough of one to admit it was true. "I'm only accepting what has been freely offered to me. In case the point was lost on you, I'm the 'him' in the 'Through him we shall do great things.'"

"Yeah, Nicholas, we get it," Hugo said, pushing up from his chair and standing. "I always wanted my own catchphrase, too."

Alice took her cue from her brother, rising and moving to the side of the chair. Suddenly tired beyond words, she grasped the top of the backrest to steady herself. To brace herself for his answer. "What do you want from us, Nicholas?"

"From him," Nicholas said with a nod to Hugo, "I want his pharmaceutical know-how." He looked over to his son. "You have experience with using psychotropics to take yourself into the astral, where it's easier to move magical power."

"I no longer have magic," Hugo said. "I no longer want magic."

Nicholas's lips curled up, then opened as he let out a caustic laugh. "You say that now, flesh of my flesh, but you're going to miss it, and miss it more and sooner than you are, in this moment, ready to believe. But," his expression softened, "I don't want you to flounce around the astral. I want you to send others there."

"You want me to drug your little acolytes, so you can shift the power of their potentiality more easily."

"Yes. Once they have been adequately prepared. I also want you to assist me with smoothing out the jagged remnants of who they were, to help them become who they were born to be."

"Your batteries."

"Precisely."

"The Dreaming Road," Alice said, an awareness of his scheme dawning on her.

"*A*"—Nicholas emphasized the article—"Dreaming Road. A new Dreaming Road." He fell silent and studied her. "That is where you come in."

Alice released the chair and, shaking her head, began backing away.

"You know more about the Dreaming Road than anyone. Together we can build these unfortunates their own private paradises."

"Go to hell." Alice turned, almost lunging for the door. She felt as if she couldn't breathe, as if she were trapped in a vacuum. She grasped the doorknob and yanked the door open. The wake, the drink, the Twins. The entire long night caught up with her in an instant.

"That goes double for me, Pops," Hugo said, catching up to her, slipping his arm around her, supporting her. His eyes met hers, a silent inquiry. Her answer was to lean into him. He placed a peck on her temple, and together they headed down the hall toward the front door.

"'Better to reign in hell . . . ,'" Nicholas's voice followed on their heels.

Alice glanced back to see him standing outside his study, his stance loose and confident, his arms folded across his chest. "You flatter yourself, . . . 'Father.'"

Power surged through her, and she slipped free of Hugo's grasp. She stepped forward on her own and used her magic to will the door open. It flung wide and slammed into the wall behind it. She reached back for Hugo's hand and together they stepped out into the glorious night.

TWENTY

Night had fallen, and Nathalie sat on the thin, stained mattress in the mildewy air of the room she now considered her cell. The fan still rattled the window blinds' metal slats, but the faint glow beyond the shifting blinds had faded away.

Nathalie felt like she could sleep a hundred years—and she also felt ready to jump out of her skin. They'd given her something, something first offered as a hot drink "to warm her up." Warm her up, hell. When she refused, three of the fatigue-wearing goons from the yard had marched in and held her down, pouring the earthy-smelling, almost tasteless liquid into her mouth, ounce by ounce, then forcing her mouth shut and squeezing her nostrils closed. She'd tried to fight back. Any one of them, she could have fought off with either her fists or, she'd sensed, magic. Maybe even two of them. But the three had proved more than she could take, especially with Emil standing over, watching, cooing at her. *"Calme-toi, chérie. Reste-tranquille."*

Darnedest thing was, Nathalie's reminiscences of hanging out with her cousins, of wrestling with them and swimming at the old white house with the above-ground pool, had always filled her with nostalgia.

She'd often thought of going back, of looking some of her relatives up, but she'd never understood what had happened between her mother and the Boudreaus. She did remember hearing her mother scream into the phone after her father's death, insisting he would be buried in New Orleans, refusing to let his body be sent back to them. If Nathalie had ever come close to guessing what the Boudreaus had planned for her first reunion with them, she would've changed her name, left the state. Hell, maybe even left the country. Beyond the odd shady comment or things left loudly unsaid, neither Lincoln nor Wiley had prepared her for these crazed militants.

What if they were a part of this? The thought didn't break her heart, but it sure did crack it some.

Wham.

The thin wall behind her back reverberated like the skin of a drum. Nathalie startled and spun sideways, her eyes fixing on the wall. *Wham.* The wall shook like its hidden side had been punched by an enormous fist.

Her captors, her cousins, were keeping her awake, keeping her on edge.

The sharp, dark tones of a fiddle filtered into the room. The tune was one she could have gone the rest of her life without hearing again. Memory piled on top of memory as the image of Frank Demagnan's mangled form crawling across the floor of the mortuary slid beneath an earlier recollection of a man who'd once terrified her by dedicating a wild, frightening rendition of "The Axman's Jazz" to "little Nat."

It struck her that she *did* know Emil. He was her father's great-uncle, though he seemed to be aging in reverse. Nathalie suspected that might have more than a little to do with the ring he wore. Not so very long ago, she would've laughed the idea off as impossible, but there wasn't much left these days that didn't seem like it could happen. The music shrieked to a stop. Nathalie felt Emil had been angry with her, that it had hurt his vanity not to be recognized. Now that she remembered, he was satisfied.

◆ ◆ ◆

Once again, he was with her.

A pendulum swung back and forth before Nathalie's eyes, though Emil suggested it wasn't just a pendulum, that she ought to look closer.

Without taking a step, she did as he suggested, her vision zooming in on the blurry object until it shimmered into fine detail. Her mother's corpse swayed before her. Accusatory, bloodshot, bulging eyes glared at Nathalie from a deep burgundy face. Ashen fingers clawed at the noose as her mother's feet danced a desperate jig in air, trying to find solid purchase.

This is on you.

Her mother's fingers loosened their grip on the noose and slipped up to her face. Nails pointed inward and clawed at skin until her face pulled away in strips to reveal another's features.

Alice's face glistened beneath a sheen of blood. Her eyes glowed like fat rubies, like a lamprey's, her mouth gaping open to reveal a spiraling circle of teeth.

Nathalie came to, alone, sticky with sweat and sick from terror.

The night wore on as Nathalie tried to force the image of the round, ruby-like stone from her mind. She kept her eyes trained on the door, her ears pricking up at every sound; there were a lot of sounds. Some came from the yard—car engines revving to life, wheels crunching over gravel, whispers that sounded more like the relaying of orders than conversation.

She fell asleep. She must have. Rough, calloused hands jerked her awake.

The guys from earlier had returned. They stood over her, the cup they'd used before filled with another dose of the same murky liquid. One of them, a kid who looked like he couldn't be more than sixteen, knelt behind her, caught her neck in the bend of his right arm, and wove the fingers of his left hand through her hair, tugging her head back. Nathalie felt nauseated by the rough movement and the three-day funk of the boy's musk wrestling with a too-liberal application of one of those canned sprays. Body heat, excitement, and exertion worked together to ensure neither scent would admit defeat.

Another of the three, one who looked enough like the boy to be his father, pried open her mouth and began to spill the liquid into it. Nathalie refused to cooperate. She made them put in the effort of forcing the liquid down her throat, but there was no denying the fight had gone out of her.

"Tu vois." Emil stood before her, resting against a plastic folding chair that hadn't been there a moment before. *"C'est pas si grave."*

The others were gone.

"No more," Nathalie said, gagging as the liquid started to work its way back up.

She heard it before she felt it. A sudden, hard backhand across her left cheek. She reached up and placed her palm over the sting. The shock settled her stomach.

Emil smiled. *"Tonton* gonna make you strong." He unfolded the chair and turned it so the back faced Nathalie. He sat, resting his arms on the chair's backrest. "Gonna make you see the truth."

He pulled the ring from his finger, and as he moved it back and forth before her eyes, Nathalie noticed a dim light radiating from within the stone. Even as she looked at it, she sensed something inside it was watching *her.* "Yeah, you right, girl. She's still in there. A bit of her. The whole may be in pieces, but there's a memory of the whole in every piece." He lifted the stone to his lips and kissed it. "Ain't that right, *ma minette?*" he said to the gem, though his eyes never released Nathalie's as he spoke.

A single glint of the stone showed Nathalie a whole history. This Emil, red-faced, eyes bulging, had flung the now lost woman against the wall to make the point that he could. He'd made every decision for her. He'd changed his mind. He'd lied about changing his mind. He'd cut her off from the world, controlling her every contact. She'd never been a strong witch, but as talk of the Dreaming Road reached her ears, she decided to use what little power she had in her to escape. She should have known such talk would never have reached her if he hadn't wanted her to learn of it. She'd been a game to him. An experiment. There was nothing left of the woman, only the rage. And the rage would bide its time, if it took until the end of the world, to tear this man to shreds.

"Wasn't easy to find her. To pick her out from the other shades slithering back and forth between here and the Dreaming Road. Took me fifteen goddamned years." He said it with a wide, wild smile, like he expected Nathalie to admire him for his stick-to-itiveness. His real goal was more artful. Nathalie sensed he was trying to break her down with his wife's story, trying to make what he wanted her to do seem normal. "But I did what I had to. What she was wasn't right. She might've been my woman at one time, but she'd become an abomination. I considered it my duty to end her."

"Why?" Nathalie said the word, though it seemed to take several minutes to form. "Are you doing"—she noticed he was now across the room, peeking out from behind the blind—"this?" He was gone by the time she finished the words.

And then, just as suddenly, he was back. The boy from earlier stood beside him. "You think the bitch is ready?" the boy said. Nathalie saw the boy's words. They were neon orange, and they turned everything they touched the same sickening, unwholesome color. When she was little, she used to open every new box of crayons and throw out anything

197

resembling the shade. Nathalie realized she was perceiving his threatening, repulsive words in the color she hated most in the world.

Nathalie felt something on her tongue, and she stuck her finger in her mouth to peel it off. She pulled out a small square of paper with a smiley face printed on it.

Emil laughed. "Don't she look ready to you?" He waved his hand before her face. The red stone of his ring became a dragon, breathing fire, and then the image faded. He looked away, addressing the boy. "You make sure you ready, too." The boy risked one last look at Nathalie before hauling out of the room.

Emil crossed to the fan, switching it off with a loud click. Nathalie hadn't thought the fan was doing much, but within seconds the air in the room felt thick enough to swim through and heavy enough to bury her. Emil went to the wall switch and killed the light. They were alone together in what should have been blackness, though Nathalie perceived it as an emptiness, like they'd been swallowed by a blank page.

She heard a scratching sound, then realized from the sulfur smell that Emil had struck a match. The world rebuilt itself around them, first two-dimensional and in black and white like an intricately detailed sketch. The color returned, and then the depth, and then the uncomfortable nearness of Emil's face as he leaned in, holding the candle under his chin. A ghoulish, campfire-ghost-story grin carved into his face.

"I brought you here to help you help your girl, your *chère* Alice." He whistled a few bars of the old song, then let the tune trail off. "To really help her, in the only way you got left." He set the candle on the floor between them before easing back down into his plastic chair. "Old Nick, he's got plans for her, big plans."

"Old Nick?" Nathalie repeated the words. For the briefest of moments, she was standing in her mother's house, looking through the door at the neighbor boy in his Halloween costume, his excited eyes staring out through a red-horned half mask on his face, his hand gripping a plastic pitchfork.

"Nicholas Marin," Emil said with a snicker, like he could see the image floating through her mind. "Her papa, or least the one who was supposed to be. He may not have sent the girl to the Dreaming Road himself, but the *couillon* being who he is, he figured out right quick how to profit from her coming back."

"We brought her back."

"You brung back a demon. You ain't seen it in her yet, but you will." He shifted in the seat, the squeaks made by the cheap chair twining up around his legs like vines. "Tomorrow night. You'll see it then.

"Nicholas, he's been goin' around bending some ears, putting little bugs in others." He held up his hand and moved it around in a zigzag. *"Zzzt, zzzt, zzzt."* He lowered his hand and rested it on his knee. "Damn Chanticleer, promising he's gonna put a chicken in every pot. Telling them fool witches he's found a way to put the magic back in them. He's gonna put something in them all right. Those demons. The ones that started out as witches before they went to the Dreaming Road. Gonna make himself king, he is. Plans to start by building himself an army, and finish by picking magic from the bones of everyone who's left. Only thing standing in his way is that he can't control those demons. But your Alice can. She was born and bred to lead those demons. Nicholas Marin can't control them, but he *can* control your girl.

"He knows we been watching. We've let him think we're coming for his sister, Fleur. That one, she killed another witch to work a resurrection spell. She had to to make it work. Sure, back in the day it might register as a capital offense, might've even got her burned, but these days, what with witches carving each other up, a resurrection spell counts as misdemeanor."

Nathalie focused on the candle's flame. Soon, she wasn't seeing the burning wick; she was seeing its negative afterimage, which seemed to have burned itself into her corneas.

"Alice, you think she the light, but she ain't the light."

The dark images left on her eyes by the candlelight grew animated. Slithering like the tiniest of snakes, they joined together into one of the shadow figures like the one that had followed Alice back into the common world, like the demons who'd invaded the Perraults' landscaping business. It slipped somehow out of her inner vision into the physical world of the sweltering, musty room.

"This is what she is now, *ma fille.*" He bent over and pulled a small, ancient-looking dagger from his boot. He lifted the candle in his other hand, ignoring the slithering beast pushing itself along only feet behind him. He pressed the dagger into her hand. "You gonna have to learn to kill it, or have it kill you." With that, he blew out the candle and was gone.

Now Nathalie was in true darkness, an inky blackness that washed around her. She could only tell where the beast was by the flashes of its glowing ruby-red eyes, the snapping of its ephemeral teeth. She forced herself up, began spinning and slashing around in every direction, aiming the point of the blade at indiscriminate angles.

A gray light began to slip in between the slats of the blinds, and Nathalie stood in the center of the room, bathed in cold sweat and gasping. A man's scream from behind her nearly stopped her heart. She spun around to find Lincoln in the corner, his face toward the wall. He knelt, hunched over something. Protecting it. Nathalie felt the slick dagger fall from her sticky hand. So sticky. She looked down at her hands. They were covered with a sheen of blood.

She stumbled over to Lincoln's side. He was lying over a smaller man. Wiley. It was Wiley. She turned toward the wider room, seeing every square inch of it, floor to ceiling, had been splattered with blood and gore. She began screaming now herself.

Suddenly Lincoln was standing behind her, bending back her arms. Forcing her to look at Wiley's butchered body. Wiley's eyes popped open—they were dead, empty. He sat up, then lifted to his feet as if he'd been pulled by a puppeteer's string. He staggered toward her, coming closer and closer, forcing his fingers into her mouth, open now in a wild howl. He placed another tab of paper on her tongue, and Lincoln nearly broke her jaw forcing her mouth closed.

She caught the scent of the teenage boy's body spray, and Wiley's dead face melted, then rebuilt itself into that of the boy. Nathalie bent her head back far enough to see the head of the man holding her. It wasn't Lincoln. It was the boy's father. She tilted forward to discover the blood and gore had all disappeared. She swallowed, the paper slipping down her throat.

Her body went slack, and the man let her drop. Nathalie fell with a heavy thump to the room's rotting floor, her pulse slowing.

Two glowing ruby stones lay before her.

DECEMBER 21

TWENTY-ONE

The section of Chartres that ran between the cathedral and Jackson Square had long ago been turned over to pedestrians, and Alice found herself weaving her way through tourists who zigzagged back and forth, seemingly tantalized by the fortune-tellers who'd lined up their folding tables one after the other along the stone walk but also chastened by the nearness of the church.

Alice, too, could use a bit of insight. The thought of a thirty-thousand-foot vantage point on her street-level drama tempted her. She considered stopping at one of the tables, if only to see if any of these purported psychics had a real gift. As she drew near, one of the card readers, a Rubenesque woman in her late twenties, maybe early thirties, pushed herself up out of her chair. The woman wore a scarlet Lolita dress, its brilliant red muted by a black-lace outer layer. Full-figured, yet of diminutive stature, she gained a few inches in height with the help of her patent leather platform combat boots. She'd curled her jet dyed hair into two large victory waves, streaked with a crimson nearly as bright as that of her colored contacts—at least Alice hoped she was wearing contacts. The reader's crimson eyes widened as they regarded Alice, and she snatched up her cards. She bound them with a thick rubber band, then marched off in the direction of the Presbytère, leaving behind her table, folding chair, and a plastic placard that read "Cartomancer, Clairvoyant, Haruspex."

The other readers looked up, surprised by their colleague's sudden flight, but none of them set eyes on the cause of it, Alice herself. If Alice ever did decide to consult a psychic, this woman in red, she decided, would be the one to receive her patronage. Provided, that was, she could convince the cartomancer not to flee at the very sight of her.

Alice turned aside and mounted the three short steps leading to the plaza. She paused for a moment to rest her hand against the base of one of the quartet of cast-iron lampposts guarding its entrance. Dressed for the holidays, the lampposts all wore red velveteen ribbons around their necks. The bright ribbons were meant to be festive, but Alice had the distinct impression that, like in the story of the mysterious bride, if she were to undo a ribbon, the head of the lamppost would slip off its ladder rail and tumble to the ground.

"Is she alive or not? It's just a mess." The complaint of one of the duller children from the library reading circle where Alice had first encountered the story resurrected itself in her memory. Some souls, Alice reflected, weren't built to cope with ambiguity, which was a shame, as those who are the most certain are, almost without fail, the most wrong.

Alice remembered the dread the story had inspired in her but couldn't remember the fate of the bride. Did a new knot in the kerchief make her as good as new, or had her groom's selfish disregard killed her?

"Marley was dead: to begin with. There is no doubt whatever about that."

The words came to her in Daniel's voice, a hangover from last night. A different story, but still apropos. Luc, too, was dead. There could be no doubt about that one either.

Only now it seemed there might be. That solid fact had been jarred loose by Evangeline Caissy, who'd called her this morning to summon her here to Jackson Square. Evangeline had told her a centuries-old witch known as Marceline had passed "through the heart of madness itself" and returned to the common world with news of Alice's older brother, the brother who now only counted as a half-brother, but who made up for the demotion by being her nephew as well.

Alice had stashed away a handful of pleasant recollections of Luc, protecting them from the warping therapies of the psychiatrists and psychologists and, quite literally, witch doctors of the hospital on Sinclair Isle. She'd even managed to keep them separate, inviolate, from the false memories of years spent on the Dreaming Road.

Most of these memories of Luc—the good ones—centered on ruby-red, cherry-flavored sno-balls and bike rides to Storyland, melting ice cream in Jackson Square, and pocket-change treasures from the French Market. Some, the later, sharper ones, included Evangeline. Those were the happiest of Alice's memories of Luc, as Luc had only ever seemed truly happy when with Evangeline.

Alice tried never to linger on these bright memories. The joyous moments were tricks, malicious *fifolets* intent on leading her into darkness. Along with these lighthearted souvenirs, Alice carried a well-rehearsed, cheerless litany of memories, strung together like the beads of her rosary and enumerated by rote. From the false memory she'd woven from a long-lost family portrait, the only one to include Astrid, to her final horrific image of Luc, his hand wrapped around a pistol and Babau Jean's hand wrapped around his. In between, scenes of Luc's red-faced fury crashing into Nicholas's white-faced rage. The day in the attic when he'd revealed to her that her beloved Daniel had been conjured, not born.

Alice passed beneath the statue of Jackson on horseback. Like the gnomon of a sundial, the sculpture cast its shadow over Alice, its touch palpable. A tickle traced down the nape of her neck, a gloom tapped her on the shoulder and whispered in her ear that Art was right. The trap had been sprung. Stars were aligning to bring them all full circle to the end.

The end. Of late, it seemed even the fat and happy were hell-bent on Armageddon. Alice didn't believe in destiny, but she'd come to question whether Daniel might have been onto something with his theory of people and events following a natural trajectory.

She stepped into the sunlight and folded her arms over her chest, rubbing them to drive out the chill. Turning to keep the statue in her field of vision, she stepped backward until she arrived at one of the long, curved benches that spanned each quadrant of the middle ring of the plaza.

She took a seat and began studying the sculpture. The one here in New Orleans was a replica, one of three. After Katrina, during the months she and Hugo had stayed with Fleur and the senator, they had visited the original statue in D.C. The original, it seemed, had lacked something in comparison. This one was somehow special, not due to its subject or the quality of its execution, but because of its placement. The statue took a charge from the land on which it stood, and the power of place imbued it with a meaning the artist had probably never intended for his work, a significance beyond that of the original sculpture in the nation's capital.

The bells of the cathedral rang the hour even as Evangeline appeared at the park's gate. The child whose hand she held, a tiny waif of a girl, broke away and began chasing back and forth between a pair of palmettos, circling each time to pass Evangeline before speeding off again.

A bit pale, too thin, but other than that the child looked like any of the others profiting from the freedom of the winter break. She wore blue jeans, a black-and-white striped T-shirt, and brand-new, from the look of them, red sneakers. Her long blonde hair was styled, like Evangeline's, in a loose French braid. Anyone else would imagine the two, so alike in appearance, to be mother and daughter.

The girl noticed her and came to a stop in front of her, gazing up at her with wide, cautious eyes. Alice's own eyes lied to her heart, telling her the girl standing before her needed her protection, not her scorn, but Alice forced herself to recognize this as a falsehood. This was no child.

As fantastical as it seemed, this seeming innocent was in fact an ancient and deadly witch. Defanged and diminished, yes, but perhaps even more dangerous in this new guise. Reflexively, Alice's hand jerked up. She could feel the energy racing through it, ready to burst forth and destroy.

Evangeline rushed forward, placing herself in front of the girl. *She's protecting her from me.* Alice had to fight back a bitter laugh.

"Thank you for coming," Evangeline said, her gaze fixed on the fiery glow at Alice's fingertips. "That won't be necessary," she said, her eyes rising to meet Alice's. "Really, it won't."

Alice turned her focus back to the counterfeit child, who'd shifted out from behind Evangeline.

Marceline drifted closer. "This," she said, gesturing from her head to her toes, "is for your benefit. I've been reborn to this world in a form that might arouse your sympathies, or at least reassure you I am of no danger to you."

As the little girl regarded Alice, her pale complexion reddened with mounting pique. "You await an expression of regret. My exterior has changed, but my heart remains the same." Her head rocked back as she huffed out a sound of disgust. "You wish to hear of my regrets? Bargaining with the Dark Man without combing through each and every intricacy, thinking He might, if only once, look upon me with favor for the centuries of faithful service rendered to Him, rather than see me as an amusement. *De cette bêtise, je m'en mords les doigts.*" Her robin's-egg eyes flashed like blue flames jumping to life. She glared at Alice over her hands as she mimed biting off the tips of her fingers. But in the next instant, her heat faded to a gray despondency. She lowered her hands and focused on her empty palms. "I am here, but my sisters are dead. I've been defenseless before, but never alone."

Marceline stood only an arm's length away, her expression sober, her body tensed as if preparing for an attack. Alice understood far too well how this type of trepidation felt, but the old witch could rest easy. Alice had given into her rage once, and the bitter aftertaste still hadn't left her. If she continued to cede to her anger, she might find herself walking in Marceline's shoes, and that was not a trek she cared to make.

"I'm . . . ," Alice began, intending to express her satisfaction over the sister witches' demise and Marceline's well-deserved comeuppance. The moment before the words slipped out, she realized there was already far too much cruelty in the world. Justified or not, she wasn't going to add to it. "I'm sorry for your loss."

Marceline's eyes popped wide with shock. "Mercy, even now," she said, studying Alice's face, searching, Alice sensed, for a scorn she did not feel. The reborn ancient seemed disconcerted by her sincerity. "It doesn't suit you," Marceline said as she regained her composure. "You are a warrior, *une femme-chevalier*, not a nun. Not that nuns are known for extravagant displays of mercy."

"You said," Evangeline said, addressing her aunt, "that you had information about Luc."

"Of course," Marceline said, and Alice felt the full focus of the foul child fall squarely on her. "You will follow me?" The way she posed the question made Alice wonder whether she doubted Alice's willingness to do so or her own safety with her back turned.

"Lead the way," Alice said, rising.

Marceline nodded, then set out in a straight line across the grass toward the statue of Jackson. She stopped and looked up, contemplating it. Alice sensed that growing chill once more, the sense that everything was coming to a head, although neither of her companions reacted to it. As they drew near to the statue, Marceline looked over her shoulder at Evangeline.

"Long before this dashing fellow drew his first breath, this square was known as le Place d'Armes. We would come here, you know, your mother and I. Mathilde and Margot, too. We'd purchase pecan pralines from the vendors who lined up along there." She traced a line with her finger along the Decatur Street edge of the park. "We never missed an execution." The wistful nostalgia in her voice held a gruesome incongruity to her words. "Margot always preferred the hangings to the firing squad." Marceline spun around, rising up on her toes and rocking back and forth. *"La pendaison sans cagoule, surtout."* She laughed, bugging out her eyes and twitching her face muscles to imitate the condemned who died from strangulation rather than a broken neck.

She seemed to take their lack of response as reproach. Perhaps she was right.

"Do not regard me as if we were savages. Were they to resume the public executions today, your contemporaries would wait hours in line to purchase tickets. 'Make Executions Public Again,'" she said, miming tugging down the bill of a baseball cap. She then doffed the imaginary hat to them. "A winning slogan, of this I am most certain."

Alice couldn't argue the point. The uncanny ancient wasn't wrong. Civilization had proved itself to be no more than a thin veneer on a myriad of occasions in the intervening decades. She was ready to say as much, but Marceline had already moved on.

"You know, don't you," Marceline said in a child's piping voice, "the river created this land, this thin crescent of earth, by carrying silt and soil with its flow and depositing sediment where we now stand. The land on which this square, with the horse and rider at its heart, is situated is younger than the Great Sphinx of Giza. *Man merged with beast. Man merged with beast.*" She repeated the words with reverence, as if they formed a benediction—or, more likely considering their source, a malediction. "The Sphinx sits approximately six and a half thousand miles to the east of New Orleans's iconic centaur at this same latitude.

"As above, so below." She repeated the most famous dictum of magic. She placed her hand over her heart. "As without, so within."

"This square, the lines and curves of its paths. These buildings"— she nodded at the older Pontalba building, then at the younger twin facing it—"along with the fine cathedral, Presbytère, and Cabildo. Church and state and commerce positioned around the central square. Their presence to be expected, but their arrangement far from haphazard."

As she spoke, Alice imagined she could see silver threads of energy linking the buildings together, forming a familiar pattern she nonetheless could not fix in her memory.

"What does this have to do with us?" Evangeline said, prodding the girl, her tone that of a parent losing patience with her precocious child. "With Luc?"

"Why, everything," Marceline responded. "It's about you, and her"—she nodded in Alice's direction—"and your Luc. It's about the fate of magic in this world, but if you feel I'm wasting your time . . ." She fell silent, crossing her arms and glowering like the petulant child she appeared to be would.

"Go on," Alice said with a cautioning glance to Evangeline, "we're listening."

Marceline hesitated, looking to Evangeline.

"All right," Evangeline said. "I'm sorry. I'm listening."

Marceline gave a satisfied nod, then leaned in toward them. "Despite what you've been told," she said in a loud stage whisper, "magic is not fading, nor is it dying. Magic comes to us through a tear in the fabric of this reality, a wound, if you will. That wound is healing. This land, right where we are standing, is the best place to create a new wound, to open a new artery."

TWENTY-TWO

"Good morning," Lucy said, the greeting sounding a tad too perky to Fleur's ears after the invectives they'd endured the night before.

Fleur released the hem of the dress she was preparing to baste and pushed the needle back into the pincushion she wore on her wrist. "We're on speaking terms again?" She looked up to find her daughter leaning against the doorframe, her long hair piled up on her head.

"I'm good with the arrangement if you are."

Fleur gazed at her daughter and found herself suddenly awash in ambivalent feelings that had little to do with Lucy or the holes her sharp tongue had poked in Fleur's heart.

"You're still mad."

"No," Fleur said, then rethought. "Well, yes, I am a little, but it isn't that. It's only with your hair up like that, you look so much like your grandmother Laure." It was to be expected that blood would tell, that Lucy should resemble Fleur's own mother, but here, in her mother's house, in her mother's favorite room, Fleur knew it was more than that. Her mother had at last found a way to haunt her.

Lucy tugged the clip from her hair and shook her hair out. "Oh, great. I look like the lunatic."

"Please don't call her that." Fleur felt her cheeks flush, but she couldn't decide if the heat was sparked by an offended sense of decorum or shame. Perhaps she'd tapped into the dregs of her filial loyalty.

"I'm sorry," Lucy said, and Fleur recognized true regret in her voice. Her daughter dropped her hair clip on a side table and drew closer. She laid a hand on Fleur's shoulder. "I didn't mean it. Well, I did, but I didn't mean to hurt you. Do you ever worry it might run in the family, the mental illness thing? Sometimes I worry that maybe it's in me, too."

Fleur felt a flash of anger meet a long-repressed sense of abandonment. "Your grandmother's condition was not hereditary. She brought it on herself." Fleur patted Lucy's hand. "She chose it. You do share much with your grandmother, but you do not share her madness."

"Like what?"

"Well, to start, your grandmother was a legendary beauty. Fiery and independent, I've been told, when she was young. She was spirited like you. But unlike you, she was selfish, and incapable of saying those two little words: 'I'm sorry.' You've gotten the best parts of her. Be glad of that and keep a guard against her less enviable characteristics."

Her daughter's face took on an inscrutable look. "But I'm a lot like you, too, right?"

In spite of all the to-be-expected teenage rebellion, and the entitled hellfire Lucy had let loose last night, Fleur sensed her daughter did in fact admire her. Lucy needed to feel she reflected the best of her mother— ironic really, as Fleur turned to her daughter for proof of her own worth. "I see your open heart and hope that came from me." She rose and leaned in for a quick hug, then stepped back. "Enough." She nodded at her work. "Let's have it, then. What do you think of the dress?"

She'd tried to sound playful, but in truth she was afraid of Lucy's opinion, terrified it would echo Laure's patronizing dismissal of the drawings Fleur had shown her years ago, back when she first told her she wanted to study design. *"Tu es bien une couturière douée, mais le modélisme, c'est la quête incessante d'originalité. Toi, ma jolie chatonne, tu es une pasticheuse."*

"My mother," Fleur dared, "thought me to be an excellent seamstress, but found my designs too derivative of the works of others. She called me a *pasticheuse*, a hopeless imitator."

"Yeah. This from the woman who thought the eighties was a good opportunity to retrofit her mothballed Cassinis with shoulder pads." Lucy held up a hand. "Don't bother defending her, I've seen the photos."

A tiny smile curled up on Fleur's lips as Lucy took a few steps backward, studying the dress first from a distance, then spiraled in on it, judging it from every angle. "Not terrible," she said, her tone signaling the approval she couldn't bring herself to convey directly. She touched the bodice. "Silk. V-neckline and back. Deep enough to be alluring, but with enough coverage to pass as demure."

She circled around once more. "High waist seam, but not too high. Gives the illusion of an hourglass figure." Her hand dropped to the skirt. "Tulle. Nice geometric cutouts. Oooh. Hand-sewn. Genuine couture." She paused to offer an appreciative nod that was only tinged with the mildest sarcasm. "A-line, ankle-length, perfect for an afternoon high tea or a wicker man torching." She paused for a quick, self-satisfied smile. "The black is a tad severe, but overall not bad." Fleur took this as a grade of A. "I might even wear it." No, A plus. "The right shoes could make it work." A summary statement to make it clear Fleur shouldn't let one success go to her head.

Fleur realized she'd been holding her breath. She exhaled, grateful and relieved. "I'm happy it passes muster, if only by a hair. I designed it for you. For tonight." She brushed back her daughter's bangs. "Tell me you really love it, because I haven't slept a wink."

"I . . . ," Lucy began, sounding a bit reticent. "I do. Love it. Really." But Lucy wasn't even looking at the dress. Instead, she drifted over to Fleur's ersatz desk. She circled around it, examining the drawings and fabric samples littering its surface. She paused and picked up the large round millefiori paperweight Fleur had taken from Celestin's study. This she carried with her as she returned to Fleur's side.

"I brought that back from Italy as a souvenir for Celestin. It's called 'millefiori.'" She gave a slight nod at the globe in her daughter's hand. "That's why I chose it for Father. He was once fond of saying he wished he had a thousand little flowers just like me." She smiled at the sentiment. Perhaps at one time Celestin had been capable of love. "I was only four or so, but I remember the trip well. Mother, Vincent, and I." She paused to reflect. "I don't remember why Father and Nicholas stayed home." She shrugged. "We were in Rome," she said and laughed. "All I remember from Rome was ice cream at the Trevi Fountain. But Venice. There is no forgetting Venice."

"Remy broke up with me."

Fleur couldn't hide her surprise. She shook her head to signal her confusion and opened her mouth to speak.

"The day after Thanksgiving," Lucy continued. "Not a big surprise."

"I'm sorry. I wish you would have come to me."

"I . . . ," Lucy began, then fell silent. "You were already having to deal with Dad." She shrugged.

Fleur felt like a total failure as a parent. "I'm sorry," she said. "I'm sorry I wasn't there for you." There was something else. She could almost hear the wheels spinning in her daughter's mind. "What happened?"

"Nothing," she said, sighing. "He got all weird after his mom's stroke. That's all."

"Weird how?"

"At first, I thought Remy was blaming me . . . well, you, for what happened to Mrs. Perrault. He'd started filling in for his mom at her shop. He and his granddad—even though Remy swore Mr. Simeon hates the place."

"Alcide is certainly no fan of the Marin family, that's certain, but—"

"Can you blame him?"

Fleur shook her head. She couldn't blame him. In fact, she'd wondered at the expert-level parental aplomb with which Lisette had accepted, or at least pretended to accept, her son's relationship with Lucy. Fleur could only hope her own performance had been equally convincing.

"Yeah," Lucy continued, "I know what you're thinking, but Remy and I both knew what you and his mom were up to, making nice even though you'd both rather chew off your arms than see us together."

"I have nothing against Remy, but anyone could see you two would have a difficult path to tread, given that—"

"My grandma murdered his. Yeah, I get it. I'm not stupid." She looked away, the way she did when she felt ashamed. "I wasn't sorry he did it. I was relieved.

"I was only fifteen when I met him. Not gonna lie, it was the Shakespearean, forbidden-romance aspect of it that first attracted me to him. It didn't seem like it would be long-term. Then you said we were staying, and I was kind of stuck in it. I wanted to want him. I wanted to love him even. But I didn't." She focused on Fleur. "A person can change a lot in two years." She spoke as if conveying a nearly unfathomable truth.

Fleur spared Lucy the condescension of adding "especially at your age" to Lucy's thought. Instead, she nodded in agreement.

"It doesn't bother me he broke up with me. What bothers me is the way he looked at me. Like he was looking through me . . . and seeing something wrong."

Fleur blanched. "There is nothing wrong with you."

Lucy lifted her chin and looked down her nose at Fleur, the expression betraying her doubt. Had Lucy begun to sense something? Was it possible she had begun to realize her time on this earth had been borrowed—stolen—from another?

"I've been thinking . . . ," Lucy began, then fell silent, biting her lower lip, focusing on the paperweight as if it were a religious icon.

"Yes?" Fleur prompted her, even as she knelt again before the dress, turning her attention back to the tulle.

"I'm old enough to make up my own mind. About the wedding. I'm going, and I won't be coming back to New Orleans."

Fleur froze. At first a surprised, wounded "oh" was all she could muster. She looked up at Lucy. "What do you mean, you aren't coming back?"

"I mean I'm staying in D.C."

Fleur's face flushed hot. Lucy had conspired with her father, who had gone along with her plan because he was too weak to speak the truth, knowing it would fall on Fleur to act as the disciplinarian. The foolish coward. He knew it was impossible. He knew what Fleur was up against trying to keep their daughter alive. "Perhaps," she allowed her fear to flame into a wounded anger, "we should call your father together and discuss this little plan you've been cooking up. He can clarify whether the party invitation includes an offer to stay on indefinitely. Trust me, he doesn't want you horning in on his new life. At least not for long. And even if he does, I guarantee you young Meredith doesn't." Her words came out sharp. *This,* she thought, *this is how Warren repays me for giving him his freedom without fanfare.*

"I don't plan to 'horn in' on Dad, or either one of his fetuses," Lucy said, crossing her arms and beginning to cry. "I spoke to Hailey last night." This didn't surprise Fleur. The two had been friends since preschool. If Lucy wanted to complain to someone about her terrible mother, Hailey would be the most likely choice. "To her parents, too. They said I could stay with them." She brushed away her tears. "I don't want to leave you, Mom, but I want to go home. I want to finish school with my friends."

Of course. Fleur realized how selfish she must appear to Lucy. Fleur had insisted on remaining here long past the point any reasonable woman would. She'd blamed her decision to stay on the pull of home, joked she was less intimidated by bloodthirsty bayou witches seeking revenge on Celestin's kin than she was by the backbiting Potomac bitches waiting for her in what she and Lucy had come to call "the real world." But for them, for both of them, New Orleans was "the real world" now, the only world where Fleur felt any confidence in her ability to keep her daughter alive.

Lucy couldn't learn the real reason they needed to remain in New Orleans. Fleur had felt the need to return to her source, sensing her magic would hold out the longest, remain the strongest, here in the city of her birth. Someday, long after Fleur had found a lasting solution, Lucy might learn everything Fleur did—everything—was for her. Until then, she might have to let her daughter hate her.

"I want to go home. I need to go home. We haven't been gone six months and already everyone's forgotten me. They're ghosting me. Not because they're mad at me, but because I don't exist."

Fleur understood. Her own D.C. friends had taken to returning her texts a day or two late, if at all. She hadn't believed her world could move on so easily without her, but it had, almost like she'd never belonged in it.

"I'm sorry, *ma chère*, but this"—she motioned around the oval room, though she meant to imply New Orleans—"is our home now."

"Maybe this is your home, but it never was mine. It never will be." Fleur had realized all along Lucy was keeping one foot out the door, resisting making new connections other than to Remy. She'd hoped a sense of family would give Lucy enough gravity to keep her happy. "I'm an adult. Almost."

Fleur shook her head. "You are still a minor. Your father and I agreed. Your place is with me." She felt a flash of inspiration. "I was planning to capitulate to your wish to attend your father's wedding," she lied, "but I can't now. You will not be returning to D.C. At least not before your eighteenth birthday." That tack could at most only buy Fleur seven months.

"I know you're angry with Daddy. Embarrassed about his affair. But you're Fleur frigging Marin." Fleur recognized the progression of Lucy's campaign. A full-on frontal attack was failing, so she was moving on to stage two, flattery. "It's been months now. You should rise like a phoenix from the Endicott ashes and carry us back to civilization on first class, if not private, wings. But instead you're here building a nest out of paint strips and fabric swatches, getting ready to put a new face on the old Marin mausoleum. You deserve more than this."

"I said no." She braced herself for the knife.

"God. You can be such a bitch. No wonder Daddy started banging Meredith. No wonder Eli is hiding from you." Lucy's last-ditch effort—cruelty. "Your life might be over, but that doesn't mean mine has to be." There it was, the brilliant summation intended to knock the fight out of Fleur. It succeeded in bringing tears to her eyes, but Fleur was prepared to fight to her last breath for Lucy, even if that fight was with Lucy.

She stood and took the paperweight from Lucy's hand. "I realize you're disappointed," she said. "Angry with me. But I hope you know how much I do love you."

Lucy snorted at her words. "Right."

She began to search Lucy's eyes, trying to gauge how long it would be before the storm passed. A couple of days, maybe a week? A chill began to tickle the base of her spine. Something was wrong.

Lucy was there. With her. Walking. Talking. Breathing. But something, some vital spark was missing. The thing that had made her Lucy was gone. Her beloved Lucy was already dead.

Fleur stumbled backward from shock and fell to the floor, dropping the paperweight. It bounced on the rug and rolled to a stop at Lucy's feet.

"I'm okay, I'm okay," she said reflexively as she pushed herself up onto her elbows.

Lucy didn't respond. Instead, she bent over and picked up the paperweight. She came closer and dropped to her knees beside Fleur.

"Your life might be over, but mine doesn't have to be."

Fleur saw a bright streak as Lucy brought the heavy glass globe down on her forehead once, then again, then all fell to darkness.

TWENTY-THREE

"Here?" Evangeline said, incredulity playing in her voice as she held out her hands and turned as if trying to take in the whole of the city and not just the festooned square around them. "New Orleans is where magic will be reborn?"

"It will certainly die here." Marceline shrugged. "But whether it will be reborn is yet to be decided. I can assure you New Orleans was molded from inception for this very purpose."

"Molded by whom?" Alice said. The "why" was obvious, the "how" no doubt arcane. The agency seemed the loosest thread to pull.

"An excellent question," Marceline said. The arch of her eyebrow and her conspiratorial tone caused Alice to abandon hope for a concise answer. "You will indulge me in a brief history lesson, yes?"

Evangeline cast Alice a nervous glance. She seemed worried the reborn sorceress would push Alice to the limits of her patience—perhaps because she herself was losing patience.

Alice gave Evangeline a nod to reassure her, then turned to Marceline and said, "Of course." It might take Alice years to sort through the facts and fictions of Marceline's story, but she could overlook a little dishonesty if it meant hearing the history of the city from a woman who'd lived most of it.

Marceline's face brightened with what struck Alice as true pleasure. The old witch, Alice realized, was lonely. This was her chance to reminisce.

"One might," Marceline said, diving into her ruminations, "look to de Pauger, the despotic little bureaucrat who drew up the plan of the Vieux Carré. *Celui-là, il était un vrai zob.*" She leaned in toward Alice, her smooth brow furrowing. "Do you know he pulled down a man's house so he could superimpose his new grid system? When the poor fellow complained, de Pauger imprisoned him in darkness with shackles around his ankles. The man was nearly blind by the time he was released. But then again, de Pauger was a draftsman, not an artist, and all witches are, at least to a small degree, artists.

"I believe we must move a bit farther afield—all the way back to France—if we are to discover the spider at the center of this web. The man after whom the city was named, le Duc d'Orléans, or as I like to think of him, 'Philippe le Branleur.' He was the regent of France between the death of Louis XIV and when Louis XV reached his maturity at the ripe old age of thirteen."

At the mention of the Bourbon kings, Alice's mind flashed back to her first impression of the Dreaming Road—a facsimile of Versailles's Galerie des Glaces. Had Alice's interpretation of the Dreaming Road as Louis XIV's famed Hall of Mirrors been a clue to the Dreaming Road's origin, a marker of its DNA?

"No," Marceline continued to muse, "Philippe was not a mastermind. He was a tool." She chuckled at her own choice of words, an accidental pun on the French "*zob.*"

"But," she held up a hand as if to fend off a protest, "a useful tool all the same, as he does bring us one step closer to Françoise Marie, le Branleur's wife . . . and cousin." She winked at Alice. "Even the branches of the Marin family tree aren't nearly as twisted as those of the late French aristocracy."

Alice felt Evangeline tense by her side. She held out her hand to reassure her all was well.

"She was a drunken hellcat, our Françoise." Marceline carried on, seemingly oblivious to the fact her last quip could have indeed been her last. "Her sot of a husband made a habit of referring to her as 'Madame Lucifer.'"

It seemed that name was on the tip of everyone's tongue.

"A pleasing coincidence, as she was, in fact, the daughter of the Sun King." Marceline paused as if giving Alice and Evangeline a chance to make the connection. Alice got the link immediately, the message of Art's sermon feeling a tad too pertinent to Marceline's history lesson for her comfort.

"Sun King? Lucifer? No?" Marceline shrugged when neither reacted. "Françoise Marie's mother," she continued, "was Louis's headmistress—no, that doesn't sound right." Her head tilted to the side. *"Maîtresse-en-titre?"*

She posed the question to them both, but it was Alice who responded. "Official mistress."

"Yes. His official mistress, Madame de Montespan, who celebrated many a black mass with the sorceress known as 'La Voisin,' and the abbé Étienne Guibourg." She nodded at Alice. "You might despise me, but in comparison to those three . . ." Her words drifted away as her eyes fell to the ground. "I have never harmed a child." She looked back up, her brow furrowing and her eyes set in preparation to take on any challenge from them. Then her features softened in a flash, and she turned to face Evangeline. "Other than you, *ma chère.*"

For the briefest moment, Alice felt Marceline stood on the verge of begging forgiveness, and Evangeline on the edge of granting it. But the silence held, the urgency in their eyes cooled, and the moment passed.

Marceline coughed, pretending to clear her throat. "It's rumored," she continued, assuming a pedagogical air, "Guibourg introduced

Madame de Montespan to *The Lesser Key of Darkness*, and through her hands the tome fell to her daughter. *Telle mère, telle fille?* Did the apple fall close to the tree? You be the judge. But the mother, de Montespan," she drew out the name, "she is our Arachne, the nimble weaver at the center of the web. I have no proof to offer, but still I am sure."

Two clear and seemingly contradictory thoughts hit Alice at once. Marceline was a consummate liar, and Marceline was speaking the unbridled truth. "How," Alice began, "can the city be used to restore magic?"

"Through the Law of Correspondence. This city, at least the older parts of it, form a kind of effigy, if you will. Like the magical *poupée*—"

"A Voodoo doll," Evangeline said, turning, oddly, to Alice rather than her aunt for confirmation.

"Yes," Marceline responded, "and no. Regardless of what the movies show us, they don't use dolls in Voodoo, at least not to harm. The magic of the effigy belongs to European witches, as taught to us in the old forests by the Dark Man Himself."

It struck Alice that the wicker man Nicholas was so intent on torching during the Longest Night celebration, too, was an effigy—a representation of the dying solar god, a stand-in for the King of Bones and Ashes. She began to wonder if Nicholas was acting of his own accord, as he believed, or as another's puppet.

"This city," Marceline said, doing a slow turn, "is like one of those dolls in the sense that any magic enacted on it will affect the corresponding target, or targets, it was created to symbolize."

"Targets?"

"The seven Gates of Guinee. Papa Legba is the first to be approached. This park and its immediate environs, they were laid out along the lines of his vèvè. Through Legba, one arrives at the seven gates—the seven wounds—guarded by Baron Samedi and his assistants. This area, Legba's vèvè, lies within a greater design—one that corresponds to the

Baron's vèvè. Seven of the second symbol's stars equate to the Gates of Guinee."

"But that's just nonsense they shell out for tourists," Evangeline said. Again, she turned to Alice, her expression incredulous. "It's rumored you can find the locations of the gates by aligning the center of Samedi's vèvè with Canal Street. The first is in the oldest cemetery."

"What is New Orleans's oldest cemetery?"

"St. Louis Number One. Everyone knows that." Evangeline responded as if her aunt had asked her to calculate two plus two.

"Ah," Marceline said, "but what 'everyone knows' to be true is more often than not patently false. St. Louis Cemetery was the work of the Spanish. There was an earlier French burial ground. The St. Peter Street Cemetery." Marceline motioned with both hands to either side of the cathedral. "Baron Samedi's vèvè links the heart of New Orleans Voodoo, Congo Square, to the heart of the Catholic faith, the cathedral." She turned back to them. "There are no dichotomies. Only polarities."

Alice knew Voodoo had been a part of New Orleans's culture from its earliest days, but decades had passed between the founding of the city and the rise of the Voodoo queens. "But," she said, raising her hand to shield her eyes as she turned a full circle, "none of this makes sense." She stopped as she again faced the statue. She jabbed a finger at Jackson. "That has only been here since around 1850 or so. And most of the Quarter has burned twice since New Orleans was founded. Still, you're alleging adherents to the religion of Voodoo plotted this city?"

"I'm saying no such thing." She sounded almost offended. "It wasn't the acolytes of Voodoo, but those who wished to attack the forces represented by their loa. Us," she said, pounding her fist against her chest, "the witches of New Orleans. We designed this city."

"But why would you . . . would we . . . want to take on those forces?"

"Just as your Dreaming Road lies between dreaming and death, the world of spirits is like a film separating the reality we know as 'the common world' from the realm of infinite possibility. From magic. It seeps into our world through the seven wounds."

"And witches want to reopen the wounds."

Marceline nodded. "They aren't separate entities, the Dark Man and Legba. They are two polarities of the same force—the one tears rifts into the fabric of our reality, the other mends them. It is our Dark Man who siphons the madness that is magic from the realm of pure potential, and their Legba who regulates its flow through the realm of spirit into the common world.

"The story of Inanna and Damuzi, the Queen of Heaven and the King of Bones and Ashes, tells us how to renew these wounds, through love or betrayal, though love creates the deepest, longest-lasting wounds. Our world has seen more than one Queen, and myriad Kings. But your Luc can be the last sacrifice, the greatest King. He's waiting now for the both of you, a mere hairsbreadth beyond the seven gates. With your help, he can return to this world. Together you can conquer the force that is strangling the flow of magic—conquer it for all time."

"I don't know," Alice said, her rational mind refusing to accept she might have been born into a living myth.

"Then the layout of this city, the attraction between your family and *The Lesser Key*, perhaps it is all a matter of coincidence?" Marceline's lips pulled down into a frown as her eyebrows rose. She was, it appeared, incredulous at Alice's resistance. "Yes, one could argue that viewpoint. Even as one can insist it's mere coincidence the speed of light as it passes through a vacuum is echoed by the latitude of the Great Pyramid of Giza, or on that selfsame latitude a little girl named Alice once noticed a ray of light coming from her *tatie* Fleur's rhinestone shoe buckle."

Alice caught her breath, and Marceline gave her a sly smile. It had happened the day the levees fell, the day of Alice's first encounter with Babau Jean. Fleur had projected herself into Nicholas's study, and Alice had indeed noticed the reflection of a beam of light off the buckle on Fleur's shoe. It should have been impossible, as Fleur wasn't truly there. The incident had long since passed from Alice's memory. To be reminded of it all these years later, by someone who'd somehow gained access to a private moment, took her breath away.

"Oh, *ma chère fille*, don't be surprised. New Orleans was groomed to act as the stage of magic, and you were groomed as well. From here to the asylum on Sinclair. To the Dreaming Road and back again. The Dark Man has watched over you ever since the day your mother dedicated you to His service. Did you really think a mere servitor spirit would be capable of freeing you unless he had the help of a greater power working behind the scenes? A few more days on the Dreaming Road, and this conversation wouldn't have been necessary. Only you weren't quite baked before your nanny came to fetch you. I suspect He wants you to choose Him as an act of free will. Perhaps your doing so is a requisite of His plan, or perhaps it simply plays to His sense of pageantry. After all, darkness has always had a penchant for the romantic gesture."

"Astrid dedicated me to His service?"

"She did, but not entirely alone. Astrid worked under His guidance. He chose you, *ma petite*, as *la Pucelle de Nouvelle Orléans*, our new Joan of Arc. It's your destiny."

Again with the destiny. "There's a big difference between fate and manipulation."

Marceline laughed. "Not when the entity that's pulling the strings is capable of shredding the fabric of reality. You are the maiden knight, born and bred to lead an army. An army you encountered on the Dreaming Road."

"The shadows," Evangeline said, turning on her, looking at Alice as if she were a dangerous stranger.

"Demons," Marceline corrected her. "Not the kind they"—she gave a quick nod toward the cathedral—"talk about. The Dreaming Road was never an escape, nor was it intended as a trap. It's a kind of factory, or perhaps refinery is the better term, that burns away a witch's humanity, leaving nothing more than a sentient, remorseless power.

"The Dark Man has done us a tremendous service, though. Your army might prove to be unnecessary. Through His splendid works He has created an alternative to a great sacrifice. There is a much simpler, less devastating way to open the gates and make way for the King if you're willing to consider it."

"I'm not sure—"

"How?" Evangeline spoke over her. "How can we save Luc?"

"The gates." Marceline raised her hands and gestured around the square. "They are no longer out here." She drew near and caught Alice's hand in her left and Evangeline's in her right. She tugged them both down as she leaned in. "The *voudouienne*," she whispered, "has taken the seven wounds into herself. All you have to do to open the gates is kill the Perrault woman."

TWENTY-FOUR

The faces in the window popped in and out of view, one moment nothing more than a flat sigil painted on a pane, the next an intelligence studying Alice with a level of wariness that matched her own. They, Alice sensed, were questioning her intentions for coming. Alice wondered at the same thing.

The interior of the shop was dark, and a sign reading "*Fermé*" hung in the door. Alice had come to get a glimpse of Lisette, to see her moving through her own world, so she could gain a sense of Lisette as a person rather than as the simple, expendable cipher described by Marceline. It was just as well Lisette Perrault wasn't there. Heaven only knew what she might have done had she spotted Alice stalking her.

Alice had left Evangeline and Marceline in Jackson Square, Evangeline kneeling before the child-crone, grasping her small hands and explaining to her that they weren't going to allow any harm to come to Lisette Perrault in much the same tone Daniel might have used to explain why a young Alice couldn't have ice cream for breakfast. Evangeline's admonition had fallen on deaf ears. Marceline had ignored her niece, looking over Evangeline's shoulder to regard Alice with a questioning gaze.

A life for a life. That was the deal Fleur had made to save Lucy, and it was the same proposal the infernal creature was now offering her. A vague, perhaps paranoid suspicion began to gnaw at the edges of Alice's mind. Could Fleur have been influenced to resurrect Lucy for this very purpose? So that Alice might one day be given a sense of precedence?

Lisette Perrault was a stranger to Alice, but Luc was family. Alice felt sure that to Marceline the trade would seem irresistible. To have Luc returned to them, flesh and blood and spirit, at the low cost of the erasure of a woman to whom Alice owed no loyalty.

Alice had to hand it to Marceline. In many ways her plan approached perfection.

The witch had either been bestowed her current form as a power-less, pitiable child, perhaps as a joke or punishment, or burned through the last of her power to assume it. Her sisters were gone, reduced to ash. She was alone and helpless. In her present state only a heart carved from stone could resist feeling at least a modicum of sympathy for her. Looking into the waif's eyes, it was almost possible to forget that Marceline and her sisters had conspired with Celestin to sacrifice a good portion of the region's witches. Almost.

But Marceline was trying too hard to win Alice to her cause, with her composite message of "You're special. You're powerful. You have been chosen." The subtext being that Alice could do as she wished without guilt or fear of recrimination. Marceline had lost all, but Alice could rebuild her family, rebuild her life.

All it would take was murdering the woman who'd defeated Celestin.

The woman who'd prevented Marceline and her sisters from collecting their due.

Alice laughed, her laughter causing the spirit faces to spark briefly to life.

Marceline had an agenda, no doubt about that.

Only Alice wouldn't play her game. She wouldn't bring Luc back.

For years, Alice had wondered what Luc would have become, considered who he might have been to her, if he hadn't been murdered. Her heart had tried to whitewash his character, to smooth away his sharp edges by lingering on the outings to City Park and the zoo, but Luc the big brother was only a sliver of a more complicated man.

Luc had been no innocent. He'd allowed himself to get caught up in Celestin's scheme to humiliate and kill Nicholas, related in equal measure to Celestin's search for the damnable *The Book of the Unwinding* and to his hunger for revenge against Nicholas for having wrested control of the Chanticleers from him.

Luc had hungered for power and been willing to kill to get it. He'd wanted to be in control at all costs.

He would have sacrificed her and Evangeline to be King, no question.

He was just like Nicholas, and like Celestin, too.

After all, blood will tell.

TWENTY-FIVE

"Cette putaine, Madame John," Marceline said, gazing up at the ceramic *Calle del Maine* placard affixed to the drab olive and cream two-story structure known as Madame John's Legacy, one of the few remaining examples of Louisiana Creole architecture in the Quarter. The old witch had insisted on coming here after they parted ways with Alice—or rather after Alice parted ways with them. *"Elle n'avait jamais existé de vrai."* Evangeline didn't respond, prompting, it seemed, Marceline to assume she hadn't understood.

"She never existed. Madame John. They got the name from a story." Marceline placed her palm flat against the lower floor's cream-colored masonry wall. "I used to know the name of the owner, the man who had these old walls built. But now it's forgotten. Poof. Like so many other tidbits I've lost over the centuries. I do remember another house stood on this spot when my sisters and I first arrived here. The owner of the earlier house was a Francois Marin." She gave Evangeline a sly smile. "A relative?" she said with a shrug. "I won't avow one way or the other, but I will point out a portion of the original Marin house is said to have been incorporated into a second structure that was later built on this same spot. That interim building was almost completely destroyed by the great fire of 1788, but the remaining portion of it was, in turn, incorporated into the current structure—and this house survived the great fire of 1794 unscathed. It's almost as if a residual magic remained to protect the house. Or at least the part of it that was once owned by *a* Marin.

"It was kind of you to take me in," Marceline said, changing the subject abruptly and without taking her eyes off the house. "I, a person you've long feared and despised. It was kind of you to feed me and give me shelter."

"It was nothing," Evangeline said, though in fact it had taken a great effort to divorce the murderous witch from the needy child.

"A nothing for which I once sold my soul. You are," she said, looking back, "a kind woman. I'm sorry you're kind. It will make what is to come harder for you."

"We aren't going to harm Lisette Perrault."

"You reject action. You will watch many others die because of your inaction. Either way, blood will be on your hands. But you do have a choice as to how much."

Evangeline wanted to change the topic, and she jumped to the first question that came to mind. "Why did you want to come here?"

"In truth," Marceline said, turning her attention back to Madame John's Legacy, "it was partly nostalgia. Visiting the square has left me feeling sentimental."

"Yeah, public executions and pralines. Good times. Why else?"

"I wanted to make a point." She went up on tiptoe and touched the plaque. "This house is old, ancient by the standards of this country. But before this house, there was another house here, one that stood for decades before my sisters and I arrived on these shores."

"Yes?"

"You've long believed us to be the instigators of this little drama, the 'first cause' of your unhappiness, but there were forces at work long before we left Europe. My sisters and I were mere links in a chain forged long ago, before we stumbled on frostbitten feet through frozen pines into a darkened vale, perhaps even before this 'vale of tears'"—she raised a hand and gestured widely around the scene—"was fished out of the abyss."

"Poetic, but that doesn't absolve you of your sins."

"I'm not seeking absolution." She looked up at Evangeline, a crone's resolution showing through a child's eyes. "At least not for myself. I only want to help ease your conscience when the time comes."

"I'm not going—"

"*Oui, je sais, je sais,*" Marceline said. "You won't lay a finger on *la voudouienne.* I'm not speaking of *La Perrault*'s demise. I'm speaking of the future, and how one day you might look back and wonder if you should have done more. More to save me. More to save yourself." She reached out her hand. "I know you brought it. Show it to me."

There was no reason for Evangeline to pretend she didn't know what her aunt was referring to. She slipped her finger into the too-small pocket of her jeans and pulled out the chain her mother had forged. She held it up, contemplating its ugly medallion, engraved with markings that resembled bird tracks in sandy soil, and the open clasp that might as well be the fangs of a venomous snake. Evangeline held it out to Marceline, but she did not accept it. Instead, she took a step back.

Evangeline felt an energy begin to pulse through her skin, and the necklace changed once again into the exquisite collection of emeralds and diamonds.

"Polarities of the same energy," Marceline said again.

"What is special about these stones?"

"The diamonds are crystallized power. Why the emeralds are special is a bit more complicated. It begins with Thoth."

"Thoth, the Egyptian god?"

"Yes, Thoth was a big shot. He was thought to have devised the calculations necessary to build the universe, and every science and art required for the creation of civilization. He was the god of writing, the creator of the sacred symbols that eventually developed into our modern alphabets. 'In the beginning was the word,' after all. The occultists hold he created twelve tablets, but—"

"Wait, let me guess. There are really only seven."

Marceline nodded. "Each tablet not only records one of the seven principles of magic, but embodies that principle.

"All is mind.

"All is vibrational energy.

"There is no duality, only polarity.

"Between each polarity, a rhythm measures movement.

"In all matters, cause and effect are joined; coincidence does not exist.

"The essential force manifests its polarities as gender; feminine and masculine are in all.

"As above so below.

"Each of these seven principles is inscribed above its corresponding gate, engraved, if you will, above its proper 'wound.' The seven tablets are made of emerald. For centuries occultists, alchemists, kabbalists, and magicians have devoted their entire lives to the search for the emerald tablets of Thoth. You hold those tablets in your hand now. They are the emeralds in that very necklace."

"I'm sorry. I know at this point it must seem like I'm being obstinate, but I'm having a really hard time believing they were created by an ancient Egyptian god."

Marceline shrugged. "Some claim Thoth wasn't a god, that he was a man."

"That sounds a bit more—"

"A man who escaped the destruction of Atlantis—"

"Wait—"

"—and death to become a god," she finished, then looked at Evangeline with an incredulity that likely matched her own. "With all you have experienced, is the thought of this Thoth personage achieving immortality, and perhaps even divinity, so much to swallow? After all, this is exactly what the Dark Man is offering you—fall as a witch, rise as a god."

"Thanks, but no thanks."

"You came into the world for this very moment. You may think you understand what motivates you and others, but I can assure you there has always been a guiding hand. Even this necklace." She pointed at it. "The massacre the night of Celestin's ball. Celestin put his scheme into play, believing himself to be its master, but the massacre had a hidden purpose—to create enough energy to reunite the two polarities of the necklace in the common world."

"If I hadn't asked you for the necklace . . ."

"The Dark Man would have found another way, another unwitting accomplice."

"This hidden agenda. What is it?"

Marceline laughed. "I can't speak to what is in the Dark Man's heart. It would be like a thought trying to describe the mind that holds it. He isn't of this world, but this world is of Him. I play my role as given me, and you must do the same."

"My Queen, my whore," Reverend Bill's voice called out from the end of the block.

"Oh, no," Evangeline said to herself. She pointed at him and called back, "Now is not the time, Bill."

But still the old man wove and wobbled along the sidewalk, coming closer.

Marceline continued as if a drunk weren't tottering along toward them. "You must accept your role as Queen, *ma chère*. You must willingly put on the necklace Mireille's husband once forced on you." The corner of her mouth curled up. "For it is written."

"Written by whom?"

"Theodosius, of course. It was he who created the gospel."

"You mean *The Book of the Unwinding*?"

"They are one, of course, Theodosius and the Dark Man," Marceline continued as if she hadn't heard Evangeline's question. "The mad monk was how the Dark Man chose to incarnate Himself in the common world. Once. He has come many times."

Marceline lowered her head as Reverend Bill drew near. "You recognized Him, once. The night of the massacre, when I helped trigger your first transformation. You sought Him out. You flew to His side."

The old man in the dirty coat knelt before them, his shiny pate surrounded by a fringe of white hair like a monk's tonsure. "My Queen. My whore." He paused, looking up at her with wild eyes that had peered into the sea of absolute, unbounded potentiality that lay beyond this reality. A flash of repressed memory flared up within her. As Celestin's ball descended into absolute chaos, she had caught hold of Hugo and carried him to safety, but then she'd carried on, rising up into the night sky, circling, drifting, then finally dropping down to alight at Bill's side. The old, drunken street preacher had placed a gentle hand on her head. It had been his touch that changed her back to human form. "My daughter."

"Your mother married to save herself from the Dark Man. But the man your mother married didn't sire you. Your mother already carried the Dark Man's seed in her. You can be the greatest Queen, *ma chère*, because you are His."

She crossed to Bill and placed a hand on his shoulder. "You must not trust your lover, this Boudreau fellow. He came to you that night at the old amusement park for a purpose that had nothing to do with love. All of the Boudreaus are executioners. Had you chosen that night to claim the power that is rightfully yours, to accept your role as Queen, he would have murdered you . . . or died trying."

"I don't believe you."

Marceline gave a small shrug. "I never expected you to. Go ahead, then. Ask the man yourself." The air around the two roiled, and Marceline and Reverend Bill, her aunt and her father, disappeared, folding back in on themselves until they were gone.

TWENTY-SIX

Lisette and Manon arrived at the baby's room in the neonatal unit to find a doctor and two nurses leaning over the incubator. For a single horrifying moment Lisette was certain Joy had slipped away from them, but then the black-eyed nurse caught sight of the two of them standing in the doorway.

The nurse—Lisette had learned her name was Gabby—straightened and turned to face them. "Getting stronger every minute, this little one of ours."

Lisette felt her heart begin to beat again, and she released the breath she hadn't realized she had been holding. The doctor, a young woman who didn't look any older than Manon, turned back. "Hope you don't mind," she said. "We were admiring your granddaughter. She's such a little doll."

Lisette realized she was already halfway toward becoming one of those grandmothers who found every topic other than how perfect their grandchild is a complete bore, and she didn't give a damn. "I must agree with you there," she said, her arm tight around Manon's shoulders, then remembered to add, "thank you." She craned her neck to see the incubator better. "May we . . . ?"

"Of course," the doctor said, stepping back to clear the way for the mother and grandmother.

Manon slipped free of Lisette's embrace and went in first. Lisette waited, watching on as Manon approached the incubator and leaned over it, beaming down at her daughter. "Good morning, sweet girl. Mama's here. Mama loves you."

Lisette hadn't been able to peel the smile off her face since last night. If anything, it had stretched even wider this morning. She stepped into the room and drew near to the incubator, gazing down, ready to get her first peek of the day at her beautiful Joy.

"I don't understand," she said, terrified and furious at once. "Is this some kind of joke?"

"Is everything all right, Mrs. Perrault?" the doctor asked.

Manon turned back to look at her, confused. "You okay, Mama?"

Lisette stepped up beside her daughter to get a better look at the baby, sure her tired eyes had played a trick on her. But there was no baby in the incubator. What was there was a rubber doll, like one she'd spotted earlier beneath the giving tree in the hospital's lobby.

Lisette looked up from the doll to Manon, then to the doctor, then to Gabby. They all were regarding her with concerned expressions. None of them realized the thing in there wasn't alive, it wasn't a real baby at all.

Gabby moved quickly, stepping around to put her arm around Lisette, already maneuvering her to the padded bench even as she said, "Perhaps you should sit down."

"She had a stroke not long ago," Manon said, panic dawning in her voice.

"When?" the doctor said, pulling a pen flashlight from her pocket and squatting before Lisette to shine it in her eyes.

"October."

"I'm fine," Lisette said, trying to rise. "The baby—"

"You stay calm, Mrs. Perrault," the doctor said, reaching up to rest a hand on Lisette's shoulder to encourage her to sit still.

The second nurse drew closer, looking at her over the doctor's shoulder. Lisette's eyes were drawn first to the pastel-yellow blanket the nurse clutched to her chest, then up to the monstrous gleam in her eyes. The strawberry blonde witch from the world of the cold fire now stood in the common world. She held the bundle she'd been clutching out and turned it around so Lisette could see one tiny hand poking through the blanket.

"Tonight," she said, though no one else reacted to her. It dawned upon Lisette no one else was even aware of the witch's presence. "Midnight." She bent her head and kissed Joy's fingers, then looked back to Lisette as she licked her lips. "You know where." The witch's laugh started as a low chuckle and ended as a mad, screeching cackle. In the next instant, she and the baby were gone.

TWENTY-SEVEN

The longest night had come, and a shadeless floor lamp's unfiltered glare combated the darkness beyond the row of graceful bow windows opposite her, polishing their rounded panes into mildly concave mirrors. Fleur had removed the shade herself and dragged the lamp closer to the mannequin she'd used to drape Lucy's dress.

Fleur hadn't a single clue how she'd come to be kneeling on the floor of the oval room. She must have passed out, perhaps from low blood sugar. No wonder—she hadn't slept the night before, and the only thing she'd consumed was a café au lait for breakfast. She glanced at the clock on the mantel to check the time, its swinging pendulum nearly hypnotic in her hazy state. She should grab a quick bite and some coffee, but first she needed to shower and decide what to wear to the procession. Fleur had put so much energy into finishing the dress for her daughter, she hadn't given her own outfit a single thought.

I did finish the dress, didn't I?

She pushed herself up to her feet and started toward the windows, slowing as she approached a shadow stretched out along the floor. It was the toppled mannequin. Fleur gazed into the reflection in the window.

Fleur blinked, then craned her neck. She could see the room behind her, the shadeless lamp and a gilt frame on the wall, but the spot where she should appear in the reflection remained blank. She wasn't in it. Only when she moved to step over the mannequin did she realize it wasn't the mannequin. It was her own body.

Fleur's mouth gaped as she studied her form, lying supine before her, her limbs gracelessly akimbo, her head turned to the side so Fleur viewed it in profile. Her head rested in an asymmetrical pool of blood that conjured the image of the French Marianne and her scarlet liberty cap.

Her face was nearly unrecognizable—swollen, bruised black. She looked away, horrified, confused. Her gaze fell to the globe-shaped paperweight, and she remembered.

Lucy. Her Lucy. Kneeling over her. Intent on crushing her skull. Fleur spun around, her horrified eyes scanning the room for her daughter, but Fleur was alone . . . alone with herself.

She wanted to scream, but didn't, not because she was afraid Lucy might hear her, but because she feared she might not hear herself. A wave of desperation washed over her, its undertow grasping at her, preparing to pull her under. It would be easier to give in than to fight. Certainly no one could blame her.

But she was Fleur frigging Marin.

She forced herself to calm, to begin to take inventory of the situation and find a rational path out of the madness. The first horrible step was to determine if the body before her was dead.

It helped this was far from Fleur's first out-of-body experience. She had once been adept at astral projection, capable not only of projecting her awareness, but of interacting with the physical world as if she were in corporeal form.

She felt sorry for the woman before her. Though she couldn't remember the attack, it must have been agonizing . . . She surveyed the trauma to her temple from that first blow. Perhaps the second, too.

She hoped she'd been knocked unconscious by that second strike, as it appeared several others had followed.

She knelt beside the body. So still. She had to face the facts—too much damage had been done. Fleur bowed to the inescapability of death and began calculating a different next move, one that would prevent the thing that had once been her precious daughter from harming anyone else.

She cast her mind back, trying to pinpoint the moment her Lucy, the true Lucy, had been taken over by the thing in her now. Fleur would have felt it, wouldn't she, if the change had occurred all at once? It must have been gradual—Lucy's spark slipping away a bit more at a time, a shadow moving in, little by little, to take her place.

She should have sensed it anyway.

A slight movement, perhaps a shallow breath. Had she imagined it? She reached out with a quivering hand to touch the body's neck, to seek out a pulse. She gasped. There was a pulse, so thready she feared the pressure of her own touch might cause it to fail, but all the same, it was there.

To survive, Fleur's consciousness would have to return to her body. That was simple under most circumstances—the body and psyche longed for each other. It should only take a tiny push. But in her current state, the homecoming would be a risky and, Fleur was sure, agonizing proposition. The shock to her physical system might end her before she could even complete the journey.

If she could muster the power to heal the body, even slightly, it would improve her chances. But she no longer felt as if her magic were fading. It felt instead as if it had been snapped off like a branch from a tree. Fleur grasped a hard truth; Lucy had not only brutalized her, she had laid claim to her power. A difficult task, even if she'd killed Fleur outright. Her daughter's occult knowledge was at best cursory. She couldn't have garnered this degree of arcane knowledge, let alone descended to the level of depravity it would have taken to use it.

Fleur perceived movement to her side, and she spun in time to witness one of the fabric bolts she'd propped against the entrance to the hidden passageway wobble and fall with a muffled thump.

Of course. *All that's left is the forgetting.*

Thoughts of Hugo's sigil had been floating through her mind from the first stroke of his brush to the moment she'd fallen unconscious, but she wasn't the one who needed to forget it for the magic to work. If she knew her nephew, and she felt she did, he was already intoxicated, weaving his way through the Quarter to Crescent Park to meet the other revelers for the Longest Night procession. His spell would be far from his conscious thoughts.

She cast a cautious glance at the door that opened onto the main hall. It stood ajar, open about halfway. Fleur crossed to the opening, shielded herself behind the door, and paused to listen. Above, she heard footsteps, soft clack-clack-clacks of Lucy walking in flats across an uncarpeted stretch of the hall. The movement directly overhead surprised Fleur. Lucy's room was at the opposite end of the house. The room above had belonged to Celestin.

Fleur darted past the opening, only then wondering if Lucy would even be capable of seeing her in her disembodied state. Even if she couldn't "see" Fleur, there remained a strong chance she could still sense her presence and realize she hadn't as yet finished the job.

She moved with caution to the wall panel that could be pivoted on a center hinge to reveal the house's hidden passage. Nine bolts of fabric remained propped against the panel. With a bit of concentration, Fleur could ease them, one by one, to the floor. Lucy hadn't seemed to take notice of the noise from the bolt that had fallen, but nine more thumps, muffled or not, might be enough to draw her downstairs.

Fleur lay a hand on the nearest bolt. To her surprise, it shifted easily, almost as if an unseen force were helping with the effort. In no more than a minute, she had slid all of them to the floor.

She willed the door to ease open, and light from the lamp rushed into the hidden room, piercing the darkness and setting fire to the comic sparkle of Hugo's sigil, its glint having nothing to do with magic. She focused the entirety of her will on the symbol, commanding it to do what it had been designed to do, pass the bulk of Hugo's power to Fleur.

She waited, she willed, but nothing happened. No fiery rush, no quiet whisper. From beyond the painted sigil, at the far end of the passage beside the panel that opened into Celestin's former study, she could sense her father's dark, delighted amusement in her failure.

Ma belle bécasse. The thought reverberated down the passage, the length of the hidden room acting like the strike on a matchbox, causing the gibe to spark and ignite Fleur's long-suppressed rage.

Her anger focused her. She would no longer wait for power to come to her; she would reach out and claim it. She entered the shadowy room and approached the sigil. Pressing her palms against the symbol, she curled her fingers, piercing both lathe and plaster to pull the sigil itself, integral, from the wall.

Another Fleur would have taken a moment to cast a self-satisfied glance at her father's no-longer-gloating face, but this Fleur no longer gave a damn what the old man thought. Instead, she focused on the sigil, watching as it squirmed to life and began unwinding itself, revealing its essence to her. Thought by thought, letter by letter, it shared a story—Hugo's story—with her. The letters followed one after the other, each catching the tail of the one before it, melding into a fiery cursive strand. The strand wound up her right arm, over her shoulder, and rose up like a serpent to dive at her forehead and pierce her third eye.

The power yanked her from the passage and slammed her without ceremony back into her physical body. She sat up with a jerk, pulling in a raspy, burning breath of air. She flung her hand to her forehead, stopping before touching the wound gingerly. She placed her index finger against her temple. There was no pain.

She turned her legs to the side, then shifted up onto her hands and knees. She stood, her legs at first wobbly, but they regained strength with each step she made toward the flawed antique mirror over the fireplace. She still looked a mess, her face sticky with her own blood. Bruises remained, but they were light, superficial. She had healed herself.

The grievous injuries were gone, but so was Hugo's magic. It had taken the rest of his power to mend her.

An old-fashioned tune, one Fleur felt she should recognize, drifted down from above. Lucy was humming—no, singing wordlessly, loudly—as she moved back and forth down the hall, soft carpeted thuds alternating with clacking as she stepped from rug to wood and back again. The pacing stopped, and Lucy cried out, her voice wild and filled with fury. The cry was punctuated by the sound of shattering glass. Something heavy crashed to the floor above. The chandelier swayed.

The house fell silent, and the singing began again.

Soon, the tune was punctuated by a creaking on the stairs. Animal instinct kicked in, and Fleur grasped the fireplace poker, her grip tight enough to whiten her knuckles. She slid away from the fireplace over to the door, positioning herself behind it and peering through the crack into the hall.

A sense of déjà vu came over Fleur. She flashed back to a long-ago game of hide-and-seek, although it had been her tiny Lucy hiding behind the door and Fleur herself descending the stairs, passing by the ajar door, pretending she didn't know her daughter stood behind it even though Lucy couldn't stop giggling. Fleur placed her left palm against the door and eased it forward until she heard the soft click of the latch.

She froze and waited, grateful for her raspy breath even though it seemed to thunder through the house. The tread on the stairs stopped, and Fleur's heart nearly did, too. She rushed to the windows, cursing the man who'd designed the lady's parlor so its curved windows opened not onto the exterior world but onto an interior courtyard. Still, she could attempt to take cover in the overgrown greenery. Perhaps the reflection in the windows would turn Lucy's mind away from the space. She lay the poker at her feet and grabbed the sash of the nearest window, trying to force it open.

The window wouldn't budge. Nor would either of its companions. Perhaps the two centuries of paint or humidity anchored them in place, or maybe the jam was related to the cracks in the house's foundation. Either way, they offered her no escape. Rather they contained her even as they put her on display.

Fleur reached down to retrieve the poker, then rose and turned slowly, suddenly aware of footsteps passing by the door. Panic gave her heart a jolt. Her gaze darted around before landing on the game table she'd been using as a workstation. There, poking out from beneath a large swatch of porcelain-blue upholstery fabric, sat her phone. She raced toward the table and snatched the cell up. If she could only reach Nicholas, he'd be able to do something. She tapped her finger on the screen, but it didn't wake. The screen remained black, reflecting her own desperate expression back to her like an onyx mirror. The phone was worthless as anything more than a weak projectile she could launch as a last resort.

Fleur heard the loud pop of a champagne bottle.

The old melody started up again. This time it was a recording being played in the main salon. The music came from her parents' old console stereo, so outdated it had shamed her when she was a teenager, so outdated now it would be hipster chic.

Outdated. A flash—the image of the old landline phone that still sat on Celestin's desk. She'd considered having it turned off—it only ever rang when a caller misdialed or the number came up on some telemarketer's list—but she'd never gotten around to it.

Lucy began singing along, this time picking up on the lyrics, joining in on some words, singing "la, la, la" to cover for those she didn't seem to know . . . or remember. It would be too risky to creep along the hall, of course, but there was no need. She could use the hidden passage to reach it.

She imagined what she must look like—covered in blood, fireplace poker in hand, creeping along with exaggerated, almost cartoonish steps. The image didn't stop her. She slipped into the passage, then eased the panel closed behind her. Each side of the panel bore a rustic iron slide-lock at the bottom. As far as Fleur knew, they'd never been shot even once in her lifetime; perhaps they never had been. Still, they turned easily in their mounts and dropped down into the sockets in the floor. Foolish, perhaps, to even bother, but the locks might buy her a few more precious seconds than it took to set them.

She averted her eyes as she pushed past the relic and eased the panel on the other end of the passage open. She stepped into Celestin's darkened study.

"You always were resilient," Lucy said, saluting her with a raised champagne flute. Her daughter stood before her, dressed in the gown Fleur had been working on.

Fleur flung herself backward, stumbling into the passage and knocking over the pedestal that held Celestin's head. Fleur heard the awful thump as it hit the floor. She jumped forward and shot the bolts to lock this panel, too.

She found herself lost in utter darkness, certain her eyes would never adjust, until she noticed a thin line of light surrounding the panel on the other end of the passage. The dimmest glow illuminated Celestin's head, his face turned toward it.

A sound like a battering ram slammed into the opposite panel. Fleur scrambled backward and lunged at the other wall, tugging on the bent handle of the iron bolt she herself had shot, now cursing herself for having done so. Another explosive boom. The wall before her shook. She pushed away and began dragging herself with the heels of her sweating, slick palms.

Her hand landed on Celestin's head. Fleur could sense the spark of magic it still held, and rather than push it away in repulsion, she caught hold of it by its gray mane. A pale, citron-yellow luminescence shone through his eyes, though both the light and the magic it betrayed were rapidly dimming.

Another thud, then another, one from each side of the passage. The message was clear. Fleur was trapped. Terror bound her to the center of the passage; she was unable to bring herself to move even an inch in either direction. She found herself thinking of a butterfly fluttering its wings for the final time as a pin fixed it to a board.

The thudding stopped even as Fleur's ears began to throb. The air in the passage grew thick, damp, its scent muddy like the Mississippi. Her lungs began to burn.

"Always so resilient. Always so clever." Lucy's voice swam to her, though the atmosphere changed it. The timbre seemed deeper, her enunciation more polished. A moment of silence, then the voice came from the oval salon. "You could always find a way to skirt any rule." The voice was Lucy's, but the condescending reminiscence was not.

Her mother had at last found a way to haunt her.

"It's taken quite some time, *ma puce*, but I've managed to evict your little urchin from her shell." *Ma puce*—my flea. Fleur had always despised that endearment, but no matter how vehemently she'd protested, her mother had insisted on using it. "*Au fur et à mesure.* Little by little, as she weakened, I strengthened my hold. It was her father's thoughtful flowers that finally broke her, by the way. I can't wait to thank dear Warren in person."

For a while Fleur heard only the sound of pacing, then of nails being drawn down the false wall that opened into the passageway. "You figured it out, didn't you?" Fleur heard her mother's cool thought spoken in Lucy's voice. "You realized the sigils preventing the use of magic on Sinclair only worked on a witch who was physically present. But you never did need to be physically present to work your mischief, did you?"

She was right. Fleur *had* figured out how to circumvent the charms—one Christmas Eve, back when she was still in college. The discovery had been innocent enough, prompted by remorse, not ill-will. She turned twenty-one only a few weeks before returning home for winter break, and she and Vincent had planned to go out barhopping. Instead, they'd stayed home, together, alone, and baked sugar cookies. They worked hard, the two of them, to conjure up happy memories of Christmases past, resurrecting only a few, but enough to make Fleur sentimental, foolishly so.

That night, shortly after midnight, as she lay awake in her childhood room, still decorated in ridiculous pink-princess style, she'd begun to feel guilty, thinking of her mother, locked up in an asylum on Sinclair Isle, the very institution where Nicholas would later confine Alice. Nicholas had accompanied Celestin to the island to ensure their mother was properly seen to. "Seen to." Those had been Nicholas's exact words as he explained the setup to her. Magic was made inaccessible to the patients through wards linked to occult symbols. Sigils decorated various points in the halls and rooms, from the walls and ceilings to patterns on the floor. Some patients, the madder and more powerful ones who would never leave the island, wore personalized sigils tattooed on their skin.

Had Fleur visited the island in the flesh, she would have been unable to use her magic there. But warm and safe and filled with . . . not nostalgia, exactly, but a longing for what could have been, she'd allowed herself to drift, and in the next instant she stood looking down on her mother.

She occupied a private room—Celestin's pride wouldn't have allowed anything less. There was just enough light for Fleur to see they had tethered her mother to the bed with tight five-point restraints and covered every inch of her flesh in ancient symbols and contemporary sigils.

Her mother lay there murmuring, eyes closed. Fleur leaned forward to listen, trying to make out her mother's words. The once formidable Laure Marin raged on in whispers, half pleading, half cursing, trying to summon enough magic to break free of the mad dream into which her own misdeeds had plunged her. Suddenly her eyes popped open and fixed on Fleur, startling her. Fleur stumbled back and bumped into a small metal side table. It made a loud clang as it fell on its side. Without thinking, she righted it and slipped away, the sound of her mother's tortured screams ringing in her ears as she slammed back into her body two thousand miles away.

Fleur had never spoken of her misadventure, not to Vincent or Nicholas, and certainly not to Celestin. And she had never again attempted to project herself into the institution that held her mother. Until, that was, she'd needed a sacrifice. A witch's life in exchange for restarting the heart of her own unborn child. It had seemed almost a mercy to will the bedsheet to snake around her mother's neck, to will it to wind tighter and tighter, until her mother's eyes began to bulge and the face beneath the intricate and sometimes overlapping sigils turned purple.

"This is how it felt, *ma puce*." The voice that was and at the same time was not Lucy's pulled Fleur back to the present. The space around her seemed to be shrinking and filling at the same time, the walls coming in closer even as the air took on the viscosity of water. "This is how it felt, when you murdered me."

The panel that opened onto Celestin's study began to rattle, then the iron locks that held it in place groaned and snapped. The panel wrenched free of its casing to the cry of twisting lath and crumbling plaster.

"The last face I saw as I died was my daughter's"—Laure Marin looked at her through her Lucy's eyes—"and the last face you see will be that of yours. This time I'll make sure of it."

"It may be Lucy's face," Fleur said, "but it isn't her. Unlike you, you wretched bitch, my daughter loved me."

Lucy's lovely features twisted with a searing rage, and she lunged forward, determined, it seemed, to tear Fleur limb from limb with bare hands.

Fleur raised Celestin's head and, calling on every atom of love she had for her own beloved daughter whose form this demon had defiled, every shred of her animal desire to survive, and every miserable jot of anger she still carried in her breast for the monster before her, she let loose the last scintilla of the relic's magic and sent Laure Marin's spirit shrieking straight back to the hell where it belonged.

TWENTY-EIGHT

Lisette couldn't have walked farther than a hundred feet from the Perrault Landscaping pickup she'd left behind at the weed-choked entry of Grunch Road. Still she had entered another world—a world that had killed her once before.

One moment she was walking along within earshot of the semis passing by on Highway 10, the glow of the city in the western sky. The next she was crossing a narrow land bridge that disappeared behind her as she walked, an inky black sea pushing her forward, washing away any possibility of return.

Pairs of watching, incandescent ruby lights bobbed up and down within that sea. The cold, dim light of their eyes reached out through the line of sickly cypress trees, incandescent enough to reveal the swishing movement of long tails as they moved through the blackness.

A reedy whine and a beating drum that seemed to determine the rate of her own pulse filtered into her awareness. They were the only sounds. Even the black sea held its silence, the reptilian slithering of ruby-eyed demons—for that was what they were; Lisette was beyond trying to kid herself—noiseless. It wasn't a true sea, of course—it had nothing to do with water. It was a living entity, capable of reaching out across worlds, staining the one and changing it into the other.

Acrid smoke, with its familiar, repugnant scent of burning flesh, rose up around her. The last time she was brought here, she'd carried the stench of this place back with her to the common world. Her doctor had called it "phantosmia," an olfactory hallucination related to her stroke. Her doctor had been wrong.

A shrill drone reached out from beyond the trees like tendrils. As if her hearing could sense cold, the sound touched her, stroked her cheek, pressed against her pulse, slid over her breast and down her thigh. The spirit who reigned over this hell had tasted her before, but then she had held little interest for it. Now, she could sense it savoring her.

The sound of the drum seemed to shatter, the single throbbing heartbeat breaking into the thundering of thousands, their cadences spinning off in a pattern Lisette Perrault felt she should recognize—one, two, three, five, eight, thirteen, building, building—though to her ears it was a disjointed cacophony.

At the tree line sat the source of the keening, a gargantuan infant with bluish, almost moon-colored skin, sitting cross-legged, swaying. It had no eyes; the skin where eyelids should have been ran unbroken. It didn't so much play the stone flute it held as breathe through it.

She passed through the curtain of cypresses to find neither drums nor drummers. Still, Lisette noticed movement farther on, in the center of the clearing. Pale creatures who might once have been human followed one after another, hand in hand, writhing like a single serpent as they spiraled in toward the source of the beating—a dark fire Lisette had only caught glimpses of before. Now she could see it all, a sentient void so resplendent, so complete it stirred a yearning in her heart. It was absolute finality, and beyond it lay peace. Beyond it lay perfect light. Lisette felt a gravity willing her forward, willing her to join the dance.

A waiflike girl, her blonde hair almost silver in the unwholesome half glow, approached her, reaching up. "Don't fear the darkness," she said, clasping hold of Lisette's hand. The spell was broken, and Lisette trembled at the power of the dark light's seduction. "Don't fear the light." She tugged Lisette down and whispered in her ear. "The terror lies in its perfection."

Lisette leaned back to study the child. "I know you. I recognize you." It was impossible, though that particular word no longer stood for much. This sickly little girl was one of the trio of weird sisters who'd invaded her shop, the ones who had sought to murder her.

The girl shook her head slowly. "You may know me for what I was, but I no longer recognize myself."

Even knowing what this broken child had done in a different form, Lisette almost felt the stirring of compassion. In almost any other circumstance, she might have even felt a spark of sympathy for the witch. In this circumstance, that didn't have a single chance in hell of happening. "Where is my granddaughter? What have you done to my granddaughter?"

"They won't hurt your baby," the false child said, "not if you offer yourself up willingly to Him."

Lisette didn't need to ask who "they" were, for she knew who "He" was. He was the dark fire, the legion that was also one. "Why should I believe you?"

"The Master Himself told me so."

"Why should you believe Him?" The girl startled as if only then realizing she might have been played the fool. Her wary expression told Lisette it wouldn't be the first time.

A shrieking laughter pealed down from the sky.

Lisette wrenched her head up to see a nude female figure circling overhead, then spiraling down, counterclockwise, each turn in her descent revealing another aspect of the witch—a wailing banshee announcing death, a screeching harpy guarding the underworld, the strawberry blonde horror who had taken her grandchild.

The creature landed and turned, advancing on Lisette and the girl, her arms folded over her breasts, her head jerking alternately left and right with each step. The witch continued until she stood perhaps only ten or fifteen feet away. She stopped and offered Lisette a glimpse of a blanket, then slowly slid her arms open to reveal the back of the baby's head. Lisette lunged forward, her arms already outstretched to take the child.

As Lisette dove at her, the witch hissed and slid backward, clutching the child with her left hand and flinging up the right, its fingers contorted to the point they resembled talons. Lisette's thwarted momentum drove her to her knees. "Is she alive?" Lisette cried out, pleading—not caring she was pleading. She would plead. She would beg. She would do whatever it took to save Joy.

"Show her," commanded a voice that sounded like branches scraping against each other in a winter storm. A figure she recognized from an earlier living nightmare floated up behind the witch. Impossibly tall, razor-thin, razor-clawed, with a face she could never forget, the animated porcelain mask of Babau Jean.

"Celestin?" Lisette said, provoking a gale of laughter from the witch.

"Not Celestin, my pet," the witch shrieked. "Same vehicle, different driver." Babau Jean pressed a sharp fingernail against the witch's throat, and she blanched, falling instantly silent. "I told you to show it to her."

The witch took the tiny infant in both hands and turned her around. Joy's face was passive, still, tinged blue by the hellish light of this place. Lisette watched, unable to breathe until she noticed the tiniest twitch of a finger in the baby's upheld fist.

Relief nearly made her go limp.

"Satisfied?" the witch hissed, then turned Joy around, once again clutching the painfully small girl to her bare breasts.

"What," Lisette addressed Babau Jean, "do you want from me?"

"I want nothing." The creature pointed the same sharp nail it had used to threaten the witch at the pillar of dark fire burning at the center of the nightmare field. "But He . . . He wants all."

"You must make a pact with him," the little girl spoke up, "to offer what He wants in exchange for what you desire. Be careful," she cautioned, "be clear, be explicit in your demands."

Babau Jean lunged at the girl, one razor-sharp nail slicing into the child's skin from her temple to her chin. The girl fell back, placing her hand on her cheek. She didn't cry out. She didn't cry.

"You promise . . ." Lisette Perrault's eyes turned to focus on the dark fire. "*He* promises my granddaughter won't be harmed? That she'll be returned safely to her mother?" Babau Jean's hollow black eyes turned to the entity in the dim icy fire—no, the entity that *was* the fire. The two seemed to be communing in silence.

Babau Jean faced Lisette. "You have His word, and mine."

"What does he want?"

"The Gates of Guinee. The gates. He wants to open them."

"But how?"

In a blink, Babau Jean was on her. He snatched up her left arm. "This is how. You've accepted the gates into yourself." He gazed down at the gad, then leaned forward and pressed his cold, smooth lips to it. Lisette shuddered from his touch, sickened by the intimacy of his kiss. "But you have a choice. You can die here, tonight, or . . ." He released her arm and stepped back, looking once more at the pillar of dark fire. "You can do as He wishes."

Before Lisette had heard nothing as Babau Jean communicated with the fire. Now she could hear them whispering, and though the words were unintelligible, they still conjured furtive images in her mind. Flash followed brief flash, until the pieces seemed to sew themselves together into a full vision. She witnessed herself dressed in robes of scarlet and sapphire, a shining diadem of emeralds and diamonds on her brow, standing before a great and glorious light, aware she was the conduit through which all light must pass. She was . . . a goddess.

"Yes," the winter-wind voice of Babau Jean hissed. "This is what He wants for you. He wants you to become the guardian of the gates. He wants you to control the flow of magic."

Lisette felt her consciousness drift from where she stood into that transcendent version of herself. All doubt faded, all fear was vanquished. She felt a bliss she knew it would break her heart to lose.

"Beautiful, isn't it?"

"Yes," Lisette replied, the ecstasy she felt redrawing the lines between friend and enemy, between safety and danger. She could almost love the dark fire.

"You can have this, from this very moment onward. Forever. There's only the tiniest of prices to pay."

Through her rapture, another image seeped into her awareness—a vision of laying the baby on a stone. Of raising her hand high above her granddaughter and driving a blade through the infant's heart.

"No," Lisette said, at first in a whisper. "No," she repeated in a scream. But the beguiling dream refused to relinquish its grasp. It tried to pull her back into it. "No," she said. "Never." Lisette came to on the ground, clawing what passed for earth in this sickened world.

Lisette lifted her face, looking up at Babau Jean and the witch behind him, who still clung to Joy. She forced herself up to her knees, then to her feet. She began walking toward the pillar of dark fire, too angry at first to feel fear, though the closer she came, the more hesitant she grew.

The pale dancers falling into the beast's black heart wove around her, mad glee in their eyes as they burned away. Lisette came to a stop opposite that black heart, listening to its jagged beat. She could feel her pulse racing in her neck. Her arms at her side, her hand balled into tight fists, she touched the spark at her very source. Then she smiled. This thing, demon, god, whatever it was, had overshot. It could kill her a thousand times over, but she would never betray her children. Neither from fear nor for glory.

"No," she said, a simple, single-word incantation that caused the foundation of this dark world to tremble. The chain of dancers snapped apart. Those on the near end of the broken link dove into the fire, while those on the other end were flung backward, disappearing from this plane altogether.

In the next heartbeat, Lisette stood once more before Babau Jean. The creature had begun quivering, twitching faster than her eyes could follow. It appeared to bend in opposite directions at once, almost like it was breaking in two.

The witch behind him was shrieking with rage and terror. She held up Joy before her like a shield. "I will kill it," she screamed at Lisette. "I will dash its head against a stone."

It struck Lisette the witch believed she was the cause of Babau Jean's distress. For all Lisette knew, she might be. She held up her hands in surrender, even as the childlike witch rushed the strawberry blonde, screaming with a righteous rage.

"You won't hurt her. I won't let—"

Babau Jean snapped into sharp focus, his razor-nailed finger darting out like a dagger and piercing the girl's heart. He flung her aside, and she landed, dead, at Lisette's feet, her eyes still open. In them, Lisette caught a glimpse of . . . regret.

The witch now held Joy up by her ankles. "Stop," Lisette cried. "Anything," she said. "Anything." She repeated herself, sure her meaning was clear. Her life. Her soul. Whatever it took to make sure her granddaughter was unharmed.

Babau Jean pointed his bloody digit at her, touching its tip to her pulse. Lisette braced herself, expecting it to slide across her throat. Instead it fell away, as Babau Jean turned his attention to the dark fire. "Are you sure?" he said, sounding confused. "This is what you want?"

He must have heard his answer, for the eyeless white mask turned back to Lisette. "Hold out your arm," he commanded, and Lisette reached her left arm out to him, exposing the skin that held the gad. He traced his nail across the healing slashes, just enough to scratch a red line through them into her skin. She felt a tingling in her arm as the gad shimmered, then disappeared. Babau Jean released her, then turned and began walking away. "You may go."

"What about the baby?" Lisette said, stalking after him, afraid now she might somehow lose sight of him. "I've done what you've asked of me. I have offered myself to . . ." She cast a glance at the living fire. ". . . to that thing." She rushed forward and caught Babau Jean by the arm. He swung back, seeming startled by her audacity.

"We promised," the witch said, easing Joy back into a cradled position, "not to harm the child. We promised," she said, her eyes shining with cruelty, "to deliver her safely back to her mother." She held Joy out, then snatched her back with a laugh. "But," she sang out the word, "we never said when."

Lisette dug her fingers into Babau Jean.

"I will raise her as my own," the witch said, leaning her face over Joy, cooing at her. "And I will deliver her to her mother when she's grown, when she is so filled with hate for her, she will fall upon her mother and cut out her heart."

A deep rumbling sounded around them, causing even Babau Jean to tremble. "Give it to her," he said. "Give her the child."

The witch tightened her hold on the baby. "No," she said, her voice again the keening of the banshee. "The thing is mine."

"It is," Babau Jean said, the sound of cold rage building in his raspy voice, "what He commands." Still the witch hesitated. She took a step back. "Now."

The witch howled and flung Joy at them. Lisette's heart stopped beating for an instant as Babau Jean reached out and caught the child, his razor-tipped fingers folding around Joy like a cage.

The creature drew near, and without a word, his fingers opened, like a deadly flower blossoming. Lisette didn't hesitate for an instant. She snatched Joy from him and then turned and ran, moving past the line of cypresses, careening back toward the black sea, even as it parted before her.

She startled, her heart about to beat out of her chest, coming to in a recliner in the neonatal intensive care unit. She jumped up and rushed to the incubator. The baby slept peacefully inside. It was Joy, her Joy, not some enchanted doll. A small cry escaped her.

The nurse with kind black eyes appeared in the doorway. "Everything all right?"

"Will you," Lisette said, her voice cracking, "will you come in and check on her?"

"Of course," the nurse said, a look of confused concern giving way to her practiced, professional demeanor. She went first to the monitor, taking a quick glance at Joy's vitals, then she came closer and leaned over the incubator.

The nurse looked up and smiled. "She's absolutely fine. Did something frighten you?"

Lisette felt a nervous smile rise to her lips. She had been taken to that world of shadows before. She knew what she—and Joy—had experienced had been no nightmare.

"Hey," the nurse said, drawing Lisette's attention back to this world. "Her eyes are open. She's looking at you." The nurse nodded to Joy, a wide and genuine smile piercing her professional facade. "She knows you're here."

Lisette gazed down into those beautiful, trusting eyes.

"Go ahead," the nurse coaxed. "Talk to her. Tell her that her grandmother is here to take care of her."

"I am," Lisette said, relief causing tears to brim in her eyes. "I'm here for you, sweet girl. And I would give anything to keep you safe. Anything."

TWENTY-NINE

The end of the world will come in silence,
but not in stealth.

Astrid once again had full control over her vehicle. The servitor spirit Babau Jean had rebelled against her, tried to throw her, though she didn't know if his revolt had been sparked by his fear of the power they both sensed coming from the Voodoo woman, or if he had planned it. He had stopped communicating with her, closing himself off after she read *The Book of the Unwinding.*

Perhaps the power that had come surging into this plane through Lisette Perrault, though the woman hadn't seemed to recognize herself as its source, had provoked the Dark Man's volte-face concerning the infant. Perhaps the woman's presence here had never been meant as more than a ruse to test her strength, and that of the spirits who watched over her.

It was not Astrid's place to question the Dark Man's wisdom, though now another sacrifice would be required to prepare the way for the triumphant return of the King of Bones and Ashes to the common world.

Of course, she realized, the Longest Night.

A wild, rushing juggernaut in opulent, garish colors,
the people shall kneel before it
in the twinkle of intoxicating lights,
and each command his brother to be of good cheer.

The witches who gathered there would serve as the sacrifice. Perhaps that had always been His will.

With the words of *The Book of the Unwinding* burned into her, she could catch glimpses of His will, though much remained hidden. He was not of this world, but this world was of Him. He was Lord of this world, demiurge, artificer.

The beast will be welcomed first into the hearts
of those who have lusted after him,
and they shall worship his greatness.

What Astrid had once perceived as Celestin's failure to create a perfect, immortal body for her to inhabit, one that would allow her to walk freely throughout the ages in the common world, she now recognized as part of the Dark Man's plan. It had never been His intent for the sacrifice at Celestin's memorial ball to bring Astrid back to the common world. She was only meant to escort the true necklace of Inanna—the necklace worn to the ball by the haughty Julia Prosper had been made of real emeralds and diamonds but was a counterfeit all the same—into the common world so the polarities of the true necklace could be reunited. At least Rose Gramont had benefited from Astrid's disappointment; her bent old form was once again young and lithe, tender.

They shall bless the one who tears innocents
from the arms of their mothers to devour them.
And though they witness the blood on his lips,
the people shall praise his meaningless utterances.

The Dark Man drew closer as the rejuvenated crone danced through the fragile verse, oblivious to His presence, unaware of His words even though their traces clung to her youthful skin like spider-silk tattoos. Like a child placated for the loss of one toy with another, Rose had moved past the loss of her living doll by being given a jigsaw puzzle.

Rose lifted the severed head of a black Kiko goat by its impressive horns, raising it high overhead. Strange, Astrid hadn't taken note of the butchery—she'd surfaced only in time to witness Rose picking through the parts. Now the foolish witch lifted the goat's head high, as if it were an offering to the moon. Perhaps she believed it was; Rose was a fool. Astrid couldn't fault the witch. She, too, had been a fool, ignorant of the perfect, untamed darkness where nothing was, but all was possible.

He shall call out to them,
"Let the lie be the truth."
And they shall respond unto him,
"Let the truth be the lie."

Rose lay the goat's head on the ground beside the dismembered remains of those first taken. The young lovers—her torso, his groin and thighs. Michael Parrish's eyes and tongue. The black goat's hoofed back legs. Frank Demagnan's hands. Astrid hoped a little of the treacherous Demagnan's spirit remained trapped in them. Not the degree of punishment Astrid would have chosen, but a small solace to her wounded pride. Not that such things truly mattered. Not now.

The old man smiled across Rose and her jigsaw project at Astrid, His grin confirming her suspicion He'd drawn the teenage paramours to the deserted lane. Astrid couldn't help but chuckle at the memory of how the couple had reacted when Rose surprised them with her ax. Rose had so enjoyed the chase.

Astrid's laughter caused Rose to look up from her project, her expression posing cautious inquisition. Astrid gave a slight shake of Babau Jean's head and waved Rose back to her work with his sharp fingers. The witch fell back into the task with relish.

Rose had collected the parts she needed and tossed the rest in the direction of the solemn, red-eyed congregation lingering on the edge of the clearing. The writhing alligator-like shapes melded into an indistinguishable mass as they rushed forward in a single wave to collect the bounty, their dance set to the savage rhythm of snapping maws.

And he shall use the light of deception
to cast fearsome shadows upon them,
and the people shall cry out to him for protection.
He shall imprison them,
and the people shall praise his might.

Kneeling beside the assembled pieces, Rose threaded a curved surgical needle with a fine thread, the thread woven from strips of Eli Landry's skin—the binding that had once held *The Book of the Unwinding.* She began stitching the pieces together, the sum of the Baphomet certain to be so much greater than its constituent parts.

Rose carried on, stopping only occasionally to wipe away the sweat beading on her brow, smearing her forehead with a fresh coat of crimson each time, until she'd finished assembling the form. She looked up to Astrid, an expression of excited expectation in her impassioned eyes. Astrid approached the figure and knelt beside it. She pressed the nail of Babau Jean's finger between the breasts of the torso and pressed the razor tip in, cutting through flesh and bone. She had cleaved the sternum into perfect halves. Rose squatted across from her and scooped out the heart resting there. This she flung carelessly away, then wiped her hands on the earth. She stood and wandered off, then returned carrying a casket made of gold and encrusted with precious stones. Its lid was ornamented with what might appear to an untrained eye to be kneeling angels, their extended wings touching, but the figures weren't angels. They were the Queen of Heaven and the King of Bones and Ashes, Inanna and the transcendent Damuzi, Artemis and Lucifer.

Rose lifted the lid and lowered the jeweled box down to her, presenting her with her own darling Luc's heart, a relic the Dark Man Himself must have protected during her long exile. Astrid reached in, so carefully, so gently. She took it from the coffin and held it to her lips. She lowered it over the Baphomet, then laid it in the void left by the girl's discarded heart.

Astrid rose and took a step back as Rose knelt once again by the creation's side. She worked quickly, deftly, her nimble fingers looping the needle through both skin and bone, resealing the chest cavity with the thread spun from Eli's skin.

As the sutures Rose had made to bind the body together dissolved into its flesh, the chimera jerked, reflexive uncoordinated movements.

The Dark Man licked His lips.

For a moment, there was stillness.

Michael's transplanted eyes opened, the goat brain behind them firing to life one last time, a bleating scream escaping its lips. The

Baphomet's body then lurched over onto its stomach, hands pushing against earth. It forced its way up, staggering forward on hands and feet in a bastardized bear crawl—a goat's attempt to escape.

And the people shall cry out
"Let not the sweetness touch
the lips of the wicked, for their love is impure."
And dressed in white linens,
they shall lay with him as his whores.

The body's memory of its human origins overtook the animal's terror. The Baphomet rose to its feet, staggering. Rose caught hold of its hands, screaming along with the animal's horrified bleating. The witch lifted it into the air as she leaped and skipped, swinging the chimera around in quickening, widening circles. She finally released the beast and it fell back, stumbling, finding its footing at the last moment before spilling over.

Rose bent over with laughter.

Freed from Rose's grip, Frank's hands went to the side of the goat's head, digging into it. The body lurched around, spinning, falling to its knees as it struggled to separate itself from the head.

Astrid shifted her focus to the entity that had brought her to this moment. He blinked slowly like a satisfied cat, then His form fell away, shards of obsidian sloughing off and coalescing again into a cylindrical shadow, as long and black as a prize anaconda. It raised into a coil, then stretched out once more, slithering toward the beast. It wrapped around the creature's legs, around its waist and torso, climbing, its "head" splitting open and branching. One branch oozed past the lips of its gaping mouth. Two entered its ears; two pierced its eyes. The shadow disappeared into the creature, filling it completely.

Rose didn't at first notice, too busy making mocking bleats and pretending to charge the beast. When she finally saw the shadow invading the creature, her face twisted into a mask of confusion.

The creature uttered a sound unlike any Astrid had heard before—animal fear, a plea for mercy, a curse, a lament for every betrayal the world had ever seen, crescendoing to a cry of utter and perfect devastation. It stumbled and fell once again to its knees, but this time the topple failed to provoke a laugh from Rose, who had given the beast a wide berth. She rushed to Astrid's side as if hoping for protection.

The creature arched its back. Its shoulders shrugged forward with an audible crack, disjointed with such force that the arms hung limply before its chest, its hands dangling, their backs turned inward and touching. The thing swung back and forth, turning at the precise moment for Astrid to witness the murdered girl's back split open. Glutinous limbs pushed out through the wound and unfurled into enormous obsidian wings, each feather a sharpened knife.

The creature rose, teetering on its dark hooves while Astrid's attention was fixed on other parts of the metamorphosis. The shadow that had invaded it slithered out from its gaping maw and glided to Astrid's side even as Rose slipped behind her. The shadow piled in on itself, growing taller, first assuming the outline of the Dark Man's shape, then coalescing into His full figure. His focus was no longer on her. The creature held His rapt attention.

The Baphomet roared and flapped its wings, the clicking of feather against feather syncopating its cry. Its eyes flashed red, as if an inferno raged within, then turned as black as its wings. In that moment the constituent parts merged into the far greater whole, losing any residual essence of the goat, any trace of Frank.

Astrid gazed at the beast in adoring wonder. *Horrifying. Glorious.*

She shook off Rose, who was tugging at her arm, trying to pull her away, and knelt before the Baphomet. Rose took a knee beside her, grasping her hand, oblivious to the deep cuts made by Babau Jean's nails as Astrid drew away from her.

The Baphomet, now certain of its step, drew near them, its nostrils flaring as it sniffed their scents.

It was exquisite. *He* was exquisite.

And he shall lead them into a singular peace,
each following, blinded by adoration,
hand to foot along a ladder that rises
not up to the heavens,
but downward endlessly into the abyss.

"You should run, dear," Astrid said, deciding she owed Rose the benefit of a head start, if only for old times' sake. Her son would be very hungry, and Rose was the only fresh meat to be had.

THIRTY

The van bounced as if it rolled over railroad tracks, four sets in quick succession, then slowed to a stop. One of her handlers—that's the word that came to Nathalie's mind—popped a cap off a syringe. The other grasped her arm and wrapped a tight rubber tourniquet around her bicep. As the boy held her tight, the father punched the needle into her vein and squeezed his poison into her.

Nathalie's rational mind bobbed up and down from time to time, and in those rare moments of clarity, she realized they had been doping her. Psychedelics, for sure. God only knew what else. She breathed out the word "drug."

"That's right, *sha*. PCP. LSD. DMT. Emil, he's done cooked you up the whole goddamned alphabet."

A bang sounded against the side of the van. The father undid the tourniquet and nodded at his son, who hammered his fist three times on the van's wall. Nathalie heard men's voices, three or four of them, she guessed. The van's rear doors opened in unison. She could still hear the voices, but no one appeared to be there. The back of the van sank down with added weight, and the hands of the men she'd heard speaking, the ones who weren't there, grabbed hold of her and tugged her out. Nathalie landed on her feet but rocked a bit on the concrete pad. An invisible grip righted her.

The father and son climbed out of the van. The father winked at her, then placed his hand over his heart. His camouflage uniform shimmered, and he was gone, too. His son slapped his own chest and blinked out of sight.

One of the men spun Nathalie around and forced her forward—one unseen hand on her shoulder, the other bending her arm behind her back. Hot bubblegum breath feathered the nape of her neck.

The Mississippi flowed mere yards away, though now it didn't seem a river at all. It curled like a snake through the land, wrapping itself around the world, ready to squeeze the life out of it. Nathalie found herself glancing around, looking for the feet whose steps she heard slapping along the wharf. The water lay just ahead, and when Nathalie realized they were reaching the end of the wharf, she began to struggle, consumed by the sudden terror she'd been brought here to be dumped into the rushing water.

Another hard, sharp jerk, and she was aimed away from the river. They marched her alongside a copse of trees that clung to the riverbank, then cut across an empty parking lot. What Nathalie saw ahead made her stumble forward. She fell to her knees so quickly and unexpectedly the man holding her lost his grip. Raucous laughter boomed around her as several sets of rough hands descended on her, tugging her back up. Nathalie didn't resist—her mind remained fixated on the giant looming in the distance.

She blinked once, twice, and the giant before her came into clearer focus. It wasn't a man of flesh and blood. It was a statue, like ten feet tall, woven from branches and twine, tethered by ropes between four enormous concrete blocks. It was, incongruously, surrounded by folding chairs.

"I saw us together in this moment." Emil appeared beside her. She reckoned he'd been with the group all along, but she couldn't be sure. "When you were still a tiny thing. I didn't understand it then, but I saw it. Your bitch mama, she did her best to take you off your path, but your rightful destiny has a gravity to it, pulling you back no matter how hard anyone tries to tug you away."

"The gravity of rightful destiny," Nathalie repeated the words, hearing them in the chipper Irish brogue in which she'd first heard them spoken.

He pointed at the wooden sculpture. "That thing there"—he leaned in, speaking directly in her ear so she felt his hot breath—"it's more than a wicker man. It's a portal. Once Marin has got his victims all fixated on the pretty fire, on the black smoke coming from it, that's how he's planning to bring those demons through."

"But none of this makes sense." Nathalie struggled to clear her head, but she couldn't do more than grab a moment of clarity. "You could put an end to it now. I mean, if you're so worried about Nicholas, why don't you deal with him? Leave Alice out of it?" Then the truth hit her like a freight train. "Oh," she said, "you don't want to stop him from building an army."

"That's right, *ma fillette*. Marin gonna build it, and you gonna help us take it from him. The rest of our family, they up there thinking the boys and me have come down to do the wet work Lincoln and Wiley have lost their stomach for." He spat on the ground in disgust. "But my boys here and me"—Nathalie heard a soft, stealthy chorus of self-satisfied chuckles—"we got other plans. You see, girlie, up until now the Boudreaus have been content to play sheriff, but I done got it into my head I'd make one fine king."

He began stroking her hair. His touch was enough to make her want to climb out of her skin. "Though you probably wondering where you come in." He leaned in from behind her, rubbing his cheek against hers. "That Alice of yours, she's key to controlling the army, and you,

you're gonna help us control her—or at least a part of her." He held up his ruby before her eyes once more. "You're gonna bring me another one of these."

Nathalie bent forward and started to retch. A rough hand jerked her upright.

As they stood watching, older witches, a couple dozen of them, arrived by vans. The elders claimed the folding chairs set out between the parking lot and the effigy, wrapping themselves tighter in heavy coats or shivering together beneath shared blankets. Twenty or more younger people arrived en masse and fell into a semicircle before the wicker man. Combined, they didn't have the magic Alice did. All of them were, Nathalie realized, unaware of the Boudreaus' presence.

The majority of the new arrivals wore masks or costumes. Two of the younger congregants carried actual torches, the modern propane kind, made of metal, not the storm the Frankenstein family's castle kind. The torch bearers stationed themselves between the wicker man and the others, who carried far less impressive forms of light, from battery-powered camping lanterns to neon glow sticks. They milled about but didn't set fire to the effigy. They were waiting, Nathalie surmised, for others to arrive.

In the interim, they passed around bottles and vaporizers. Raucous laughter and shrieking pierced the night. Alice, she knew, was not with them. No disguise could mask Alice from her—she would feel her presence if she were here. There wasn't a doubt in her mind of it.

Three women caught hold of each other's hands and began spinning together in a circle, faster and faster till they rose up off the ground. The trio fell back to earth, laughing as they touched down. As incongruous as it seemed, the refrain of a Christmas carol reached Nathalie's ears.

A bus pulled into the parking lot, two others following it. The three came to a stop, one beside the other.

"Heads up, boys," Emil's voice hissed low but clear. She twisted her head to find he had once again become invisible. She sensed the men around her snapping to attention. "Find your stations." At his command, the men dispersed, leaving her alone with Emil.

The doors of the buses opened, and men and women, a hundred and fifty, maybe two hundred of them, piled out. They all wore matching outfits—tan pants or knee-length skirts, white button-down shirts, gray cardigans. The passengers gathered to one side of the buses—some shaking hands, others hugging each other like long-lost friends. A greeting worked through them like a wave. "Through him we shall do great things."

Nathalie saw this as her moment and hit Emil with everything she had, the power of her body and the power of her magic. She heard him hit the ground. He remained transparent, but blood flowed from nothingness to pool at her feet. It began to coat his skin with a sheen that looked almost black in the low light, rendering bits of him—his hand, his right arm, the left side of his face—visible. The parts she could make out were still. She felt sick to her stomach. She'd killed the man. She hadn't meant to; she'd only wanted to get free so she could find Alice, protect her.

Alice. Emil might no longer be a threat, but there were maybe seven men posted around the gathering, lying in wait to murder her when Nathalie didn't. Nathalie turned, preparing to dart back in the direction the other witches had come from, hoping Alice would take this same path.

Her muscles tensed, readying for a burst of speed. She lurched forward, throwing all of her force into the first step. A hand gripped her ankle, tugging her down, and she fell face-first, barely managing to catch herself with her hands. She started pulling away the second she touched earth. Emil caught her with both hands and flipped her onto her back with a single, solid jerk. She struggled, but his weight was already moving up her body. Emil growled out a string of curses as he pinned her arms beneath his knees. A drop of his blood fell into her eye, burning, blinding. She blinked.

"I won't help you," she gasped out, unable to catch a full breath. "I won't hurt her. You can't make me."

"Mais, ma fillette," Nathalie heard Emil's voice crooning the words. She felt the pinch of a hypodermic needle in her neck. "You ain't gonna be able to help yourself."

Nathalie struggled beneath his weight, but felt her strength, her will fading away. As the world around her grew smaller, duller, she took one last bit of comfort from the least expected source.

Emil was wrong. The demons weren't coming. They were already here.

THIRTY-ONE

Alice had learned the route of la Defilé des Maléfiques in New Orleans had been redrawn more than once—as the city grew, as the makeup of the population changed, as once revered landmarks faded in importance and then slipped from memory, replaced in value by others. The earliest processions, in the early part of the eighteenth century, had been simple affairs, following the bend of the river that gave the Crescent City its nickname. Later, the path grew longer, taking in the full perimeter of the Vieux Carré, but at that time the Quarter had still ended at the moat that separated Dauphine from the ancient cemetery.

The traditional path, at least the route those who'd participated in the city's last procession considered to be traditional, began at the edge of Congo Square, not far from the gates of what was now Armstrong Park, and cut through the heart of the French Quarter to the river. The straightest path would have been to follow Orleans Street, but the participants, *les Maléfiques*, with their torches held high overhead, took a detour, crossing over Rampart at St. Ann Street.

This "traditional" route, first walked in the nineteenth century, remained a sore point for some, as it was the Voodoo queen Marie

Laveau who'd determined the path, a privilege she'd claimed as one of the terms of an armistice between herself, her followers, and the witches of New Orleans. The cause of the original bad blood between the factions had been lost to memory, though if Marceline had spoken the truth about the layout of the original city, it probably grew from the covert use of vèvès in an attempt to weaken or conquer the loa they represented. Regardless, each member of the walk would pause on St. Ann Street and bow before a house that no longer stood, Laveau's former home. Alice suspected this paying of respects had little if anything to do with acknowledging the dominance of the great mambo. Rather, Laveau had probably insisted on it to goad the witches into conceding to Legba's right to control the amount of magic filtering into their reality.

Nicholas had redrawn the route of the procession once again, this time in deference to the advanced age of many of the remaining witches. The new path followed along the river on the Crescent Park Trail. Nicholas had granted them an additional dispensation by arranging for round-trip shuttle service from the foot of Elysian Fields Avenue to the bend of the river near the End of the World, where the wicker man had been built.

The park and trail had been closed for hours, but the point of the evening was to defy the rules of non-witches. This year trespassing would serve as a contemporary substitute for the assaults and vandalism of yesteryear. In the past, fear or even a begrudging respect would have staved off interference from the police. The same might hold true tonight, or perhaps Nicholas had performed his greatest act of magic by obtaining a permit from the city for a midnight romp followed by a bonfire.

Alice had been waiting now for nearly half an hour at the base of the stairs leading up to the pedestrian bridge over the railroad tracks. She stood shivering in the river breeze, feeling foolish in a long, turn-of-the-century gown Hugo had rescued earlier in the day from Celestin's attic, the borrowed cat mask in hand. A group of elderly witches lurked in a pack nearby, waiting, she surmised, for her to take the lead. The dozen or so witches anywhere near her own age who had shown up for this sad procession were already half a mile or more ahead.

Hugo, who refused to carry a phone and was as usual unreachable, had set the meeting time and place. Fleur, who always answered between the third and fifth rings—she thought it a mistake to appear too available—was letting her phone go to voice mail. Alice checked her phone for the fourth time in three minutes and was surprised to see she'd somehow missed a call. Nathalie had left a voice message. Alice smiled as she listened to the rambling, apologetic message. Yes, Nathalie had gotten her text about the Longest Night. She'd be back home tonight, but too late to join them for the procession. She'd join Alice at the End of the World.

Little does she know, Alice thought, scanning each direction from the bend where Elysian Fields Avenue curved to become North Peters Street for any sign of Hugo.

He was nowhere to be seen. Perhaps she should start the two-mile trek to the site of the bonfire even if it meant acting as sole custodian of the elders who seemed determined to make themselves her charges. A couple, a man and a woman, stragglers dressed in magnificent Baroque costumes that could have been the envy of the court of Louis XIV, approached her, not so much walking as gliding.

The male wore a gold-filigreed version of the plain, squarish half mask Alice had seen displayed on the Twins' wall; the woman wore an ornate silver mask that covered her eyes and forehead. She held a lit torch, the wind from the river causing its flame to dance and cast eerie shadows around them. As the pair came closer, Alice realized the brow of the woman's mask was ornamented with the face of Medusa.

"Your brother"—the sound of Art's voice coming from the woman's lips shocked Alice—"sent us to accompany you."

"It seems," Polly said from behind the filigreed half-mask, "Fleur and Lucy are running behind. Hugo hasn't been able to reach them, so he's gone to set a fire under them."

"So to speak," Art said and laughed.

"Yes," Polly said, joining in. "A most unfortunate turn of phrase for the evening. Let's do try to keep the burning to the effigy."

Alice smiled, suddenly feeling naked without her own mask. She held it up to her face.

"Let us help you, *chérie*," Polly said, stepping behind Alice and tying the ribbons to hold the mask.

"I didn't recognize you," Alice confessed.

"That was the point, Alice," Art said in the same admonishing tone she'd used to chastise Alice for assuming they were incapable of speech.

"I only mean I've never seen you dressed unalike."

"Oh," Polly said with a chuckle, "you have, only you don't realize it. Don't feel bad. It's rare anyone does."

"When we wish to pass incognito, we go out dressed in the costume of the common man and woman."

"Though sometimes Art plays the boy."

"The clothes aren't as fashionable," Art said, "but at least one has ample pockets. And one is treated with a level of respect the 'fairer sex' never receives."

"There," Polly said, finishing with Alice's mask. "Shall we," he began in a forced baritone, "ladies?"

It had fallen to Alice and the Twins to shepherd those elders who'd committed to going to la Defilé on foot. The half dozen elders encircled her, pushing in as close as they could, like they were clinging to the only light in a very dark night. The scent of menthol arthritis creams and stale perfume blended with the muddy scent of the river and the unspeakable aromas of magical unguents that had faded in potency, but not in reek.

The elders carried no torches, though some had flashlights—one even held a keychain penlight—in their trembling hands.

Alice resented their presence. It was uncharitable of her, she recognized that. Only she felt hemmed in, and their anxious, agitated faces triggered memories from her lost years on Sinclair. Some of the inmates had been addled by dementia—sweet one moment, wanting to stroke her hair, then striking out the next. Worse, Alice felt like these toothless witches, these *maléfiques manqués*, were draining her, feeding on her life force, much as Nicholas planned to do to his desperate and deceived acolytes.

Like the shadows of the Dreaming Road.

The thought landed in the pit of her stomach like a stone. The demons of the Dreaming Road had begun as witches such as these. Witches like her.

"In regards to the resurrection of this bit of pageantry, we witches of New Orleans are of two minds," Art said. She and Polly, one on each side of Alice, were more escorting Alice than walking with her. "There are those—"

"Many of whom," Polly spoke over Art, "like my treasured sister and I, narrowly escaped Celestin's massacre—"

"—who," Art continued as if Polly hadn't interrupted her, "are refusing to participate in la Defilé as they consider it sheer madness to put themselves in the hands of Marin *fils* after the atrocities of the Marin *père*."

"And the others?"

Art cast a glance at their entourage. "They agree it's mad, but they're too intrigued by the rumors, rumors Nicholas himself set in circulation with expert precision, that he has found a new source of magic—"

"A new source he will share tonight with those who show themselves as faithful," Polly added.

"Faithful?" Alice couldn't help but laugh. "To Nicholas?"

"Not only Nicholas," Polly said and paused in his stride, bowing and scraping before Alice. "To the family Marin."

A pair of vans continued to pass by them as they brought sorcerers to the bonfire and away from it. There were more open seats on the "to" vans than there had been at first, indicating that most of the attendees had already arrived, and a few worn-out sorcerers were already heading home on the "from" vans.

"Why did you two come?" Alice said.

The Twins looked around her at each other. Alice couldn't pick up on their silent conversation, but she could sense their ambivalence had served as a source of discord between them. It was Polly who answered. "Habit, perhaps? Our family has always been counted among the Marin loyalists."

"At least we used to be," Art added. "No offense, but the Marin family's behavior of late hasn't exactly inspired loyalty."

"Of late?" Alice echoed her words. "That's a generous qualification to make." The transgressions of the Marins, at least the ones Alice knew of, went back over five decades. She suspected in actuality they reached back to the beginning of the line.

"What about you, Alice? What brings you here?"

Alice had been posing this question to herself since last night, when she had agreed to participate. "It seemed important to Fleur," she said, adding after a moment of thought, "and Hugo, too."

Polly made a show of looking all around them. "Neither of whom is here."

"You are," Art said, "in fact here without keepers."

"I thought that's why Hugo sent the two of you."

"Don't be ridiculous, *ma petite*, we are here to act as aiders and abettors, not as chaperones."

"Still, it seems you have another reason to be walking among your fellow *maléfiques*," Polly pressed.

"Curiosity," she said, the response automatic. Alice considered this a somewhat true, if incomplete, answer.

"Really, Alice," Art said. "Are you that lacking in self-awareness, or do you believe we're too simple to see through your transparent ruse?"

Three tour buses, prowling metal behemoths, traveled along North Peters Street toward the river, each slowing, it seemed, so their passengers could get a better look at Alice's group. Each bus appeared to be completely full, scores of ogling faces pointed toward them. Alice sensed none of the passengers were witches. Still they were all headed out to the End of the World.

"Nicholas," Alice began, giving voice to a truth that was only now dawning on her, "makes a habit of practicing distraction, shifting everyone's attention from his true aim to something shiny. He's owning up to a horrific-enough plan—"

"So imagine what he's really up to," Art said, the sardonic humor her voice usually held failing her as she spoke. "I . . . *we*," she said with a nod at Polly, "have been thinking along similar lines."

"I think," Alice said, casting a glance at an out-of-place white van deserted on the concrete pad of the wharf, "I came in case Nicholas has to be stopped. In case I'm the only one who can stop him."

"Intriguing," Art said, her expression hidden by her mask, but her sincere appreciation curled around that single word.

J.D. Horn

They arrived at the bonfire site as quickly as the shuffling gait of the elders allowed them. The small stretch of land by the river was packed with people. Alice froze at the sight of the khaki-clad men and women, more than a hundred of them, lined up in perfect semicircles, seven rows deep, before the wicker man. They stood at a respectful distance from the witches already gathered there.

"I had no idea," Alice said, scanning the crowd, "he'd already collected so many of them. What could he have told them to pull them in? What could they possibly expect in return for turning their lives over to Nicholas?"

"They probably don't understand what he's planning to do to them, maybe already doing to them," Polly said. "Not really. They couldn't possibly be okay with him draining their life essence."

"I wouldn't be so sure about that," Art said. "Nicholas has offered these people the chance to be part of something greater than themselves without actually having to do a damned thing other than believe in him."

"But there has to be more to it than that," Alice said, incredulous. "They're offering up their lives, their freedom." Alice's freedom had been taken from her, twice, and each day she'd spent on the Dreaming Road had drained her life force. She would die before she allowed either to be taken from her again.

"I'd bet the one thing they share in common is they feel powerless, threatened," Art said. "Their free will is a small thing to sacrifice for security. Their great leader, I am sure, is offering them a mind-numbing cocktail of easy answers to complex questions, simple decisions in a complicated world, and complete absolution from the responsibility for making their own moral decisions." She surveyed those arrayed before the wicker man. "Most of all, he makes them feel special."

A cold hand caught Alice's forearm. "Who are these people, dear?" one of the elders asked in a much louder voice than necessary.

"They're Nicholas's attendants," Alice responded, patting the woman's hand. The woman tilted her head toward her, probably in an effort to hear more clearly, and the feather on her plastic half mask tickled Alice's cheek.

"It looks," Polly said, leaning in toward Alice and his sister, "like the 1950s vomited."

The woman turned to Polly. "They've come to help us?"

"Perhaps not us," Art said, answering the question for him. "But they have come to help Nicholas. There's no reason to fear them," she said, then added under her breath, "probably."

"What exactly is it your father is up to?" Another elder, a man leaning against an ornate, bejeweled walking stick, his face hidden behind a jester mask, stumbled forward, bumping into her.

"He isn't her father," the woman with the loud voice announced with enough gusto to catch the attention of Nicholas's followers. The khaki-clad devotees turned in a cascading wave, the rear row first, their movement alerting those in front of them. Faces lit up in expectation, then dimmed with disappointment, then rebuilt themselves into polite smiles. They had been hoping for Nicholas. Alice could feel the waves of love, some desperate, some mad, rippling out from them. The crowd parted down the center, the members falling back to create a wide aisle for the newly arrived witches, and a smattering of applause rose up from the crowd. A voice called out over the applause, and the congregants shifted and began lowering themselves, some with more agility than others, to their knees.

"You," Alice said in amazement, "have got to be kidding me."

The elders, their energy renewed and mood lightened by this show of adoration, pushed past Alice and the Twins. Backs that had been bent for the last mile straightened. Slumped shoulders pulled back. They were, it seemed to Alice, eating this up. She suspected any doubt they'd held about Nicholas's scheme had been crushed with a single blow. The woman with the booming voice slowed, then glanced back over her shoulder at Alice. The wide smile on her lips told Alice her former charge, unsettled and uneasy the entire trek, was now drunk with pleasure.

"Shall we?" Art said, addressing Alice but taking her brother's arm.

"You two go ahead." Alice shook her head. "I'm waiting for someone."

"Aren't we all, *ma chère?*" Polly said, then led his sister through the worshipful congregants and toward the wicker man.

THIRTY-TWO

Evangeline sat cross-legged in the god-awful green club chair she'd agreed to hold for one of her former dancers. Seven years had passed since Evangeline had taken the chair in, and still the eyesore remained unclaimed. She stared down at the miraculously untasted tumbler of vodka on the table before her.

Sugar wove her way through the room and rose up on her hind legs, placing her front paws on the edge of the chair. The cat trilled and fixed Evangeline with her saucer-like eyes. Evangeline leaned forward and touched the top of the cat's head, twirling her finger around the cat's ear, an action that never failed to please Sugar.

"Hello, baby," she said, and Sugar dropped down and fell back, only to leap forward onto Evangeline's lap. She pawed her way up Evangeline's chest, purring emphatically. The cat began kneading her shirt, her needlelike claws piercing the cloth, though not scratching any skin. Evangeline was familiar with the act—it was how Sugar declared ownership. A gentle reminder. "Yes, Mama knows she belongs to you."

Odd, incomplete images avalanched into Evangeline's mind. The cat was building a case for some argument, but as practiced as

Evangeline was at interpreting her pet's efforts at communication, she couldn't grasp the whole picture.

Sugar was concerned—stronger than concerned, worried—that much was clear. If anything, it was this overriding feeling of uneasiness that blurred the other images together into an indecipherable warble. "A little slower, sweetie," Evangeline said, catching the cat up in her right arm and running her left pinky from the cat's dot of a nose over her tiny head and along her spine. As far as Evangeline could make out, the cat's confused messaging boiled down to her not wanting Evangeline to set foot out of the house tonight.

"Don't worry, pretty girl," Evangeline said, "Mama isn't going any-where." She'd already decided as much. Someone from the club had called a thousand times, but she'd turned off the ringer on her phone. Bonnes Nouvelles could survive a night without her. If the dancers left the door wide open, if the fill-in bartenders robbed her blind, so be it. It had taken learning she was a devil's—if not the Devil's—daughter, and that the man with whom she'd been sharing her bed might be out to kill, sorry, to execute her, but Evangeline had finally reached her limit.

Sugar rubbed her cheek against Evangeline's finger, then slipped down off her lap. She stared for a moment longer, as if to drive her message home, before padding from the room.

Perhaps Sugar was right, and she ought to be careful. But what she'd learned had changed her. It had certainly changed her perception of herself.

She had not a single drop of the sanctimonious storefront preach-er's blood in her; she would no longer struggle beneath the weight of his name. Her sire, a cold, dark fire with many faces, had innumerable names, but the only name that mattered to her did not belong to the fire.

Evangeline Longeac. She tried on the name, surprised by how well it fit. Evangeline Longeac was fatherless.

She was the daughter of Mireille Longeac, niece of Marceline Longeac. Two innocents who, starving and dispossessed, had wandered together into the dark forest to offer all they were to any force that would save them. Two innocents who were deceived, blinded to the truth.

Evangeline could sense Lincoln getting closer. She'd been picking up random thoughts and flashes from him as he drove with his little brother back from Natchitoches in his beat-up blue pickup. He was circling now, looking for a place to park. She no longer sensed Wiley; Lincoln must have dropped him off along the way. She wanted to call Hugo, to text him, to warn him Wiley wasn't necessarily the guy he presented himself to be, but the little son of a bitch refused to carry a phone, and since there weren't any owls around to carry the message, it would have to wait till she saw him face-to-face. Better that way, anyway.

Lincoln circled once, twice, then Evangeline sensed he'd pulled over. A few minutes passed as he made his way from his parking spot. The images flashing in her mind told her he'd left his truck on Esplanade.

She followed along with Lincoln as he approached. He was tired, exhausted from the drive and a high-drama visit with the rest of the Boudreau clan. That much she picked up on as he fished in his pocket for the key.

She had given him that key. Maybe too soon.

It turned in the lock, and Lincoln stumbled in, his oversize duffel bag leading the way. He froze at the sight of her. "Oh, hey. Thought you would've already gone with Hugo. You got my text, right?" He dropped his bag by the door, almost like he expected to be sent packing with it at any moment.

She nodded.

He mistook her resignation for anger. Still, he risked leaning in to place a kiss on her forehead.

Maybe she should be angry with him, but she couldn't be. He was as much a product of his DNA as it seemed she was of hers. "We drove straight through," he said, a defense for being late. His aura shifted to a dark, muddy blue. He was tired. He could turn angry soon if she didn't toss him a lifeline. "Can we start with how sorry I am for whatever it is I've done . . . or not done?"

"It isn't you," she said, "not really. And I'm not her."

"Her who?"

"The woman who'd make you guess if she was pissed at you and why."

"No, I reckon you aren't. But are you mad at me?"

She looked up, studying his face, trying to separate the kind, gentle man she knew from the cold-blooded killer Marceline claimed him to be. "Why are you here?"

He took a step back. "Shouldn't I be?" His shoulders straightened, his spine stiffened.

"Why are you here?" She repeated herself. "In New Orleans, in my life?" This was it. This was his one and only chance to tell her the truth. She opened herself up to his energy; if he lied, she would know it.

Lincoln looked away. She knew he was calculating, weighing what he wanted to tell her against what he thought he should. Finally, he turned back to her, his jaw tightening. He knelt before her and tried to take her hand, but she pulled it away. He looked her up and down, then ran the rejected hand over his two-day stubble.

"I was sent here," he said. "Wiley and me both. That's why we came to New Orleans."

"Sent by whom?"

"By my family, of course."

"They sent you to kill me."

"The seers could only tell us a big storm was brewing. They sent us to take out the threat to our kind, but we didn't know who or what the threat was."

"And you think you know now?"

"Yeah," he said. "We think we do."

Without reflection, she folded her arms over her chest and pushed deeper into the chair's backrest. "You're ready to take that threat out."

"If we have to, but I think there's another way to handle it. I don't think she's lost. Not all the way. Not yet."

"Alice," Evangeline said, picking up on an image of her in his mind.

He nodded. "Wiley and I know how important she is to you and Hugo. That's why we had to meet with the family." He placed his hand on her knee. "They've given us permission to try to diffuse the situation before taking more drastic measures."

"What does Nathalie think about you and your more drastic measures?" She considered removing his hand from her knee, but it proved unnecessary.

He released her and rose to his feet. "Nathalie doesn't know anything about this."

"Then why was she invited to the big Boudreau confab?"

Lincoln's forehead scrunched up, his jaw jutting forward. "She wasn't invited. She wasn't there." He wasn't lying. He was confused by Evangeline's belief Nathalie had been with them.

Maybe Nathalie had gone to try to intervene on Alice's behalf. Maybe Nathalie was banging someone else. Either way, Evangeline had bigger questions. "Could you do it?" She gripped the chair's arms. "Could you kill Alice?"

"You have to understand—"

"Could you do it?" Evangeline screamed at him. He bolted back, his eyes opening wide.

Sugar ran into the room, positioning herself between them, staring up at Lincoln and chirruping.

"Yes," he said, his voice coming out low. "If I have to. If that's what it takes to protect others."

Evangeline nodded slowly, focusing on the floor between Lincoln and the cat. "What if you're wrong? What if this danger you're trying to quell isn't Alice?" She looked up, her eyes fixing on his. She recognized a glint of fear dawning in them. "What if it's me? Could you do it then?"

His faced flushed. Fear was stoking anger. "But it isn't—"

"Could you do it then?" she said, nearly growling out the words. She needed an answer. She had to know.

He blinked and fell silent. His inner debate lasted a full minute, then he spoke. "No," he said, his voice firm, sure, and honest. "I could not."

Evangeline closed her eyes, digging her nails into the arms of the chair. "Then you need to go," she said, her voice coming out in a near whisper. She opened her eyes and glared at him. "I said you need to go."

His shoulders fell. His jaw dropped open. He was hurt. Shocked. "Evangeline . . . ," he said, his voice pleading.

She jumped up from the chair and advanced on him, getting right up into his face. "You need to go, and you need to find someone who can, 'cause I don't think it's Alice. I think it's me."

A knock sounded on the door. Lincoln turned, making a move toward the door, but Evangeline's hand shot out and caught hold of him. "Wait," she said. "I'll get it." She knew who was knocking. She also knew that if Lincoln answered the knock, it would mean his death. "If you love me," she said, "if you really love me, you will find a way to stop me." She sent a pulse of energy through her hand into him. He slumped and fell to the floor.

Sugar scooted away from his falling form, looking up at her. The cat shot another cascade of images at her, demanding explanations, trying to convince her to ignore the knock and stay home where it was safe. A second, more insistent rap on the door shattered her pet's desperate attempt to hold on to her. "Mama's sorry, baby."

Evangeline crossed to the door and opened it. Her father, her true father, stood on her doorstep, holding out his hand to her. Evangeline didn't want to take it, but her hand no longer seemed in her control. As if by magnetism, it reached out to take his. Then, like an electric fence latching on to the careless hand that grasped it, she was caught. He tugged her over the threshold and down to the street.

THIRTY-THREE

The blood of Ouranos gleams eternally
on the blade held to Kronos's thigh.

They circled each other, Astrid and her eldest son, taking the other's measure.

He was magnificent. His hate for her was so perfect, so complete. "My son," she said. "My masterpiece."

Tonight, the Beast would rise and claim his crown as the King of Bones and Ashes, the greatest and perhaps the last. Never before had magic known a Queen of Heaven born of the Dark Man's seed. This Queen could reign forever, and should she do so, it would be with Astrid's son at her side.

Luc laid hands on her and maneuvered her to the center of the clearing. He presented her to the cold fire, and the Dark Man agreed to accept Astrid as the first sacrifice. This was an honor beyond anything she could have wished.

It came to her as an odd revelation that although Luc loathed her, his dark heart harbored an affection for Babau Jean. Though Astrid had promised the creature to remain forever with him, she would go alone into the fire. The vow she'd made was of no import, as Babau Jean no longer desired her company. He'd been trying to throw her ever since *The Book of the Unwinding* unfurled on Eli Landry's skin. She savored its wisdom, but it wasn't to his liking.

Hers was the darkest heart.

As the cold fire reached out to draw her in, she felt nothing but happiness. After all, she would remain a part of Luc, even if he reigned for all of eternity. It was, by her estimation, a perfect mother's revenge.

THIRTY-FOUR

A cold, low-lying fog was creeping in off the river, chilling the air as it erased the edges of the ominously named End of the World, a stubby, unremarkable peninsula that jutted out into the Industrial Canal and pointed toward Holy Cross. The fog was a natural enough phenomenon, though the timing struck Alice as contrived. She suspected its entrance was a bit of Hollywood Nicholas was employing to make an impression on his khaki-clad acolytes.

Alice milled around among Nicholas's new pets, searching for Nathalie. She could sense Nathalie's presence by using the old trick Luc had taught her, sending out tiny psychic pings that worked a bit like radar, but she'd already made two sweeps without spotting her. Alice had the odd feeling that they were circling each other. Nathalie's energy seemed off, scattered—almost cloaked—perhaps deflected by the congregants' zeal or affected by her visit with the Boudreau family. Then again, Alice couldn't get a signal on her phone either, so perhaps Nicholas had placed a magical shield over the site, like the faltering privacy spell woven long ago over Précieux Sang, back when witchcraft didn't have to make accommodations for technology.

She undid the ties of her mask and slipped it off, casting a quick glance down at the ornate cat face. The story of the goddess Artemis's pursuit of her brother Lucifer bubbling up as she did. Alice made quick work of pushing the troublesome myth back down into her psyche.

She lifted her eyes and scanned the crowd for the others—Fleur and Lucy, Hugo and Wiley. Nothing. She got a hit on Evangeline on the edge of the gathering, and another on Lincoln. They weren't together, but she suspected they were nearby, and the same bit of intuition that told her she and Nathalie were circling each other insisted Evangeline and Lincoln were drawing closer to her and each other.

She was passing by as one of Nicholas's followers nodded toward the wicker man. "They can't light that thing up soon enough for me," he said to the woman at his side. "I could do with a little heat." Alice sensed the two were strangers to each other. The woman, who was stuffed into an undersized, extra-large blouse and straining skirt, eyed him with suspicion. "Or maybe a coat," he said, his good-natured grin fading in the face of the woman's continued silence. He rubbed his upper arms and rocked up to the balls of his feet and back again, trying to generate warmth.

He stopped as he took note of Alice.

The woman turned on him, her expression at once irritated and vacuous. "Father didn't offer us coats," she said, sounding offended. "If we were supposed to be wearing coats, Father would have seen to it we had them." She looked earnestly to Alice, seeking a sign of approval for her steadfast faith in "Father." "Through him we shall do great things," she added swiftly, shivering. The blanket justification might have cheered her, but it certainly didn't warm her like a real blanket would.

"Through him we shall do great things," her nervous companion said quickly, echoing the hollow jingle.

Alice shook her head in disgust and moved on, continuing counterclockwise. Without finding any of the people she'd sought, she approached the spot where Art and Polly had positioned themselves to enjoy Nicholas's spectacle, arriving just as two of the younger witches pushed past, lit torches in hand. Alice turned, walking backward a few steps as she watched them move to the center and set light to the wicker man's foundation.

A jubilant roar went up from the crowd as the fire began to lick at the wicker man's feet. Alice's eyes followed the flames as they climbed skyward. For a moment, she thought it only a play of shadow and light, but she witnessed a darkness swooping down from above, followed by a spray of blood that shot out from nothingness.

Applause and cheers shook the site as blood sprayed out from multiple points overhead, invisible clouds bursting open like fireworks. An anguished cry rose up above the din, and a figure writhing in flames broke free of the effigy. It was a man.

It was Nicholas. He stumbled forward before falling to the ground. Only then did Alice see the army of hungry shadows, dark, grotesque human silhouettes rising up from beneath the cover of the fog, the majority positioning themselves among Nicholas's followers, but the larger, denser shadows seeming to target the gathered witches.

Whatever Nicholas's intentions had been, he'd lost control. This gathering had been appropriated by someone with, it appeared, even more diabolic notions.

Alice pushed through the oblivious spectators, advancing on Art and Polly. "Get out of here," she screamed, trying to make her voice heard over the ovations that were quickly changing into cries of terror. She grasped the hands of a pair of the older witches who'd followed her here, shepherding them toward the Twins. "You have to go," she yelled at the resisting, indignant elders. The Twins, however, had the sense to move first and ask questions later. They were already gathering those near them into a tight knot. "Get them out."

She turned back in time to see two of the shadows circling one of the witches who'd lit the effigy. His torch still burned, and he spun around, wielding the torch like a rapier as he advanced and then fell back. His erratic movements told Alice he was attempting to fend off a menace he sensed but couldn't see.

The two shadows, for the moment, ignored the boy's attempted parries, focusing their rage on each other. They circled their intended prey, swiping at each other with their razor nails, disputing the right of the kill. First one, then the other took notice of her arrival. Together they fell back, bowing to her in obeisance.

They saw her as one of them. They saw her as their leader.

Alice flashed back to Marceline's claim. She'd said Alice was to be their general, their Joan of Arc.

"Run," she called to the terrified boy. "Run," she yelled when he didn't move. He cast a quick glance right and left, and shot off, dropping his torch. She hoped he'd get enough of a head start before he attracted another of the shadows with his flight.

A movement at the center of the disintegrating effigy caught her attention. The fire was running out of fuel, but the flames rose higher instead of dying, no longer giving off light as much as devouring the light around them. Their once intense heat had turned in a heartbeat to a glacial cold.

Another figure, this one undeterred and untouched by the flames, emerged from the conflagration. She understood in a flash of insight that the pyre served as a portal, a doorway between the common world and a place of nightmare.

Alice caught a glimpse of the creature from behind, a kind of chimera, part human, part beast, but she didn't have time to process it, let alone consider what it might mean. Shadows were advancing on her, bringing with them tributes. She looked up in horror as they piled the heads of their victims at her feet. There, the woman who'd gloried in being cold. There, the man who'd dared to want a coat. And dozens more.

In the distance, beyond the fire, she saw Nathalie. Nathalie was trying to stand but could only seem to make it to her knees before tumbling back over. Three of the shadows were advancing on her.

Leader. General. Joan of Arc. Fire.

In that moment, Alice saw her purpose with absolute clarity. She was to lead this army—to lead them away from those she loved, to lead them out of the common world to a hell from which they could never return. She, like Joan of Arc, was destined to burn.

Alice threw back her head and called out to them with all the pain, all the rage, all the fear she held inside her. The shadows stopped. They listened. And then they obeyed, falling into formation and following lockstep behind her as she began to lead them into the dark, icy flames.

The center of the fire seemed an impossible distance away, but as she gained on it, she saw the common world had folded itself back around the fire. The edges hovered, shimmering like summer heat on asphalt. At last she reached the event horizon where one world ended and the other begun. She held up a hand to signal her army to stop. Then she paused at the edge to take one last breath.

THIRTY-FIVE

Evangeline was alone on this path. Reverend Bill was gone, but she felt the Dark Man all around her. Her feet were bare, but it didn't matter. They didn't actually touch the ground. The earth below her had grown thin enough to be translucent, and beneath the asphalt and soil, below the roots of ghost trees, Evangeline could see a darkness writhing like a snake, wriggling back and forth in precise, straight lines. A new gospel, a revelation waiting to be made manifest.

A pair of witches touched their torches to the dry brush at the base of the wicker man, and flames began to rise. As above, so below. The fire at the feet of the effigy was at the same time the spark of the Dark Man, burning its way into the common world—no, burning away the illusion of separateness.

Evangeline now saw the two worlds as one, not layered atop each other but each existing at once, like the two true natures of the necklace. A congregation stood between her and the fire. In the one reality, those gathered were the remnants of the pale souls who'd danced through the heart of the fire in search of oblivion. In the other, they were her former lover's sad acolytes, who—gathered together by the riverside in their matching, modest dress—resembled her former father's church group awaiting baptism.

Hungry shadows, the broken witches of the Dreaming Road, moved in silence among these fanciful, faithful congregants. The shadows' mirrors, the desperate witches of the common world, basked in the glow of the congregants' adoration.

Men, visible to none save themselves and Evangeline, played soldier like little boys among them. They moved with impunity among the others, confident they were the hunters. They failed to consider the hungry shadows' heightened sense of smell.

The shadows fell on them first.

It was an astounding sight to see thin air burst into a shower of blood. A roar rose up from the crowd, cheers and wild applause celebrating the bloody deaths. Some of the witches clearly perceived the bursts of blood as part of Nicholas's Longest Night pageantry, others perhaps thought it a sacrifice. The acolytes, she intuited, considered it a baptism, and those covered in spatter were treated with the special awe reserved for the lucky chosen.

Only one toy soldier had the time to cry out before a shadow snatched him up, and like a bird returning to the nest to feed its young, it carried the screaming man to its companions before quartering him with claws and fangs. Evangeline spotted Nathalie rising to her feet, turning a full circle, falling back to her knees.

A terrified, anguished animal cry came from the man concealed in the center of the pyre. Nicholas had planned to make a triumphant entry, bursting forth unharmed from the inferno, but the Dark Man had a vision of His own. Nicholas stumbled, burning, from the conflagration, falling and rising before he somehow, perhaps on instinct, found the water's edge. In a final desperate act, he tumbled forward into the flow and disappeared beneath its surface.

The hungry shadows fell next on Nicholas's followers, the sheep who'd agreed to sacrifice all for certainty. In the end, the Dark Man had honored the deal these poor fools had struck with Nicholas; they could hope for no purer form of certainty in their lives than having those lives snuffed out, no greater clarity than annihilation.

On the edge of the gathering Evangeline spotted Alice trying to guide a knot of confused, geriatric witches away from the slaughter. A couple Evangeline didn't recognize joined her. Alice must have deputized them to take over the rescue, for she stopped and turned back, walking in a straight line directly toward the fire.

As the last of the sacrifices, his fingers clawing the earth, was jerked upward into oblivion, another creature strode into the common world.

The head and cloven-footed legs of a goat, the breasts of a woman, the sex of a man. Man joined with beast, female joined with male, the Beast awaited her at the altar, this side of madness.

Evangeline recognized the essence at the core of the horrifying chimera. It was Luc returned to her in the form of the Beast. Luc had passed through the gates of madness, through the gates of oblivion, to touch the source of all magic—the realm where nothing was, but all was possible. In his kiss he carried the last breath of the old magic, and with that breath in her lungs, Evangeline could determine the fate of magic in the common world—if it would return or fade away forever.

The discordant drone of an ancient flute accompanied the timeless drumming of her father's heart to create her wedding march. There was no question of love. Had Luc ever loved her, he would not have conspired to bring her to this moment. No, he loved the Queen and had willingly become a monster so he could claim her for himself and through union with her become King. A beast is never reformed. A beast will forever remain a beast.

Evangeline joined him before the burning wicker man, the collection of twigs and branches and hemp that would act as officiant to the sacred union of the Queen of Heaven with the King of Bones and

Ashes. The vows the Dark Man commanded them to repeat echoed the screams of those sacrificed to bring the King into the common world.

A voice called her name, from another reality, from a few yards away.

Lincoln called to her once more. He was speaking to her, or trying to. The words held little meaning in themselves but they caused memories from her subconscious to surface, much like the images Sugar used to communicate with her. The day the electricity between the two of them had burned out the lights. The night she'd almost ripped him apart with beak and claw. The comfort they found in each other, and how it had healed them both.

Flames glinted off the sword in his hand. He'd come to stop her, just as she'd asked of him. Perhaps he believed he'd found the courage to end her, but the look on his face was evidence enough he hadn't.

He started a slow approach toward her, not like he was afraid of her, but like he feared she would take flight. *I know who you are.*

The Beast snorted and fumed but didn't move on Lincoln as she'd expected he would. Evangeline felt herself surfacing from beneath the haze that had enveloped her.

"I choose you." She heard Lincoln speak these words, rather than merely feeling their impression.

He held the sword out to her, hilt first, offering it to her. She took it from him, felt its heft, lifting it and listening to the sound its sharp blade made as it cut through the air. She could feel the Beast tensing, growing excited in the anticipation of watching the death of an unworthy rival.

"You can't change your parents," Lincoln said. "And you sure can't change your past." He knelt before her. "But you can choose your partner, and you can choose your path." He lifted his head and looked straight into the heart of the dark fire before him. He didn't flinch.

"Now, choose me or end me, but don't make me have to watch you give up on yourself."

Holding the hilt with both hands, she drew the sword back and swung it slowly forward until the edge of its blade pressed against Lincoln's neck. She sensed Luc quivering in anticipation, mentally urging her to sever Lincoln's head from his shoulders. He delighted in imagining the headless corpse falling forward at his cloven feet. It would be Evangeline's gift to him.

"I'm sorry," she said, addressing Lincoln. "I truly am."

She pulled the sword up and lunged, driving the tip of the blade through the Beast's heart. Luc stumbled backward, the goat lips opening to cry out, but no sound came, only a tiny puff of air. Evangeline could sense it coming toward her as the fire fell to darkness, forming a suctioning gravity that caught hold of the body of the Beast and pulled it back, wresting it from the common world. She reached down to grasp Lincoln's hand, to steady him as he rose on his shaking knees. But then the same irresistible force gripped her and tugged her back, too. Lincoln dove to grab her. Evangeline knew he couldn't save her, that the gravity that had claimed her was too strong. He would end up sacrificing himself for nothing. She bent his fingers back, trying to break his grasp on her.

"You have to let go of me. You have to let go." She watched as the reality of the unreal situation dawned on him.

His jaw stiffened, and he tightened his hold on her. "Get it through your head, girl," he said. "I choose you." He rushed forward, wrapping his arms around her as the common world faded away.

The last glimpse Evangeline had of the common world was of Alice as the final breath of magic claimed her.

Of course, Evangeline realized. That was how it had always been meant to be.

She tasted a bittersweet revelation, an epiphany Alice, too, would soon share—one person's strength is another's madness. Evangeline couldn't have survived the knowing, but her last wish was that Alice might.

After all, out of all the witches of New Orleans, Alice had always been the strongest.

In the final moment before Evangeline returned to the eternal fire where nothing is, but all is possible, two seemingly conflicting thoughts came to her, not as opposing ideas, but as polarities of a single truth:

There is no such thing as magic. All that there is, is made of magic.

THIRTY-SIX

Burning ice. Not a gasp. An invasion.

Alice's lungs expanded, though she felt like they might crumble to icy dust on exhale. When the breath escaped her, it came out as the spicy, bitter perfume of myrrh.

She heard Uncle Vincent's anxious voice calling her name. "Alice." The sound of it felt like a punch in the gut. "What are you doing over there?"

Alice realized she stood at the edge of Nicholas's yard. A wall of swirling water slid before her eyes, its undulating surface scintillating in the brilliant light of an impossible white sun. This was the day everything had changed. The day she'd first encountered Babau Jean.

"You know it isn't safe out here," Vincent pressed. "Come back inside."

She couldn't answer. She couldn't take a step. All she could do was turn her head to look back at him over her shoulder.

Vincent wasn't there. He'd been too good for this world, she realized, too kind. She sent out a wish he'd found a heaven with cold beer, old dogs, and an endless supply of beat-up cars to refurbish.

Like Alice herself, her uncle had always been a loner. She hoped he wasn't still alone.

Above her, the cerulean sky slid into hematite, then went full black, the diamond sun blinking out, dying as if poisoned by the sky. A heart-rending cry went up around Alice, giving her the sense that all souls, living and dead, and all objects, animate and inanimate, mourned as one.

All except Alice herself, who, alone in her wonder, could find no tears.

The cool silver-blue points of seven stars pierced the blackness above her.

A creaking caught her attention and she turned her face toward its source. The door to her father's house eased open, and a cold silver light, like that of the seven stars hanging above, spilled out of it. She felt something brush up against her leg, and she startled. A purring patch of gray fur wove around her ankles. Glowing viridescent eyes looked up at her. Sugar padded past her, then slunk back into the blinding whiteness.

A figure, a dark silhouette, appeared in the doorway, then stepped forward.

Alice recognized Daniel in an instant, even though his form was in flux, flashing back and forth between her beloved nanny and her earliest nightmare, Babau Jean. He turned—they turned—and went back into the light.

Alice sensed the answer to every question she'd ever posed lay beyond the threshold, and that realization, tantalizing and terrifying in equal measure, held her in place.

She felt a pressure build around her, as if the air itself was congealing. The horizon tightened, and the seven stars seemed to be descending, falling to the earth in slow motion, though Nicholas's house—the house of her earliest memories—remained unchanged. Alice realized the world beyond the house was shrinking, leaving her without a choice. This was not a new experience for her. She'd endured a similar constriction of her reality before, on the Dreaming Road. But this was not the

Dreaming Road. This was, as far as she could tell, the common world, the world she'd always held to be objective reality. She trod along the walk toward the house, an unseeable force sweeping her along like a gust of wind chasing fallen leaves.

Alice arrived at the doorway. She could feel the force willing her forward, but she hesitated, uncertain. The light spilling through the opening obscured what lay inside. She didn't know how long she stood there, straddling what felt like two separate worlds, but not because she lost track of time. It felt more like time stood still, waiting for her as she gathered her nerve. She didn't remember taking the step across the threshold but found herself on the other side as soon as she made the choice to cross. Beyond the threshold, she'd expected to find a world of wonder, or perhaps a world of terrors, but the only thing to shock her was the banality of what she found awaiting her. She stood in the hall of Nicholas's house. His office sat, as it always had, off to the left, and the staircase lay dead ahead.

"I'm sorry, love." Daniel's lilting voice came from the foot of the stairs, accompanied by the *shing-shing* sound of Babau Jean's grating razor teeth. "I didn't know about any of . . . this . . ." He motioned with Jean's sharp nails from the death-mask face down the gangly frame. "Not until I came to free you from the Dreaming Road and found myself stuck there instead."

"I think," Alice said as she approached him, "I did. That's why the connection Jean and I have felt so familiar." She took his hand, not fearing the nails, and in that instant the monster shimmered and turned back into Daniel. "You and Babau Jean. You aren't the same."

"No. Not the same, but not separate either. Two expressions of the same energy. Much like the relationship between Papa Legba and the Dark Man. There is no dichotomy. Only polarity."

He touched her cheek, then tapped the tip of her nose. "It's time, love," he said with a nervous smile. "Shall we?" She saw hope in his eyes, hope clouded by uncertainty. He was unsure, she realized, of her. Not of her nature, but of her strength.

Alice nodded, and he began to lead her up the steps. Halfway up the staircase, he disappeared, and then he reappeared on the landing. He smiled down at Alice, unaware he'd switched back to the appearance of a monster. It didn't matter. Alice understood the truth—if one could think in such terms—of the person she loved lay somewhere between the two extremes. She mounted the final stairs, counting the moments until—*an incandescence, a deep rumble*—there it was, the flash of lightning she'd been expecting.

"What is this place?"

"You know what it is, love. It's Nicholas's house. Your first home."

Yes, it was that. But it was something more. "What is this place?" she insisted.

Daniel breathed out the patient, impatient sigh he'd once reserved for muddy tracks across the kitchen floor. "It's the resolution."

"The resolution?"

"The point where dissonance is resolved. In short, it's the end of the world."

A shimmer, and Babau Jean was gone. Daniel once again stood before her.

"Lisette, Evangeline, and you. It could have been any one of you. But you're special. Always have been. Everything that has ever happened to you has been to strengthen you, to temper you, to prepare you for this moment."

"What are we doing here, Daniel?"

"Lisette is so strong," he continued, paying no heed to her question. "She would suffer any fate, death or even worse for herself, as long as her children and grandchildren were left untouched. That's why she couldn't be the one. The one to decide can't have children—at least not ones she loves. Lisette failed her test, or passed it, depending on your perspective.

Either way, she proved herself not to be the one. Mrs. Perrault, she has all the strength in the world, but not the right kind for this crucible."

"You wouldn't have turned against your children either," Alice said. Daniel loved the mess that was her brother Hugo, there was no denying that. Alice knew he loved her, too. His totality loved her, even his nightmare ego of Babau Jean. And Daniel also loved Luc. Even now. She knew if any possibility of redemption existed for her big brother, Daniel would lead him to it, by the nose if need be. Daniel may have had nothing to do with their conception, but they were his children.

A tear escaped his eye. "Enough of that, young lady." He wiped the tear away. "Of course, I was never to be the one."

"The one to what?"

"Evangeline. She, too, was strong, and unlike Lisette, she wasn't bound by the love of a child. But she wasn't as strong as you, my love." Alice remembered the ringing of Evangeline's laughter. "Such a sweet, generous creature, such a loving woman, she would have been a fine choice, except that she would have crumbled under the weight of the knowing. Still, she isn't really gone. She never will be, regardless of what we do here. She's a part of magic now."

Daniel paused for a moment, letting his words linger, then said, "I think in my heart, I always expected that it would come down to the two of us in the end." A loud meow from below as Sugar snaked through his legs. He stooped and scooped her up into his arms. "Yes, of course, the three of us. I stand corrected."

He scratched behind Sugar's ears and set her on the ground. Sugar circled around and stared up at Alice. Without words, Alice somehow understood the feline, too, felt something akin to pride in her.

Daniel reached out to her.

Behind him was the large landing window. Alice imagined she could see herself, a small girl on tiptoes, peering through it at the maelstrom below. This, she realized, was the image, the inspiration that had given birth to her.

She joined Daniel before the window and took his hand. Together, they turned to face the dim gray light filtering in through the panes. Beyond the glass, the dirty waters of Katrina still swirled. A white plastic lawn chair bobbed up and down, then rushed out of view. A blue tricycle followed, triggering a flash of its owner's face, a younger boy she'd pushed along on the trike.

A plastic pink flamingo. A red door. Alice took inventory of the expected objects, ticking them off on the mental checklist she'd long carried with her, cached away as if in anticipation of this very moment. A bubble of trapped air rose up through the muddy water, surfacing a kaleidoscope of bright colors Alice remembered as belonging to the covers of a collection of DVDs and paperback books. The colors rotated once, twice, then began to sink once again into the deluge.

Beneath the colors—no, through the colors, through the water itself—she could make out symbols. Only then did she discern the pattern buried beneath what she'd perceived as a random collection of flotsam.

These symbols were the sigils from the hospital on Sinclair Isle. Then the sigils melded together to become the image she'd traced on her window on the Dreaming Road. The image shattered, though Alice could see each splinter still contained the image of the whole.

Her mind turned to the vèvès, the living symbols in the windows of Lisette Perrault's shop. Yes, they, too, contained a hidden depth only hinted at by the visible.

All were two-dimensional expressions of a deeper reality.

Alice clutched Daniel's hand tighter.

One book remained afloat, its waterlogged spine giving way, its individual pages coming loose from the binding. The pages rippled on the surface of the maelstrom, their words floating up and separating from the sodden paper, unwinding themselves from the page.

"When is a book not a book?" Daniel said, and as he spoke, his words appeared on the surface of the water.

She tried to close her eyes, but Daniel pulled her to him. "You can't look away, love. You can never again not see this. The gates have opened." He kissed her cheek. "The angels have fallen. And you've been chosen as the sacrifice."

She opened her mouth to speak, to protest, her own words lining up on the pages before her, disappearing as she changed her mind.

Her memories, for the moment sharp, shocked her by disintegrating. By *changing*. Words she'd spoken, or intended to speak, came instead from the mouths of others, and their words became hers. Alternate time lines—positing infinite possibilities—collapsed into the experience she had known.

Alice began to see the world through others' eyes. She remembered crossing through Jackson Square, a brightly colored tourist map in hand, as surely as if she herself were Lisette Perrault. She saw a different symbol, one she knew through Lisette to be Papa Legba's vèvè. She registered Lisette's epiphany as if it had been her own. The square. Legba's vèvè. The one was a model of the other.

"The square," Alice heard Daniel whisper, "could be understood as a three-dimensional representation of the two-dimensional design, yes?

"Magic has long been preparing us for a truth science is only just beginning to explore. Quantum theory and the theory of gravity are finally beginning to approach the concept of a holographic reality, a truth those who know magic have long sensed."

In a flash it struck her. Two-dimensional symbols strung together to create a three-dimensional experience. Editorial conflagrations erasing earlier efforts, reworking of plots, characters coming to the page, then disappearing, deleted as if they'd never existed.

The importance of the written word to her own existence.

The Book of the Unwinding wasn't some musty tome moldering in a locked chest in a convent's attic. Nor was it only a single spark capable of burrowing into a person's soul.

Alice now stood in the heart of madness. Only there could the book's true nature be perceived. The world fell flat into a string of characters against a blank surface. Force and restraint in balance.

"*We* are *The Book of the Unwinding.*"

"The story is what matters, love," Daniel said. "There is no greater power than story. The story is all there is; it is our reality, and beyond it, nothingness."

In the face of the madness, an epiphany struck her, and Alice began laughing. "Storyville," she said. "You were trying to tell me all along."

Daniel nodded. "I think so. At least the part of me—the piece of Babau Jean—who did understand. In retrospect, it seems a fairly heavy-handed clue."

Daniel waved a hand before the symbols, which shimmered and changed shape, taking on depth and texture, and again Alice was looking at what she understood to be real. "It takes a special type of person to learn she doesn't exist, then go on living. You've been groomed, all your life, to stand firm in the face of madness.

"It's up to you, love. This can all end now, here. You can stop all suffering, end all joy. You can simply erase us all, everything and everyone you've ever known. Plunge us back into the nothingness from which we sprang. No more Nicholas, no more Celestin, no more hospital on Sinclair. But then, there'd also be no more Hugo. No more Nathalie. No more me. No more you." He paused, raising an eyebrow and looking down his nose at her, the expression she remembered him making when she was small and he was cutting her a deal such as "take your nap now, and you can go to the park this afternoon," or "finish the spinach and you can have ice cream." Somehow, in the face of this madness, discussing his own nonexistence, he was still himself. He was still Daniel. "Or . . ."

"Or?"

"You'll find the beauty, the value of creation. A speck of meaning in an endless sea of absurdity. But you'd have to be strong to let our reality continue, aware that it doesn't exist, aware that you don't exist, at least not in the concrete way you once believed. To accept what has come before—what has been written, so to speak—as fixed . . . immutable . . . and that what is to come will spring from the interaction of innumerable variables, of which the will of Alice Marin is but a single factor."

Daniel paused like he wanted to give this last bit a chance to fully sink in, pulling a serious face, another familiar expression, this the one he used whenever she would refuse to pick up her toys or brush her teeth. It meant it was time to put on her big-girl pants and get on with it. "There have been others," he continued, "before you who have stood where you now stand. Who've had to make the choice you now must make."

Alice didn't have to ask. It was self-evident those who came before had chosen to continue the illusion; they had chosen yes.

"Of course, it would be just the two . . . the three," he corrected himself, "of us who'd share the secret." She felt Sugar brush up against her leg, twining around it. "Anyone else you share the truth with will think you've gone mad, that you've lost your grip on reality. And in a way, they'd be right. But you'll always have us to share the burden."

Daniel reached out with both hands to take hers, then smiled down at her. "So, my love," he said, grasping her hands tightly, ready to plunge with her into the abyss if that was what she asked of him. "What will it be?"

She took in his mop of curly red hair, his crooked, perfectly imperfect smile, his sparkling green eyes.

They were Thoth's emerald tablets; they were the jewels of Indra's net.

THIRTY-SEVEN

A sudden flash like heat lightning, followed by a low rumbling. Lisette associated it with distant thunder even though it was less a sound than a vibration she felt deep in her bones. When the rumble died, it gave way to an almost reverential silence, or maybe more of a quiet dread. This was the moment of final judgment.

A nauseating vertigo gave way to a sweet resin scent, like the frankincense and myrrh of the incense burned at mass. A blessing then, rather than a curse.

If Lisette mentioned any of this to the nurses passing back and forth before the open door of Manon's room, she'd find herself being threaded through the hole of a CT scanner in zero time flat. But these weren't symptoms of a second stroke. These meager manifestations, along with a feeling deep down in Lisette's gut, counted as the only signs that the world had just been made anew.

She glanced over at her beautiful daughter, sleeping, peaceful, unaware, then turned back to the window. The darkness outside produced a reflection of her own features—and behind her face, that of the old man, Papa Legba.

Lisette's father had sworn that *her* Legba wasn't *the* Legba, but Lisette had just held Papa's hand as she watched the world be reborn. She knew now that the truth was a tricky beast to pin down. Her manifestation of Legba was different than her mother's, but he, too, was *the* Legba—at least for now.

She sharpened her focus and looked beyond herself, through Papa Legba, to take in a sliver of the night sky. The seven stars of the Big Dipper hung low on the horizon but shone bright enough to be seen through the big-city glare. But they, too, had changed. She no longer saw them as the seven gates or as the seven wounds of the gad. They were, at least to her mind, a family—her family.

She selected a star for Remy. A star for Manon. One star for each of her parents. One for her beloved Isadore and one for herself. She saved the brightest of all of them for Joy.

Around their constellation, other stars gained in brightness, and she knew them for the ancestors who came before, and the children who would come after.

Lisette felt a hand touch her own and looked over to find Isadore squatting before her.

"I think maybe you should go home," he whispered. "Get some rest. Remy's waiting for you downstairs." He patted her hand. "Come on now. I got this."

Lisette looked at her husband, and in that moment her heart felt so full of love for him, so proud of the life they'd built together, she began to cry.

His brow scrunched up with worry. "Is everything okay?"

She lifted his hand to her lips and kissed it. "Yes, you sweet man. *Everything* is okay." She touched his hand to her cheek. "For the first time in one hell of a long one."

DECEMBER 22

THIRTY-EIGHT

Nathalie came to, standing across from Bonnes Nouvelles, her eyes fixed on a mass of flowers and candles that spilled from the sidewalk in front of the club out into the street. She blinked and scanned the faces of the people milling about in the neon-lit night. Some passed by, slowing and bending to add to the collection. Others watched on, acting almost hypnotized by the bright white beam illuminating a familiar-looking stranger in the street, in front of the sea of tributes. A man pointed a video camera at her as she pressed a hand to her ear, seeming to be mid-conversation with someone not there. Nathalie's eyes drifted to a van that sat a bit farther down the street. She read the words "Five Alive" printed in a large, italic font on its side. Of course. Five Alive. The woman standing before the camera was Katie Cunningham, the same reporter who'd reported on Frank Demagnan's dollhouse.

Nathalie couldn't join the pieces together. Flowers and candles and Katie speaking to the camera, her manner animated yet reverent.

"She was my friend," a woman with eighty-six-proof breath said into Nathalie's ear, causing her to startle.

"I'm sorry?" Nathalie said, asking for clarification.

The woman seemed to misunderstand. "Thank you," she said, then tipped a bottle to her lips with one hand, grasping Nathalie's forearm with the other.

"I mean, who?" Nathalie said, removing the woman's hand.

The woman's eyebrows rose in surprise. "Well, Vangie, of course. I used to dance there, but we were more than employer-employee, if you know what I mean. We were like . . ." She held up her hand and managed to fumble twisting her middle finger around her index. "Ah, hell," she said, discouraged by her own lack of coordination. "Vangie was my girl."

"You mean Evangeline?"

"'Course, sugar." She stopped and studied Nathalie's face. The woman's mouth pursed as her raised brows lowered and came together. "You mean you haven't heard?"

Nathalie couldn't respond. If she said anything, this woman would speak again, and if she spoke, she would make something Nathalie didn't want to be real, real. She stepped back and began to turn.

"She's gone," the woman said, her voice suddenly quiet, but not quiet enough.

It was too late. Nathalie felt as if an inescapable spell had been cast upon her.

"There was an accident," the woman continued, "out on Highway 10." Her voice drifted up as she glanced toward the east. "About a quarter mile from the old Michoud Boulevard exit."

Nathalie knew the exit well. A southward turn took you to a long-abandoned theme park. A turn north led to Grunch Road. What had happened to Evangeline was no accident. Any more than what had happened to Nathalie near the same stretch of road.

Nathalie heard newscaster Katie speak the name Lincoln Boudreau. She turned back, and the woman leaned into her. "Yeah, Vangie and her boyfriend, too. I used to date him, but he took up with Vangie after I broke it off with him. Nice guy. Pretty, too. But . . . ," she said with a faraway gaze, "it wasn't right." She shrugged. "Accident only happened about an hour ago, but look at all this." She gestured with her whiskey bottle toward the bouquets and votive candles in glass holders. "Vangie used to look after everybody. People loved her." She took another drink. "Yes, everybody loved Evangeline." She lifted the bottle in salute. "Here's to you, Vangie," she called out at the top of her lungs, then she started crying.

Nathalie could feel the spinning of the earth pressing her against its surface, like one of those carnival rotor rides the moment before the floor drops away. She felt sick to her stomach. She turned away from the woman and started walking, then running, toward the river. Her breath came more quickly, and perspiration broke out on her forehead, but no matter how fast she ran, she couldn't escape the stench of smoke. It rode her skin; it twined through her hair.

It brought her back to the horrors at the burning of the wicker man.

She'd watched the torches touch down. A man's laughter, full of pride and triumph, had filled the air as the flames shot high, though the laugh had slid seamlessly into fearful, animal shrieks. Emil had clutched her in an icy, unyielding grip, until a shadow had swooped in from overhead. It snatched Emil up and away, his curses ringing out over the stunned gathering as the demon carried him alive into the heart of the fire.

Then all hell had broken loose. Nathalie's mind was filled with horrors beyond what it could contain. The shadows feeding. Showers of blood and shreds of khaki.

From the far side of the burning pyre, Nathalie had caught sight of Alice, walking in her direction, though not toward her. Alice had continued without hesitation, like she was in some kind of trance, into the heart of the fire, and then she was gone.

As the nightmare vision faded, Nathalie found herself before Vèvè, focusing intently on the symbols painted on the panes of its windows.

But it wasn't like it used to be. Nothing was like it had been. The faces that had always gazed out at her—some fearful, some jubilant—were gone. Nothing remained for her eyes other than the flat painted sigils.

Had they lost their power during the Longest Night, or had she herself moved to a different frequency, one that left her incapable of recognizing the forces embodied by the symbols? There was nothing for her here now. Neither fear nor comfort.

Nathalie caught sight of her own reflection playing hide and seek with her through the vèvès, and she began to scream, the sound turning deep and guttural as rage seeped up through the earth into her feet, climbing like sap through her legs, through her core, and finally releasing itself through her mouth.

The world spun around her again, and the longest night was done. Somehow the world had decided to lurch forward into another day. She stood on Decatur Street, grasping the bars of the locked gates of Jackson Square. She heard the Mississippi flowing a couple of hundred feet behind her, whispering its never-ending story beneath the honking of horns and the banging of garbage trucks, adding its own ancient perfume to the aroma of deep-fried dough and the scent of diesel fumes.

The sky in the distance was blue, but patchy fog still filled the park, blurring, although not erasing, the palmettos and the statue of Jackson on horseback, as well as the lower half of the cathedral. Nathalie watched on as four crows rose up from the foggy ground and took together to the sky. The light of the rising sun caught them, setting them ablaze, their wingtips catching first, their own wings fanning the flames as they flapped harder, rose higher.

They circled overhead, rising and diving, like kids playing tag. Nathalie sensed no pain, no fear. If anything, they seemed happy. The wind rose, lifting them higher, and as they fell away to ash, Nathalie felt a sense of peace, of a long-hoped-for release. Their happiness was infectious, and Nathalie felt her own heart lightening.

Something fell from above, landing a foot inside the gate. Nathalie knelt and reached through the bars to catch hold of the object. She drew it out between them.

She held a necklace, like from a child's play set, made of plastic with fake gold plating and plastic crystals resembling diamonds and emeralds. Nathalie gazed up from the necklace to the rising sun, her eyes fixed on its brightness, its shadow image tattooed on her eyelids when she blinked.

She felt a hand on her shoulder and dropped the toy necklace.

"Come with me," Alice said, taking her hand. "I've been looking for you." Alice lifted her hand and kissed it, her warm brown eyes never releasing Nathalie's own. "From the beginning."

EPILOGUE

April 30

Hoping to beat the crush and inevitable confusion at the Canal and Carondelet stop, Fleur excused herself to her fellow passengers, then squeezed between the streetcar's mahogany bench-style seats, making her way to the door. She held an oversize shopping bag filled with sample linens in each hand. The riders were mostly tourists for whom the short St. Charles line ride was both an adventure and a slight disappointment. Always expecting more, they tended to rise slowly and clog the aisle once the streetcar reached the end of the line at Canal. The rest of the passengers were New Orleans residents who chatted with the visitors, offering directions, advice, tips on the restaurants other tourists hadn't yet discovered. Fleur smiled as she descended from the car. The visitors were happy to be here, and the people of New Orleans were happy to have them, remembering it wasn't so very long ago some were arguing the city should be abandoned.

Canal Street still acted as the dividing line between Carondelet and Bourbon, even as it had once provided a buffer between New Orleans's long-established Vieux Carré and the upstart American Quarter, the median between its lanes becoming the original "common ground," since it offered a neutral territory between the two entrenched groups. Of course, borders once established will be crossed, and Fleur's own ancestors counted among the first wealthy French-Creole families to abandon the French Quarter and build a grand house among the English-speaking newcomers. "*Fidélité et Tradition*"—loyalty and tradition—might be the motto emblazoned on the Marin family crest, but the Marins had always known how to divine shifts in power and had always done whatever they deemed necessary, regardless of what had to be sacrificed, to ensconce themselves in the heart of the new order.

Fleur had long felt no loyalty to tradition or to New Orleans. At least not until it seemed that it might all be lost. Fleur had loved the city from afar, holiday visits and anonymous six-figure donations to aid recovery, but never a thought of homecoming. As Fleur crossed the common ground of Canal Street, the bags she carried bumping into her knees, she wondered if things had been different, if she hadn't needed to return to New Orleans for Lucy's sake, would she have come home? It meant something, Fleur reckoned, that she did still think of the city as "home." It meant something that Fleur wished Lucy could have loved New Orleans more. Maybe under different circumstances, maybe with more time . . . Nothing more than moot conjectures now.

A young man wearing a pocketed red apron stood on the corner of Canal and Bourbon, scanning the faces of passersby, the golden fleur-de-lis embroidered on his Saints cap catching the sun as he did. "Swamp tours," he called out to no one in particular, holding up a handful of glossy trifold pamphlets. "Plantation tours," he continued his chant. "Ghost tour, lady?" he said, addressing Fleur as she passed before him.

Fleur managed to offer him a quick smile and shake her head before the tears started. She didn't need a tour. She knew firsthand spirits did indeed pass along the streets of New Orleans, only they were never the one you'd wish to see. The gods knew she'd been trying. Reaching out, and waiting, waiting, waiting for any sign of her dear Lucy.

For nearly a month after Lucy's final death, Fleur hadn't been able to bring herself to leave the house, as if she expected at any moment her daughter might return, dropping her latest unnecessary and extravagant purchases at the foot of the stairs and demanding Fleur to take her "somewhere nice for a change" for dinner.

The one kindness the universe offered was that the liquor store had one-hour delivery.

Fleur was doing her best to rewrite her memories, to substitute in her mind the pious lie she'd hatched for the world in place of the actual horror she had faced. The lie itself was horrible enough. Fleur had dressed for the party they were to attend, then gone downstairs to look for Lucy, only to find her lying on the floor of her grandfather's former study. Gone. In the gown Fleur had made for her.

Such a beautiful girl. Such a healthy girl. Such a shame. The neighbors had sometimes spoken these words behind her back, sometimes to her face.

Sometimes, when her loss was still juicy news, they'd used it to fill the lull in party conversation. *You've heard about the Marin girl?*

Sometimes, they had been unable to say anything at all, their own hearts breaking in sympathy for Fleur's devastation.

It might have been because the coroner's office was long accustomed to turning a blind eye to any aberrations surrounding deaths associated with the witches of New Orleans. Or perhaps Warren had used his political clout. Or maybe it was only the approaching holiday, and the coroner didn't want to take on any more paperwork than he had to. Regardless, the coroner had identified Lucy's congenital heart disorder as the cause of death and released her body for burial.

Within hours of the release, Fleur had boarded the plane Warren had chartered to carry her and Hugo, along with Lucy's remains, to D.C. Warren and Meredith had canceled the large wedding they'd planned and married instead after the new year in the office of a judge friend. Ironic, really, that Fleur had found herself at Lucy's graveside, holding the very pregnant Meredith as the woman sobbed into her shoulder. The galling truth was that Meredith, too, was shattered by the loss of Lucy. Fleur had left D.C. knowing she couldn't bring herself to hate the woman. At least not any longer. In time she might not despise Warren either.

January followed, a string of bleak and hazy hours, curtains drawn, a single lamp burning in her bedroom day and night. Perfunctory, level responses to the ringing phone. Pots of tea whenever anyone dropped by, "to see how you're doing." She found it almost funny, watching her visitors try to maintain their cheerful expressions as their eyes took inventory of the mess she'd become.

Only Hugo understood, for he hadn't just lost Lucy, he'd lost Evangeline, too.

The day after Christmas, when most people were still basking in the goodwill afterglow of the holiday, Evangeline's friends had gathered for a memorial. Evangeline, with her generosity and faith in people, had made many friends in her lifetime. Mourners from all walks of life had come. At least that was what she'd heard.

Fleur had gotten dressed to attend, then taken her dress off again. It would remain one of her greatest shames that she hadn't pulled it together for long enough to help Hugo through the service. He'd told her he understood, and he truly seemed to.

Hugo would come and go, unannounced in each direction. He'd show up with heavy bags of greasy hangover-cure food like Chinese takeout and donuts, or those odd little square burgers smothered in what had to be synthetic onions, or fried apple turnovers. Most visits included a fresh large plastic bottle of off-brand bourbon, or box wine with a tap on the side. The food sat untouched more often than not.

She and Hugo would sit with each other for hours without speaking, sometimes without so much as a greeting. She would fall asleep to the sound of the television he'd turned on to do the talking for them, then wake alone to the silence, the television's screen still giving off its flickering blue light, its sound muted.

Finally, on a hushed, gray day toward the start of February, Fleur had gathered the courage to step back into the world. She had pulled on a pair of blue jeans she'd forgotten she owned and a fuzzy slate turtleneck that still held Lucy's perfume and headed to a café on Prytania that Lucy had frequented. Lucy had graded the cafe as "adequate," not a soaring recommendation in most circumstances, but an important distinction given that Lucy had failed all others south of Alexandria, Virginia, and west of Annandale, Maryland. Still, as the café was situated diagonally across from Lafayette Number One Cemetery and located in the same shopping complex as a bookstore, Lucy had branded the place as "the Triple B"—books, beans, and bones.

Going to Lucy's café had felt like a way to both hold on to her and take the first step toward moving on. She'd ordered her drink, a ghastly cinnamon-peach-mocha combination of Lucy's own invention. She could almost hear Lucy's voice as she directed the barista—a mocha with two pumps of cinnamon syrup and one pump of peach. The thought brought a smile to her lips. She was able to share this first true smile with the barista as she paid for the coffee and echoed the barista's hope that she'd have a good day.

An arriving patron held the door open for her, and Fleur had been happy, though surprised, the smile had held long enough to carry her through that encounter, too. She'd almost made it through the outing without incident; she had one foot over the threshold of the café when she heard a rising baritone voice coming from behind her. She didn't have to turn around. She recognized it as belonging to one of her neighbors, a kindly old retired doctor she'd known her entire life.

"The Marin girl, poor thing. She was living on borrowed time."

Not borrowed time, Fleur thought to herself, *stolen time.*

Fleur had felt like she had slammed into a brick wall at a hundred miles an hour. She dropped her paper cup and it fell to the ground, its contents shooting out like a geyser.

Fleur didn't remember how she made it home that day. One moment she was teetering outside the café, the next she was sitting alone in that mausoleum of a house, in the rarely used grand parlor, in front of a bottle of unopened scotch that twenty years ago had cost Celestin, she was sure, more than most people make in a year. She stared at the scotch and tried to steady her trembling hand so she could open it, but then lifted the bottle and flung it with all her strength against the perfect white marble neoclassical fireplace. She watched the bottle shatter, then went to the kitchen to make a cup of tea.

After that, she hadn't left the house again, not even for a walk, until this project had come along to save her life.

Fleur hefted her bags as she carried on down Bourbon Street until she arrived across the street from Bonnes Nouvelles. Hugo owned the building, though it was held in a trust he'd set up to conceal the fact he'd purchased it until he could present the papers to Evangeline on Christmas Day for her signature. Those papers would have transferred the ownership to Evangeline. But Bonnes Nouvelles had remained dark that day, as it had since the Longest Night.

She paused there, allowing herself a moment to take in the transformation that had occurred since she'd last been here, only two days earlier. The building had been an unattractive tawny brown, the favorite color of its former owner, but no more. Brilliant, bright white had taken its place, and the window frames, doors, and twin balconies had been updated from a grimy flat white to a black enamel. In a step Fleur would have avoided, had she been left entirely to her own devices, the vault of the recessed arch over the center doors had been painted amethyst, and the rectangular inset below it had been rendered emerald green. The surrounding framework of the arch as well as the rosettes adorning the vault had been ornamented with actual gold leaf.

But what the hell? It was still Bourbon Street, not the Avenue Montaigne.

Still, the most striking change was the absence of the boxy electric sign that used to hang down from the lower balcony displaying the name of the club.

Evangeline Caissy's Bonnes Nouvelles was no more.

Although as popular as ever with the tourist trade, gritty Bourbon Street clubs like Bonnes Nouvelles had fallen out of favor with the powers that be. It was rumored municipal leaders were making it hard to open new clubs, and harder for the existing establishments to stay afloat. The city wanted restaurants along Bourbon now—nice, respectable venues like the holy Creole quaternity of Brennan's, Arnaud's, Broussard's, and Antoine's. And that was exactly what the former club was to become. The gold and jewel-toned display over the entrance was the idea of the new chef, a nod to the King of Mardi Gras, a figure, it seemed, created by his own fancy. Fleur had proven incapable of disabusing him of either the notion of the king's existence or the idea of the garish tribute.

Hugo was bankrolling the renovation. He'd given Fleur a blank check, several of them. He couldn't bring himself to let the building go, but he knew Evangeline wouldn't want the place left empty. Fleur believed him, but she also recognized this renovation was a lifeline he'd tossed out to her. She'd caught it with both hands.

Fleur waited for a car to pass, then crossed over Bourbon.

She didn't have a key to the space. She didn't need one. Whereas six months ago, witches had resorted to collecting grotesque relics to prop up their failing powers, now, magic was everywhere. The witches who had managed to hold on were now using it with little discretion, tossing it about like nouveaux riches burning through their newfound cash. Once again, it seemed everything ran on magic. Ironic, really, that after how hideously wrong Nicholas's scheme had gone, these foolish, power-drunk witches hailed him as the hero who'd restored magic to them.

Her big brother had undoubtedly planned a grand entrance, emerging whole from the flames of the burning effigy, but something had gone wrong. A normal man would have most likely been dead by the time he dropped to the ground, but Nicholas's will had allowed him to survive long enough to rise and stumble toward the river. She thought of Nicholas in the newly reopened hospital on Sinclair Isle. A poetic fate, a fate well-earned. Still, as he lay there slowly recovering, in a magically, medically induced coma, she hoped his dreams were not the ones he deserved.

As Fleur approached the door, she heard the lock click, and the door eased open.

Fleur could feel her own power pulsing through her, a vitality like she'd never known before. The magic had returned at a terrible cost, the lives of Evangeline and Lincoln and Nicholas's pathetic acolytes, but what sickened her most was that it had returned too late. Fleur couldn't bring herself to use magic, though, as with the automatic opening of this door, she occasionally triggered that of others.

This magic, she recognized at first touch, was Wiley Boudreau's.

Hugo had contracted for the renovation with the man who'd taken over Vincent's company without even asking for an estimate first. Hugo had only insisted on two requisites. The first, Fleur knew, was that she would design it. The second was that Wiley, who had only minimal experience in construction, be placed in charge of the subcontractors.

Hugo being Hugo, he'd found a way to hold on to Wiley while still keeping him at arm's length. Hugo had lost Evangeline, his best friend, the cornerstone of his world, and it would be a long while before he'd open himself up to hurt again. Fleur hoped Wiley was a patient man.

Fleur stepped over the threshold and cast a quick glance around. Wiley and the framers had managed to carve out a good-sized main dining room and two private dining rooms, one for up to twenty guests, the other an intimate space for two.

Her design took inspiration from the heydays of Storyville. New dark oak flooring had been floated over the chipped concrete. The black lacquered walls had received a fresh skim coat to hide dings and cracks, then they'd been primed and covered with what had seemed like endless coats of ivory paint. Wiley had sourced an exquisite period Brunswick mahogany bar with a brass footrest, a dentiled cornice, and an original back mirror flanked by columns with intricately carved capitals.

Fleur wouldn't have a hand in the installation of the new kitchen. The chef himself would be seeing to those details. From what she could make out by craning her neck, he'd better get a move on, as the restaurant was scheduled for a soft opening on Independence Day. The event would include an early dinner seating before the fireworks, followed by cocktails on the rooftop to watch the dueling pyrotechnic displays shot from barges on the river. Friends and family and influencers, friendly influencers, by invitation only. An opportunity to get the figurative, but—Fleur shuddered—no longer literal bugs out. Evangeline had always kept the club spotless, which took more than magic. In the intervening months between the closure of the club and the beginning of the renovations, however, it seemed every manner of vermin and insect and, worse, spider, had sought sanctuary within its walls.

"Is that you, Fleur, love?" Daniel's voice drifted down to her from the upper floors. With the resurgence of magic, Daniel had blazed back into this reality, as real to the eye and to the touch as any man Fleur had ever known, and—given the circles in which she'd traveled over the last two decades—more real than many.

"You know it is," she called back, sounding impatient, not intending to. She shifted her bags and headed to the foot of the newly installed interior stairway. Evangeline had only leased the street-level space, and until now the upper floor could only be accessed from a stairway at the back of the building, which itself could only be reached via a narrow, gated alley on the building's right side.

"Of course I do, love," Daniel replied, "but it would seem rude to leave you knocking about down there by yourself without acknowledging your presence. Pop on up. I'm in the kitchen preparing a wee bite for you." Thanks to Daniel and his "wee bites," Fleur had put on four pounds in a week. Her pride protested, but she'd caught sight of her own reflection enough to realize she had gone from a disciplined petite to skeletal since last December. Daniel was waging an undeclared campaign to bring her back to a normal weight.

The scent of vanilla wafted down from the upper floor, the space Daniel had reserved for his own private living quarters. Fleur continued up, stopping when she noticed the glow of peridot eyes on the landing above. "Well, hello, pretty girl," Fleur called up to the cat, who if not for the shining eyes, might have been invisible in the gray shadow. Sugar purred in appreciation, it seemed, of the compliment, then performed a corkscrew turn and disappeared through the doorway into Daniel's apartment.

The doorway opened into an enormous, at least for one, combination living and dining room that was full of natural light thanks to the new skylight they'd installed. On one side of the living space were two bedrooms. Daniel had claimed the smaller one, leaving the larger of the two for "the children," as he still called Hugo and Alice, for whenever either of them felt a need to get a taste of "home." A full bath sat between the bedrooms, and the small kitchen with its eat-in breakfast space was tucked into the far corner next to Daniel's room.

"Come through, love," Daniel called from the kitchen. "Hugo called to say he's running a little late."

"I hope that means Wiley will be detained as well."

"Knowing our Hugo, more like *restrained.*"

"Yes, thank you for that image," she said, trying to sound disapproving, but undermining it by choking back a chuckle. "I've brought the samples to show you." Fleur set her shopping bags beside the dining table, pausing there to take note of the postcards scattered over the tabletop. Daniel seemed to be trying to arrange them in some order, though Fleur couldn't decide if it was a temporal timeline or a chromatic scale that served as his guide.

Lisbon. Madrid. Barcelona. Andorra. Toulouse. Bordeaux.

Alice and Nathalie were on their grand tour. For the longest time, neither of them had ever been anywhere. Now it seemed the two young women were determined to go everywhere. They'd left six weeks ago; they'd be gone twenty more. "What is this, then?" she asked Daniel, whose head popped through the doorway.

A wide grin cracked his face. "Oh, those. Postcards." His head disappeared back into the kitchen.

"I can see they're postcards," she said, beginning to flip them over. The upper left quadrant of each was covered in a detailed description of the place and customs, printed in Alice's neat, careful hand, while the lower quadrant contained the same nearly identical scrawled sentiment. "Wish you were here. Love, Nathalie." Sometimes the word "Love" included, and other times was superseded by, a heart.

"Then why did you ask?" She heard an oven door open and close, a pan being placed on the stove top. "Scones," he announced. "Lemon–poppy seed and plain, clotted cream."

Fleur felt herself roll her eyes, as her Lucy had always done. "I meant what are you doing with them?" She was worried he'd planned to unleash a decoupage monstrosity on the restaurant space below.

She could hear him moving about in the kitchen, no doubt sliding the pastries from a parchment-lined pan to a cooling rack. "A little present for Alice and Nattie." He had hung the nickname on poor Nathalie, and she'd seemed unable to resist him. Daniel poked his head back out. "The postcards, not the scones. Raspberry or marmalade?"

"You know the answer is both," Fleur responded. "The postcards?"

"I made them promise to send poor old keep-the-home-fires-burning Daniel a postcard from every place they visit. I'm putting together a scrapbook for them as a welcome-home gift."

"I'm sure they'll love it."

He flashed a bright, crooked smile. "I do hope so." The smile faded, and he bit his lower lip. "I've had a bit of an inspiration," he said, his eyebrows rising as a line formed between them, "about the name for the restaurant." Fleur tilted her head and raised her own brows, a signal to continue. "I was thinking, perhaps . . . if Hugo doesn't mind . . . we could call it 'Evangeline's Rest.'"

"I think it's perfect," she said. "I'm sure Hugo will agree."

Another broad smile. "Do make yourself comfortable, love." He nodded to the sofa at the same moment Sugar came padding out of the larger of the two bedrooms. The cat sat and looked up at them, issuing a commanding yowl. Daniel jolted. "Yes, it was your idea." His brow lowered as his lips pulled into a tight pucker. "I was going to give you full credit—"

Sugar cut him off with a dismissive mewling, and turned away from him.

"I have most certainly not forgotten your bowl is almost empty," Daniel said, his voice indignant. He looked up at Fleur. "I'm five minutes late with the can opener once, and I'm never allowed to live it down." Another yowl. "Why don't you call the ASPCA, then? Tell them how misused you are. *Really.*" He turned on his heel and went back into the kitchen in a huff. A cabinet door thumped. The sound of a can opener biting through metal followed.

Fleur took a seat on the sofa, and Sugar looked up at her, her eyes shining with triumph. A quick leap and the cat landed by her side.

"I interviewed someone for the manager position yesterday."

"Oh?" Fleur said, wondering if she should have asked to be part of the interview process for Daniel's sake.

"Bright young woman," he said to the sound of clattering plates and clinking silverware. "College degree. Good experience. A native New Orleanian, even."

It seemed he'd found an ideal hire. Fleur was impressed. "She sounds perfect. What's her name?"

The kitchen fell silent, and Daniel poked his head sheepishly through the door. "Manon Perrault."

"Oh, Daniel," Fleur said, unable to believe her ears. "Her parents will not be happy about that. And Alcide—"

"I know, love, I know," he said. "Not to worry—she excused herself with the utmost politeness the moment she learned my last name was Marin." He disappeared once more into the kitchen. "A shame, really . . ."

"A shame that is ours," Fleur said.

Sugar bumped Fleur's hand with her head, a clear demand to be petted. Fleur obliged. "I'm sorry, *ma petite*. It's my fault you were pulled into this madness in the first place." The cat pushed back and stared at her, as if looking to her for an explanation. "It's only when I first saw you, a tiny speck of gray fur with that perfect pink dot of a nose"—she risked touching her index finger to that nose—"and beautiful eyes, well, I had a premonition Alice would need you." It was true. It had seemed an odd idea at the time, but she had taken the kitten anyway.

Fleur stroked her hand down the cat's head and back. "Do you think you'll ever forgive me?" Sugar stepped up on her lap and began purring as she gently kneaded Fleur's skirt. The cat fixed her with her magical green eyes, willing Fleur to meet her gaze. It seemed ridiculous, really, but once their eyes locked, Fleur found she couldn't look away. Sugar peered deep into Fleur, touching the hurt in her heart. Then, to Fleur's amazement, the cat opened herself to Fleur, revealing her own bereavement.

Mama.

"I know, you miss Evangeline."

Sugar moved forward, reaching up and resting her paws against Fleur's chest.

Girl who shines.

The image of Lucy, her bright essence not quite contained within her form, impressed itself into Fleur's mind. Sugar leaned in and rubbed her head against Fleur's cheek.

Gone not gone.

As the skylight overhead flooded with warm sunlight, the cat dropped from Fleur's lap onto the floor. The sun's rays touched Fleur's skin, and all at once she understood. "You're right," she said, her voice catching, sensing Lucy's love as it enveloped her. "I can feel her . . . everywhere."

Sugar looked up at Fleur, blinked her peridot eyes slowly twice, then turned. With a proprietary purr, as if the sun were hers alone, the cat eased into the golden light.

ACKNOWLEDGMENTS

In 2011, when I began writing the manuscript that was to become *The Line*, I never dreamed I would spend the next seven years writing about witches. Now that I've arrived at *my* final days of magic—at least for the time being—I'd like to thank David Pomerico once again for seeing the potential in that first odd little book.

I'd also like to thank Angela Polidoro, who has been with me since the beginning of this journey, making me look a thousand times better than I really am. No, seriously, maybe even two thousand times better.

Beginning with *The Source*, I've had the incredible fortune to have Jason Kirk as my head editor. I will always be grateful to him for the freedom he has granted me, the trust he has shown me, and the friendship I've been lucky to share with him.

One of the greatest pleasures I've had while writing these books has been getting to know Pat Allen Werths, a beta (and sometimes even gamma) reader whose sharp eyes have helped spot many a typo.

I'd like to thank my spouse, Rich Weissman—my cheerleader, my rock, my friend, my most ardent promoter, and my love—for putting up with this writer's insanity and occasional—okay, habitual—surliness.

I also couldn't do this without the love and emotional support of the best little dog in the world, Kirby Seamus Weissman-Horn, rescue Chihuahua extraordinaire. (Adopt, Don't Shop.)

And finally, I'd like to thank Sugar Chloe Weissman for inspiring the character of Sugar Chloe Caissy. You'll always live on in Daddy's heart. *(Uh, uh, yesssssssss.)*

ABOUT THE AUTHOR

Photo © 2017 Mark Davidson Photography

J.D. Horn is the *Wall Street Journal* bestselling author of the Witching Savannah series. A world traveler and student of French and Russian literature, Horn also has an MBA in international business and formerly held a career as a financial analyst before turning his talent to crafting chilling stories and unforgettable characters. His novels have received global attention and have been translated into more than half a dozen languages. Originally from Tennessee, he currently lives in California with his spouse, Rich. Visit www.JDHornAuthor.com.